MW01698258

AFTER the DANCE

AFTER the DANCE

LORI JOHNSON

KENSINGTON PUBLISHING CORP.

DAFINA BOOKS are published by

Kensington Publishing Corp.
850 Third Avenue
New York, NY 10022

Copyright © 2008 by Lori D. Johnson

All rights reserved. No part of this book may be reproduced in any form or by any means without the prior written consent of the Publisher, excepting brief quotes used in reviews.

Dafina Books and the Dafina logo Reg. U.S. Pat. & TM Off.

ISBN: 978-0-7394-9490-5

Printed in the United States of America

For Al
Who never stopped believing

Acknowledgments

I'd first like to thank the Muse-Maker for blessing me with a passion for the written word; my parents (Bobbie and Leo Johnson) and my brother (D. Steven Johnson) for nurturing my addiction to books and storytelling; my extended family (the Johnsons, Hunters, Hawkins, and Hams) and in particular, my grandparents (Ethel V. and Larther Johnson and Zenna and Edgar Hawkins) for providing me with so much great material and unconditional love; and my in-laws (the Morris family) for their support and encouragement.

I'd like to thank the following for always being in my corner; my LeMoyne-Owen sisterfriends (Charlotte P., Violet S., and Susan B.); my play-cousin and all-around bud (Dr. Yvonne Newsome); my Memphis writing pals (Alice Faye Duncan, Ayo Jalani, and Dwight Fryer); Da Fellas in my circle (Stanford L. and Martin W.); my Memphis Go-To-Girl (Michelle F.); my Memphis Go-To-Guy (Michael R.); and Dee-Dee, my North Memphis confidante.

To all of the guys and gals who "worked" the magazine's desk with me at the main branch of the Memphis Public Library when it was still on Peabody & McClean (Cathy B., Griff, Astrid B., Pam B., Michael S., and Joy B.), I am deeply indebted to every one of you for all of the laughs and moments of inspiration—especially Joy B., who helped plant the seed for this project and who was among the first to give it a big thumbs-up.

I'd like to offer a special thanks to *Memphis Magazine* (former editors, Leanne Kleinmann and Ed Weathers in particular) for publishing my first short story; Robert P. Kleinmann, Jr. for penning my first fan letter; Sharon J., Shelley S., Sandra P., and Angelia L. for being a part of my Cleveland Crew and Dr. Sara and Mr. Nate Wilder (of Cleveland, OH) for treating me and mine like blood kin.

I will be forever grateful to Arthur Flowers for pointing me in the right direction; Anita Diggs for the advice that made all of the difference; Stacey Barney for inviting me to Kensington; my current editor, Selena James, for guiding me through the process; and my agent, Janell Walden Agyeman, for all of her ongoing reassurance, advice, and tireless efforts on my behalf.

A thousand thanks to all of those unnamed and nameless folks I've encountered along the way who've encouraged me, prayed for me and believed in my dreams. This book is as much yours as it is mine.

Last, but not least, I want to thank my husband, Al, for putting up with me and all of my idiosyncrasies for the past twenty plus years and my son, Aaron, for being my best work ever.

Part One

HER

I had never really paid that much attention to him before, even though he lived right next door. Usually when we ran into each other we'd nod, speak our hellos, and keep on 'bout our business.

Nora, my roommate, was the one who told me his name was Carl. She'd talked to him on several different occasions. She also told me he'd tried to hit on her—like I wouldn't have guessed it. Nora's got this, well, this sluttish quality about her. And I'm not trying to talk bad about the girl or anything, it's just that I don't know how else to describe it. She kind of puts you in mind of some of those girls you see dancing on *Soul Train.* You know, the ones who look like their titties are about to shake outta their clothes? Or, the ones who are always turning their asses up to the camera? And that's cool when you're twenty-three and under, and don't have the good sense to know any better.

Anyway, according to Nora, our tall, dark-skinned, bearded neighbor was sweet, but not her type. I kind of looked at her sideways when she said that, but I didn't say anything. Me and Nora go way back. I know all about her "type." It's dog. Straight up and down, dog. I'm telling you, she's not satisfied unless some guy's smacking her upside the head, taking her money, whoring all over town, or some combination of the three.

Problem with Nora is that she's still under the impression that there's actually something called love out there, and if she searches long and hard enough, she'll eventually find it. I don't have any such illusions. See, I know ain't nothing out there but game. And having played hardball with the best of them, I also know the secret to winning is knowing how not to get played—something Nora has yet to learn. That's why every other month, just like clockwork, you can find her sitting up in the living room of the condo we share trying her best to kill off a fifth of scotch, looking crazier than Bette Davis did in *Whatever Happened to Baby Jane?* and playing them same old sad-ass songs over and over and over again. And Lord knows I'd go to bat for my girl Phyllis Hyman (God rest her beautiful soul) any durn day of the week, but listening to "Living All Alone" fifty times straight on a Friday night, with no interruption, is enough to drive even the sanest sister out of her cotton-picking mind.

And that's how it happened that Carl and I had our first real conversation—if you want to call it that. I had just stepped outside for a break from the music and the madness and was settling comfortably into my patio chair with my pack of Kools, a chilled glass of wine, and a romance novel, when he opened up his back door, stepped outside, and noticed me sitting on the other side of the fence.

He said "Hey" and I said "Hey," and I thought that was gonna be the extent of it before he went on his merry little way. But no! He decided he was going to be sociable.

"Must be Nora in there jamming to Hyman."

I said, "Yes. If it's disturbing you, I'll ask her to turn it down."

He said, "No, I was just wondering 'cause you don't exactly look like the Hyman type to me. No, you look more like a—let's see—Millie Jackson. Yeah, you look like the kind of woman who could really get into some Millie Jackson. Am I right?"

I guess he was banking on me not knowing about Miss Millie, the late '70s and early '80s trash-talking forerunner to the likes of today's Lil' Kim and Foxy Brown.

No, you ain't right, smartass, and you must be blind is what I started to say but didn't. Instead I blew my smoke, swirled the wine in my glass, cut my eyes, and said in my coolest "don't mess with me, man" voice, "Is that supposed to be funny?"

HIM

I knew I was taking a risk when I opened my mouth. My Uncle Westbrook was the first to warn me, way back in the day. "Son," he told me, "you never know how a woman's gonna react to what you say. Sometimes you'll get a smile, sometimes you'll get an attitude."

But really, I should have known better 'cause every time I see this chick, she looks like she's got her jaws tight about something. I mean, we've been neighbors for nearly six months now, and she still acts like she don't hardly want to speak.

Some women are like that, man. If you didn't know any better you'd swear they were born with permanently poked lips. Have to say, though, I've noticed it more in fat women. Not that I have anything in particular against fat chicks. Matter of fact, I've gotten right close to one or two. But a fat chick with an attitude—hey, that's something else altogether.

Yeah, she's one of them feisty big-boned girls, man. She's got a pretty face, though. Actually, she'd probably be a stone-cold fox if she lost, say, thirty or forty pounds and smiled every once in a while. But I guess that'd be asking for too much, huh?

So I was standing there, right, trying to figure out how I was going to work my way out from under this Millie Jackson comment, when Nora came out and got me off the hook by informing the fat would-be-fox with the pretty but unsmiling face that she had a telephone call.

Now, me and Nora, we're cool. She kinda puts you in mind of a young Lola Falana with a double dose of spunk, you know? Though I'll be damned if she ain't always crying the blues over some dude. And this particular evening was no exception. Before I could even get out a proper hello, she'd launched into an all-too-vivid, blow-by-blow account of her latest hellacious affair. I don't know, man, I guess it's just something about me that brings out the worst in a woman. But being the polite fool that I am, I stood there nodding, grinning and grunting in all the right places, until both boredom and curiosity got the best of me and I walked over and picked up the book left by her roommate.

Call me a proper bourgeois if you want to, but I still say you can tell a lot about a person by what they read. And it wasn't like I was expecting the big sister with the bad attitude to be into something as heavy as Fanon's *Wretched of the Earth* or anything, 'cause I'd seen her sitting out on the patio enough times with her head propped up behind a Harlequin to know better. But yet and still, I wasn't at all prepared for anything on the level of a *Jungle Passions* either. I mean, the title alone was a bit much, but on the cover was this crazy Tarzan-looking character who's got this even crazier-looking, big-breasted blonde wrapped up in one of those back-breaking, humanly impossible embraces. And you know me, I wasn't about to let something like that pass without comment.

"Excuse me for interrupting, Nora," I said, "but might this be the type of relationship you're looking for?"

She glanced at the book and rolled her eyes. "Honey, don't even try it! I'm into real-life, flesh-and-blood romances, not paperback ones. But yeah, Faye, she's always reading that junk. And then got the nerve to tell me I live in a dream world. Ain't that a blip?"

HER

I heard them out there talking about me. Didn't faze me any more than him taking the book did. Yeah, girl, when I went back out there the next morning, the book had mysteriously vanished into thin air. Nora tried to play dumb and acted like she didn't know what I was talking about when I asked if she had seen it anywhere. I guess the way they had it figured, I'd eventually get around to asking him—you know, Carl—about it. Give me a break. Like I said before, I know all about games, and anybody with half a brain could peep that one a mile away. And as far as my indulgence in romance novels is concerned, let it suffice to say that I read them purely for their entertainment value, and I'm perfectly capable of distinguishing the carefully drawn lines between fiction and reality.

I didn't bother to listen long enough to find out, but I'm pretty sure their trite little conversation concerning *moi* ended somewhere along the lines of "Poor, poor Faye, if only she had a man . . ."

Yeah, I've heard it all before and really couldn't care less. It's not hard to get a man—if that's what you want. I just don't happen to want one—not to keep, anyway. To me, having a man is about as emotionally satisfying as having a fish in an aquarium or some other kind of pet. I'm not into pets. That's not to say that I don't have, well, certain needs and desires. Yes, there are those times in a woman's life when all the tender finger-stroking in the world just ain't gonna get it. Okay? But I've yet to meet the man whose stuff was so good I wanted to trade my heart in for it. Uh-huh, when I go out, I do what any sensible woman would—I leave my heart at home, locked away for safekeeping.

Really, it's better that way. It evens out the exchange. And in my book that's about all a *relationship* boils down to anyway—a simple exchange of goods and/or services, a sexual contract, if you will. I think my deal's a pretty simple and fair one. I don't expect them to take me out to expensive places or buy me gifts. I don't expect any displays of affection outside the bedroom. And they don't have to worry about any discussions having to do with commitment, babies, or the like. In turn, I fully expect them to come equipped with adequate protection. I expect them to make an honest attempt to satisfy my sexual needs. But most important of all, I expect them to exit my life promptly after the contract's expiration, which with absolutely no exceptions is after the third lay.

Why three? Well, to be perfectly honest, after the third time, the thrill of it all has begun to dissipate. And if you think about it, that's about the point at which most guys want to try and take the game to another level. I don't play that. So I'm very careful about whom I choose to negotiate with.

HIM

We've bumped into each other a couple of times since the night of the infamous Millie Jackson comment, but she has yet to say anything to me about the book. I know she knows I have it. The chick really baffles me, man. There's something 'bout her game I haven't quite figured out. As it stands now, I'm putting my money on split personality because the last time I saw her she did an almost complete about-face.

It was another Friday evening, right, and I was just getting back from the video store with a weekend's worth of entertainment—a soft porn flick, a couple of Eddie Murphy movies, and something educational for the kids to watch when they came over Saturday night. I was getting out of my ride with my goods when I saw homegirl hunched down beside her car trying to change a tire.

So, thinking man that I am, I paused and deliberated on the situation a moment before deciding upon an appropriate course of action. Like, should I (a) do the honorable thing and offer my humble assistance? Or (b) keep on walking and pretend like I don't see her big ass all pressed up against the curb? Yeah, you know me, man, sucker city all the way, I went for (a) and asked the chick if I could give her a hand.

Instead of thanking me with a big pretty smile and a few kind words, she said—without even looking up, mind you—"I'm perfectly capable." Can you believe that?! "I'm perfectly capable." You know I wanted to cuss, man, but hey, I played it off like a gent.

I said, "Well, I can see that, Ms. Fix-it, but it certainly wouldn't hurt to have a couple more hands on the job. Or would it?"

Chick hoisted her big butt off the ground, tightened her grip on the wrench she'd been using, looked me dead in my eye, and said, "Look, the name's Faye, okay?"

Now, I could see the sister was 'bout ready to go into this nut act on me, so I backed up a bit, but I wasn't about to be deterred from my program. I said, "Okay, Faye, okay! I'm Carl. Nice to finally make your acquaintance. So tell me, Faye—are you planning on handing me that wrench or smacking me with it? No offense intended, mind you, just thought I'd ask."

So I was standing there waiting for her to take a swing at me, when the miracle happened. I'm not lying, man, the chick actually smiled. Came right out of nowhere! And it was so quick I almost didn't catch it. But it was definitely a smile. Okay, if that wasn't strange enough, after we'd finished the job, she actually thanked me and invited me inside for some lemonade.

Heck, yeah, I accepted—though out of curiosity more than anything else. I think deep down a part of me really wanted to be there when she morphed back into Dorothy's wicked witch of west Tennessee. But no, she was cool. We even chit-chatted a bit—general stuff like car repairs, the weather, our jobs. And get this, man, I was helping the sister take her things inside when I noticed the "Dr. Abrahams" name tag pinned to the front of the lab jacket she'd given me to carry. Come to find out ol' girl is a pharmacist, of all things. She's only been out of school a little over a year and she works up at the veterans hospital. The fact that she deals with old and crazy, doped-up vets on a daily basis might certainly account for her funky little mood swings, huh?

Anyway, I followed her inside, had a couple tall glasses of lemonade, and had more than a few slices of some of the best carrot cake I've ever had in my mouth. But not wanting to overstay my welcome, I got up to leave after twenty minutes or so. I was in the living room and almost out the door when I realized I'd left my videos in her kitchen. While she went back to get them, I mosied on across the room and started browsing through the bookcase that housed a huge CD and album collection and covered one of Faye and Nora's living room walls. Now as you well know, what a person listens to says as much about them as what they read. So I'm busy trying to figure out how all these Al Jarreau, Cassandra Wilson, Dianne Reeves, and Rachelle Ferrell numbers fit in with Nora's round-the-way-girl personality when Faye comes back in with my package of videos. Completely forgetting my previous musical misinterpretation, I say right off the top of my head, "Nora's got quite a selection of music here."

Faye gave me one of those looks sisters are famous for around the world and said, "Those aren't Nora's. They're mine. And if you look closely I'm sure you'll notice there's not a Millie Jackson, a Lil' Kim, or a Foxy Brown in the bunch."

So to get out of it, what did I do? Quite naturally the next fool thing that comes to mind, which for some reason was to invite her over to watch the flicks with me. Of course she promptly refused with one of those "thanks, but I don't think so" lines and ushered me out the door. But get this, man, later on that evening when I was going through the tapes trying to decide which one to watch first, I noticed my porn flick was missing. Now, what do you make of that?

HER

Yeah, I took his ol' nasty flick—*Wanda Does Watts*—just to even the score and show him that two can play that game. Now I'm wondering what he's got up his sleeve to do next. I told you about his latest ploy, right? How he's been inviting me over to watch videos with him?

You know, the first time he asked, I didn't take him too seriously. Videos? I mean really, hasn't everybody with an extra ninety-nine dollars to spare gone out and bought themselves a DVD player? Still, I figured he was just trying to be nice and what have you. But then he asked a second time the following week, and again I politely declined. Well, last night he up and asked again. He was like, "Check it out, Faye, it's gonna be a Spike Lee night tonight—I'm talking classics like *She's Gotta Have It*, *Do the Right Thing*, *Crooklyn*—better join me."

Girl, please, who wants to sit up and look at all that old, tired mess? It's not that I've got anything against Spike. I'm just saying, if the brother had really been out to tempt a sister he would have skipped the Forty Acres and a Mule section altogether and come at me with something along the lines of a Taye Diggs, Boris Kodjoe, and Morris Chestnut kind of sampler. You know what I'm saying?

Anyway, I told dude I had laundry to do—a couple of loads, as a matter of fact. He gave me one of those "Yeah, right, tell me anything" looks and said, "Well, showtime's at eight if you change your mind."

Really and truly, I had no intention of going. But it just so happened that Nora came home that evening in one of her Friday black-and-blue moods. Walked in the door reaching for the vodka with one hand and my Aretha albums with the other. Yeah, I could tell by the looks of things it was going to be another one of those "Ain't No Way," "Chain of Fools," "The Thrill Is Gone" nights—and I was most definitely not in the mood.

See, what you have to understand about me and Nora is—even as night-and-day different as we can sometimes be—we've been hanging with each other since durn near kindergarten. Over the years, not only have we seen each other through the good and the bad, but Nora was once there for me when I absolutely had nowhere else to turn. And for that alone I owe her and will forever be truly grateful.

So sure, I tried to be a friend in this particular instance and talk sense to the girl, but to absolutely no avail. Between the sniffing and the snotting, she started telling me about these three gray hairs she found the other night. And I was like, three gray hairs? So what's the big deal?! Hell, we're both well within that thirty-and-over age bracket. It's not like we're still teenagers or anything. But before I could get my lecture off the ground and to the podium, she said, "Not just any three gray hairs, Faye. Three gray pubic hairs."

Now, don't get me wrong. I love Nora like a blood sister, but I'll be damned if I'm gonna sit around with her crazy ass and discuss pubic hairs—much less count them. I poured sistergirl another drink and told her she needed to get some professional help and quick, because there wasn't a thing I could do for her. That's when I decided to go next door and ask Carl if his invitation was still open.

HIM

I almost fell out when I opened the door and saw her standing there. Even though I had invited her over a couple times, the fact that she might actually take me up on the offer was something I hadn't really banked on. The shock must have registered on my face, because she asked if I was expecting someone else.

"No, no," I said. "Come on in and have a seat." And all the while I'm thinking to myself—*now that I've got this chick over here, what am I going to do with her?*

You know what a creature of habit I am, man, and how I hate being forced to make a sudden change in plans. Not that I had made what you might call major plans for the evening. These days a typical Friday night for me is one where I kick back with a video or two, pigging out on popcorn, chips, and soda or beer until I conk out in front of the tube. Yes, sad but true. And I'll thank you to save your snide commentary concerning my social life until you've signed over your share of triple-digit child support and alimony checks.

Anyway, I'd sort of halfway planned on watching *She's*

Gotta Have It that evening. That was my first choice, simple reason being that it was the sole one of the bunch I had only seen once as opposed to a couple times already. But being that Faye was my guest and all, I went ahead and let her choose which flick we'd watch. Naturally she said she'd watch anything but *She's Gotta Have It.* Anything but that.

"Hold on a minute, Faye," I said. "You mean to tell me you actually wanna pass on a movie that deals with the exploits of a sexually liberated Black woman?"

She looked at me like I was a fool and said, "Liberated?! I guess that depends on how you choose to define the word. Rape is not exactly my idea of a liberating experience. And lest you've forgotten, that is unquestionably what happens to the female lead at the end of this quote-unquote funny, lighthearted flick. Man, you and Spike both need to quit. *She's Gotta Have It* wasn't nothing new. The message is essentially the same ol' mess we've been hearing since the day y'all stumbled outta the caves and realized you'd lost a rib."

See, a lesser man might have tried to hurry up and move on to another topic. But me? I couldn't resist. I had to ask, "And what message would that be?"

Without so much as a blink of an eye, she said, "That any woman who dares to exercise the same sexual freedoms taken for granted by men is honor-bound to 'get it,' whether figuratively or literally, 'in the end.' "

Well, need I say the conversation took off from there? Yeah, man, we got into this real heavy discussion about Black filmmakers, pop culture, the depiction of women and minorities in various media—all kinds of heady-type stuff—and ended up not watching anything. I found out the chick is capable of conversing quite intelligently on a whole range of issues. Not that I was in total agreement with everything she had to say. But still, it was kind of nice talking to a woman whose worldly knowledge and educated opinions extended beyond whatever happened to be in *Jet* or on *Entertainment Tonight* this week.

And if that wasn't tough enough, man, toward the end of the evening, I even got her to slow dance with me. Now, tell me I ain't smooth! No, I'm not going to get into any of the dirty little details. A brother's got to keep some things to himself. I will say this, though—much as I hate to admit it, we actually had a pretty good time. Really. Or maybe I should speak for myself.

HER

Far as I can tell, Carl's pretty much your typical middle-aged divorcé, with a rapidly receding hairline, an old school rap, and a smug, settled look about him. And his personality fits somewhere in that tight space between nerd and intellectual. But on the other hand, he's got a boyish quality about him that's almost, I don't know, charming, I guess, for a lack of a better word. And keep in mind, I said almost. The jury is still out.

The first thing he did that night I went over to watch videos was introduce me to his cat. You know how I feel about pets, especially cats. And this Negro's got the audacity to have one named Sapphire. Yeah, girl, and I know he was just waiting for me to make some kind of comment or inquiry as to why this silky black feline with her sadiddy, cattish ways was called Sapphire. Huh! I let him keep that trip all to himself. His comments concerning *She's Gotta Have It* told me all I needed to know about his level of enlightenment when it comes to Black women.

We never did get around to watching any videos. We talked most of the night. And while I deliberately steered around his repeated attempts to get me to talk about myself, he was quick to volunteer all kinds of info about himself. I found out he's a manager in one of FedEx's courier divisions, he's a couple semesters shy of earning an MBA, he's divorced, and he has three kids whom he absolutely adores.

At some point during the course of the evening, the topic got around to music—that seems to be a particular favorite of his. When I asked what kind he liked, he told me he was into love songs. Or as he put it, "Those old, slow dance tunes we used to bump and grind to when we were kids." Then he jumped up, put on "Baby, I'm For Real" by the Originals, and said, "Now, tell me that doesn't bring back memories of sweaty palms, bangs gone back, and youthful nights of innocent pleasure?"

Then, girl, he turned his back to me, wrapped his arms around himself, and launched into this solo slow-dance routine that was absolutely hilarious. After he'd finished tripping he looked at me real funny-like and said, "That's nice. You oughta do that more often."

I said, "What? What are you talking about?"

He said, "You know, smile. Something happens to you when you smile. Your personality, your whole aura softens when you smile."

After he laid down that line, I figured it was about time to call it a night. I said, "Yeah, well, it's getting late, Carl. I think I'd best be going."

But before I could make a clean getaway, he said, "Wait—I bet I've got something you'll like." He fumbled through his records while I stood there thinking to myself—if this man puts on some Millie Jackson, we're going to fight. And get this, girl, he put on some Luther. And not just any ol' Luther, mind you, but one of my personal all-time favorites—"Make Me a Believer." Uh-huh, tell me about it, chile, Luther V. know he be *sanging* that song!

Then Carl did something that totally threw me—he asked

me to dance. Yes, dance. And, well—I did. But don't go getting any ideas. Dance is all we did and dance is all we're ever going to do. Carl's just not the kind of guy I'd want to get involved with. I mean, we're neighbors, for goodness' sake. It'd cause too many problems. Anyway, I haven't decided whether he was actually trying to come on to me or whether he was just trying to see how I'd respond. You know how some guys like to see just how far you're willing to go. It's one of those male ego things. The trick is to only give them so much. They want a mile, you give them an inch or two—a yard if you're feeling generous. So sure, I gave the brother some leeway and the benefit of the doubt. And when he asked if I was going to join him next Friday, I told him maybe. Maybe . . .

HIM

Maybe?! Get out of here! She knew as well as I did that she was coming back. Come next Friday, she was at my door, eight o'clock sharp, cradling a bottle of wine and trying hard to deny me the pleasure of her smile.

Yeah, but see, I was ready this time. Having taken extensive mental notes on the occasion of our last conversation, I knew *Glory* and *Training Day* would be safe and mutually appreciated choices. We'd both had nothing but praise for Denzel and his Oscar-winning portrayals. And being that I'm undeniably a man starved for female company, I wasn't about to let another bad video choice muck up what thus far had all the makings of a pretty good time.

I never thought I'd be saying this, but I'm actually starting to take a shine to ol' girl. To tell you the truth, in a lot of ways she reminds me of Betty, my ex. Yeah, man, slim as Bet is today you'd probably never guess it, but back when I married ol' girl she was more than just a few pounds heavier than Faye is now. And talk about feisty! Hey, being a preacher's daughter ain't never stopped Bet from speaking her mind, especially if you get her mad.

But what I like most about Faye, man, is that unlike a lot of these Memphis chicks who've educated themselves and managed to get a handful of change in their pockets and some little title before or after their names, she's not always up in a brother's face flossing, flaunting, and trying to pull rank. You know the type. First thing outta their mouths is "I'm Director So and So. I belong to such and such sorority, alumni chapter, civil rights organization, or civics club. I've got a Jag, an Expedition, a ski club membership, and a summer home in Martha's Vineyard." And ol' girl is coming at you with all this, man, in an accent so thick you'd swear that instead of having lived most of her life deep in the heart of North Memphis, she'd just jumped off the boat from England after having spent years hobnobbing with the likes of Tina Turner or somebody.

And don't get me wrong, I'm not trying to hate on a sister for having "come up" and then gone out and snagged herself a nice chunk of the American pie. It's not like I myself don't have a liberal arts degree, a managerial position, and a healthy appetite for the nicer things in life. All I'm saying is, I have yet to buy in to the notion that being a card-carrying member of the Black middle class means I've got to be out here 24/7 wearing my upward mobility like another doggone layer of skin.

Far as I can tell, Faye comes from a similar school of thought. She's the kind of woman who knows how to bounce between the King's English and Southern Black street vernacular without getting bogged down on either side. That's the kind of down-to-earth flavor and versatility that a hardworking brother like myself can appreciate—so much so that I'm willing to go ahead and invest what little free time I have in getting to know her better.

'Cause the real of it is, man, just when I think I've got ol' girl figured out, she goes and whips something new out the hat on me. Take the other night, for example. She was scanning the shelves at my place and complimenting me on my collection of books (most of which I either borrowed or outright stole from Dr. Tucker, my literature-teaching baby sis) when right off the top of her head Faye starts reciting lines from two of my all-time favorite poems—Langston's "Dream Variation" and Margaret Walker's "For My People." I'm saying, I'd been under the impression that Harlequin was the extent of her literary repertoire. But no, come to find out ol' girl is extremely well versed in the African American literary canon and no doubt could hold her own in Doc Tuck's class.

Yeah, just like the time before, me and Faye did a lot of talking. Matter of fact, we didn't part company until way up in the wee hours of the morning. And this time around, in addition to being much more relaxed, the conversation was also much more personal.

At one point she asked me straight out about my marriage and the reasons behind its demise. And I came right out and told her. I told her how I strayed one time too many, and ended up getting someone other than my wife pregnant. Told her how at age ten, my twins, Renita and Renee, knew more than I wished they did about things like affairs, mistresses, and divorce. Told her about the pain, man, the pain of having destroyed my family, of having betrayed the trust of my children, of having hurt so many innocent people unnecessarily. Even told her about the other woman, Clarice, and the other child, my son, Benjamin, and how strange it felt to be a man with two families, but no place to really call home.

After all that emotional retching I should have ended the

evening with some soul-cleansing music—some Johnnie Taylor or some Bobby Womack—but instead I opted for a smoother sound—the Friends of Distinction and their "You've Got Me Going in Circles."

Yeah, she danced with me again that night, man. And I held her a little closer than the last time. Close enough to feel her heartbeat. Close enough to smell the faint traces of the cologne she must have put on earlier in the day. And all the while we danced, her eyes never left mine, her facial expression never once changed. I don't know, man. I don't know if it was gratitude, temporary insanity, or just the wine gone to my head, but something made me want to kiss her. And before I could even think twice about it, I had.

HER

It wasn't just the kiss. It was the kiss and everything that led up to the kiss that gave me good reason to pause. I guess I should have known better than to think for even one quick second that Carl and I might be able to have a nice, friendly, uncomplicated, platonic relationship.

Not that I'm excusing myself from any responsibility for what happened that evening. I did make the mistake of asking about the breakup of his marriage. Really, it was an innocent line of questioning that I thought might lead to a general discussion on the current status of male-female relationships. Unfortunately, he mistook it for an invitation to disclose just how big a 'ho he'd been during his eight-year hitch.

I have to give the brother this much, though, he doesn't believe in making any excuses for himself or his behavior. He readily admits that what he did was wrong, and acknowledges that his lying, cheating ways were what got him thrown out and living all by his lonesome. But even more admirably, not once did he ever blame his ex or attempt to verbally trash the woman. Course now, he did run a variation of that "but, baby, I've changed" line on me. I'll be durned if every man I know doesn't keep some form of this line shined, polished, and tucked beneath the tip of his tongue, as if this is supposed to make you feel more at ease about all the evil, trifling mess he's done in the past.

Then there was the dance and the kiss. Yeah, I know you been waiting on that part. So I danced with him again, okay—shoot me already. I didn't have the heart to turn him down. You remember how it was back in junior high when the guys were still shy about asking us to dance at the sock hops? Well, Carl kind of reminds me of one of those guys. Guess it's that boyish charm I told you about. Anyway, he seems to get such a kick out of the whole thing, and he's not at all vulgar about it—none of those pelvis digs and wandering hands that you have to watch out for with most guys. So we danced, and just as the song was ending he leaned over and kissed me. Yes, on the lips and, similar to the dance, it wasn't at all vulgar. And no, I'm not going to lie; it was, well, kind of nice. Not wonderful, not earthshaking, but nice as far as kisses go.

But after all that, I felt it best to put some distance between us. What do you mean "why?" The disclosures, the dance, the kiss, the glazed look in his eyes—they all spelled trouble, girl. Carl, nice guy that he is—or seems to be—is simply moving too fast in a direction that I have absolutely no interest in exploring with him. So when he asked if I was coming back next Friday, I lied and said I'd already made plans. As it stands now, I don't see where I have any choice.

Course now, if circumstances were different—like, if he lived across town somewhere—I probably wouldn't be so quick to rule out a quiet jaunt in the boudoir. But the reality is, the man lives next door—a distance that would be much too close for comfort when it all came crashing to an end, as it ultimately would. I told you, girl, "three strikes and you're out." That's the policy. And until I run into the man who causes me to think otherwise, there will be no exceptions. Romance? Yes, it makes for good reading, but really—I have no illusions. None whatsoever.

HIM

Okay, I'd be lying if I said that Faye's company hasn't meant a lot to me. Hanging out with her on Friday nights most definitely beats the heck out of spending them alone. I really thought we were starting to connect and I was hoping she felt the same. But lately she's been avoiding me. For two weeks straight now, she's given me the brush-off when I've asked her about coming over to watch videos.

"Sorry, Carl, I've already made plans for the evening."

Plans, my foot! Who does she think I am, Sam Sausage Head or somebody? I know she's not doing anything other than sitting over there with her head propped up behind one of those doggone Harlequins. Sure, my feelings are hurt. When was the last time a woman told you that she'd rather spend time with a paperback than with you?

At first I was fairly levelheaded about it. I said, hey, there are plenty of available women in the world. If she doesn't want to be bothered with me, cool, later for her then. But then it started to irk me. I mean, one day we're laughing, talking, and having a good time, and the next day it's back to the curt hellos and cold good-byes, and not a moment to spare for anything in between. I think, at the least, I deserve an explanation.

I know the whole thing is pretty petty, man, but I just can't seem to get her off my mind. Just the other day when I was picking up around the place I noticed her book, *Jungle Passions,* sitting on top of a small stack of books in my bookcase. It was right there in plain view. And I thought about that night when she had browsed the shelves. There was no way she couldn't have seen the book, man, not with that cover jumping out at you like the neon lights in front of some strip joint. But she never said a word about it.

Looking back on everything that's transpired between us, I can't help but wonder if me laying that lip action on her might have been just a little bit too much too soon. And I'm saying, it's not like I stuck my tongue all down the chick's throat or even tried to cop a quick feel. Still, she may very well think I'm out to do a "take the coochie and run" number on her. And granted, once upon a time I might have done just that.

But my days of indiscriminate tail-chasing have long since ended. All that stuff that went down with the ex, Clarice, and the kids made me realize a lot of things—number one being that it's high time I started searching for that something or someone that will add years to my life, not take them away. I'm tired of waking up and wondering if the chick lying next to me is going to give me crabs, herpes, AIDS, or yet another child to support on my already meager income. I thought I'd already told Faye as much. But then again, maybe it's what I haven't told her that's making her back off.

I don't know, man. What do you think? Should I go over and tell this girl straight up that I'm digging her and that I'm more than willing to slow this thing down to whatever speed works best for her? Do I sit back and give her a chance to come back around on her own accord? Or, hell, do I just move on and forget about the whole thing?

HER

I could tell the rejection was getting to him, but I never expected a personal confrontation. After two weeks of declining his video invitations and slamming a tight lid on the small talk, I figured he'd take the hint and turn his attention elsewhere. Well, I was wrong. When the third week rolled around, he didn't ask me over—no, girl, he asked me out—as in date—as in dinner and a movie. And I said no—as in "I'm not interested"—as in "I don't want to be bothered."

Girl, you would have thought I called his mama a 'ho or something. This big cloud of fury dropped down over his face and I did what any smart, right-thinking woman would have—I beat a hasty retreat before all hell had a chance to break loose.

That would have been more than enough for most guys. But not Carl, honey. I'm telling you, this is a man who is not easily deterred. Paid me a personal visit that very same evening. I was stretched out on my bed, listening to the jazz station, and trying to unwind when I heard Nora outside my bedroom door. "Yo, Faye. You got company."

Hell, I thought maybe it was you or Terri or Wilma or somebody. But then Nora poked her head inside my room and told me it was none other than video man himself. I said, "Look, Nora, you've got to get rid of him for me. Tell him I'm taking a bath. I'm indisposed."

"Indi—who?" Nora said with her ignorant self. "Girl, you better stop tripping and bring your fat butt on out here. What you dodging him for? Uh-huh, I knew y'all was doing more than watching videos over there." Then the cow turned around, went back out, and told the man I'd be out in a minute. Wait and see if I don't pay her back!

There wasn't anything left for me to do but go and face

the music. So I went out and said a polite hello, which he, of course, returned. And then there was this god-awful moment of silence as the three of us—me, Carl, and Nora—stood there gawking at one another, before Carl cleared his throat and said, "If you've got a moment I'd like to talk to you—in private." Nora flashed me one of those, "Who?! I ain't going nowhere" looks, so I didn't have any choice but to invite the man into my bedroom.

Once there he didn't waste any time getting right to the point. "So what's with the cold-shoulder bit? It's obvious you've been avoiding me like the plague for the past couple of weeks, and I think it's time we cleared the air."

I said, "Don't take it personal, Carl, 'cause believe me, it's not. I'm simply not interested in getting emotionally involved—with you or anyone else, for that matter."

He shook his head and was like, "Emotionally involved? We've been emotionally involved, Faye, ever since day one. What human interaction is ever without some emotional involvement? Look, if you don't want to spend any more time with me, fine, but could you at least tell me where I overstepped the boundaries? Was it the kiss? My breath? Something I said? Was it the way I touched you or didn't touch you?"

Excusing his breath, it was, of course, all of those things and more. But what was I going to say, and how was I going to say it without doing any more damage to his already bruised ego? I ended up copping a plea—told him I didn't know exactly how to explain it, but I was sorry if I had hurt his feelings.

Then I stood back and waited for him to spit fire, but he just gave me this little polite schoolboy grin and said, "Okay, Faye, if that's how it's gonna be, what's there left to say? It's just that I'll be moving soon and I didn't want to leave with all of these question marks hanging in the air between us. But since you're obviously not interested in shedding any light on the situation, I guess I'll just have to go through life wondering just what it was I did to earn myself the boot."

HIM

After my soul-sapping encounter with Faye, it seemed like the rest of my weekend went steadily downhill. I swear, it was like a chain reaction or something, man, 'cause all the women in my life just plain started acting a fool.

The very next day I got into this big shouting match with Clarice after I found out she'd been letting my son, Benjamin, call some dude she's been laying up with "daddy." I'm saying, man, some gold-toothed runt of a fool named Bull-Dog. I let her know, not only was it not right, but I wasn't gonna have it. I mean, come on, my son is almost three and has yet to act like he even knows he and I are some kinda kin. But I'm supposed to just step aside and let her slowly poison my boy's mind against me? I don't think so.

Man, Clarice went off and accused me of not spending enough time with Ben and being negligent in my duties as a father. Like that's my fault! She's the one who won't hardly let me take the boy out of her sight, which pretty much limits my role to that of a checkbook papa, some dude who rolls through every once in a while to drop off a check, a box of Pull-Ups, and maybe a Tonka toy or two.

Well, the name-calling and insults escalated to the point where I said, hey, enough already. I snatched up Ben—who by this time had joined in with some screaming and wailing of his own—and told Clarice she could call me when she came to her senses, and maybe then we could sit down and figure out some sort of sensible visitation schedule.

Oh yeah, man, she howled up a storm then. Threatened to call the cops and have my butt thrown in jail for kidnapping! But I was way too far past mad to let that detour me any.

Next thing I know, I'm driving around the city with this screaming kid who don't know me from Santa Claus, when outta nowhere I get this bright idea to run by the ex's and pick up my girls. After all, it's a nice sunny, spring day in May. What better way to spend it than with all of my kids? I could take them downtown, treat them to a ride on the Main Street Trolley, show them the Pyramid, zip on over to Tom Lee Park and let them watch the boats on the river . . . Yeah, man, I went over to my ex's all ready to play this daddy thing to the hilt—only to have Bet promptly pitch a fit and curse me out for having the "negrified audacity," as she put it, "to bring that stank tramp's child" up in her house.

In hindsight, I don't know what I was thinking. The fact that Benjamin even exists is still very much a sore point between me and Bet. That's not to say that my ex is at all a hateful woman. Really, for the most part, she's the sweetest person you'd ever want to meet. It's just that in a lot of ways Benjamin's birth was the straw that broke the camel's back in our already troubled marriage. I keep praying that time will eventually ease some of the pain for her and maybe even one day allow her to forgive me for it. But needless to say, that wasn't the day.

Anyway, instead of the girls, all I got was a good chewing out. That's how I ended up back at my place trying to bribe my hardheaded, inconsolable son with a doggone Happy Meal and just about on the brink of bawling some myself.

HER

There's nothing I hate more than the sound of a crying baby. And this child was over there screaming like his whole little world was about to come to some catastrophic end.

After fifteen minutes of trying to tune it out, I went over and asked Carl if everything was all right, only to have him spit a nasty "Yeah!" at me before slamming the freaking door in my face.

Hump, he can play crazy if he wants to is what I told myself, but I wasn't going anywhere until I'd verified with my own two eyes that the kid was okay. So after a couple of deep breaths and a quick count to ten, I banged on the brother's door again. And this time when he swung it open, I jumped in his face. "Look here, man," I told him, "if you don't let me up in here, I'm calling 911 and reporting your behind for suspected child abuse."

Something must have told homeboy I was more than ready to make good on the threat 'cause he checked the flip attitude, backed his butt on up, and let me in. The first thing I saw on entering the living room was this little boy who was Carl's spitting image: big square head, pouting lower lip, and all. The kid, who by this time had boo-hooed so hard he could hardly catch his breath, was seated in a thick puddle of what turned out to be strawberry milkshake, he had gobs of mustard decorating the top of his head, and he had a gooey ketchup, tears, and slobber mix setting up a right nice tie-dye down the front of his shirt.

I threw Carl a look, which he obviously interpreted as some kind of accusation.

"What?!" he said. "I haven't done anything. He's upset about the stupid toy. It broke when we took it from the package."

I knelt down next to the kid and on closer inspection saw the plastic doohickey he had in his little balled-up fist. I unsnapped the miniature hourglass I keep on my key chain and held it out to him. "Look, sweetie, why don't you play with this? What do you say? You wanna make a trade?"

I think for a few seconds there, Carl and I both were holding our breaths. But after wiping his nose on his sleeve and peering around me to sneak a peek at Daddy Dearest, he decided to take me up on the deal.

Figuring my job there was done, I looked at Carl and said, "Well, don't just stand there. Clean him up."

I watched in amazement as this fool went and got a couple sheets of paper towel and then tried to dry-mop the boy down.

"Man, please," I said. I grabbed the child's hand, led him away from his ol' crazy daddy and toward the bathroom. I helped myself to a clean towel and a bar of soap, ran the sink full of warm water, and started disrobing the boy.

"Don't you have a change of clothes?" I asked Carl, who was standing there staring at me like I was the one who'd lost my ever-loving mind.

"No, I don't," he said, jumping back into his Mr. Snot-Butt routine.

"Well, find him something to put on 'cause this stuff is gonna have to be washed. You can do that, can't you?" I said, getting snotty right back at him.

He snatched the baby's clothes from the floor and disappeared for a moment. When he returned, instead of cutting him any slack, I went in for the kill. "You don't have a diaper bag? I can't believe his mama would send him over here without a change of clothes."

Oooh, girl, that got him good and pissed. He stepped in the bathroom and said, "Hold up a second, okay? You don't know me and judging from what you said last night, you don't wanna know me. So why are you over here trying to be all up in my business?"

He tossed a shirt that must have belonged to one of his daughters at me, then stormed out. So there I was alone with his son, who, frightened by the bass in his daddy's voice bouncing all off the shower curtains and ricocheting against the tiled walls, had up and started bawling again.

HIM

I was down on the floor cleaning up the mess Ben had made and working out my frustrations with the help of a rag and a bucket of water when I heard ol' girl clear her throat. Before I stopped and turned to look at her I asked the good Lord to forgive me in advance. Why? 'Cause I knew, man, if ol' girl started talking crazy to me again, I was going straight for the jugular.

But she was cool. All she said was, "He's tired. If you've got a rocking chair I'll see if I can't get him to go to sleep." My boy Ben played up the point by poking his thumb in his mouth and nestling his head on her shoulder.

I had her follow me to my bedroom, where I keep this rattan rocker my ex was decent enough to let me take after we split. I stretched out across the bed and watched while my son alternated between fighting to stay awake and falling headfirst into the rhythmic rock and hum Faye was pressing on him.

After a few minutes Faye peeled her eyes off the boy and laid them on me. Having braced myself for something mean-spirited to come flying outta her mouth, I was a bit taken aback when she asked if the drama between me and Ben was always so intense. After a moment of sincere contemplation, I told her what I thought was the God's honest truth. "I don't think he knows what to make of me. His mother doesn't let me see him that often."

True to form, Faye shot back at me with, "Why is that? Payback for something you did or something you didn't do?"

"The only thing I ever *did* to her was get her pregnant" is what I said. "And believe me, if I could take it back, I would. Thus far, it's been the biggest mistake of my life, bar none."

She looked at Ben and said, "Maybe that's why he's having such a hard time warming to you. Kids pick up on negative stuff like that, you know."

She didn't say it in a nasty way or anything, but still, I wasn't up to hearing that some of the difficulties I'd been having with my son might in part be my own fault. "I didn't say I didn't love him or that I wasn't committed to his well-being" is what I told her in my defense.

"No, just that he was the biggest mistake of your life," she said, glaring at me through squinted eyes.

Gnawing on the inside of my jaw to keep from cussing, I was quick to tell her, "That's not what I meant. And anyway, who are you to tell me how to parent, when you don't have child the first?"

I saw her eyes widen and had it not been for Ben, who came to my rescue with a well-timed squirm and whine, I'm pretty sure a verbal beat-down is what would have followed. But rather than waste another breath in my direction, Faye turned her attention back to my boy. While stroking his face and head she started singing the words to one of the tunes she'd been humming earlier.

It sounded like something from either the motherland or the islands. And don't you know, little dude took to it like a shot of morphine. He settled right on down. I was impressed, really I was. But rather than come right out and give the girl her props, I went the buster route.

"Hoodoo, huh?" I said, trying to play the whole thing off. "Now, why didn't I think of that?"

Instead of smiling or getting mad, all Faye did for what seemed like an eternity was stare at me, like I was the most ignorant so-and-so she'd stumbled across in a long time. Then, in a voice barely above a whisper, she laid it out for me. "It's Yoruba," she said. "It means 'God's work will never be spoiled.' "

HER

Ise olowa, kole baje-oh. Ise olowa, kole baje-oh. It's just a little something I picked up a couple years ago at a Sweet Honey in the Rock concert. It means "God's work will never be spoiled." I don't know if Carl felt stupid, ashamed, or some combination of the two, but he got real quiet after I told him that.

While he and the kid chilled, I lowered my guard just enough to kick back and get taken in by the room's decor. I'm saying, it was weird, girl, because not in a zillion years would I have ever guessed Carl to have such an eye for style—especially given the rest of his apartment's barren state. But eyes don't lie and in a glance I could tell a considerable amount of thought, time, and energy had gone into the creation of the African safari/jungle kind of ambience he had going on up in there. And before you start thinking tacky, no, I'm here to tell you, girl, the room was laid. I'm talking live plants everywhere, including two big-leaf banana trees and a collection of clay pots, wicker baskets, hand-carved knickknacks, and the whole nine.

But the clincher was the bed. When it comes to what men will sleep on, I thought I'd seen it all, from old, funky futons to foam-rubber floor mats. But, honey, let me tell you, Carl is the first brother I've ever run across who actually owns—by choice, mind you—a canopy-style bed. His is a black, towering, single-rail number with two draping sheers that spill into a perfect triangle over the wrought-iron headboard. And then he's got the nerve to have the entire thing covered in not one but three plump layers of chocolate mud-cloth print pillows.

But before you go getting any ideas, I assure you, the closest I got to the bed or Carl was when it came time to lay the baby down. Carl helped me arrange the pillows around the kid and cover him with a blanket.

As we both stood there gazing down at the little fella, I couldn't help but comment, "He looks just like you. Kinda acts like you, too."

Carl smiled and told me that was the same thing the child's mama was in the habit of saying and he was pretty sure she didn't mean it as a compliment.

I was headed for the front door and was in the process of advising Carl to get the boy back home to his mama before he woke up hollering again, when I was interrupted by what sounded like a pot boiling over in the kitchen. I followed Carl to the kitchen, just to make sure he didn't need my help in putting out a fire.

On discovering that it was just a pot of water for some tea he'd put on and forgotten about, I spun around and was two seconds short of being gone when he said, "You're welcome to join me for a cup. Or, you know, if you'd rather, I could fix you some to take with you."

Yeah, girl, I know. I should have stuck to my guns and kept right on out the door. See, but you don't know Carl. He's got this subtle way of soliciting sympathy that I'm sure draws him a fair amount of play from those susceptible to that sort of thing. And while copping an attitude with him is one thing, I'm slowly learning that maintaining it for any length of time is proving to be quite another. So to make a long story short, even though tea ain't even my drink, I stayed and let him fix me a hot cup.

HIM

I didn't really think she'd stick around. It wasn't until she pulled her cigarettes from the front pocket of her blue-jean jumper and climbed atop one of the kitchen bar stools that I realized she planned to hang for a minute. While I poured the tea, I tried to think of something to say that wouldn't have us right back at each other's throats. We sat there for the longest, neither of us saying anything, just leaning over the kitchen island, sipping tea and listening to the loud *tick-tocks* coming from the rickety clock on my wall, until finally she blurted out, "So how long were you involved with Benjamin's mother?"

At the risk of making myself sound even more morally bankrupt than I am, I took another stab at the truth and just came out and told her, "Technically, all of one night. I met Clarice at this party my cousin Squirrel drug me to. We hit it off, ended up back at her place, kicked a little sumthin'-sumthin', and, well, nine months later along came Ben."

She took a moment to digest the information, then blew out a cloud of smoke, smiled, and said, "In other words, it wasn't a relationship you were interested in with this woman, just sex?"

Since I wasn't exactly sure where she was coming from or headed to, I said, "Listen, don't go getting it twisted. That whole Friday-night thing that transpired between us with the videos, the slow dances, and all, that wasn't just about me trying to get you in my bed."

"No?" she said, still wearing what looked like a grin.

Personally, I didn't see what was so funny. I told her, "No, I mean, I just thought, like me, you were having a good time. And I just figured, like me, you'd be interested in having an even better time. I know I'm not the most exciting guy in the world, or necessarily the best looking, but, dog, don't hate a brother for trying."

Apparently, that was even funnier to her. She laughed outright and said, "Carl, it's not that I don't find you attractive . . ."

Oh, man, I thought for sure the next thing outta her mouth was gonna be that doggone "why can't we just be friends?" speech I've been hearing from chicks since the seventh grade. So before she could get going good, I said, "Yeah, I know. You just don't want things to get too physical between us. And hey, like I told you the other night, if you don't want to get involved, cool. It's all good."

That's when she dropped the bomb. "Actually, Carl, if you remember correctly, what I said was I didn't want to get emotionally involved. I never said anything about us having a physical relationship. And given the tale you just shared with me in regards to you and Clarice, I take it you're well aware of the difference."

When I asked her to come again, homegirl broke it down something like this: "If you wanna play, fine, let's play. The only thing is, in order to remain an active participant for the duration of this particular game, you have to be willing to abide by my rules."

Per my humble request, she stopped blowing smoke long enough to run me down a whole list of things, the most peculiar of which involved her "three times and you're out" policy. Yeah, man, according to Faye's golden rules of sexual etiquette, we can bump it once, twice, three times even. But after the third swing, the game's over and the deal's done.

At the end of her spiel, I just looked at her and said, "You're serious?"

She looked back at me and said, "Why wouldn't I be?"

I said, " 'Cause it's pretty darn cold, that's why."

Ol' girl sucked on her cigarette a moment, then said, "Yeah? I bet you didn't think that when you were out there running around behind your wife's back, buck-jumping from one bed to another. I don't get guys like you. Why bother with the pretense of a quote-unquote relationship when all you want is sex anyway?"

In an attempt to steer the spotlight off me, I asked, "Is that all you want?"

She frowned and said, "Carl, I'm a realist. I know from experience that's about all there is to have."

Then, man, if that didn't beat all, the sister snuffed out her smoke, stood up to leave, and said, "Thanks for the tea. And if you decide you still wanna play, you know where to find me."

After she left, about all I could do was sit there and think, *Damn, maybe I ought to just leave that alone.* But after having slept on it a couple of nights, I'm not so sure backing out is the thing to do—not now, when it's just starting to get interesting.

Besides, you ever wonder what a fly would choose if given a choice between sugar and shit? Would it prefer one over the other? Or does it really make a difference? What I'm saying is, I have yet to determine if Faye is something sweet or something foul. And I'm not sure I wouldn't want her, one way or the other.

HER

The man is moving, all right? So, rather than keep pulling punches, I went ahead and hit him with the truth. I told him point-blank if a relationship is what you're looking for, sweetheart, I'm not the one. But if it's only fun and games you're after, we might be able to work a little something out. So I ran him down the deal and watched as he struggled to hold back his horror.

Don't get me wrong, I like Carl. If I didn't, I never would have bothered to give him so much as the time of day. But I should have known better than to think he'd be up to the challenge. After a couple of days passed without me hearing another peep out of him, I figured he'd wised up and decided it best not to mess with what he obviously couldn't handle.

So along comes Wednesday night, right? After my volunteering gig up at the hospital I decided to stop by the mall and check out the sale going on at the Bad Lady Boutique. I'd made my purchase and was meandering toward one of the mall's exits when I heard this voice behind me.

"Faye? Margaret Faye Abrahams?"

I didn't have to turn around. Recognition washed over me like a big ol' bucket of ice water. Had I been a stronger woman maybe I could have just shaken it off and kept on strutting. But when it comes to this particular voice, and more specifically, this particular man, I've always had what can only be described as an irrepressible weakness.

"Scoobie, Scoobie, Scoobie" was all I could say as I turned to face his still super-fine behind.

He spread his arms and, with a smile that was even more gorgeous than I remembered, said, "It's been, what? Eleven? Twelve years? Don't tell me after all this time that's the best you can do."

And like the simple fool that being around him frequently makes me, I couldn't help but grin and give him a hug.

He said, "Damn, girl, I can't tell you how good it is to see you again." Then he had to go and add, "Put on a little weight, though, haven't you?"

Being that I was considerably smaller the last time Scoobie saw me, I probably wouldn't have minded the comment had he not been the main somebody to blame for me picking up and holding on to the forty pounds of extra flab. Or if he hadn't been so compelled to drive the point home by slapping, squeezing, and jiggling my ass in a way that made me feel like a farm animal he intended either to mount or to ship off to market.

"Show a girl some decency and a little respect," I said. "In case you haven't noticed, this is a public place."

He ran his fingers alongside my jawline and said in that same soft, sweet, sexy voice that used to make me tremble, "I see the years have made you modest. That's good, because I distinctly remember a time when there wasn't much shame in your game when it came to me."

"Yes, and let's both be glad I finally grew up" is what I said on backing away from him. "Nice seeing you again, Scoobie. Who knows, maybe our paths will cross again one day when you're ready to own up to some of that treacherous crap you did to me."

I know the truth can hurt sometimes, but, girl, had you seen his face you'da thought I'd just hauled off and slapped him upside the head with a hammer or something. "Baby, wait," he said. "How do you know today's not that day? The least you could do is give me an opportunity to redeem myself. Have dinner with me tonight. My treat."

Honey, please. I know all about Scoobie's treats. In the past a "Scoobie treat" typically involved me paying in the end with money, time, tears, and quite frequently all three. I looked at him like he was crazy and said, "I guess you think we big girls are always on the lookout for an easy meal and a quick bone-jumping. Well, you'd best think again, because I'm neither hungry nor that durn desperate anymore, thank you."

Really, I wasn't trying to play hard, I just know this man. My infatuation with him dates all the way back to the summer I turned twelve, and ended the same number of years ago when he borrowed—excuse me—suckered a couple grand from me and used it to treat some other woman to a weekend in the Bahamas.

Dude told me I had him pegged all wrong. Told me there had been a lot of changes in his life since he and I were together, changes for the better. He said, "If nothing else, have a cup of coffee with me and I'll tell you all about them."

I told him, "Sorry, maybe some other time."

He dashed in front of me and said, "Okay, coffee, an admittedly long overdue apology and"—he pulled out a checkbook and a pen and started scribbling—"and this, a good-faith down payment on what I owe you."

Girl, when he ripped out that check and handed it to me, I was almost too afraid to look. But you know I did and there it was—cha-ching! Fifteen hundred big ones!

I'm sorry, girl, but between my student loans, my car payment, the mortgage, what I owe Nora, what I send to my folks, and every other durn thing that comes out of my paycheck on a monthly basis, my first instinct was to pocket the dough and hit the floor running. Instead I gathered my wits about me, handed him back the check, and just told him, "Look, there's a Starbucks on the second floor. One cup of coffee. An apology. And no games. Got it?"

HIM

I think I told you about my Uncle Westbrook and his little handyman business, right? And how he's kind enough to let his two favorite nephews—me and my equally broke cousin Squirrel—earn extra ends by helping him out on different projects? Even though it makes for a pretty decent part-time gig, it can still be kind of rough on an already hardworking brother, especially when it falls on the heels of his regular nine to five.

Anyway, this past Wednesday turned out to be one of those days for me. I had just clocked out of my full-time grind and was on my way home when I got word via my cousin Squirrel that Unc had some floors that needed refinishing and some walls that needed painting if I was interested. Being that I've got bills to pay and a whole host of mouths to feed, I could hardly say no, so I sucked it up like any real man would and went on to make that paper.

Tired, sore, and funky as I was when I finally stumbled in later that evening, about all I had in mind was a thorough scrub down, a few dabs of Ben-Gay, and a long conversation with my pillow. I was in the process of shedding my shorts when I heard a bunch of banging at my door. Turned out to be Nora wanting to know if I'd seen her ol' fickle friend Faye.

In between sniffles she told me, "I've tried reaching her on her cell, but she's not answering. It's just not like her to be out this late on a weeknight without trying to call and tell me what's up." Then she grabbed my arm and said, "You heard about that woman that got kidnapped from that barbecue joint up on Third last week, didn't you? And the one that got snatched a couple nights ago coming out of the library on Poplar? Well, I just heard on the news that they think it's the same guy who grabbed both of them."

Rather than buy into Nora's panic, I opted for the less strenuous role of the concerned yet cautious optimist. Besides, a part of me couldn't help but feel sorry for the joker who would unwittingly make the mistake of trying to snatch Faye up from somewhere. Hell, he'd more than likely come off better trying to wrestle with a doggone porcupine. I looked at my watch and was like, "Okay, Nora, calm down a second. It's, what, 9:45? Have you tried calling up to the church?"

Nora screwed her face all up and said, "The church? Carl, what in the hell would Faye be doing up at church this time of night?"

Excuse me? Having noticed Faye leaving outta there round about the same time every Wednesday evening, I'd just assumed that like most good Black Baptists—excluding myself, of course—that her Wednesday-night forays had something to do with midweek Bible study.

But Nora was quick to set me straight. "Carl, Wednesday night is the night Faye goes up to the hospital."

"The hospital? Oh, so maybe she's just working some extra overtime or something," I said, thinking I had it all figured out.

But that only seemed to make Nora all the more flustered. "Look, man, what Faye does every Wednesday night ain't got nuthin' to do with work or overtime, okay? And that's all I'm finna say about it. If you wanna know anything else, you need to take it up with her. All right?"

"Tell you what," I said, seeing that she was on the verge of falling apart on me. "Let me grab a quick shower and after I'm cleaned up I'll come over and hold your hand, help you call some folks, organize a search party, or whatever it is you think we need to do."

I was sincere about that, man. Like I told you, me and Nora are cool. Whatever thoughts I mighta once entertained about trying to ease up on her, I'd long since abandoned in deference to her total lack of interest in a straitlaced, broke-butt brother like myself.

Anyway, by the time I got over to her place, she'd calmed down considerably. She told me she wanted to give Faye another thirty minutes or more before we called the police or went out looking for a body. I told her "cool" and plopped down on the couch with her to wait. Having never known Nora's conversation to extend too far beyond the latest dude she'd let dog her, I was kind of surprised when she inquired as to what Faye and I had been doing besides watching videos on all those Friday nights we'd spent together at my place.

Not knowing if ol' girl was out to implicate me in Faye's disappearance or what, I did like she'd done when she thought I was pressing her about Faye's Wednesday-night routine. I played dumb and kicked the question back to her. "What she tell you?"

"That's just the thing," Nora said. "Me and Faye talk about some of everything, especially when it comes to men. But I've noticed when the subject turns to you, she'll only share so much. I'm starting to think it just might be because she likes you a lot more than she wants to let on."

Interesting, huh? I thought so. Didn't take much prodding to get Nora to feed me a whole host of other juicy tidbits about her friend. Among other things, she verified Faye's skank-ti-fied "hit it and quit it" credo and put forth as its inspiration some bad-news boyfriend who'd obviously been the major love of ol' girl's life. She even showed me snapshots of the sparkling-eyed, slim-figured babe Faye had been before the years of getting jaded and jacked around had taken their toll.

By the time Faye finally strutted through the door that night, not only had I begun to view her in a different light, but I also knew I wasn't gonna be satisfied until I'd uncovered whatever else lay hidden beneath the mask she always seemed to slip behind around me.

HER

Twenty minutes max was all I'd planned to waste. I figured that would be more than enough time for the Scoobmeister to spin whatever lies he intended to tell me. After ordering a latte and finding us a table in the crowded food court, I sat down, glanced at my watch, and said, "Okay, Scoobie, out with it already. What wondrous series of turns has your sordid little life taken in the years since we both went our separate ways?"

He laughed and said, "First off, hardly anyone calls me Scoobie anymore." Then he passed me his business card and proudly proclaimed that most of the folks he dealt with these days referred to him either as "Chef Venard Payne," or "Chef Payne" for short.

Wearing the sweetest smile I could muster, I leaned over, fingered what looked to be a real Rolex on his wrist, and asked him to explain exactly how one goes from being too trifling to hold down a job flipping burgers at Mickey D's to being the executive chef for the dining room of a reputable financial institution like Morris-Morgan?

He was like, "What? You saying you don't believe me?" Before I could answer, he wrapped his hand around mine, looked me dead in the eyes, and said, "Faye, everything I have now—from this watch, to the Hilfiger on my back, to the Benz I drive—I earned the hard way. After I left Memphis, I went back to school, busted my tail, and kissed all the right behinds. If you're anywhere near as ambitious and driven as you used to be, my success is something you ought to be able to appreciate."

I told him I was happy for him. I just couldn't help but think that maybe I'd have a success story of my own to share if someone hadn't ruined my credit and left me with a bunch of bills before skipping town with what little money I had left. "Did you know I had to file bankruptcy?" is what I asked him. "Did you know things got so bad for me that had it not been for Nora I probably would have ended up dead, strung out, or locked up in an asylum somewhere? Did you ever once stop to care?"

He had the nerve to tear up, like he was actually fixing to cry, and said, "Faye, I'm sorry for all that I did and all that I should have done. But something tells me I could sit here all night apologizing and explaining until I ran out of spit and wind and you still wouldn't take me seriously. So come and go for a ride with me and I'll prove it to you."

I couldn't help but get tickled. Even with the mustache and goatee dude is sporting these days, at that moment he looked so much like the baby-faced boy who'd way-back-when dropped down on his knees and asked me to go with him that I just had to laugh and ask exactly what it was he intended to show me that I hadn't already seen more times than I cared to admit or remember.

He pulled out the check he'd handed me earlier and said, "For starters, that I'm more than able to make good on this. And that I will pay back everything I owe you, with interest, even if I have to go into debt doing it."

Anyway, girl, to make a long story short, that's how I ended up taking a late-night tour of Morris-Morgan's dining hall, the kitchen facilities, and the private office bearing the nameplate of one "Chef Venard Nathaniel Payne." It all looked too legit to be a lie, as did Scoobie's demeanor when he started talking to me about church and how he'd been looking for one to attend. Of course, you know, the latter I'm still not trying to believe until I actually see it. But most shocking of all, not once throughout the entire evening did the brother make a single play for the panties.

Talk about impressed. I couldn't wait to get home and tell Nora. But when I finally stepped through my front door at around 10:45 that evening, guess who I discovered sitting up on my sofa, eating Redenbacher's and looking like he didn't have anything better to do than worry the heck out of me?

HIM

I know good and well the sight of me all reared back on her sofa, straight-cold kicking it with her roomie, had to have come as a shock. But Faye, as always, played it cool. She even went so far as to extend a nod and a "What's up?" my way before Nora jumped into the mix with her mad-mama tirade.

"And just where in the hell were you, Ms. Thang, that you couldn't pick up the phone and call somebody? Got folks sitting 'round here wondering if some fool done gone and bopped you upside the head and left you lying in a ditch somewhere. And you know good and well I got to be up at the Bulk Mail Center early in the morning."

Faye apologized and tried to tell Nora about someone she'd run into at the mall, but homegirl wasn't having it. She said, "Uh-uh, if you're not fixing to tell me about an accident, a carjacking, or a death in the family, I ain't trying hear it. Maybe tomorrow I'll be in a better frame of mind, but right now, I'm taking me a B.C. and calling it a night."

Without further ado, Nora proceeded to make good on her threat, leaving me and Faye alone to face off with each other. I told her, "She was really worried about you," only to have Faye sorta shrug and saunter off to the kitchen, like she couldn't have cared less.

As I fell in step behind her, I was struck by a few things that up until then I hadn't really noticed before, like the fact that I'd never seen the chick without makeup and how she always looked like she'd just come in from having her hair and nails done.

While I watched, she puttered around the kitchen, checking her mail, pouring herself a glass of water from the fridge, and occasionally eyeballing me. I wasn't really leering, I was just, you know, taking note of a few things, like the pantsuit she had on that was hugging and tugging in all the right places. It was one of these beige and cream pinstriped numbers, cut dangerously low in front. And even though I'm not typically what you might call a "boob man" I couldn't resist the urge to take a visual stroll across the honey-colored terrain laid out so wondrously before me.

But when my gaze rose up outta her cleavage only to crash into the hardened glare she was aiming at me, the most I could come up with, man, was a shamefaced "You look nice."

She rolled her eyes and, in one of those tired "I ain't got time for this type of mess" tones of voice, asked if there was something I wanted.

Realizing I was 'bout to get run off, I said, "Yeah, I want in."

She scrunched up her face and said, "Beg your pardon?"

I'm not gonna lie, man. I had to swallow a couple of times to drive back the flock of butterflies I felt fluttering around in my belly. But once done, I stepped to her again. "The game," I said. "The one you're playing. I want in."

"Why?" she asked.

I told her, "Intrigue, I suppose. You're one big elaborate puzzle to me. I like puzzles. The more difficult, the better."

I could tell by the way she raised her eyebrows and set down her glass she didn't care for my answer. She sashayed that big butt past me, slanging yang all the while. "As much as I hate spoiling anyone's fun, Carl, I think you're better off knowing that a hump-buddy is what I'm looking for, not a shrink. And that's pretty much the big picture, in a nutshell. It's nowhere near as complicated as you're trying to make it."

Like a puppy eager for some petting, I trailed her to her bedroom, where I pulled up short at the door. I watched for a moment as she removed her jewelry and shoes and started rummaging through her closets and drawers. After summoning the proper amount of courage, I said, "Can I ask you a question? Why'd you proposition me?"

She stopped moving long enough to say something to the effect of "Because you told me you were moving, and I figured the distance would help circumvent any silly notions you might try to entertain about us having anything other than something quick and casual."

I told her, "Hey, I know the deal. And like I said before, I'm game. The ball, sweetheart, is officially back in your court. So do you still want to do this or what?"

She laughed like I'd really said something funny. Then she walked over to me and was like, "You know, I think it's time we said good night."

Now for all practical purposes she was telling me, "Go away, little boy. You can't even handle the likes of this."

But having already come so far, I wasn't 'bout to just walk away with my tail tucked. Besides, I figured if some thug-loving was what she wanted, then damn it, some thug-loving was what I'd give her. I told her, "You're right, it is getting late. But I'm not leaving here until I find out what I need to know."

She squinted her eyes and said, "Which is?"

"This," I said, making my move and hoping all the while it wouldn't get me slapped. I didn't grab her, or pull her against me, or try to feel her up. No, man, all I wanted was a kiss, the kind that, if she cooperated, would let me know whether pursuing this thing was gonna be worth my while. And being that she didn't do much by the way of resistance, I think she must have wanted it, too.

Matter of fact, after a quick quivering of the lips and a brief flutter of lashes, the girl held her ground, opened her mouth against mine, and matched me stroke for stroke.

When our tongues finally came undone, she looked at me and said, "You mind telling me what that was all about?"

"Oh, like you don't know," I said, wanting for all the world to go at it again but figuring it best to bide my time.

Looking like she wanted to laugh again, she insisted she didn't have a clue. I played along with her and said, "Yeah, but you liked it, didn't you?"

She tried to stop smiling but couldn't. And finally she said, "If you wanna know the truth . . . yeah . . . I did."

I backed away from her and in a whisper that was pure "wannabe Wesley," as in Snipes, I said, "Well, then, let's just call it a sampling of what's yet to come."

HER

Had any other brother rolled up on me like that, he would have straight got clocked. I don't know, bad as I hate to admit it, I guess there's just something about Carl that appeals to my softer side.

You'd never suspect it, but as silly and goofy as he is, the brother really can kiss. And ever since he's shown himself capable of more than just one type of lip service, I've been sort of looking forward to checking out some of his other skills. But who knows when that's liable to happen. Unlike durn near every other fool I've invited to play in the park, Carl isn't acting in too big a hurry to run beyond first base. Matter of fact, he let another whole weekend slide by before he brought up the topic again.

I'm trying my best to be patient and understanding. And really, given his willingness to accept my terms, it's only fair I let him set the pace. But, girl, you know I'm most definitely tired of being kept awake at night by a body that's throbbing from a lack of attention. And as much as I hate the thought of screening and cultivating another potential player at this late stage in the game—a woman has to do what a woman has to do, especially when her needs aren't being properly attended to.

Part of the problem, I know, is time and his apparent lack of it. In addition to his regular nine to five, he's trying to juggle night classes at the university, some kind of part-time handyman gig, and on top of all that, his kids.

I met his daughters the other day. They're ten-year-old twins whose gift of gab comes close to matching their motor-mouth old man's.

I was leaving my place just as Carl and the girls were piling out of his. He put on the brakes and said, "Ladies, I want you say 'hi' to Ms. Faye."

After their "Hey, Ms. Faye," Carl introduced them to me as his daughters, Renita and Renee, better known to their proud papa as Princess Ren and Princess Nay-Nay. The twins promptly followed up their pop's royal introduction with an all-too-cute curtsy.

Carl told me they were going out for ice cream and invited me to tag along. Since it was Wednesday night and I already had other plans, I opted for a rain check.

"That's right," Carl said. "Tonight's the night you go up to the hospital. So what exactly do you do up there every Wednesday night, if you don't mind me asking?"

Uh-huh, right then and there I knew Nora had been running her big mouth again. But rather than come right out and tell the brother to mind his own, I cut him some slack because of his kids. It wasn't any big deal, I told him. Just some volunteer work I've been doing for years.

At that point, one of the twins butted in with an "Excuse me, Ms. Faye, but could we get your opinion about something? Do you think ten is too young to start wearing nail polish?"

Taking my cue from the scowl that flared up on Carl's face, I said, "I think that depends on what the ten-year-old's daddy has to say on the matter."

Carl clapped and shouted, "Good answer, good answer." Come to find out his daughters are scheduled to be in some wedding in a couple of weeks and they've been hounding him about having their nails done for the occasion.

You could tell these were girls used to having their way, especially with their daddy, because his negative stance didn't alter a note in either of their tunes. "Aww, Daddy, you're so old school. How come we can't at least get manicures?"

I had to bite my lip to keep from laughing when Carl said, "A manicure? Please, what y'all need to do is concentrate on your schoolwork. Either one of you need pretty nails to open up a book? No, I didn't think so."

He sent them off to the car and waited until they were out of earshot before offering me an apologetic list of reasons why he probably wouldn't have time to hook up with me until later in the week—Sunday at the earliest. Then he asked if there was anyplace in particular I'd like to go, forcing me to restate what I'd told him previously about the non-necessity of any prebedroom formalities.

I said, "Look, Carl, other than someplace that has clean sheets, you really don't have to take me anywhere."

He said, "I know I don't have to. But I would like to. If it helps any, don't think of it as a date. Think of it as an extended version of foreplay."

"Tell you what," I told him. "Let me get back with you about all that."

See, girl, homeboy is trying to complicate matters. My thing is, why waste his money or my time? His best bet is to save the wining and dining for somebody who's trying to care, because like I've already told him, I am not the one. And furthermore, if he doesn't hurry up and come on with it, I may just have to let him go in lieu of the next acceptable somebody who will.

HIM

Nora's coyness about the quote-unquote volunteer work Faye supposedly does up at the hospital every Wednesday night can mean only one thing—somebody's trying to hide something. My question is, why?

When Nora inadvertently gave up some of the goods on ol' girl, I just automatically assumed the hospital in question was the Veterans Administration where Faye works. Then I got to thinking how the VA is west of where we live and how every time I've seen Faye jetting outta here on a Wednesday night, she's been headed east. Hmm . . . interesting, huh?

Yeah, I know it really wasn't none of my business, but the bloodhound in me wouldn't let me leave it alone, man. And that night me and the girls bumped into Faye on our way out to get ice cream seemed like the perfect opportunity to slap on my detective's cap and hit the trail.

I let her get a good couple minutes' head start, then after announcing to the girls that we were taking the long route to the ice cream parlor, I set out after her. And guess what I discovered? The trail dead ends at the hospital, all right. Just not the VA. Nope, whatever Faye's doing involves the folks and the facilities at Baptist Medical Center's eastern division.

First I was just curious. Now I'm really starting to wonder what the chick is up to, and all sorts of possibilities have crossed my mind. I mean, ol' girl just might have some chemical dependency issues she's trying to work on, could be she's a schizophrenic, a manic-depressive, or quite possibly some sort of sex addict.

When I made the mistake of peeping my cousin Squirrel to the mystery, he volunteered to pick up the scent where I'd left off, and all for the very reasonable price of a forty ounce and a hot slab of Corky's ribs. "Come on, man," he said. "Ain't like 'Big Red' know who I am. And the building is open to the public. Wouldn't be no thang for me to follow her up in da joint and find out just what in the devil it is she be doing up in there every Wednesday night."

It wasn't a bad plan, except for the one thing Squirrel overlooked—the fact that his nickname fits him to a T. And don't get me wrong, 'cause I ain't got nothin' but love for the brother. Having grown up with the boy, I can readily vouch for his inability to hurt anyone, outside of himself. Yet and still, he's this scrawny, pinched face, shifty-eyed rat of a dude. The type folks are apt to suspect is up to something, even when he's not. Shoot, the last thing I needed was for him to go and get his squirrelly tail arrested for stalking on my account.

After having given it some thought, I've pretty much decided even if Faye is trying to hide some sort of secret addiction or affliction, I doubt that it's something contagious. As callous as she comes across sometimes, she just doesn't strike me as the deliberately malicious type. It's a gut feeling, if you will, and one I'm content to roll with for now.

But don't worry, man, I'm not about to let my fascination with this woman or any other wreak havoc on my physical, mental, or spiritual well-being. It's not like I'm out looking to get hooked, hitched, or hung-up. All I'm after is what ol' girl said she was offering—a little action, no strings attached. Trust me, first real noose I see, I'm out.

HER

Nora and I haven't been on the best of terms lately. Did I tell you how hard she tripped after I gave her the 411 on

Scoobie and the new turn his life has apparently taken? Girl, she had the nerve to call me sick, twisted, and hopelessly pathetic. I mean, like she's really in a position to talk about somebody when it comes to men.

I guess I should have seen it coming, though. Nora never liked Scoobie from day one, a sentiment that over the years has only intensified. "Scoobie ain't nothing but a user, Faye. You can do better" is what I can remember her telling me as far back as junior high. And she was right, of course. Scoobie was a user and I his most willing and gullible usee. But that was then and this is now.

Whether Scoobie has changed or not remains to be seen. What I do know for sure is that I have—changed, that is—and even Nora can attest to that. My stint with Scoobie, though long and torturous, was a lesson well learned and one that I have yet to repeat with any other canine. Girlfriend, on the other hand, can still be found durn near every other week bad-mouthing and boo-hooing over some new breed of mangy mutt she done let lick and maul her.

But it's not like I don't know where she's coming from. She simply doesn't want to see me get weak and fall for the okey-doke again. After all, she was the main somebody right there with me through it all—the pain, the tears, the senseless drama, even the time when I thought there'd be no getting back up. The truth is, if anybody's earned the right to call me on my madness, it's Nora. But that doesn't mean I've durn well got to like it or take it lying down.

When she jumped in my face about the little bit of time I spent with Scoobie the other night, I told her I was perfectly capable of deciding whether or not I should be dealing with dude and without her help, thank you! Well, after a fairly heated exchange, we both decided it might be best to just stop speaking altogether for a while. That's why when she marched in Saturday afternoon and commenced to yanking my ear about the importance of being neighborly, I pretty much ignored her.

I was sitting in the kitchen, just as content as I wanted to be, flipping through the pages of my latest romance novel and waiting for the cookies I had in the oven to brown, when Nora busted up in the place talking about, "Guess what? Carl and his girls are throwing some burgers and franks on the grill and they've invited us to come over around six and help them eat 'em."

Skinny as Nora's narrow behind is, you'd never guess the chile eats like a 280-pound linebacker and is always the first somebody looking to get her grub on. And the way she kept carrying on about going next door, you would have thought the brother had offered to fire us up a couple of filets mignons.

When I didn't say anything she said, "Come on and go with me, Faye, please. You are going, right?"

Without bothering to look up from my book, I told her, "We're not talking, remember?"

Rather than move on, she pulled up a chair, sat down, and said, "Listen, I know you ain't trying to hear this, but I'm gonna say it anyway. Our next door neighbor, Carl? Not only is he a nice guy, but every time I see him these days, you're all he's trying to talk about. I'm saying, on the real Faye, I think this boy's starting to have genuine feelings for you, so maybe you oughta think twice about playing games with him."

I started to tell her I ought to go if only to keep her big blabbermouth from telling dude whatever there was left to tell about my business. Instead, I just glared at her a second before dropping my head back into my book.

Nora knows better than anyone how I'm only too content to spend an evening entertaining a warm batch of cookies and a good book without feeling like I've missed out on anything. Which makes all the more inexcusable her mumbling something about my lack of congeniality (big word for her) when six o'clock finally rolled around and she found herself making the trip next door without me.

Left alone to enjoy the peace and quiet of my own company, I probably would have hung tight there for the rest of the night had it not been for all the racket they started making next door. Wasn't any use of me trying to read any more. I could barely hear myself think over all the music, loud talk, and laughter leaking through the flimsy walls between our condos.

I drew myself a tub of water in hopes that a nice hot bath would help relax me. No such luck, honey. Even with the door closed, my eyes fastened shut, and the Dianne Reeves I'd put on in an effort to drown out some of the rhythmic thumping sounds coming from next door, I could still hear Nora over there cackling like some kinda crazed hyena.

Oh yeah, you and I both know it was a deliberate ploy on girlfriend's part to get me riled. It worked too, 'cause after about fifteen minutes of the carrying on, I was ready to run over and snatch the heifer up by her scrawny little neck. Then I got a better idea.

How's the saying go? If you can't win, join 'em and beat the heck out of 'em at their own game. Well, anyway, after I got out of the tub I slipped into some fresh duds, grabbed a few essential items, and mosied on over as if arriving nearly an hour late had been part of my plan from the git.

Carl greeted me at the door with a "Hey! What a nice surprise. Nora said you weren't coming."

I swung past him like it wasn't no thang and said, "Just goes to show you, Nora doesn't know half as much as she thinks she does."

Game face intact, I popped the lid on the plastic container I was holding, waved it past Nora's nose, then handed it to Carl, and in the sweetest voice I could muster said, "I brought cookies. Chocolate chip. Fresh from the oven."

Honey, you should have seen them. With Carl's two little ones taking the lead, they pounced on the bait—chewing, smacking, drooling, and whining like a bunch of sugar-sprung junkies who'd been fiending all night for a fix.

HIM

I'm trying to figure out what's up with all the baked goodies Faye keeps feeding me. Remember the carrot cake? Well, the other night it was homemade chocolate chip cookies. In the past when a woman's given me something she's crafted by hand and thrown a bit of hip into, I've typically read it as a pretty good sign of her affection for me. But with all the changes this sister's put me through, I don't know whether to view her sweet offerings as genuine acts of kindness or part of a more sinister plan to fatten a brother up before the kill.

Now, I was down with the sweets. I'll even confess to having gobbled down the greatest portion of 'em myself. But when ol' girl broke out the manicure kit she just so happened to have tucked away in her bag, I was kinda slow to bite.

Call me an old head if you want to, but if there's one thing me and the ex both agree on it's that our little girls should remain little girls for as long as possible. Having grown up in a house with three fast-tail sisters myself, I'm a firsthand witness to where too early a start in the dolling up and adornment process is liable to lead.

But with the twins "pretty-pleasing" the devil outta me, I was eventually convinced, coerced, corralled, or whatever you want to call it into running the idea by Bet. Feeling for all the world like some poor sap who'd just let himself get talked into bungee-jumping off the Hernando de Soto bridge, I got her on the phone, hurriedly pitched the plan to her, then braced myself for the verbal head-bashing I figured would follow. Yeah, I ended up with my face broke all right, but only because Bet pulled a fast one. Man, instead of launching into a lengthy questioning of my sanity, she did something far worse—she asked to speak to Faye.

Now, you know, those two birds cackling at each other was the last thing I wanted. To be perfectly honest, the thought that a lady friend of mine and my ex might actually be capable of indulging in a civil conversation was, for me, totally inconceivable. But I went ahead and handed over the phone, and to my total astonishment, after Faye got through running down the deal, Bet was cool with it. She even went so far as to okay an application of the clear nail polish the girls had been lobbying so hard for. What can I say, man? Just when you think you've got them all figured out, they switch up on you.

I certainly never would have pegged Ms. Faye as the type who'd spend an entire evening at my place playing Scrabble with my daughters, doing their nails, and sitting on the floor between them while they watched some silly kid show on Nickelodeon. But she did. And she seemed pretty content doing it.

Even after Nora skipped out on us to don her managerial cloak for the good folks down at the Bulk Mail Center, Faye stuck around. Actually, I was really digging her company and after I'd sent the twins off to get washed up and ready for bed, I told her as much. But when I asked if she'd decided where she wanted to go prior to the rendezvous I thought we'd tentatively scheduled for Sunday, her answer snatched my happy butt back into the bitter reality.

After lighting up a cigarette and taking a couple of puffs, she looked at me through the smoky haze and said, "You're still interested in going out?"

"Heck, yeah," I said. "Matter of fact, there's gonna be an Al Jarreau concert on Mud Island next weekend. I could get us tickets if you want to go."

A nice jazz set would be right down her alley, is what I figured. But nooo! Instead of getting bubbly behind the suggestion, she sighed, like just the very thought made her tired. "Carl, I hope you're not forgetting what I said about not trying to take this relationship any place other than the bedroom" is what she had the nerve to up and tell me.

I told her, "No, I haven't forgotten. And the bedroom is ultimately where I'd like to see us end up, too. I guess I'm just operating from the premise that getting there is half the fun. The way I look at it, the only thing the two of us going out and having a good time together is bound to do is make the passion between us all the more intense."

Now, after a rap that sweet, any other sister would have at least cracked a smile. Not Faye. She just sat there puffing like a chimney and eyeballing me like I'd just passed gas without saying "excuse me" or something. Man, I'm telling you, sometimes it just doesn't pay for a brother to try and play nice.

HER

Girl, what was I supposed to do, applaud? I just sat there, like most any other intelligent woman would have, and tried to figure out just what percentage of the brother's rap was real and what percentage was the usual rot.

Something about my silence must have unnerved him because no less than ten seconds into it, he jumped up and said, "Look, if you really don't want to do the date thing, it's cool. Sleep on it, why don't you, and get back with me about it later. Either way it goes, though, I'd still like to see you sometime tomorrow."

I could tell by the expression on his face I'd hurt his feelings again, which hadn't been at all my intent. To make up for it, I told him, "Well, you know the early part of my day is pretty much gonna be spent in church. But maybe we can catch a movie or something, sometime tomorrow evening. I'll check the paper in the morning and see what's playing."

Keep in mind, though, I did say "maybe." It wasn't like I promised him anything. A wise woman is always going to leave her options open just in case the need for an easy out should happen to arise.

But anyway, about that time Renita and Renee came back in to say their good nights. And you want to know something? Watching Carl interact with his daughters was surprisingly one of the highlights of the evening.

He's good with his girls. Maybe it's because they're older or maybe the high regard in which he seems to hold their mother is a factor, but whatever the reason, it was both nice and a relief to know his relationship with the twins lacked all the tension and drama I'd witnessed between him and his son.

So yeah, girl, despite my initial reservations, hanging out with Carl and his crew wasn't all that bad. The twins got a real kick out of me doing their nails. You should have seen how big their baby browns got when I whipped out that manicure kit.

Of course, that little stunt only opened the door to a whole 'nother something. Now not only do they want me to do their nails for this wedding they're supposed to be in, but they've also invited me to attend so I can see them all dressed up, looking cute and doing the flower-girl thing.

Carl didn't waste a second in leaping aboard the bandwagon, but I've got some serious reservations about the four of us charging down that particular path together. I don't know if I ought to be getting in that deep with them, especially since me and dude aren't even trying to be a couple. The last thing I'd want to do is give him or his girls the wrong impression about the nature of my intentions.

But like I said, the night had its moments, the most memorable of which occurred when it was time for the girls to head off to bed. In the process of saying their good nights and without any prompting from Carl, the twins took it upon themselves to thank me with hugs and kisses for both the cookies I'd brought over as well as the time and attention I'd given to their nails. Well-mannered children I can appreciate, but I'm not used to being around such touchy-feely types. All the fuss only made me have to go to the bathroom.

While Carl marched the kids off to bed, I headed for the john with every intention of emptying the ol' bladder before squaring things up with dude and heading on home. But on my way there, I couldn't resist the urge to stop for a quick peek into the girls' bedroom. That's when I caught them, all three of them, down on their knees quietly reciting the Lord's Prayer.

It's not like I haven't seen folks pray before. I'm a churchgoing girl from way back. But there was just something about the sight of this man and his children huddled together on the floor, eyes closed, heads bowed, and hands clasped, that moved me. I was touched, so much so, I forgot all about having to pee.

Even after they'd finished their amens I just stood there and watched as Carl helped them into bed, smoothed their covers, and then kissed one of the girls' eyebrows, the tip of her nose, and her chin before leaning over and doing the exact same to the other child.

The smile he flashed me when he finally turned and caught me standing there helped alleviate some of the embarrassment I felt at having intruded.

I knew I was busted, plain and simple. I thought he was getting ready to rub it in, so I said, "I wasn't trying to spy or anything. I just—" But before I could spit out the rest of my defense, he hushed me by placing his fingers against his lips. After he turned out the light and closed the girls' bedroom door, he looked at me and whispered, "So you gonna stay awhile or what?"

I'm sorry, girl. I know I shouldn't have, but I let myself get all caught up in the sappy sweetness of the moment and before it even occurred to me to think about it twice, I'd told him, "Sure, I can stay for a little while."

HIM

It's probably safe to say that listening to me vent my frustrations about being a father isn't what Faye had in mind when she sat down and cuddled up next to me on the couch. And hey, it's not like I didn't want to give the sister a little play. I just knew I wouldn't have wanted to stop at a little is all.

And what would that have looked like? Me and ol' girl getting busy with the twins right around the corner and subject to pop in on us at any second? Oh sure, I could have waited until the girls were sound asleep, snuck Faye back into my bedroom, locked the door, and coaxed her into keeping the moaning to a minimum. Maybe I would've, had the understanding between the five of us—meaning me, her, the kids, and my ex—been that Faye was gonna be my lady on something like a full-time, permanent basis. But that wasn't the case, and wasn't no good bound to come out of any of us pretending otherwise. Besides, these days I'm all about trying to set a better example for my girls, and exposing them to the sad, sordid details of my sex life is definitely not the road that's most liable to lead me there.

I took Faye telling me how much she admired my no-nonsense approach to raising my two princesses as a sure sign that she not only understood my position but felt the same way, too. Looking back on things, that may have been where I made my mistake.

Man, an honest-to-goodness, old-fashioned purging is what I pulled on this girl. I let it all out—my feelings of inadequacy about my son, my fears of having already done irreparable damage to my daughters by virtue of the divorce, and my inability to give as much of myself as I'd like to any of my kids. After unloading all my baggage on her I was too spent to do much of anything but sit there quietly, soaking up bits and pieces of the ten o'clock news.

I bet the only reason she didn't run screaming from the room is that I'd probably bored her to the point of being too stiff to move. Stupid me, I thought her silence was some sort of indication that we'd finally made a real connection. Man, little did I know that what I thought was the sound of me and Faye clicking was actually the sound of ol' girl ticking.

To borrow a line from one of the Gap Band's greatest hits, "she dropped a bomb on me." I'm serious, man, come Sunday not only did the sister stand me up without even bothering to extend me the simple courtesy of a phone call, but when I finally did catch up with her jive behind, she was flapping her jaws and grinning all up in some other dude's face.

HER

Carl needs to stop tripping. Why after spending four and a half hours with him and his kids on a Saturday night would I turn around the next day and deliberately leave him hanging? I had every intention of seeing him that Sunday. But the real of it is, things happen sometimes—things over which we often have little or no control.

Girl, please, had anybody told me when I woke up that morning I was destined to spend durn near half my day with the likes of one Scoobie, aka Venard Nathaniel Payne,

I would have called them a bald-faced liar and then crawled back into bed to make sure it didn't happen.

My first mistake, besides leaving the house at all that Sunday, was arriving at church with a thirst that couldn't wait to be quenched. So there I was in the vestibule, right, bent over the water fountain getting my drink on, when I felt this presence behind me and heard this gravelly voice.

"My, my, Sistah Abrahams. Aren't we looking mighty blessed this morning?"

No, it wasn't Scoobie. Worse. It was old lecherous Deacon Jones, who, though very much married and supposedly sanctified, is always trying to hit on somebody—as if his seventy-some-year-old, ancient behind would even be able to handle it if somebody was crazy enough to try and give him some.

Anyway, when I turned around, I realized he had me trapped against the water fountain with nowhere to run. "Deacon Jones," I said, acting all surprised. "Isn't that your lovely wife I see over there?"

Honey, I might as well have saved my breath. That old buzzard's big pop-eyes never once left my chest as he wagged his head and said, "No, no, 'fraid not. Sistah Jones, praise the Lord, decided to visit with her kinfolk over at Greater Blessings this morning." Then, dabbing sweat and drooling all the while, he leaned over and added, "Not to change the subject but, ah, I was wondering, Sistah Abrahams, if you've given any thought as to when we might get together for that cup of coffee? As you know, I'm quite eager to discuss with you how you might grow closer in your relationship with the Lord."

Yeah, right. Girl, I was stuttering and fumbling and trying to come up with just the right lie when Scoobie walked up and spared me the trouble.

"Morning, love. Sorry I'm late," he said as he squeezed between me and the deacon to plant a soft one on my cheek. He smiled at the old man and said, "How are you this morning, sir? Forgive me for interrupting. I just didn't want Ms. Abrahams to think I'd declined her kind invitation to join her in worship this morning."

The freaky deke pulled on his suspenders and reared back on his ol' run-down heels before he said, "Oh, tha's quite all right, son. It's a pleasure and a sho' 'nuff blessing to have you with us today. Y'all go on and enjoy the service. Me and the good sistah can get together on our business some other time."

While the deacon strutted off in pursuit of his next victim, I peeled my butt off the water fountain, brushed off my clothes, and asked Scoobie, who was trying hard not to crack up, "What are you doing here?"

He held out his arm and as we walked toward the sanctuary he said, "Is that any way to greet the chap who just spared you the trauma of being felt up and slobbed on by old man Methuselah?"

I might have laughed had I not been so distracted by all the heads I noticed swiveling in our direction. Not that I could blame folks for gawking, 'cause when it comes to Venard Nathaniel, we're not talking just your average, good-looking brother. No, ma'am, we're talking exceptionally pretty—big brown eyes, thick, wavy hair, broad shoulders, tight buns—the whole nine. And on top of that, the brother had stepped up in the place sharp as a military crease. Shoot, had I not known him I probably would have been sitting up somewhere with my eyes bucked and swinging from the sockets as well.

Acting totally oblivious to it all, Scoobie said, "Shame on you. Obviously, you thought I was joking when I told you I'd been looking for a church home."

"Joking? No, I wouldn't say that," I whispered back at him. "Try lying."

It's the truth, girl. Bottom line when it comes to Scoobie and the tales he tells—if I can't see, touch, taste, or smell it, I'm not hardly likely to believe it.

But yeah, I did recall him asking me where I was attending church these days. Of course, I never expected the exchange would lead to him showing up at New Hope, Love, and Deliverance looking to join. But that's exactly what happened. Not only did the brother join, but he stood up and made one of those full-fledged testimonies about the horrible wretch he'd been before he'd seen the light.

The congregation bought it hook, line, and sinker. Girl, you should have seen all the women young and old alike he had up in there weeping and wailing and falling all out in the aisles. Even though I made a point of giving him a congratulatory hug and welcoming him to the fold, I was praying all the while that the good Lord would give me a chance to get up out of there before he threw down the lightning strike.

With all the meeting, greeting, gabbing, and grabbing going on at the end of the service, I figured Scoobie would be much too preoccupied to care if I split. Just as soon as the crowd around him got good and thick, I let the twenty or more hussies shamelessly vying for my spot next to the brother have at it.

I'd strolled back out into the vestibule and was about to kick up my heels when I be dog if I didn't hear him call my name. "Faye! Faye, hold up a minute."

He came and said, "Listen, I'm going to chat with the pastor and meet with some of the deacons. You have time to wait for me?"

I said, "Now, why would I want to do that?"

Brother acted like he wasn't even fazed. He said, "Well, I was planning to stop by the gym after I left here. I thought you might like to come along."

Girl, I had to cough to keep from laughing. He obviously had me confused with one of those starry-eyed groupies he'd just gotten through flirting with. Never one to mince words, I told him, "Honey, please. Watching you work out is hardly my idea of an afternoon well spent."

His snappy comeback was, "So who says you have to watch? You're welcome to join me. Matter of fact, I've got a personal trainer I'd be happy to hook you up with. Come on, I promise to make it worth your while."

Baby, don't you know I've got a standing Sunday appointment with a chicken three-piece and a Big K Cola? is what I started to say. Instead, I just shook my head and told him, "Thanks, but no thanks."

That's when he called himself trying to get ugly with me. He said, "Oh, it's like that, huh? You can take my money, but you can't spend any time with me?"

I said, "Your money? I beg your pardon, don't you mean *my* money? The money you stole from me umpteen-some years ago? Man, don't make me lose my religion up in here!"

He jerked open his jacket and said, "Fine. You want me to just write you another check? If that's what it's going to take to mend what's broken between us, then maybe you just ought to name your price so we can be done with it."

Who? Don't think I wasn't tempted. But you know, being in the Lord's house and all, I opted to take the high road. I told him, "Scoobie, sweetheart, if nothing else, let's just get this one thing straight. There's not enough money in this world or the next to mend all that's broke between us. Okay?"

"Baby, I know that," he said, looking right contrite. "All I want is a chance to give you back at least some of what I took. Will you let me do that? Please?"

Yeah, girl, that's when I got weak and went ahead and cut the brother some slack. "Look," I told him, "I have to stop by the church nursery to see if there's anything I can help the director with. It'll probably take me a few minutes. So swing by when you get finished and if I'm still there, maybe we can talk."

HIM

I'm not ashamed to admit that I'd been keeping an eye out for Faye. She'd told me she'd try to set something up with me after she got home from church. So quite naturally every car I heard that afternoon had me running to the window. That's how I'd first caught a glimpse of her and dude. She'd pulled up in her car and not more than two seconds later, he'd pulled up in his—a spotless, vanilla ice cream–colored, brand-spanking-new Benz, no less.

Even though he looked vaguely familiar, initially I just figured dude was one of her church members, some harmless, nonfornicating, effeminate type whose business with ol' girl would take only a few minutes—a half hour at best.

So I sat there twiddling my fingers and checking my watch, and ten minutes later when I heard Faye's front door open, I thought, *Great, wonderful, fantastic—he's out and I'm in.* But get this, man, when I peeked out the window, instead of seeing her bidding brotherman a brisk adieu, what I clearly saw was that Faye had traded in her Sunday best for some kind of hip-hugging jogging gear, she was toting a big-ass gym bag, and rather than standing on her stoop waving, she was bebopping right alongside dude.

At that point I was a bit steamed, but I was still willing to give the girl some time to do whatever it was she had to do. But after a couple of hours had drug by without so much as a peep from her, I was starting to feel just a little on the pissed side.

I know confessing to having made other plans or accepting a better offer probably wouldn't have been the easiest thing in the world for her to do, but hell, I would have been happy to settle for a lie. I mean, tell me something, don't just have me sitting up somewhere waiting and wondering if you're ever gonna show at all.

Another hour or so ticked by before I heard a car pull up again. Only this time instead of Faye and dude, it was Nora. She looked tired and run-down, like she'd just gotten off after pulling an all-nighter at the Bulk Mail Center, and I almost started not to bother her. But after giving her a couple minutes to get in the house and settle down, I went over and tapped on her door.

She greeted me with her usual "Hey, sweetie, what's up?"

When I asked if she had any idea when Faye would be back, she told me she didn't know Faye was gone. She'd seen her car and just assumed she was with me.

I told her, "No, she left outta here a couple hours ago with some dude in a white Benz."

That's when Nora's cheery disposition disappeared and her voice climbed an octave. "A guy in a white Benz? Was he a skinny, good-looking guy? Light-skinned? About my height?"

"Yeah, all of the above," I said. "Why? What's wrong? That her boyfriend or something?"

She didn't have to say a word, man. Everything I needed to know was right there in her eyes. When she finally did cough up an answer, she couldn't even look at me. "Ah, Carl, that's sorta, kinda another one of those things you need to take up with Faye. Were you two supposed to go out or something?" she asked with more pity in her voice than I felt necessary.

I'm a grown-ass man. It ain't like I don't know how to get up and brush myself off when I've been knocked down. So rather than let Nora in on the extent of my disappointment, I just smiled, buried my feelings beneath a thick layer of nonchalance, and said, "That was my understanding, but you know, maybe there was some kind of mix-up. If you happen to see or talk to her before I do, just let her know that I stopped by."

Then I went home, man, and started plotting my revenge.

HER

I should have called. And had I been in my right mind, I would have. But you know how it is when you get tied up with something—or in this case, someone—and you lose track of everything but the "now" you're in at that moment.

I was at the gym, thoroughly engaged in the process of killing myself on the stair-climber when the thought first crossed my mind. And I was like, wait, wasn't I supposed to touch base with Carl? My next thought was, well, maybe it's not too late. Maybe if I call him now the gesture alone will be enough to keep him from pitching too big a fit. But the thing was, I didn't have the piece of paper he'd given me with his number on it. I'd left it someplace at home.

That only left me with the option of calling Nora—which I'll be darned if I didn't attempt to do on four separate occasions over the span of a three-hour period. By the time she and I finally connected, not only had I finished working out and washing up, but I had already agreed to let the ever-so-generous Brother Payne take my sore, tired, starving behind somewhere to get something to eat.

Quite naturally, the first thing out of Nora's mouth was, "Carl's been by here looking for you."

"Do something for me," I said. "Go next door and tell him something came up and I'll try to catch up with him later this evening."

Nora sucked her teeth, then after an exceptionally long period of silence she said, "You laid up somewhere with that fool Scoobie, aren't you?"

Given how she feels about our old childhood friend, I wasn't about to waste my time trying to set her straight, so I said, "Look, would you just stay outta my business?"

That's when she went off. "Heifer, you the one going out your way to put me all up in it! Some nerve you've got asking me to run over and do your dirty work for you. Since you so bad, why don't you dial him up your damn self?"

The best I could do was reach for the sympathy card. "Nora, please, just this one time. I'm in a jam. You know I'd do it for you."

She huffed and puffed until finally she blew out an "Oh, all right! But I swear, Faye, I'm through bailing you out of some mess you done let Scoobie trick you into. Next time you're on your own."

Girl, I'm not worried about Nora. Just because she's not ready to summon the Christian fortitude necessary to forgive Scoobie doesn't mean I can't. And mind you, I did say forgive, not forget.

We were right in the middle of our meal at the posh little Germantown cafe he'd taken me to, when all of a sudden he popped up with "You and me back together again. Who would have ever thunk it?"

Not wanting him to slip up and get it twisted, I was quick to assure him there wasn't a chance in hell of us ever resurrecting our quote-unquote relationship or whatever the heck it was we'd had for all those years.

When he started laughing I got hot and told him, "I'm not playing with you, Scoobie. If nothing else, understand this—ain't no more booty here for you to get today, tomorrow, or any other time."

He got serious behind that and said, "Let me let you in on a little something. And please don't take this the wrong way, but believe me, even if you were giving it away, I wouldn't want it. For your information, I've been celibate for a little over a year now and I have every intention of staying that way until the good Lord sends me the woman he means for me to take as my wife."

Girl, what you talking 'bout? I durn near choked on the

chicken wing I'd been gnawing on. As big a hound as Scoobie used to be, it's just hard for me to imagine him cold turkey giving it up.

I looked at him and said, "You're not sick, are you?"

He started laughing again and was like, "What? I have to be sick in order to be celibate? Like I told you, I'm a changed man. I'm ready to settle down and live a righteous life with one woman to whom I can be a helpmate as well as a loving, faithful, and devoted husband."

I have to give this much to the boy—if he's pretending, he's doing a durn good job of it. But to tell you the truth, I really don't care one way or the other. As far as my current dealings with Scoobie go, my primary aim is to collect as much as I can on the debt he stuck me with all those years ago. Nora doesn't have a thing to worry about. Once I feel like I've been sufficiently reimbursed, Venard Nathaniel Payne's presence in my life will once again be a thing of the past.

HIM

Get this—no less than fifteen minutes after I'd spoken with Nora, she came tripping over with a message from Faye. She said ol' girl had called to say she'd gotten hung up and she'd try to get with me later in the evening.

I wasn't buying it. Hung up! Yeah, I bet she got hung up all right. Hung up on whatever homeboy happened to be throwing down. I told Nora, "She's got my number. Why couldn't she have called over here and told me that herself?"

Nora hunched her shoulders and looked like she wanted to say, "My name is Bennett and I ain't even in it."

It wasn't her fault, but even so, I broke her off a little

something to take back and share with her friend. "Next time you talk to Faye, you tell her I said to just forget about it. I guess she thinks she can just treat a brother any old kinda way. Well, I've got news for her. I ain't the one!"

Wasn't no call for ol' girl to do me like that, man, not when she knows full well I've always gone outta my way to treat her with the utmost respect. Well, okay, there was that time when she came over to see why my son was making all that racket, and I slammed the door in her face. But, hell, you know what I'm saying.

I'm not trying to player-hate. Even when I was out there living foul and juggling women, two and three at a time, at least I had enough decency and common sense not to parade them past one another. In my book, anybody who stoops that low is either looking for a fight or thinks they've already got the other person good and whipped.

I'm still not sure what category Faye fits into, but by the time she and slick pulled into the parking lot and slithered out of his pretty ride, I'd decided if a show is what ol' girl wanted, then doggone it, a show is exactly what I was gonna give her. Even now, I don't regret what I did. They brought it on themselves, man, standing out there lollygagging, like neither of 'em had a doggone care in the world, while I was sitting inside with my drawers twisted and working on a seven-hour seethe.

HER

When Scoobie and I arrived back at the condo, it was pushing 7:30. We might have been back sooner, but after leaving the restaurant Scoobie took it upon himself to make an unannounced detour. Yeah, girl, we were riding along, making small talk, when before I knew anything we were pulling into the long circular drive of what looked to me like some rich good ol' boy's plantation estate.

Scoobie parked in front of the antebellum mansion with its thick columns and sprawling veranda, then turned to me with a self-satisfied grin and said, "This is where I live. You like it?"

I stared at the white-on-white monstrosity, fully expecting at any second for some Butterfly McQueen type to come bustling out the front door, waving her apron and hollering, "Lord, chile, where is y'all been? Massa John and da missus is all fit to be tied. Hurry up and pull dat dere buggy on 'round yonder 'fore we all gets a tail lash or two."

But before I could say anything, Scoobie said, "I just thought you'd like to see what lots of hard work, sound investments, and a firm commitment to walking on the right side of the Lord can do for a brother."

Honey, please. I rolled my eyes and said, "Huh, I'm happy for you. We should all be so blessed."

When he rolled down the car's windows and started rattling off details about the house's square footage, the number of bedrooms, baths, fireplaces, and other amenities, I said, "Hold up! Aren't we getting out?"

He said, "What? And have you misinterpret something I say or do as an attempt to get some? Not a chance. Maybe later when you've come to trust me a little more."

"Scoobie, quit," I said. "This isn't even your place, is it?"

He fished out his driver's license, showed me the address, then said, "Faye, you really think I'd bring you all the way out here to tell you a lie?"

I looked at him sideways and was like, "Is money green?"

"See, my point exactly," he said. "You don't trust me. But that's okay, 'cause I've got faith. And I know it's only a matter of time before you're singing a totally different tune."

Then dude up and started talking about inviting me and Nora to this book party he was having at his place a couple weeks from now. Yup, just when I thought I'd heard and seen it all, the brother pulled another something out on me. Supposedly he'd put together a collection of recipes, entertaining ideas, and etiquette tips. From what I gather, his goal is to evolve into the Black man's version of Martha Stewart, B. Smith, and Miss Manners, all rolled into one.

Anyway, that's how we spent the next twenty minutes cruising the grounds of homeboy's property with him steadfastly refusing to take me inside for even the quickest of look-sees. We'd spent so much time together that day I thought for sure he'd be anxious to be on his merry little way when we finally returned to my humble abode. But nooo, not Scoobie. He still had plenty more he felt needed to be said before the day was done.

Yeah, girl, so there I was in the parking lot, patiently listening to dude attempt to sell me on letting him come inside and try to make nice with Nora, when who but Carl should decide to make an appearance.

And, honey, you should have seen him. Instead of his usual quick-footed gait, he'd adopted one of those leg-dragging, pimp-daddy kind of struts, which only accentuated the fact that his pants were hanging all off his behind, like some middle-age gangster wannabe.

And his hair, girl, it was just plain awful. Remember James Evans from the *Good Times* series and how messed up his 'do would look on those shows when he was supposed to be mad, frustrated, tired, and having a bad day? Well, that's what Carl's poor head looked like—with possibly a few more naps, matted patches, and clusters of lint.

As if all that wasn't bad enough, the scowl on the brother's face reminded me so much of Mr. T's, I thought for sure the first thing out of his mouth would be, "What you looking at, fool?!"

I nodded, still hoping to keep things pleasant, but the three seconds' worth of teeth Carl flashed me in return looked more like a grimace than a smile. He didn't say a word, but I could tell by the way his eyes never left mine as he pimp-walked to his car that he'd come outside for no other reason than to clown.

Soon as I realized Carl's intent I should have sent Scoobie packing, hightailed my butt on into the house and locked the door behind me. The reason I have for not doing so is the same as I mentioned before—I wasn't in my right mind. I couldn't have been, because the thought that any serious trouble might arise didn't occur to me until Carl had flung open the trunk of his car and started rummaging around inside.

And by then, it was too late to do much of anything besides map out the best direction in which to duck, dive, and roll.

HIM

I'm not the violent type. A physical confrontation isn't what I set out looking for. Not that I couldn't have served up a serious beat-down, if push had come to shove and I'd been so inclined. But man, dude wasn't even worth all that with his scrawny, high yella, Shemar Moore–looking, homemade wave-wearing behind.

And as far as Ms. Faye is concerned, she best be glad she didn't say anything when I stepped outside, 'cause I probably would have gone off. There's nothing more potentially explosive than an angry Black man who doesn't have plan the first.

Yeah, that was me. Even after all those hours I'd spent brooding, I was still without a proper clue as to how I might get ol' girl to recognize and acknowledge that she'd messed with the wrong somebody this time around. How else you think I ended up barefoot in the parking lot, thoroughly hacked and rutting 'round in the trunk of my car, like I actually knew what I was searching for besides an excuse to be out there?

Likewise, me grabbing up the crowbar wasn't anything beyond a mindless macho act of complete desperation. Tell me what man hasn't found himself caught up in the middle of something he knows is totally stupid, but pride won't let him back up off it? Well, that's what happened to me. Having already put myself out there, like a fool, I didn't know what else to do but see the act on through to the end.

HER

Girl, when Carl came up out that trunk with a crowbar, I literally stopped breathing for a few seconds.

Scoobie had been standing with his back to the brother and initially was too engrossed in his own game to give too big a flip about what might have been going on behind him. But the loud bang Carl's car trunk made when he slammed it shut cut into Scoobie's blabbering and made him swivel around for a look.

Even then, he obviously didn't see what I did—an angry, deranged Black man with a weapon in his hand and murder on his mind. Scoobie even went so far as to say, "Hey" to the fool and ask how he was doing before he swung back around and said, "So, where was I?"

Oh, only on the verge of getting your freaking head bashed in is what I might have said, had I not been scrounging around in my purse for my canister of mace. Seriously, girl, I'd all but made up my mind to give my crowbar-toting buddy one good blast to the eyes before making a run for it. Fortunately, rather than get ignorant enough to make me hurt him, Carl took his pimp-daddy macking self back into his condo.

After breathing a sigh of relief, I switched my attention back to Scoobie only to discover that he was trying to ask me out—on a date—and to the Al Jarreau concert, no less. He promised to take care of everything, from the tickets to the backstage passes and VIP party afterward. He even offered to arrange for a limo to take us there.

I hemmed and hawed and finally just broke down and told him the truth—well, most of it, anyway—which was that I'd sorta, kinda already been asked by someone.

"Is this somebody you're serious about?" Scoobie asked, just as Carl decided to bring his crazy self back outside again.

"Serious? No, I wouldn't say that. We're barely even friends" is what I told him as I watched Carl go into his trunk again and this time drag out the spare.

According to Scoobie, that was all the more reason for me to go out with him. He took out a business card and proceeded to jot down all the numbers I'd ever need to reach him—at home, at work, or by cell.

Meanwhile, spare-tire-toting Carl is about halfway through act two of his award-winning performance. Unfortunately for him, he was so busy glaring at me that he wasn't mindful of where he was walking. And before I knew anything, girl, blam! Brother had misstepped and hit the curb. The tire went spinning in one direction and poor Carl in another—hopping, cursing, and reaching down to soothe his stubbed toes.

Probably wouldn't have been so bad if he'd had sense enough to put some durn shoes on before showing out. But noo, homeboy was out there stomp-barefoot, trying to act a clown.

You know it took everything in me not to burst out laughing, especially when Scoobie glanced over at him, then back at me with a frown and said, "What's up with your neighbor?"

All I could do was shake my head and tell him, "I don't even know."

While Carl gathered his spare and limped into the house with it, I went ahead and gave in to Scoobie's request for my number, sparing us both the fifteen extra minutes he undoubtedly would have spent pestering me for it.

After he finally got up out of there, I went inside and quite naturally the first somebody I saw was Nora. She'd kicked back in one of our living room recliners with her legs crossed and her face buried in the pages of an *Essence* as if I was really supposed to believe she'd been reading all this time instead of peeking out the blinds and tripping off me. Her tired little scam might have gone over better had she not been sitting there with her reading material turned all upside down.

I snatched the magazine from her, handed it back right side up, and asked if she'd given Carl my message.

"Yep," she said, still acting like it wasn't no thang.

I said, "So what did he say?"

She raised the magazine back over her face and said, "Pretty much that for all he cared you could jump in a lake, kiss a snake, and crawl out on your stomach with a bellyache." She went on to ask why I'd want to hurt Carl when all he'd ever done was try to be nice to me.

I told her I couldn't see what the fuss was all about. Carl and I were just kicking it. Wasn't like we'd had what you'd call a "real" date planned. Matter of fact, a good solid fifteen minutes would have been more than enough to take care of all I'd had in mind to do with him that day.

Nora shot me a look and lowered her voice to just barely above a whisper, like she does when she's about to dispense a bit of her own special brand of advice and wants to be taken seriously, which, thank goodness, isn't very often. "Faye, how many times am I gonna have to say this? You just can't be playing with folks' feelings. One of these days while you're out there, just kicking it, you're bound to trip up and fall so hard on your face, even I won't be able to help you put all the pieces back together again."

"So what would you have me do?" I asked her. "Go over and apologize to him?"

"Sure, why not?" she said. "It couldn't hurt."

HIM

Hey, man, as hard as I ran up on that doggone curb, it's a wonder I didn't break a toe or two. After a stunt that stupid, wasn't nothin' left for me to do but tuck tail and hop on into the house, where I could drop the bad-boy act and express the full extent of my pain in private.

I'd all but finished my cursing and crying and was in the process of doctoring my busted foot, nursing my wounded pride, and trying to convince myself that the crowbar and the spare I had sitting up in the center of my living room were all the company I needed, when who but Ms. Thang should show up at my door looking to do even more damage.

Still full of herself, she came in talking 'bout "I take it you're upset."

I told her, "You've got a hell of a lot of nerve, you know that?"

"What?" she said, trying to act all innocent. "I told Nora to tell you something had come up."

"Oh, she told me all right," I said. "And I told her to tell you to just forget about it. So why are you here? What part of 'forget about it' do you not understand?"

The sister pulled the old hands-on-hips routine on me and said, "I know you're not fixing to cop an attitude over this."

I snapped back at her with, "And why shouldn't I? It's bad enough you didn't tell me you already had a boyfriend, but then you had to go and flaunt him all up in my face. You ever heard the word 'discretion'?"

At that point she dropped what little was left of her polite veneer and came at me swinging hard, fast, and loud, like a straight-up gangsta "b". "First of all, he's not my boyfriend. And secondly, even if he was I don't owe you an accounting of my time or who I choose to spend it with. I told you from the git, I wasn't trying to be down with you like that."

"True dat," I said. "I know it's your game, but I mean, come on, Faye. Before I step up to the plate, I think the least you could do is let me know just how many players you've got out here running the bases."

Her face softened for a second and in a more conciliatory tone she said, "Carl, for all it's worth, the guy you saw me with tonight is an old acquaintance. And what happened between us was over with a long time ago."

I have to give it to her—the girl tried, at least in that particular instance. And if anybody's to blame for what quickly turned into a failed attempt at a peace negotiation, it's me for being knuckleheaded enough to try and sneak in a sucker punch.

"Well, of course," I said, dishing out the sarcasm with a smile, like it was ice cream. "I suppose that explains why you stood me up to spend half the doggone day with dude. Hey, if you want to hump slick for old times' sake, that's your business. Who am I to say anything, right?"

"Right," she said, slinging a big scoop of my own mean-spiritedness right back at me. "Especially given the fact I had every intention of humping your tired, stuck-in-the-past behind, and you're definitely not all that."

Hopping around her on my one good foot, I said, "No, but you, my dear, most definitely are all that and a big, fat bag of cheese puffs to boot!"

My intent had only been to crank it up a notch and show her I wasn't about to be shouted down in my own house. But I could tell by the way her eyes went from glimmer to glass that she'd taken my comment the wrong way.

With a noticeable quiver in her cheeks she pushed past me and said, "Yeah, I figured the 'fat girl' jokes would be next."

"See, you're wrong, Faye. You're wrong," I tried to tell her. "I didn't even mean it like that."

"Man, whatever," she said, looking for all the world like she was going to backhand the taste out my mouth if I didn't let go of her arm, which I'd grabbed to keep her from heading out the door.

What I should have done was gone ahead and apologized for what she'd wrongly perceived as me making a wisecrack about her weight. Instead I told her, "Faye, listen, I've already bought the tickets for the concert. If you don't want to go I'd appreciate you letting me know now so I can make other arrangements."

"Negro, please," she said, before jerking away from me and storming a trail out my door.

HER

I left the brother's apartment mad as all get-out and vowing never, ever to speak to his ignorant ass again. So you know the first thing I did when I got home was find his number and call him up. Yeah, girl, there were still a few more things I wanted to share with him, none of them too nice, mind you. But about all I managed to get out after his "hello" were a few choice expletives before he hung up in my face.

Later I remember thinking to myself, *Why am I even*

wasting my breath, much less my body on this lunatic? Please, there are plenty more deserving men out there who'd be only too happy to spend some quality time with me. I'll just call Scoobie . . . then I caught myself. Call Scoobie? Oh, hell no!

I stretched out across my bed, eager for a moment of peace and hoping to put the events of the day behind me. Of course, as soon as I laid down and closed my eyes, all I ended up doing was falling asleep and having the weirdest dream.

I dreamed I'd accepted Scoobie's invitation to the concert. We'd strolled up in there arm-in-arm, both of us dressed to the nines—Scoobie in a tux and me in a full-length mink. Yeah, like I don't know it's almost June and in this Memphis heat I would have durn near cooked to death. It was a dream, girl! Anyway, not only was I sharp, but I was my old slim self again—the fine, sleek mamma jamma I used to be before I ate my way into the forty or more extra pounds I lug around with me now.

So there I was, strutting and flaunting my stuff as Scoobie and I made our way to our front-row seats when Carl's big head popped into the picture. He was there with his little boy on his lap and the twins on either side of him, and they were all laughing and having a good ol' time until they spotted me and my date. As we glided past them, I heard, first the baby crying, and then one of the twins ask, "Hey, isn't that Ms. Faye?"

And, girl, when I turned around to wave and flash them my best Diana Ross "Some Day We'll Be Together" grin, the kids had all disappeared. It was just Carl sitting there with his bandaged foot, the crowbar, the spare tire, the James Evans hair, and this sad-sack expression on his face. With Scoobie tugging at my sleeve, I stood there and watched until Carl finally picked himself up and limped out the amphitheater, head hung, like some scolded and whupped puppy.

I woke up with a start, like I have in the past when I've dreamed about falling. And crazy as it sounds, I knew if I tried to go back to sleep without first making a genuine effort to clear the air between me and Carl, I was only going to have the same durn dream, or some variation thereof, all over again.

A couple hours had passed since I'd last dialed his number, but I didn't really expect him to be any more receptive than he'd been when I'd called earlier to express my sentiments. And sure enough, after a couple of rings, his answering machine clicked on.

At the beep I said, "Pick up, Carl. I know you're there. And I know you know it's me." When he didn't respond I said, "Fine. Be that way. I was just calling to apologize . . ."

He picked up and said, "Go 'head. I'm listening."

I told him that I hadn't planned for things to turn out the way they had and that if I could do it all differently, I would. "You still mad?" I finally ventured to ask after about thirty seconds of waiting for him to say something.

He said, "Why? You got more salt you want to rub in my wounds?"

Rather than let him bait me into another battle, I went into my Iyanla Vanzant "save yourself" bit. I smacked myself on the forehead, sucked in a deep cleansing breath, blew it out slowly, then told him in a voice totally devoid of all spite and rancor, "You know, Carl, maybe it would be best to call the whole thing off and just forget about trying to be anything other than friends."

"Is that what you want?" he asked, this time sounding more hurt than angry.

I took a moment before telling him point-blank, "I told you last week, and in no uncertain terms, exactly what it was I wanted."

He was like, "So what's changed? I still want that too."

I said, "Yeah, but if the way you were acting tonight is

any indication, Carl, that's not all you want. How are you going to act when this game we're playing is over?"

He jumped from my inquiry to one of his own. "You dumping me so you can get with him?"

I told him, "See, there you go acting like a jealous boyfriend again. Didn't I already tell you there wasn't anything between me and dude?"

He mumbled something about seeing Scoobie kiss me. "Sure," I said. "On the cheek. And did you by any chance see me kiss him back? No, case closed."

He wasn't about to let me off that easy, though. He said, "Tell the truth, Faye."

I said, "I am telling the truth, Carl."

Homeboy kept on. He said, "He's the one, isn't he?"

I was like, "The one what?"

Then in a voice so serious I couldn't laugh, even though I wanted to, Carl said, "You know, the one Nora told me about. The one who ran roughshod over your heart, forever ruining you for the rest of us."

HIM

Yes, "roughshod." Look, don't hate me 'cause I've got a vocabulary and I'm not afraid to use it. Faye thought it funny too. I could feel her cheesing through the phone. But rather than give in to her urge to giggle, she said, "Is that what you think I am, ruined?"

"You're not answering the question," I said, sinking even deeper into my "I ain't playing" voice. "Is he or isn't he?"

See, by then I'd figured it out. Having gotten a good look at dude up close and personal, it had gradually dawned on me that he was the joker from the pictures Nora had shown me that night we'd sat around waiting on Faye.

Finally, ol' girl went ahead and fessed up. She told me she'd known him about as long as she'd known Nora. "And yes," she finally admitted, "he was the first guy I ever fell head over heels for. The first guy I ever made . . ."

Right there in midsentence she slammed on the brakes and changed gears. "Well, he was the guy I lost my innocence to. We had an off-and-on relationship for years. But like I told you, that's all ancient history now. And that's exactly how I'd like to leave it."

I asked why she'd stopped short of saying he was the first she'd ever made love to.

"Because that's not what it was," she said. "We didn't make love. And we certainly weren't in love. Even though there was a time I thought differently, I know better now."

Never one to step clear of an obvious challenge, I said, "Do you? What could you possibly know about love when from the looks of things you've spent half a lifetime running from it?"

Her response to that was, "Well, maybe one day we can sit down and you can tell me all about it—being you're such an expert and all."

Rather than go there, I laughed her off and asked, "So what exactly did you and Scrotty do today?"

She made a big deal about correcting my mispronunciation of dude's name, like I was supposed to care. "Scoobie, Scrotty, hump buddy, boyfriend—what difference does it make?" I asked. "All I want to know is where you went with him that I couldn't have taken you?"

Her story involved running into dude at church and him supposedly talking her into going to meet his fitness trainer. Quite naturally that led to a workout, after which he took her to get something to eat, and so on and so forth.

All in all, it sounded pretty lame to me, but it did provide me with an opportunity to clear my name. I told her even though I thought her timing pretty lousy, I didn't see anything wrong with her striving to get toned. "But for the record," I said, "I was not, I repeat, I was not making fun of your weight when you were over here earlier."

Man, I might as well have been talking to myself. "If you say so," she said. "But for future references, I'm well aware that I could stand to shed a few pounds. It's not like I don't own a mirror or a scale."

And if that didn't beat all, right in the midst of me trying to tell her that I thought she looked fine, she jumped in and said, "Let's just drop it, okay? It's late and I need to get off this phone so I can get ready for work tomorrow."

You get the picture? Pretty much she was aiming to tell a brother to hurry up, shut up, and be gone already. What she didn't know is that Keith Sweat don't have nothing on me when it comes to begging. I said, "Faye, you know I still want to see you—even if it means I have to take a number and stand in line in order to do it. So come on, don't have me laying over here wondering if you want me to go away, wait for you to wrap up your unfinished business with this brother, or what."

"Are you through?" she asked in the pause I took to catch my breath.

"I don't know," I said. "Are we?"

I'd closed my eyes and was waiting for her to verbally nail my balls to the wall when she started laughing. When she finally stopped, she said, "Carl, I've just got two questions for you. Number one, what time does the concert start? And two, next time, instead of the spare, why not go for something a little less dramatic, something a little less injurious to your health—like, say, the jack or the jumper cables?"

Ha, ha. Let her make jokes. Ain't no black off my back. Man, long as I get what I'm after, I don't even care. Believe that!

Part Two

HER

Finally, all systems were fired up and ready to go! For the rest of that week I was darn near beside myself with anticipation. The wham-bam-thank-you-ma'am I'd been wanting and needing for oh, so long was finally about to come to fruition. At least, that's what I thought.

So not only did I agree to let homeboy treat me to dinner before the show, but like a trouper I played along with the sappy-sweet talk over the meal, and the hand-holding afterward, even though public displays of affection typically make me ill. Call it my way of compromising, if you will. And the truth is, it really wasn't that bad.

The brother's choice of restaurants—an upscale Italian eatery in the heart of downtown—went a long way in launching the evening on a high note. The food was absolutely wonderful, the service excellent, and Carl did quite a commendable job of playing up his boyish charm for all it was worth.

And the concert, girl, was pure heaven. The night was clear and cool with a slight breeze. The lights from the city's bluffs were flickering across the water. Jarreau and his band were jazzing it up on stage, filling the air with nothing but good music. And of course Carl was there treating me to a steady flow of wine coolers and compliments, and an occasional hand across my thigh. Chile, let me tell you, by the time we got back home I was feeling real good.

Still, I didn't want to seem too eager. Not yet, anyway. So after we got out of the car, I led him over to the front door of my condo, as if I was ready to turn in for the evening. "I had a good time tonight," I told him.

He raised his eyebrows and said, "Had? The night's not over yet. According to my copy of the rule book, the night's not over until after the dance."

"Oh yeah?" I said, real casual-like. "I thought it was after the kiss."

He leaned over and whispered in my ear, "Well, what do you say tonight we break some of the old rules and make up a few new ones?"

And then he kissed me. Yeah, girl, he kissed me like there was no doubt in his mind that he could deliver on everything I'd been wanting and needing and then some. When he finally let up, he said, "So what do you say? Is the night over, or has it just begun?"

"Well, since you put it that way," I said, still choosing to play it cool but waiting eagerly for just the right moment to heat things up.

And so without further ado, we went over to his place, where instead of heading straight for the bedroom, which I personally would have preferred, homeboy poured us some wine, dimmed the lights, and then surprised me by opting to play the CD of Jarreau classics I'd purchased after the concert, rather than something from his collection of R&B moldy oldies.

After a couple sips of the merlot, we slipped into the familiar comfort of our old slow-dance groove, except on this particular occasion there was only so much of the hip bone–to–hip bone, cheek-to-cheek either one of us could take. Somewhere in the middle of brother Al's "Like a Lover" we ended up on the sofa necking, like two inexperienced teens, easily distracted by the slightest noise, and still somewhat unsure about just how far the other was willing to go.

Carl's kisses, like his hands, were soft, full, caressing, and prone to wander. He seemed thoroughly engaged, if not fully aroused by what we were doing, which only made all the more confusing what happened next.

We'd been at it for a couple of minutes, with homeboy's fingers cruising the full terrain of my body. Now, while my right hand enjoyed a similar freedom, my left pretty much stayed where homeboy wanted it—in his lap, keeping company with the surprisingly larger than average endowment that he, unlike most similarly blessed brothers, had never once bothered to brag about.

And before I'm accused of any unnecessary roughness, let me just say that if I was putting a hurting on the man, it must have been one he liked, because every time I tried to move my hand away, he always pulled it right back.

But for some unknown reason, right while I was in the process of unzipping his fly, Carl jerked away from me, a move that nearly landed him butt-first on the floor, while simultaneously offering me a glimpse of what looked like sheer panic in his eyes.

"I—I'm sorry," he said, on repositioning himself. "I'm just a little uncomfortable."

I watched as he first slipped out of his shoes, then untucked his shirt. He was wrestling loose the cuffs on his sleeves when I decided to go ahead and put my dignity on the line.

"Here, let me help you with that," I said, trying to play innocent as I leaned over and started undoing the buttons along the front of his shirt, making it a point to "accidentally" brush my nails against his chest as I worked my way down to his navel. Oh yeah, girl, as tense as he was, he grinned big-time and said, "That kind of gives you an unfair advantage, don't you think?"

"Maybe. But that can easily be remedied," I said as I proceeded to unfasten my own blouse with a direct frontal assault in mind. Really, sometimes a woman simply has to take matters into her own hands. The bra I had on hooked up in the front, and with one quick twist I'd unsnapped the clasp and unleashed the full fury of these high-riding, 42 double Ds.

Well, let it suffice to say, it was a move that aroused more than just his curiosity. He peeled back the lace cups and ran an appraising eye over my twin sisterfriends before subjecting them to a much more physically pleasurable type of scrutiny.

Girl, let me tell you—it was heaven all over again. My head was spinning, my blood was racing, and my body was practically screaming, "Yeah! Yeah! Git it! Git it!" when all of a sudden he stopped.

The brother stopped, girl! Got up, changed the music, replenished his wineglass, came back to the couch, and then started a conversation.

Hell, I durn near croaked. I mean, I'm sitting there, titties bared to the world, my every nerve in an uproar, and he's quizzing me about my plans for the rest of the weekend. I'm thinking to myself, this man is either crazy, confused, or a latent homosexual. But since I had already come that far, I decided to play along. Okay? Maybe he just wanted to slow things up a bit before the real action began, right? Uh-uh.

I made the mistake of telling him that Nora and I were planning a trip to Water Valley to visit Mama 'nem. Honey, that just prompted him to launch into this long, mindless monologue about his own mama. And how wonderful she was. And how much he loved her. And how much he missed her. Which is all fine and dandy, but not at all the type of lip action I was particularly interested in at that moment.

He went on, and on, and on, and I listened until I felt my head about to explode. Finally, I just had to come right out and ask him, "Carl, why in the hell are you sitting up here talking about your mama?"

He looked at me like I had just slapped him or something and said, "What?"

And I told him. I said, "I just find it rather unnerving, if not downright perverse, for you to be suckling at my breast one minute and talking about your mama the next."

He frowned all up and said, "What's with the funky attitude? You got something against mothers or something?"

That's when I let him have it, girl. Read his ass, chapter and verse, straight from the Book of Black Women! Told him that was the problem with most Black men—they're all hung up on their mamas. Think their mamas are the only durn women in the world worthy of being treated with any degree of decency. Every other woman they want to treat like a 'ho."

After I'd finished my piece, Carl shook his head and said, "Just tell me this, why'd you have to pick tonight of all nights to change back into the bitch?"

Well, that did it for me. I grabbed my bag and said, "Maybe I just ought to leave."

Without so much as blinking an eye, Carl stood up, rehooked my bra, and said, "Yeah, maybe you just ought to."

HIM

I'm not out to make excuses for myself. The truth is, I just got scared. And fear, like lust, will drive a man to do a lot of silly, stupid, and foolish things—especially if he's predisposed to being all those things to some extent anyway.

But heaven forbid, man, should those two things—lust and fear—ever collide on any other joker like they did on me, and at the most inopportune moment. There I was in full throttle, ready to whip the bad boy out and lay it on her, when I'll be doggone if some of the conversation I'd had with my cousin Squirrel about Faye's weekly trips up to the hospital didn't replay itself in my head.

"Whatcha gon' do, man," I remember him saying to me at one point, "if come to find out 'Big Red' is hiding sumthin' really horrible? Like, say, turns out she's some bipolar, post-op transsexual who's got an extreme case of herpes?"

If that wasn't bad enough, I started hearing what my Uncle Westbrook had told me after I'd peeped him to the deal between me and Faye. He'd looked at me kinda funny and said, "I don't know, Carl. Ol' girl sounds like she plays a pretty tough hand. You step outta line and ain't no telling what kinda hurting she's liable to lay on you."

Now, unlike my cousin Squirrel, my Uncle Westbrook's got sixty-five-some years' worth of wisdom under his belt. I figure if anybody, he ought to know a li'l sumthin'-sumthin' about love and life and redbone gals whose game involves giving it up to a brother with seemingly no strings attached.

Man, with all those voices in my head, straight up wrecking my flow, wasn't nuthin' I could do but ease up off the gas and slam on the brakes. Faye was cool about it at first. She even gave me a few seconds to make the necessary adjustments before reaching over and literally giving me a hand. And it wasn't long before we were both bare-chested, breathing hard, and working toward getting our groan on.

I'm serious, man, I was handling everything that needed handling. I was coming up on third and had my sights set on home when—blip, bam, boom—it hit me out of nowhere with all of the ferocity of a freight train—the overwhelming realization that over and beyond my blatantly doggish desire for a good hump, I really do like this woman. I do. And I want to please her. But what if I can't? I mean, hell, when it comes to experience she's probably been 'round the world and back. What if I don't have what it takes to get her where she wants to go? Sure, it sounds irrational. Other people's fears generally do.

But being able to accompany a woman to the land of ooh-la-la? Well, that's what you might call a sensitive area for me, a sensitivity that was born the day my wife, a woman I loved dearly, up and confessed that in all the years we'd been kicking it, I'd yet to take her there. I'm saying, man, all those times when I thought I'd really been up in there wearing it out—had her sweating, squirming, and singing a right nasty version of Donna Summer's "Love to Love You, Baby"—shoot, ol' girl had been straight faking it!

And before you go writing me off as some sort of sexually retarded Neanderthal, let me just say that in Bet's case, it wasn't even about me. Of course, you couldn't have told me that at the time. But come to find out, an orgasm wasn't something Bet had ever experienced with me or anyone else for that matter.

Anyway, there I was on the couch, still fully aiming to do right by Faye and the two big, pretty titties she'd so graciously unveiled for me. I'd gotten her sufficiently hot and bothered and I could tell she was about ready for me to go on and make that next move. But instead of me focusing all of my attention on making that final push up on her, I'd become much more intent on pushing back all the fears and doubts I had swirling around in my subconscious.

Well, I'm sure I don't have to tell you what happens when a joker can't keep his mind on what his ace is supposed to be doing. Uh-uh, after a certain point junior just says to hell with it, drops the proud salute, and marches south with all deliberate speed. I don't know 'bout you, man, but in my book, the only thing worse than not being able to get the bad boy up at all is having the son-of-a-gun bail out on you in the heated throes of passion.

See, what Faye wrongly assumed was me tripping was actually me trying to spare myself some embarrassment and buy myself some time to get myself together. And besides not wanting the girl to bear witness to my partner's all-too swift shrinkage and untimely descent, I also didn't want her thinking I wasn't totally into her or that I didn't want her, 'cause on the strength, man, I was and I did.

In the end, though, balking didn't get me anywhere but back on chick's bad side again. And afterward, wasn't nuthin' left to do but own up, face the fire, and be a man about the whole lousy situation.

HER

I'd come home, changed my clothes, and crawled into bed. About thirty minutes had passed since the nasty episode with Carl and I'd pretty much resigned myself to another sexless night. But it was cool. I had a nice tall stack of Arabesques to keep me company. I was laying up, flipping through the pages of one, and working on my fourth or fifth cigarette when he called.

Even though I didn't bother to reach for the phone, it wasn't like I was actually trying to avoid him. It's just that Nora and I have separate phone lines. And to keep from disturbing each other in the evenings, we have our answering machines programmed to pick up after the first ring. Plus, having already exerted myself on Carl's behalf that evening, I was perfectly content to just lie there and listen while brotherman said what he had to say.

"Faye, it's me, Carl. Look, you've got every right to be upset. The only thing I can say is, I got a little nervous and started worrying about whether or not I was gonna be able to—you know—please you. But it's all good now. Really, it is. And if you wanna come back over I'd be only too happy to try and make it up to you.

"Come on, Faye, just give me another chance. Please? Okay, tell you what. Just think about it. I'll leave my door unlocked and if you decide to come back I'll be here waiting. All right? So if somebody should happen to come in here and knock me in my head, it's gonna be on you. And I'm sure that's not something you'd want, or is it? Well, I don't know what else to say. Come back over if you want. Okay? Bye."

Girl, I'm telling you, this is one brother who's got begging down to a sho' 'nuff natural science. But as bad as I still wanted me some, wasn't like I was about to jump up and run right back over there. Hell, even a woman as brazenly hot-blooded as myself has to maintain some sense of pride and decorum, right? So I made him sweat another full hour before trudging back that way with my lips fixed to tell him I wasn't 'bout to take no more junk.

Honey, please. I pushed open the door only to find the brother all laid out in a corner of the couch, head thrown back, mouth hanging open, and snoring like somebody who'd worked hard all day out in the fields. Believe me, endeared as I was by the sight of him sitting there waiting on me with the phone clutched tight in his lap, it was all I could do not to walk over and dash some of our leftover wine in his face.

And his place—all I can say is, you should have seen it. I guess he called himself setting the mood or something. But instead of him worrying about getting bopped upside the head, he should have given more thought to laying up there and falling asleep without first extinguishing the half dozen or more candles he'd lit. I'm not playing, girl, between his "dead to the world" behind and Sapphire, that spastic cat of his, the whole durn complex could have gone up in a freaking four-alarm blaze.

I blew out the candles, turned off the TV, and was about to shake Carl awake when I got a better idea. I tipped into his bedroom and changed into the slinky nighttime attire

I'd brought along in my bag, before slipping between the sheets of that big pretty bed and giving Carl a buzz. Yeah, you heard me right. I had my cell phone with me and his number finally committed to memory, so I rung the brother up.

After his groggy "Hello?" I jumped straight to the point and said, "Apology accepted."

He was like, "Does that mean you're coming back over?"

I waited a few seconds before telling him, "Why don't you go to bed and maybe we can discuss it in the morning."

He woke all the way up behind that and said, "In the morning?! Come on, Faye, don't do me like this."

I said, "Carl, blow out the candles and go to bed. Just do that for me, okay?"

"All right," he said, sounding like that was the last thing in the world he wanted to do. "Good night."

So I waited. And waited. And waited some more until finally I figured the fool must have drifted back off to sleep. Aiming to go in there and thump him in the head, I'd just thrown back the covers when his slow-moving tail showed up at the bedroom door, carrying a candle and wearing a smile.

He said, "That was a good one. You got me. But that's all right. Wait 'til you see what I've got in store for you."

I told him, "Yeah, I've heard all the talk. But I can't say I've seen much by way of action. And what took you so long, anyway?"

Still grinning, he set down the candle and started taking off his clothes. "Oh, it only took me a minute to figure it out. But I didn't want to get caught trying to step to you with dragon breath, so I made a brief pit stop along the way."

The brother is a mess, I'm telling you. For some reason, after stripping down to his shorts, he decided to entertain me with a few bodybuilding poses and martial arts moves.

Girl, I was ready, willing, eager, and tired of waiting, hear me? So I just told him, "I'm glad to see you've got your confidence back, but if you don't hurry up and quit with all that Arnold Schwarzenegger, Bruce Lee mess and bring your butt on over here, I'm rolling over and going to sleep."

He peeled off his shorts and said, "Oh, you want some action? Girl, I'm fixin' to give you some action you ain't never gonna forget."

Honey, there wasn't anything I could say to that but "Umm-uh, have mercy."

HIM

Okay, how do I say this without sounding insensitive or coming off like a complete jerk? Let me just put it to you like this—my first impression of Faye's bedroom behavior was that she made love like a woman who's accustomed to being in total control. But after it was over and I was lying there trying to make sense of it all, I realized I'd been mistaken. In actuality, Faye makes love the same way she lives her life—like a woman who's desperately afraid of losing control or being somehow forced to relinquish it.

The only reason I opted for compliance over protest—when no less than five minutes into the smooching, squeezing, and stroking, ol' girl indicated that she was ready to saddle up and ride—was that I assumed there'd be plenty of time for a few slow strolls here and there before we charged off into the wild blue yonder together. Man, not in a million years would I have ever expected ol' girl to leap on top of me, dig in her heels, and take off in full gallop. I'm saying, she wasn't even playing. And every time I tried to alter her course with something along the lines of either a kiss or a caress, she'd either brush me off or shove me back against the mattress, as if to say that if it wasn't 'bout the straight-up hump and grind, she wasn't having it.

But after a few minutes of listening to my teeth rattle around in my head, I just up and told her, "Baby, I don't mean no harm, but unless we slow this train down, I'm gonna reach my peak and that's gonna be all she wrote."

Ol' girl paused for all of three seconds, then leaned over, looked at me like my name was Dudley Doofus, and said, "Correct me if I'm wrong, but I thought that was the whole point."

Man, at that particular juncture in the road, it wasn't in me to argue with her. I just grabbed hold of the side of the bed, closed my eyes, and pretty much let her have her way with me. When it was over I just laid there for a moment, like I told you, wiping sweat, trying to catch my breath, and wondering what in the world had just happened.

Faye as usual wasn't exactly bubbling over with answers. After a speedy dismount she'd rolled onto her side and was lying there with her back to me. I wasn't sure what to read in to her reaction. So I reached out and rubbed her shoulder, hoping for a moan, a groan, a grunt, or something, only to feel her stiffen beneath my touch, like I was some kind of stranger whom she'd suddenly found guilty of having violated her space. And rather than turning over to face me, she got up and started gathering her things.

I shot straight up in bed and said, "What? You're leaving?"

She said, "Yeah, I was gonna take a shower first, if that's okay."

I asked if everything had been all right. "I mean, did I miss something? Did I do something wrong?"

She was like, "No, everything was fine, Carl. Really."

So I asked her, "Then how come you don't want to spend the night?"

She sighed and told me it just wasn't something she generally did.

I could have left it at that. Maybe I should have. But something deep down inside wouldn't let me. I said, "Faye, I'm sure to you this is gonna sound incredibly needy and pathetic, but I was really hoping you'd stay. I kinda miss having someone to sleep next to. You think maybe you could make an exception, just this once? Please?"

Hell, she acted like she hadn't even heard me. Instead of coughing up a reluctant "yes" or even spitting out a sassified "I don't think so," she snuffed out the candle on her side of the room, then went into the bathroom and locked the door behind her.

I just sat there for a while with my head in my hands before finally piecing back together the shredded bits of my ego and drawing together enough strength to get up and make a trip to the hallway john. After a brief stop by the kitchen for a quick sip of water, I headed back to the bedroom, fully expecting to be greeted by the sound of a running shower. Instead there was only silence, a faint hint of cigarette smoke, and surprisingly enough, Faye.

"I sorta prefer this side of the bed" is all the explanation she offered as she leaned over and blew out the last remaining candle, before settling beneath the covers in the spot I'd occupied just minutes before.

Hey, that was fine by me, and I said as much before maneuvering my way 'round to the other side of the mattress and lying down beside her. Even though the room was now pitch-black, I could tell that like me, Faye was positioned on her back. After a few minutes of lying there listening to her breathing and mine, I mustered up enough courage to reach out to her again.

My wandering hand lucked up and landed on the curve of one of ol' girl's silky brown thighs. I eased my fingers into the warmth I found there, kneading the softness ever so gently but fully expecting her to go into withdrawal on me at any moment. Sure enough I felt her stir beneath my hand, but rather than break the contact, she indulged it—even went so far as to cover the spread of my fingers with her own.

Curious as to just how far I could push my luck, I said, "You think I could get a good-night kiss? Or would that be asking too much?"

She turned toward me and after a few seconds I felt her hand on my chest. "Just don't forget, Carl," she whispered, "we made an agreement. You can't go getting serious on me."

"I know," I said, bypassing the opportunity to target her lips to give her the kind of royal treatment I generally reserve for my two princesses before tucking them in at night. "Three times and I'm out, right?" Then, using my fingers as a guide, I planted a soft peck on both her eyebrows, the tip of her nose, and in the curved space just below her lower lip.

She didn't say anything, but if I'm not mistaken, I think I felt her smiling next to me in the darkened room. And when she rolled over on her side, instead of hugging the edge of the bed like I thought she might, she actually eased her body back toward mine and drew my arm around her.

Now, that part felt right, man. Ol' girl's behind pressed all up against my groin. My lips brushing against her neck and shoulder. My fingers freely navigating the wondrous stretch between her left breast, hip, and thigh. Her reaching back every now and then to pull me even closer. We fit together like two puzzle pieces—two lost puzzle pieces that had finally found each other amid all the other ill-fitting matches.

Yeah, ol' girl's got issues, man, and from the looks of things, big-time issues, to say the least. But don't think I'm about to let that discourage me from getting to know her better. If anything, I'm even more enchanted with the whole notion of having crossed paths with someone who actually seems more emotionally messed up than me.

I can't help but wonder if perhaps there's a reason fate brought us together. Maybe there's a part for me to play in the soothing of her pain—and vice versa. Perhaps there's even a part for her to play in the easing of mine.

HER

I can't remember the last time I spent the night—I mean the entire night—with anyone. Typically my preference is to wake up alone and in my own bed, irrespective of how good, bad, or indifferent the boot-knocking was. But there was something about Carl and, moreover, something about the way he asked me to stay that made me, well, that made me want to.

The God's honest truth is, I didn't really know which way I was going to swing until after I'd ventured into the brother's bathroom, found myself lighting up a cigarette, and calling Nora from my cell phone. When I told her not to look for me because I was at Carl's and wouldn't be coming home, you know she had to trip.

After she finished cracking up, she said, "So what y'all doing over there? Having an all-night-long video marathon?"

I told her I'd thank her to mind her own durn business, to which she replied, "Well, just don't hurt the poor boy, Faye. I know you ain't had none in ages."

See, she don't even know. And if she was going to tell me anything it should have been to snap out of it and bring my big butt on home before I allowed myself to be sucked in any deeper than I already had been.

When I woke up the following morning I found the spot next to where Carl had lain empty and cold. He'd left a note on his pillow telling me he'd be right back and asking me not to leave before he returned.

Even though I had him to thank, in part, for some of the best sleep I'd enjoyed in quite some time, waiting around on his slow-as-molasses behind wasn't something I planned to do. Uh-uh, it was already after nine and despite my hedonistic performance the night before, I still had an eleven o'clock Sunday service I had every intention of making.

After showering, I was sorting through the bundle of clothes I'd deposited on top of the hamper the night before when I realized all my toiletry items were still in the purse I'd left on the floor next to Carl's bed. My plan was just to dart out, grab the bag, and dart back in again. But something told me I'd better cover up. So, I grabbed Carl's robe from the back of the door and sure enough when I tipped out, there he was cradling a cup of coffee and waiting on me with that big, silly grin.

I might have smiled back at him, had I not been so distracted by the spread he'd set up in my absence. On the dresser, not too far from where Carl stood beaming, sat a silver-plated coffee urn, with a matching sugar bowl and creamer. On a small table that Carl had moved next to the bed was a bowl of fruit and a basket of assorted muffins and croissants.

Too stunned to do much of anything else, I went over and peeled back the napkin covering the pastries. He'd just taken them out of the oven and he warned me that they were hot.

On closer inspection I noticed both the white carnation he'd laid across my pillow and the surprising fact that he'd actually changed the linens.

"Well, just don't stand there gawking," he said. "Go on and help yourself. At least have a seat."

I shook my head and, hoping I didn't sound too ungrateful, told him I wasn't too big on breakfast. While he poured me some coffee, I made a big to-do of thanking him for his efforts before stuttering through an explanation of my desire to make New Hope's eleven o'clock morning service.

Looking disappointed, he handed me the coffee, then shuffled over to the bed, sat down, and said, "I wasn't trying to keep you. This was just my way of, you know, trying to be hospitable."

Oh yeah, that's when the guilt grabbed hold of my ankles, and instead of racing from the room, I stayed planted long enough to sugar and cream the cup of brew Carl had poured me, before dragging my weighted feet across the carpet and settling down next to him. I told him he really shouldn't have gone through all the trouble and asked if he went to similar lengths for every woman who happened to spend the night.

He looked at me funny for a second, then in a quiet voice said, "You're the first I've ever asked to stay overnight."

Girl, I wasn't about to touch that. The implications were much too profound. So I just left it out there hanging while I blew on my coffee, nibbled on a muffin, and proceeded to bury my head deep within the folds of the Sunday paper.

HIM

I knew at a glance the window of opportunity Faye had so begrudgingly granted me was a small one with a worn sash and a faulty jamb. Even with my talent for laying on the butter thick, and in all the right places, I understood at any given moment the whole thing could come crashing down on me like a double-edged guillotine. But I figured what the hell, it was worth the pain if only to get another glimpse of ol' girl's ever-elusive "soft and gentle side."

So while she sat there pretending to be engaged by the news of the day, I went ahead and stuck my neck out. I nudged her and said, "You sure everything was all right last night?"

She rustled the paper before clearing her throat and saying, "That's the second time you've asked. Might you be just a tad insecure about your abilities, or lack thereof?"

There'd been a twinge of amusement in her voice, but I told her in all seriousness, "If you ever meet a man who tells you he's not—he's a liar."

She cut her eyes at me and said, "Like I told you last night, Carl, everything was fine."

I let her take a couple swigs of the coffee before I eased up on her with a "Well, don't you want to know how it was for me?"

The entire right side of her face drew up like a fist and a big ol' vein in her neck popped out and started pulsating. Still, rather than confront me head-on, she kept her gaze fixed in front of her as she issued me a right frigid "No, not if you're getting ready to tell me you didn't get yours."

I said, "Is that all there is to it for you—getting yours?"

She slapped the paper shut and said, "Basically, yes. And let me clue you in on another little secret—had I known there'd be a 'morning-after critique' I wouldn't have opted to stick around."

When she jumped up I grabbed her hand and said, "Faye, don't be like that. I'm glad you stayed. That was the best part of the night for me."

She got loud behind that. "And what was so unsatisfactory about the rest?"

I'll be dog if I was just gonna come right out and tell her that for all it was worth, I might as well have kicked it with a porno and a doggone party doll. So I niced it up. I told her, "Faye, in a lot of ways you were everything I could have hoped for—soft, warm, eager . . ."

"But?" she said in a way that let me know she wasn't 'bout to take too much more of my beating 'round her bush.

So I said, "But it's just some things I think are meant to be both savored and shared, like good books, fine wines, sunsets in autumn . . . sex. I just think last night could have been better for both of us if things hadn't been so . . . rushed."

After speaking my piece I waited a couple seconds for her to fly into a fit. When she didn't, I squeezed her hand and asked, "Aren't you going to say anything?"

She stared at me like I was a two-headed alien with a double set of nostrils and a big green booger hanging outta each. Then she plopped down next to me and said, "What you want me to say, Carl? I'm sorry it was so awful for you, all right?"

I was like, "Awful?! Who said anything about it being awful?"

"Well, maybe you need to go ahead and break it down for me," she said, "because besides a moment or two of pleasure, I'm not exactly sure what it is you're looking to get out of this relationship."

I said, "Faye, I know this thing between us isn't supposed to last more than a minute. And I don't have any qualms with that. I just think the interaction between us could be a hell of a lot more intense and mutually gratifying than it has been. Write it off as me being vain, if you like, but all I'm saying is, years from now when you look back on this experience, I want you to smile and I want your pleasure to have my name written on it."

She made a gagging noise and said, "Not only is that vain, it's asinine, it's insane, it's . . . it's . . ."

"Pretty damn scary," I filled in for her, knowing full well the truth was something she was hardly ready to admit, much less hear aloud. But I threw it out there anyway. "It frightens you, doesn't it? Just the mere possibility that I might be capable of taking you someplace you've never been before."

She blinked a couple times and said, "You know something? I don't have any idea what you're talking about."

"Oh, I know you don't," I told her. "But you could if you wanted to. The thing is you have to want to, Faye. Now, when and if you ever decide you do, I'll be more than happy to school you."

She said, "Yeah, well, that's terribly generous of you, but like I told you, right now I've got a few other things of a more spiritual nature to be tending to."

"And like I told you," I said, lowering my voice to just above a whisper and riding my mack for all it was worth, "hospitality aside, I'm not out to keep you anyplace you don't want to be."

Then she was like, "Besides, what makes you think you even have what it takes to school me?"

Man, as much yak as this girl was slinging, you'da thought her tail would have been halfway out the door already. But she'd barely budged. That was my tip-off. That's when I realized that something about my game intrigued her, and the task left to me was coming up with the right combination of words and deeds that would draw her into the full swing of things.

HER

In all the years I've been kicking it, no man has ever indicated that my stuff wasn't up to snuff. So, heck yeah, I took offense at Carl's suggestion that I might need some tutoring in the sexual-arts arena. What made him think he was *all that* in the sack or, moreover, owned the proper skills necessary to bring me up to par?

Keep in mind that all throughout the course of our conversation, Carl was cutting up and nibbling on bits and pieces of fruit. He was right in the middle of slicing into one of the large strawberries when I asked him to come with some proof that he could walk it like he talked it.

When he lifted his hand and extended his arm toward me, my first thought was, *Please, what does he think this is? One of those freaking B-movies he rents every Friday night? I know he is not fixing to try and feed my behind.*

But as it turned out, it wasn't my mouth the brother wanted just yet. Uh-uh, his first target was, of all places, my left earlobe. And like a newborn whose instinct it is to turn his or her head toward the source when touched on the cheek, my initial reflex when I felt the hairs on the back of Carl's hand brush against the side of my face was to close my eyes and lean into the sensation.

It was a momentary lapse. Three seconds if that. But as any player worth his or her pepper knows, one slip, however slight, is all it takes to ruin a cover. And on spying the crack he'd so skillfully coaxed into creation, Carl didn't waste any time in trying to see just how much wider he could pry it.

He pressed the wet fruit to my flesh and a cool shock wave of pleasure flooded my system and swept open durn near every closed pore in my body. He bent his head toward mine and whispered, "I'm pretty sure I could show you better than I could tell you. But since you don't have the time and I'm not into crash courses, I guess we'll just have to save our lesson for later."

Girl, I had my lips fixed to tell the brother where and exactly how he could get off without me, when all of a sudden I felt the caterpillar-like creep of his mustache and the warmth of his tongue picking up where the cool wetness of the strawberry left off. Honey, in all of one smooth suck, that man had drawn my earlobe into his mouth and my "you'd better go on somewhere" response back into the far recesses of my throat, where it near 'bout choked me.

And you'd best believe, in those few seconds I gained a greater appreciation for what sister Eve must have wrestled with that day in the garden when she ran upon Mister Snake and got gamed into taking a bite out that durn apple. Like, girlfriend, I knew the deal, but at that point I was too far gone to wanna do right.

When I finally stopped gurgling and regained my voice, instead of yelling for Carl to stop, about all I found the strength to mutter was, "I know what you're doing, Carl. You're trying to make me lose my religion, aren't you?"

"To the contrary," he said before easing open the top of the robe I'd borrowed and, with fruit in hand, commenced a slow downward zigzag to the fleshiest portion of my shoulder. On finding a spot he liked, he stopped and drew a series of strawberry-scented circles, one inside the other, while winding up his explanation.

"I'm a God-fearing man. And after all the shouting is done, rest assured, I'm going to be the first to proclaim that to Him goes all the glory." And with that bit of blasphemy, the brother proceeded to plant his mouth on the fruit-drawn target and swirl his tongue in the bull's-eye.

It was all good, girl, and I'd be lying if I sat up here and said otherwise. But I must confess to getting just a little nervous when the brother started untying the robe. Bouncing around in the dark with him was one thing, but being butt-ass naked with him in the light of day was quite another.

I pushed away his hands, but instead of getting riled like I thought he might, Carl said, "It's okay. Just lay back and relax." Then he kissed me, a long lingering one on the lips this time, and in the process reached for the belt again.

But still, I wasn't ready to give it up just yet. I told him, "You know if we do this, you'll only have one strike left."

He leaned across me, pressed a button on the tape player situated on the nightstand closest to us, and said, "Here, maybe this will help."

Girl, when Barry White's "Playing Your Game, Baby" came oozing out the speakers, it took every ounce of restraint in me not to holler. Carl, with his crazy self, jumped up and started doing a slow dance/striptease around the room. He said, "You like that, don't you? Uh-huh, I knew you would."

"You're a nut" is all I could say when he crawled into the bed with me and reached for the robe's ties again.

I held my breath as he peeled back the terry cloth and, with his eyes still focused on my face, cruised his fingertips over my lower forty-eight, like a man who knew where he aimed to go and wasn't in any particular hurry to get there.

"It's show-and-tell time," he said, his voice seemingly caught up somewhere in that crowded space between mumble and moan.

I told him I got the "show" part, "But what exactly is it I'm supposed to be telling you?" I asked.

He got another strawberry, bit into it, and smiled. And, girl, before I could summon forth so much as the warm blush of a single self-conscious thought, this man was squeezing droplets of juice in and around my navel.

"Why not start with what I need to know" is what I think I heard him say. His tongue-twirling chase of the strawberry rivulets sliding across my skin had me more than just a little distracted, if you know what I mean. But if memory serves me right, the brother's rap went something like, "You've got to talk to me, baby. Tell me what I need to know. If it's too fast, I'll slow it down. If it's too hard, I'll make it soft. The only way I'm gonna know is if you tell me. The only way you're gonna know I can is if you let me."

So . . . I let him, as much as I could. And . . . he did

what he said he would, girl. The man *showed me something*. And there are no words to describe just how truly . . . truly wonderful, it really, really was.

HIM

I could tell Faye wasn't used to giving instructions. But in order for me to do right by ol' girl, I had to get her to tell me what she liked where. Wasn't it Johnny Taylor who said you gotta give a woman "what she wants, when she wants it, how she wants it, every single time she needs it"? Well, essentially that's the thrust of my whole program.

A few minutes of exposure is all I was asking and a willingness to hang back and let me take the lead some. But like a lot of women who've been hurt, Faye thinks if a man finds out where and how she's vulnerable, he's gonna make it his primary goal and official business to somehow use that information against her. I'm not that guy. She ought to know that by now. Why would I want to hurt her? There's nothing of value for me to gain by bringing her pain. But pleasure, hey, now that's another story altogether. These young dogs out here can say what they want, but any true player for real knows it's all about the "feel good"—his, as well as his woman's.

My sole aim that morning with the whole strawberry escapade thing was to show Faye that my desire for her was earnest-felt and that I could please her if she'd let me. I'm saying, man, I went so far as to suck the girl's toes and kiss the bottoms of her feet. After I'd popped what was left of the spent berry into my mouth, I diced us up a fresh one and invited ol' girl to take a stab at doing for me what I'd just done for her.

I pointed out a nice place on my neck for her to start,

trusting that her sense of give and take would keep her from opting to just walk off and leave a brother hanging. Her first few attempts were kinda shy and awkward, but I kept encouraging her and it wasn't long before ol' girl was giving it as good as she'd gotten.

The grand finale seemed well within reach. But no sooner had I positioned my body above hers did I see this look on her face that told me she was about to be sick. I hovered over her for a moment, waiting to see if she was fixing to start throwing up, having heart palpitations or somethin'. Man, the last thing in the world I wanted was chick freakin' out on me.

So I told her, "If you're not ready to do this, then we won't."

For a second I could have sworn she was about to tell me to get up offa her, but then her eyes softened, and I felt her hands, one on my hip and the other you know where. She pulled me toward her, and in the process of leading me in she whispered, "Oh, I'm ready. You'd just better make this worth my while."

Now, a lesser man might have shriveled up in the face of such an ominous and potentially threatening task. Not me. You'd better believe if I hadn't thought myself up for the challenge, I wouldn't have put myself in that position, especially in light of my previous bit of floundering. But really, at that point, man, it wasn't about the sex or even me liking the mean ol' gal. At that point, it was more about my need to prove myself capable of giving her something . . . something beyond the simple mechanics of a good time.

I knew I'd done something right when she arched her back and said, "Oooh, Carl!" rolling the *r* and wrapping the *l* around her tongue, like a young Eartha Kitt.

And when we were through and she was lying there with her face buried in my chest, her body still twitching and jerking from the series of aftershocks that generally come in the wake of a job well done, I got the distinct impression that I'd taken her someplace she hadn't visited in quite some time.

HER

Sure, I felt guilty afterward. Incredibly so. It was a Sunday morning, after all, and there I was laid up next to Carl, butt-ass naked and bathed in the soft-scented blend of strawberries and sex circulating beneath the sheets. But it had been years since my body had been treated with that kind of reverence and affection, you know, the kind brothers generally reserve for the care, handling, and maintenance of a new car. And no woman with any sense of decency just up and walks away from that kind of tenderness. It's funny, but I almost felt like I owed him something.

I got up shortly after 12:30 and washed up again. Another hot cup of coffee awaited me on my exit from the bathroom. Only this time when I went to pick it up, I couldn't help but smile at the little something extra I saw sitting on the saucer. I glanced over at Carl, who was still lying undressed beneath the sheets, and told him, "Enough with the strawberries already."

He said, "Aww, girl, you know you loved it." And he was right. I had. But I wasn't about to let him know that.

I'd plopped down near the end of the bed and was lotioning my legs when he started poking me with his foot. At first I ignored him, but my lack of response only seemed to make him even more determined to coax a rise out of me. He eased his foot out from under the covers, pressed it against me, and started wiggling his toes all up on my behind.

I turned around, looked at him, looked at his big crusty

claw of a foot, and politely asked if a nail clipper was something he'd ever owned.

He poked me again, but this time instead of letting him get away with it, I grabbed hold of his big clodhopper, wrestled it into submission, and with homeboy screaming and laughing like a woman, I tweaked his toes, pinched his heels, and raked my nails up and down his instep. Just as I was about to grab the other one, he caught my hands and, looking all serious said, "Careful now, that's the foot you made me slam into the curb last weekend."

I was like, "Oh, so I made you do that?"

He said, "Don't play dumb. You know what I mean."

I reached for the foot again and told him to relax, I'd play nice.

He looked skeptical when I reached into my purse and pulled out my oversize nail clippers. But as soon as I started massaging lotion into the dry, cracked skin on his feet, he stretched out on his back, like some big, shaggy overfed house dog who was only too happy to entertain a little petting and grooming.

I lotioned, massaged, and trimmed the nails of first one foot and then the other. A few minutes went by with neither of us saying anything. The peace and quiet suited me just fine. But being that I was with Carl, I knew it wasn't likely to last. Sure enough, after about five minutes he raised up on his elbows and said, "I've got to go pick up my son around two and take him to get some shoes. Why don't you come with me?"

"What?" I said. "And end up in the middle of some baby's mama drama? Ah, thanks, but no thanks." I let go of his foot and started collecting my things.

He reached out and took me by the hand. "Don't worry about Clarice. The only somebody she's got beef with is me. She's not going to give you any problems. Besides, since it was you who so kindly suggested that I keep him a change of clothes around here, I thought maybe you'd like to come along and help me pick something out at the mall."

He looked so cute sitting there, staring up at me with his big puppy-dog eyes and the covers bunched up in his lap, that I almost leaned over and kissed him. But you know that would have been too freaking big a jump for me. I hedged and told him, "I don't know, Carl."

He let go of my hand and then with a mischievous grin said, "So how's about I throw in a little extra something to sweeten the deal?"

As I waited to hear the rest of his proposition, I couldn't help but stand there and think to myself, *Man, if you think I'm about to crawl my butt back into bed with you for yet another round of the freak-nasty, you'd best put away them Viagra pills you're obviously popping and think again.*

He said, "You know, something along the lines of a pack of cigarettes and a handful of Harlequins?"

I laughed with him before I said, "Oh, so is that all you think a sister's time is worth, or are you just out to play me cheap?"

In a tone that let me know he was totally serious, he said, "It may come as some surprise to you, Faye, but I'm not out to play you at all. This is your game, remember?"

I said, "And what's that supposed to mean?"

After tossing aside the sheet he'd been using to cover his nakedness, he stood up and said, "What it means, Faye, is that I don't have a whole lot of extra money or time, but what little I do have I'd very much like to spend and share with you. So needless to say, whatever price you set is the one I'm damn well gonna try to pay."

When I didn't say anything, he leaned over and kissed me on the forehead a couple times. Then he looked at me and said, "I can play the game, baby, but I can't help the way I feel, rules or no rules."

He caressed the side of my face with his hand and eased his thumb over the quiver in my bottom lip, but rather than kiss me again he nodded at the basket of pastries on the TV tray next to us and said, "If you want to take any of this stuff with you when you leave, be my guest, okay?" Then he turned and headed off for the bathroom.

HIM

I didn't really expect Faye to be there when I came out the bathroom. And she wasn't. The bedroom was empty, quiet, and a whole lot tidier than when I'd left it. I was a little surprised to see that ol' girl had actually taken time to straighten up. The bed had been made, the food removed, and all of her gear was gone.

So thoroughly stunned is the only way I can describe how I felt when I wandered into the kitchen and found her seated at the breakfast bar, staring down at the carnation I'd given her. She looked up at me and said, "I've only got three things to say, so listen up and hear me good. Number one . . . exactly what time do you plan on leaving? Two—is it okay if I go dressed like this? And three, despite what you might want to believe, not everything has a price for me."

Without stopping to think about it, I threw my responses back at her in a manner similar to the way she'd hurled them at me. "To answer your first question—about fifteen minutes. Secondly, you look fine. And as for the third, well . . . that's good to know."

Thin ice is what we were skating on, man. One good push, twist, or slip in the wrong direction and one, if not the both of us, would go crashing through the delicate surface, never to be seen or heard from ever again. That's not at all what I was aiming for. So rather than haul off and try to finish reeling Faye's contrary butt in, I stepped back some and gave the girl space to move, breathe and even change her mind if she wanted.

Ain't like I haven't been out here long enough to know that it's all about timing, patience, and owning the wherewithal to pace oneself when it comes to winning a woman's trust. Besides, Faye's decision to hang around, rather than to simply leave me hanging, let me know something. It let me know that slowly but surely she was warming to the possibility of there being something deeper and more meaningful between us.

HER

Even though Carl assured me that Clarice, his baby's mama, wasn't the type to trip over seeing him with another woman, when we finally pulled up to girlfriend's house, I thought it best for me to just stay put while he went inside to fetch the young'un. The way I saw it, why push my luck? Besides, given the limited amount of time me and Carl were going to kick it, there wasn't any need for me to meet Ms. Clarice or her me.

But I knew at a glance when she tripped out the house behind Carl and their screaming kid, our coming together was bound to prove unavoidable. My first impression was—my, my, isn't she a cute, skinny little thang, and barely a baby herself. My second thought was—Carl really needs to have his tail-wagging butt kicked.

And as the laws of divine retribution would have it, his son, Benjamin, was doing just that. Not only was the kid yelling at the top of his lungs, he had Carl wrapped in a headlock and looked pretty intent on gouging the poor man's eyes out. In spite of my apprehensions, I got out of the car hoping to lend a hand.

I jangled my keys, thinking maybe I could distract Ben with the hourglass, like I had the first time we met. Fortunately, it worked, and to everyone's relief not only did the boy quiet down, but he even let me help him into the car's backseat. After I'd secured him, I turned to face his silly parents, only to find them engaged in some sort of disagreement about the amount of time Carl was going to spend with his son that day.

I was about to slip my butt back into the car when Carl took it upon himself to introduce us. "Uh, Faye, this is Clarice. Clarice, this is my friend Faye."

Homegirl said, "Hey," did a little wave thing, and showed me some teeth. I was quick to return the favor before following through on my disappearing act.

After Carl ducked in on the driver's side, I thought that was going to be the end of it. But before we could drive off, Clarice started tapping on the passenger's side window.

When I rolled it down, she leaned over, cut her eyes at Carl, then looked at me and said, "Just a few words of advice. Carl's a pretty decent guy in most respects. But take it from me, you're better off not buying anything he says about being allergic to condoms, being sterile, or working with the Freakmasters, that god-awful singing group his cousin Squirrel calls himself managing."

I nodded, girl, even though I didn't have clue the first. So when Carl finally pulled off, I asked him, "What exactly was she talking about?"

But all I got from him was a shamefaced "Ah, well, you know, I was drunk that night and, ah, it's a long story. I'll have to explain it to you later."

HIM

Man, as we drove off I made the mistake of asking, "So what'd you think of Clarice?"

Faye's snout drew up into a snarl. "For one, I think she's young. Too durn young for your old behind to have been messing with. She couldn't have but what—eight or nine years on your daughters? What on God's green earth were you thinking?"

Now, why'd she have to try and make it sound like I'm some kind of pervert? I mean, come on, if I'd have been sober I'da never got myself in a jam like that in the first place. In an attempt to defend myself, I said, "Hey, I'll have you know that was a twenty-three-year-old woman you just met, which made her all of . . . well, all of twenty when I met her. And don't think she hadn't already been 'round the block and back a few times before I met her. Besides, what's her age got to do with anything? As far as I'm concerned, she was old enough to know better, same as me."

Rather than turn toward me and cut loose with some lip, Faye didn't say anything and kept her eyes glued to the road. And given the look of utter contempt and disgust I saw on her face I probably wouldn't have been able to bear it if she'd done otherwise.

She didn't say anything, not a word. But after about five minutes, the silence started eating at me. Finally, I said, "Faye, correct me if I'm wrong, but not once have I ever tried to convince you I was some kinda saint who'd lived a perfect life. Yeah, I've lied, I've cheated, I've hurt a lot of people unnecessarily. It goes without saying that when I met Clarice, I was trying to live anything but a righteous life. But sometimes experiences do change people. And whether you choose to believe it or not, I know I'm a much better man than I was back then. Furthermore, the only thing I can do about my past is apologize for it, learn from it, and move on. Ain't a damn thing I can do to change it."

It was a mouthful and I hadn't pulled any punches. When she drew in a breath, I braced myself for the fierce cussing out I felt coming on, only to almost slam on the brakes when she followed through with "Well, you know something, Carl . . . you're right. I don't have any business trying to judge you. The only real difference between you and me is that thanks to your big mouth, I've got plenty of firsthand knowledge about your transgressions, whereas you don't have much insight to speak of into mine."

I don't know if it was the kid, the fact that it was Sunday, or just a by-product of some of that good loving I'd laid on her, but ol' girl actually managed to keep the attitude in check for the rest of the day. To say she was a big help to me at the mall is a gross understatement. Truth is, the whole doggone experience probably would have turned into one big hellacious affair had Faye not been there to keep everybody calm.

Even though ol' girl's champagne taste oftentimes ran counter to my beer budget, she chose to pass on the many opportunities I presented her to call me cheap. I mean, come on, man, it's ridiculous the prices these retailers are demanding for things that most kids are either gonna tear up or grow out of in three months' time. And all that so-called designer crap is outta the question. I don't spend that kind of money for my own duds.

Faye tried, though. At the shoe store she got all ga-ga over these little-boy boots that were sharp, no lie, but would have required me to shell out no less than sixty-five big ones, nearly half of what I'd already planned to spend on the kid that day.

I told her, "Unless you're prepared to sweet-talk these folks into a twenty-dollar discount, you need to go 'head and put those things right back where you found them."

She pulled the same stunt on me when we went to look

at clothes. After helping me pick out a few reasonably priced items that the kid could spill juice on and roll around in the dirt in—this sister had the nerve to come stepping up to me with some Little Lord Fauntleroy getup that she claimed was "so adorable." I probably would have broken down and bought the darn thing too if I hadn't peeped the price tag and nearly upchucked all those strawberries I'd downed earlier.

But instead of asking her if she'd flipped, I was like, "Uh, yeah, baby, that's awfully cute and everything, but a brother's ends will only stretch so far. And besides the fact that I can buy him three outfits for the price of that one, I really don't have any place to take him all jacked up—I mean, dressed up—like that."

She seemed sympathetic, but when we went to the register to pay, I saw she was still holding tight to the cutesie gear. When she noticed me scratching my head and frowning, she said, "Don't worry, I'll pay for it. I suggest you give it to Clarice and tell her it was just a little something extra you decided to throw in with the shoes. Who knows? It might help improve your status with her."

It wasn't a line of reasoning that particularly moved me, but since ol' girl seemed so insistent, I checked both my pride and my ego and went ahead and let her have her way.

HER

Yes, I did spend the rest of the day with Carl, but only because he needed me to help him with his kid. I mean, please, you know good and well I'm not the type to go out of my way to spend a Sunday evening at some durn amusement park.

If anybody's to blame, it's the child's mama, Clarice. She's the one who instructed Carl to drop the boy off at the park when we finished shopping. He offered to take me home first, but I figured what the heck, I'd come that far, why not go the rest of the way. Besides, I thought Carl was going to stay only long enough to see his son safely deposited back into the arms of his mama. And had Ms. Clarice been where she said she was going to be when we got there, that might have happened.

As it was, we'd been waiting outside the park's entrance a good fifteen minutes when me and Ben both started getting restless. I fished out my cell phone and suggested Carl use it to call homegirl and tell her she could catch up with us in Kiddyland because we were going to go ahead and take the child in. I thought he might balk at me trying to call the shots, but he seemed only too happy to comply. Of course, I'm sure the fact that the park was admitting folks free on this particular Sunday went a long way in keeping the brother's mood on the upswing.

He also lucked up and ran into some old partner of his who just so happened to be managing one of the ticket booths. That's how we got hooked up with a handful of free coupons for the kiddy rides, as well as a discounted handful for the other section of the park.

In a lot of ways I'm glad I stayed. It did give me an opportunity to see something just short of a miracle—this man and his son actually bonding. Carl was all into it, cheering Ben on when he braved a ride by himself, giving him a hand to hold and/or a shoulder to lean into when he got intimidated, coaching him on the kiddy games. He even managed to help the kid win a couple of stuffed animals. By the time Clarice and her girls and their umpteen kids finally showed up, the two had practically become bosom buddies.

Carl racked up a good number of points with his baby's mama and her friends when he forked over the extra

Kiddyland tickets along with the shoes he'd purchased at the mall. But just like I knew he would, he scored double bonus points when he handed homegirl the outfit I'd bought for him. After oohing and ahhing, Clarice looked at me like she knew I must have had something to do with the matter. But she didn't say anything and I didn't either. I mean, hey, why not let the brother enjoy his moment?

I waited until Clarice and her cronies had wandered off before asking Carl why he hadn't given them the other tickets, the ones designated for the adult and big kid section of the park.

He hunched his shoulders and said, "I don't know. I figured you might want to ride something."

I said, "Oh yeah? Like what?"

He said, "Well, ah, for one, they've got that train that circles around the grounds."

I was like, "What, that tired putt-putt number all the old folks get on with their grandbabies? So what you trying to say, Carl? Is that about all the excitement you think a big girl like me can handle?"

A little good-natured teasing was all I was doing, but he didn't take it that way. He said, "Look, woman, don't start that stuff with me again. I was just throwing something out there. If you don't want to ride the doggone train, fine, we won't ride the doggone train."

"Uh-uh," I told him as he followed me over to one of my all-time fairground favorites. "If we're going to ride something, the least we could do is ride something with a little get-up-and-go to it."

But as soon as Carl caught sight of the roller coaster as it raced around the bend, he got all bug-eyed and started backing up. "You can't be serious. Oh, hell no. I'm not getting on that."

He got on it, all right. Three times, to be exact. Not in a row—that would have been too cruel, even for me. No, in between coaster rides we went for a wet slide down the

Log, did the haunted-house thing, chased each other on the bumper cars, and ended the evening with a slow spin on the Ferris wheel.

As much as I hate to admit it, girl, I actually had a lot of fun munching on candied apples and corn dogs, laughing at all the crazy expressions on Carl's face and walking side by side with him as we strolled through the crowds trying to decide what to get into next. We were sitting at the top of the Ferris wheel when I realized that the last time I'd spent an entire afternoon at this amusement park, I'd been a pimply faced teenager on the verge of my first major heartbreak.

When I glanced over at Carl and smiled, he was like, "What?! What did I do?"

I informed him that my very first kiss had come at the top of a Ferris wheel at this exact same park some eighteen years ago.

"Yeah? Was it something sorta like this?" he said, prior to leaning over and planting a soft one on my lips.

I told him, "No, it was more like this," before placing my mouth back against his and giving him a good solid twenty seconds' worth of slow and steady tongue.

When I was through, the most the brother could do was make a quick adjustment to his crotch before looking back over at me, shaking his head, and saying, "Daammn . . ."

HIM

I witnessed yet another side of Faye that afternoon at the amusement park—her playful side. Even though the kiss she laid on me while we were dangling at the top of the Ferris wheel was unmistakably that of a well-seasoned woman, she's still got quite a bit of little girl left in her. I wish you could have seen her out there laughing hysterically after she'd managed to push and jam my bumper car all up in the corner or waving her arms all up in the air, as if she was seated front row center at some doggone Prince concert instead of just barely strapped into the rickety cart on that two hundred–year-old roller coaster she kept making me get on.

Ol' girl played so hard she fell asleep on me during the drive back home. She looked so peaceful and content with her eyes closed and her head gently rocking from side to side that I didn't even bother to wake her until after I'd parked the car and pulled the key from the ignition.

I reached over and with my thumb stroked the dimple in her cheek. When she opened her eyes and looked at me, I told her, "You were smiling in your sleep. Thinking about that kiss on the Ferris wheel again, huh?"

She batted her lashes at me, wet her lips, and said, "Hmmm . . . that and more."

She'd turned away from me, grabbed hold of the car door's latch, and was getting ready to bail when I said, "Hey!" I threw an arm across her lap and told her, "Hold up a second, why don't you?"

She sighed and said, "Carl, as hot, tired, and funky as I am, I sincerely hope you're not about to ask me back over to your place again. I told you—I've got to get up in the morning and drive to Water Valley. I promised my folks I'd be there for Memorial Day."

"I know all of that" is what I told her. "I just wanted to talk for a minute."

She squirmed for a second, then picked up the container of orange soda in the cup holder. After downing a couple of sips she sighed again, leaned back against the headrest, and said, "So what is it you want to talk about?"

"You and me and this whole weird 'three times and you're out' scenario you've got us locked into."

Her eyebrows jumped up on her forehead and she said,

"Look, Carl, I told you from the git how it was with me. So don't go acting like—"

"I know," I said, cutting her off. "I know what you said, Faye. And all I'm asking is that you give some thought to easing off these artificial constraints and cut us both some slack. I like spending time with you. I do. And I can't help but wonder what might happen if you gave this thing between us a real chance at being something more than just friendship and occasional sex. I'm not asking you to make a decision now. All I want is for you to think about it."

She'd been staring out the window the whole time I'd been talking. When I finally shut up is when she turned and looked at me for what seemed like an eternity before she said, "Okay."

My heart flew up against my chest and I was like, "Okay? Okay, what?"

She said, "Okay . . . I'll think about it."

HER

Yeah, I know what I said. "Three times and you're out. That's the policy. And there are no exceptions." Well . . . under ordinary circumstances and with the average guy, there aren't any exceptions.

I guess what makes this thing with Carl different is that he's the first man to ever come forward and straight out ask me to think about bending the rules on his behalf. That fact, in and of itself, sets Carl apart from all the other knuckleheads I've invited to come over with their balls and play with me for a while. Outside of those who think they can trick a sister into serving up a little something extra, most brothers seem only too content to accept the rules as they are and don't have any problems with vacating the premises after the last pitch has been thrown. In all fairness, I couldn't do anything but grant Carl an "I'll think about it." I mean, if I'm going to tell the truth, the brother has more than proved himself capable of showing me a good time—in bed and out. And he does make me laugh, even when he's not trying. He's not all that hard on the eyes. And rather than be out here fronting and carrying on, Carl's been excruciatingly candid with me about both his adulterous past and the fact that it's probably going to be a while before he's not struggling financially to keep his head above water.

But as much as I'd like to buy into all the honesty and candor Carl's been projecting, in the back of my head lurks the nagging suspicion that the brother can't be for real. He's got to be keeping something on the down low, you know?!

I was weighing all of those things and more when I finally stumbled in that Sunday evening. My weekend romp with Carl had taken a lot out of me both physically and emotionally. But any plans I might have had about taking a load off and temporarily clearing my mind were immediately snatched away and cast aside by Nora, who met me at the door, cracking her gum and popping her jaws.

" 'Bout time your fast behind came up for some air," she said. "In another hour, I was gonna call and ask if you wanted me to bring you a clean change of drawers."

I cut my eyes at her and kept right on stepping, hoping she'd at least let me make it to my bedroom, where I could kick back and relax for a spell.

But she spun me around and was like, "Oh, no, girlfriend. I want all the dirty little details, right here and right now."

Too pooped to protest, I fell into the closest chair, kicked off my shoes, and said, "Fine. Where do you want to start, Nora? The sex?"

She pushed an ottoman beneath my legs before having

a seat on it herself and saying, "Hey, that's about as good a place as any in my book."

I couldn't help but smile when I got hit by the flashback of Carl working my body into a righteous frenzy with those durn strawberries. But rather than go ahead and give Nora the goods, I closed my eyes and told her, "It was . . . you know . . . all right."

Nora cracked her gum and all but snarled before she said, "Honey, please. You and I both know it takes a whole lot more than some 'all right' to keep a sister's ass voluntarily holed up with a Negro for damn near two days straight. I know you can come up with something better than that."

So after I got through laughing at her crazy behind, I told her everything I just told you, plus a little bit extra. I mean, after all, Nora's my girl and we go back like that. For the most part, she just nodded and smiled without much comment. It wasn't until I told her about how Carl had asked me to consider shucking my standard modus operandi for a trial run at something more along the lines of a more traditional relationship that homegirl's jaw nearly fell off its hinges and hit the floor.

"What?" I said.

"Look at you!" she said, screaming and jumping up at the same time. "You're seriously thinking about this thing, aren't you?"

"Why?" I said, suddenly feeling a case of cold feet coming on. "You don't think I should? It is kind of soon—"

She said, "Girl, now you know I've been in Carl's corner since day one. Besides, I always knew it was only a matter of time before you ran into the brother whose shit was so tight, you weren't gonna be able to do anything but drop all that 'three times and you're out' foolishness and deal with dude like a grown-ass woman deals with a grown-ass man. So heck, yeah, I think you ought to go on and give this boy the fair shake he's asking you for. I was just wondering what you planned on doing about that fool Scoobie is all."

I was like, "Scoobie?! What's his trifling behind got to do with anything?"

Nora snorted and said, "You might want to check your answering machine, but my guess is that he's called here at least six or seven times in the last twenty-four hours. He's even swung by here and tried to entice me into giving up the info on your whereabouts."

She tried to fill me in on Scoobie's visit, but by then I was so good and tired, I really didn't feel like hearing it. Having indulged Carl to the extent that I had, I already had too much on my mind as it was. After a long soak in a tub of hot suds, I took my broke-down butt straight to bed and would have durn well stayed there until dawn, had it not been for Nora.

It must have been around 9:30 when girlfriend came a-knocking at my door with a loud, "Yo, Faye! Your boy is out here and he says he's not leaving until he talks to you."

Girl, you know I got up ready to spit fire, don't you? I could appreciate the man digging my company and all, but this was getting downright ridiculous. I'd thrown on my robe and was still busy adjusting the sash when I stumbled into the living room and said, "Listen, Carl, I told you I needed some time . . ."

On looking up, I quickly realized there wasn't any need for me to finish the statement. Instead I sighed and said, "What the hell are you doing here?"

Scoobie smiled and said, "Carl? Is that his name? I saw the two of you at the concert the other night. No wonder the chump was acting so strange that time in the parking lot. I suppose he's the reason you skipped church on Sunday?"

You know that made me mad. I said, "Look, man, I don't have time for this. What exactly is it that you want?"

"A chance to make things right between us, Faye. How many times do I have to say it already?"

"You can stop now, as far as I'm concerned, because in case you haven't noticed, sweetheart, I'm really not trying to hear it." With that, I twirled on my heels and headed back from whence I'd come. It was a move that earned me both a big grin and a quick thumbs-up from Nora, who'd been standing there the whole time with her head swinging from one side to the other, as if she were courtside somewhere, watching Venus and Serena battle it out, instead of me and the Scoob.

Of course, I don't think either one of us was banking on dude up and following me. With Nora in hot pursuit, he came busting up in the room behind me and not only closed the door in homegirl's face but had the nerve to lock it.

"Oh, no, he didn't!" Nora said as she rattled the doorknob. "You all right in there, Faye? You want me to dial 911?"

"We need to talk," Scoobie said, over Nora's banging and shouting.

Shaking my head at the insanity of it all, I went over and unlocked the door. "It's okay," I told Nora. "Let me just go ahead and talk to this man so he can hurry up and be up out of here."

She shot Scoobie the ol' evil eye and said, "Yeah, okay, but first time I hear anything that sounds like a struggle, I'm calling the police."

While Scoobie invited himself to a seat on my bed, I lit up a cigarette and started pacing.

He followed me with his eyes for a couple of seconds, then said, "Whatever possessed you to start that nasty little habit? In the event that no one's ever told you, it's incredibly unattractive."

"Good," I said, blowing a big cloud of smoke in his direction. "I'm glad you hate it. Now go ahead and state your case, if you would, so we can say good night already."

He grabbed my hand as I walked by him and made me sit down on the bed next to him. "This boy, Carl," he said. "I mean, what could you possibly see in him? He drives a ten-year-old Toyota Corolla, for goodness' sake. And where'd he take you for dinner, huh? Taco Bell or Burger King?"

Scoobie knew he was wrong for that. I shouldn't have dignified it with a response, but you know I did. I told him, "Look, Carl and I are friends and that's all you need to know—period. End of discussion."

"Fine," Scoobie said. "So let's talk about us."

I stared at him, shocked that he could even look me in the eye and say that shit. Ever since our paths had crossed that night in the mall, I'd been waiting for Scoobie to come all the way correct with me. His apologies, his cash offerings, his nonstop testimonies to the many wondrous changes the Lord had made in his life were all fine and dandy. But there remained one white elephant of an issue between us that Scoobie in all of his newfound righteousness had yet to even acknowledge. The time had come for us to stop dancing around the bad boy and tackle it head-on.

I took one final drag on my cigarette before I got up and buried it in an ashtray. "Fine, you want to talk about us, Scoobie? Then let's do that. Let's talk about *us*—all of us—me, you . . . and *our son*."

HIM

Even though I'm not the type to go out looking for trouble, for whatever reason, man, trouble never seems to have any problem finding me. There I was sitting in my own living room, minding my own business, when I heard this car pull up.

The only reason I ventured outside at all was because I

assumed it was my ex. She'd called earlier, while I'd been out with Faye. She'd left a message asking if I'd mind her stopping over and making some warm-weather adjustments to the wardrobe the girls keep at my place. When I finally caught up with her to give her the okay, she told me she wouldn't be able to make it by until late.

So on hearing a car drive up to the condo around 9:30, I stepped outside to make sure she got in all right. But instead of Bet, who do I spy, sliding out of his pretty vanilla-colored ride, but Faye's old flame.

I'm standing there thinking to myself, *Now, I know this joker is not out here delivering Fudgesicles and Mr. Goodbars this time of night, or is he?*

I was on my way back into the house when dude called out to me, "What up, chief?"

Thinking he was only trying to be polite, I told him, "You got it, man."

That's when dude paused and then, with what was most definitely a smirk plastered across his smug, high yella mug, said, "That I do, my brother. That I do."

Who does this joker think he is? Like it wasn't bad enough that he was slipping by after dark to see my woman, but then he's gonna turn around and try to sell a brother wolf tickets, to boot? Oh, hell, no!

I spent the next thirty minutes peeping out the window and wondering what ol' boy was doing over there and just how long he planned to stay. By the time Bet rolled up, I had worked myself into a full-fledged steam.

She took one look at me and said, "What's wrong? I warned you I'd be late. If you had something else to do, Carl, you should have said something."

"It's not you" is what I told her before hurriedly relieving her of the empty box and the stack of summer wear she'd pulled out of the car.

"How come the kids aren't with you?" I asked, hoping to steer the conversation away from me and my problems as I led Bet to the room our daughters share on the nights and weekends they spend with me.

She launched into a whole big to-do about the twins and some pajama party, but you know how women are, man. Even though ol' girl was running her mouth a mile a minute, it didn't stop her from immediately noticing the clothing I'd bought Ben and foolishly left laying across one of the girls' beds.

"You been out shopping today?" she asked, after a quick look at the outfits and their still-attached price tags.

"Yeah," I told her. "My friend Faye suggested I keep a few extra things over here for Ben."

Generally all it takes is the mere mention of my son's name for Bet's jaws to start getting tight, so I was surprised when she broke into a smile and said, "Sounds like things between you and your friend are starting to heat up. Squirrel told me you were taking her to the Jarreau concert."

Leave it to my cousin Squirrel to be out spilling the beans behind my back. "Yeah, we went," I said, not really sure if I was ready to let Bet in on my feelings for Faye.

Bet opened the girls' closet and started pulling items out, but I could tell she was eager for me to fill her in. When I didn't, she said, "So . . . when do I get to meet her?"

I was like, "Uh, I don't know about that, Bet. This thing is still fairly new. I don't want to rush anything or make Faye feel like I'm out to jump the gun on her."

"Carl, I'm not out to cause you any trouble. I just think that if Faye is going to be spending time with our two girls it might not be such a bad idea if she and I had at least one face-to-face meeting. After all, I didn't waste any time in introducing you to my friend Charles."

Yeah, I met Bet's new man, all right. And don't think I'm not still having nightmares about it. As hypocritical as I know it sounds, just the thought of some joker other than myself being all up in the ex's Kool-Aid makes me downright ill. It doesn't help that this dude—*Charles*—is one of these six-four, Armani suit–wearing, proper-talking types who before you can even finish shaking his doggone hand is shoving all up in your face the fact that he's rolling with a brand-new, fully loaded Hummer and an f-ing "esquire" behind his name.

I don't doubt Bet's motives when it comes to her desire to meet Faye. In the two years since we've been divorced, she's told me on numerous occasions that she'd love to see me stop humping around and make a serious commitment to one woman. To continue to do otherwise, in her opinion, is to only put myself at risk for contracting something that'll permanently take me out of commission and ultimately break our little girls' hearts.

In yet another feeble attempt to redirect the course of our conversation, I said, "Hey, you want me to come over tomorrow and fire up the grill for you and the girls like I did last year on Memorial Day?"

Bet shook her head and said, "No, actually Charles is having us over to his place for dinner tomorrow. That's why I was out so late this evening. I've been over there helping him season the meat and what have you."

Yeah, I bet you were over there seasoning his meat and what have you is what I mumbled to myself. I'm saying, man, that's what I call TMDI—too much damn information!

Rather than stick around and let the heifer continue to gag me, I politely excused myself and went back into the living room, where I resumed my pathetic peek-and-pout by the window.

HER

Yes, I do have a child, a son, who on his next birthday should be turning all of twelve. His entrance into my life was marked by his father's all-too-sudden exit. Instead of dealing with me or our situation head-on, Scoobie took off on a cruise to the Caribbean with a handful of my credit cards and everything I had left in the bank, and in the company of some other woman.

Suffice to say, neither the child nor the circumstances surrounding his birth is something I'm generally open to discussing. Until now God, Nora, and my gynecologist are about the only ones I've ever fully trusted with any of the details. Although they shouldn't have, the facts came as news to Scoobie as well.

"*Our son?!*" he said, jumping up from the bed as if it had teeth and had just bitten him solidly in the behind. "What do you mean *our son?* Didn't you—I mean, damn, Faye, all these years I just assumed you went ahead and had an abortion."

You know it took everything in me not to clue homeboy in on the word "assume" and its nasty little habit of making a right natural ass out of "u" and "me." But rather than take that route, I just hit him full-fledged upside the head with the truth of the matter—"Well, you assumed wrong. He was born in Oklahoma, where I'll have you know, I moved with Nora's help in order to keep my folks from finding out."

"Is that where he is now?"

"Don't you get it, Scoobie? You left me a wreck in more ways than one. I wasn't in any condition to take care of a child—financially, emotionally, or otherwise. I gave him up for adoption. Where he is now is anybody's guess."

Scoobie sank back down on my bed, buried his head in

his hands, and moaned, "I didn't know, Faye. I didn't know."

"And if you had known," I said, "you really think it would have made a difference?"

To my utter shock and disbelief, he looked up at me with his eyes red, his face wet, and said, "Back then? To be honest, no, probably not. But that was then, Faye, this is now. If we've got a son floating around out there somewhere, then we need to find him."

"Find him for what?" I said. "Haven't we complicated his life enough as it is? Face it, Scoobie, it's too late. The boy is twelve. I'm sure by now he's settled in with some nice family who loves him and—"

He cut me off with, "But what if he's not? What if he's stuck in the system somewhere, bouncing from one foster home to the next? What if he's been neglected? Mistreated? Abused?"

I told him, "Like I haven't spent more than one sleepless night thinking about all those things and more? But what's the use, Scoobie? It was a closed adoption. Finding out anything with regards to either his well-being or his whereabouts is virtually impossible. Don't think I haven't tried."

"I don't doubt you have," he said. "But I haven't. I run in a lot of different circles these days. Chances are better than good that I can come up with a connection to someone who can help us."

"Yeah? And then what? We find him and the three of us reunite to become one big freaking dysfunctional family, destined to live unhappily ever after? Man, get real—"

He jumped up again, only this time he grabbed me, locked his arms around me, and whispered, "Faye, I've been in love with you since I was fourteen years old. All it took was bumping into you that night at the mall for me to realize that not much has changed as far as my feelings for you are concerned."

This wasn't anything like the brief exchange we'd had at the mall. It had been years since he'd held me that close. A part of me wanted to pull away and never look back. Another part of me longed to feel him even closer. Durn near choking on all the days and nights of hurt I'd endured because of him and his trifling ways, I said, "What? And that's supposed to make it all right? After twelve years and all the dirt you did, I'm just supposed to forgive, forget, and welcome your sorry ass back with open arms just because you say you love me?"

With tears streaming down his face like rain, Scoobie said, "You want the truth? Well, the truth is, Faye, yes, I was a low-down, dirty dog for leaving you when you needed me most. But you know what? I was scared. I thought you'd gotten pregnant deliberately as a way of tying me down and keeping me from realizing my dreams. So yeah, I ran. That's what boys do. But I'm a man now—ten times the man I was before. And as a man, I'm coming to you and asking—no, not asking—I'm begging you, baby, for just one chance—one chance to try and make this right."

Okay, before you go getting it twisted, let me just say that it wasn't all the crying or even the fact that the brother broke down and used the L-word that sucked me in and kept me there. More than just a few of the things we touched on that night struck sensitive nerves with me—from Scoobie's long-overdue admission to having been both a dog and a coward, to my own confession to indeed having gotten knocked up in a weak, illogical, and totally immature attempt to keep dude in check. And then there was the guilt we now both feel about the birth and subsequent abandonment of the little boy who carries our DNA but neither of our names.

In essence, what Scoobie and I had was our very first ever no-holds-barred conversation. We dumped it all out there—the good, the bad, the ugly—and sorted through each and every one of the messy bits and pieces until we were both satisfied. It was extremely cathartic, if nothing else.

But I told Scoobie before he left, "Just because we've talked doesn't necessarily mean I'm ready to let you back into my life just yet." We'd been standing outside under the porch light saying our goodbyes, and his quick response had come in the form of a kiss—a soft, wet, and teasingly sweet kiss, followed by an all-too-sincere-sounding "Take all the time you need, baby. I'm not going anywhere anytime soon."

HIM

It was close to eleven when dude finally brought his rusty butt up outta there. I might have been willing and able to just let it go if I hadn't seen them kiss. Yeah, she kissed him, and unlike the time before it wasn't any of that quick, friendly peck on the cheek kind of action either. As far as I could tell, it was all lip and quite possibly more than just a little bit of tongue.

To say I was disappointed in ol' girl is putting it mildly. After having spent nearly a full day and a half with me, and a good portion of that laid up in my doggone bed, she turns around and lets dude slip up in the mix like it ain't no thang. I had a good mind to call her up and ask if her revolving door was gonna be spinning through the night or what? But you'll be happy to know, I didn't show out this time.

No, rather than venture outside and give either of them the satisfaction of knowing just how much they'd managed to get me riled, I left my window peeking post and spent the rest of the night drifting back and forth between sleep and trying not to speculate on what all the two of them might have been doing over there.

I can't help it, man. I dig the girl, okay? Even after what I'd just witnessed, I was still wanting very much to extend her the full benefit of the doubt. I mean, after all, what reason would she have to lie about what's been going down between her and dude? But as far as slick is concerned—man, I should have known from the jump his yella ass wasn't up to nothing good. And the next time he fixes his mouth to say something foul in my direction? All I can say is, he'd best bring his "A" game and come ready to play hard 'cause I'm 'bout through being Mista Nice Guy.

HER

And to think, I woke up the next morning in a good mood. Really, all I had on my mind was kicking it with the kinfolk, eating some ribs, and savoring the sweet taste of my Aunt Bessie's homemade ice cream. All that worrisome stuff having to do with brother Scoobie and Mr. Carl, I'd resolved to put on the back burner to be dealt with some other day.

So I was in my room getting ready for the trip when Nora started pounding on my door. "Yo, Faye. You up? Loverboy's here to see you and he's got flowers."

Hell, girl, my mood took an immediate turn for the worse. I marched out of my room and into the kitchen with every intention of pulling the brother to the side and tactfully reminding him of some of the promises that had come out of his mouth just last night. Please, if only it could have been that simple. First of all, the brother in question wasn't Scoobie.

An eyeful of his back and Nora's big moon-pie face were what greeted my entry into the room. I should have known by the slick grin on the heifer's face, she was up to something. She was cheesing hard and looking dead at me when she said, "So, Carl, what you got planned for this fine Memorial Day?"

I cleared my throat, hoping to distract him, and he did turn around and smile, but he also kept right on gabbing with my traitorous roomie. He said, "Not a whole lot. My girls are hanging out with my ex and her new man; my cousin Squirrel rode up to Chicago yesterday with my Uncle Westbrook; and all of my other friends are spending time with their families, or you know, have made plans that don't include me, so . . ."

And like the low-down cow that she can be sometimes, Nora giggled and said ever so sweetly, "So why don't you come and go with us? Faye won't mind. The more the merrier, she always says. Isn't that right, Faye?"

I could have choked her. Strangled her dead right there on the kitchen floor. She knew I didn't have the heart to veto her invitation—not with Carl standing there holding a durn armful of yellow carnations and wearing a smile of my making.

HIM

Hey, it wasn't like I went over there looking for an invite. All I called myself doing was letting the sister know that one, I wanted to be taken seriously, and two, I didn't intend to let her late-night caller's challenge to me go unanswered.

If she didn't fancy the idea of me tagging along, she should have doggone well gone ahead and put her foot down. All she had to say in so many words was, "Look, man, I'm feeling pressured, okay? You need to back off and give me the space I need to think this thing through," and I would have been more than happy to oblige her.

Instead she took my doggone flowers and led me to believe everything was on the up-and-up—until we're all set to hit the road. Being that it was her car we were taking, I did the gentlemanly thing and offered to both drive and put a couple dollars' worth of gas in her tank. Though she nodded her consent and tossed me the keys, rather than join me in the front seat, she climbed her big butt into the back, claiming she was tired and in need of some room to stretch.

I tried to convince myself that after having kicked it with me for most of the weekend, she probably was feeling a bit drained. What I didn't want to think about was how the time she'd wasted doing Lord knows what with her late-night guest might have fit into her fatigue equation. And then there was the silence. While Nora, as usual, talked her fool head off, Faye was pretty quiet the whole way down. But every once in a while I'd glance at her in the rearview window and notice her eyebrows all scrunched up, as if she were brooding about something.

The only saving grace was that the trip wasn't a long one. Water Valley is, thankfully, only an hour and a half or so drive from Memphis. Once we got there I figured it best to just temporarily put aside my concerns about the bad vibes I was picking up from Faye. I wasn't about to let her funky little attitude keep me from being anything less than cordial when it came to meeting and greeting her folks.

She comes from a nice enough clan—mom, dad, couple of brothers, and the usual assortment of elders, cousins, and kids. They're somewhat on the loud and country side, but you don't have to be around them for longer than a minute to know that they're basically good people who care about one another. Her old man is a semiretired truck driver and a pretty easygoing sort of guy. He gave me the usual interrogation concerning my intentions towards his "babygirl," but it was fairly laid-back and lighthearted kind of stuff. On the other hand, Faye's two older brothers, Frank and Grant, let it be known in so many words and gestures that they weren't above whupping the black off my ass if they found out I wasn't doing right by their li'l sis. And then there was Mrs. Abrahams, Faye's mom, who treated me like I was already a member of the family—called me "son," waited on me hand and foot, and kept asking if Faye had been taking good care of me.

It also didn't take me long to hone in on the fact that ol' girl's family had anointed her their "chosen one." You know, the one most everybody tries to push out in front of the pack and encourages to go forth and do well; the one all the old folk pin their own deferred dreams of a better life on; the one thought of as smart and talented enough to one day do not only the family but the whole damn race proud! Doesn't every decent, working-class, God-fearing Black family have at least one? I know amongst my own kin, it's my sister Sheila, the serious scholar and tenured English professor, who proudly wears the crown.

But getting back to ol' girl's peeps, overall I'd have to say that hanging out with them was a whole lot of fun. To tell the truth, at one point I was having such a good time feeding my face, sipping on Uncle Chester's evil-tasting homemade wine, playing cards, and swapping lies with the fellas that I damn near forgot all about Faye. Who knows when I would have noted her absence if Nora hadn't come over and whispered into my ear, "Better go check on your girl. I think she might be needing some attention—if you know what I mean."

So, dutiful lover that I am, I went inside and found Faye sitting alone in the den, blowing smoke into the hum of the air conditioner.

When I asked what was wrong, she gave me one of

those curt "nothings" that usually mean something. So I said, "Then why are you sitting here in the dark puffing yourself full of nicotine?"

She took a moment to snuff out her cigarette before she said, "I came in to get out the heat."

I said, "Come on now, Faye. You've hardly said ten words to me all day. Are you upset with me about something? Is it that you didn't want me to come?"

She shook her head and said, "I've just got a few things on my mind, is all."

I took a chance and asked, "Might I be one of those things?"

With a sad little smile creasing her lips, she said, "You might."

After squaring my shoulders, I said, "And what about your friend? The one I saw over at your place last night?"

Rather than answer, she sighed, leaned back in her chair, and closed her eyes.

Even though I wasn't completely sure I'd be able to stomach the truth, I went after it anyway. "Something happened, didn't it? Something between you and him that changes the way you feel about you and me?"

With her eyes still fastened shut, she said, "If you want to know the truth, Carl, yes, something did happen. But like I told you already, it was a long time ago. How I feel about you and me is a totally separate issue."

She sounded earnest enough, but just to be sure I said, "So does that mean you're still open to what we discussed the other day—a one-on-one, I'm your man, you're my woman type of scenario?"

Before she said anything, she blinked open her eyes and focused them on me. Then, in a soft voice she said, "Sure, I'm still open to that, Carl. It's just that . . . well, it's complicated. I still need some time. It's not the kind of decision I can just turn around and make in a day."

Feeling better, now that some of my fears had been

openly addressed, I plopped down on the floor in front of the chair where ol' girl was seated and said, "Well, what about a night, then? I'm saying, when we get back home, you could come on over to my place, I could draw you a warm bath, give your back a nice rub, your feet a slow, sensuous massage—and then, if you act right, I could even throw in a little toe-sucking here and there."

I slid off one of her shoes, nibbled on her big toe, and pretended like I was fixin' to make good on the promise, right then and there. And for the first time that day I got a genuine smile out of her.

"You play too much," she said. "Now give me back my shoe."

"No, the problem is you don't play enough," I said as I rose up on my knees and shoved her shoe down the front of my pants. "Now come down here and give me some sugar and I'll give it to you."

She laughed and said, "If one of my brothers should happen to walk up in here you're gonna have a whole lot of explaining to do."

I said, "So what you waiting on? Hurry up and get your butt down here."

To my surprise, she did. She eased herself onto the floor next to me, plucked her shoe from my pants, and when I leaned over to collect on my end of the deal, ol' girl laid 'em on me—long, sweet, keep-a-brother-coming-back-for-more kind of kisses that almost made me forget we were still in her parents' house.

There was an urgency in her kisses, an urgency that both thrilled and scared me in much the same way the look I saw in her eyes did when we finally paused to catch our breaths.

But before either of us could say anything, Nora poked her head around the corner and said, "Ooh wee, I'ma sho'll tell it! Mr. and Mrs. Abrahams, you better get in here quick. Faye and Carl in your den, down on the floor, fixin' to straight get freaky with it!"

HER

The trip to Water Valley couldn't have been more perfect—for Carl, that is. He got rave reviews and durn near a standing ovation from the home folk—especially my mama, who made a big show of fawning all over the man, like he was royalty or something. And Carl seemed right at home sitting out under the shade tree, drinking wine out of a jelly jar, and backslapping with my big-headed brothers.

But out of everybody, I'd have to say it was my father who really surprised me. I was in the kitchen stirring up a big pitcher of lemonade to replace the one we'd already finished when he strolled in and said, "How you like your mama's new refrigerator?"

At first glance, the question came off as an entirely legitimate one. My mama had been needing a new refrigerator for the longest, but given the shaky state of my finances, I'd been hard pressed to come up with the cash—that is, until that fateful night in the mall when I'd bumped into Scoobie with his open checkbook and guilty conscience. I'd taken half of the money and turned it over to Nora as an extra payment over and beyond what I already give and owe her. The other half I'd sent on to my mama with instructions for her to make Daddy or one of my big-headed brothers take her to pick out the fridge she wanted. But it wasn't long after I assured my dad that as long as Mama was happy with her choice of appliances, I was too, that I realized his true motive for wanting to talk to me.

"So . . . Carl tells me he's a FedEx man. You know, ever since you got on down at the VA your mama's kind of had her heart set on you bringing home some nice doctor, one of them smart, good-looking Ben Carson/Marcus Welby types."

Rather than let my daddy in on the fact that I'd hardly

be interested in such a beast, I just played along with him. "Well, if the way she's been doting on him is any indication, she's either changed her mind or else is looking to trade you in."

My daddy laughed and without skipping a beat, turned around and asked, "You known him long?"

I told him the truth, which was, "He's been subletting the condo next to ours for close to eight months now."

Looking all serious, my daddy came over and stood next to me before he said, "From what I gather he's more than just a few years older than you, isn't he? Been married before and he's got, what? Two or three kids?"

I didn't know if he was asking or telling, but in any case my response was, "I wouldn't go reading too much into his having come along with us, if I were you. By no means is this some sort of 'let's go meet the folks' kind of visit. At the moment and until further notice, all we are is friends, okay?"

My dad grunted and said, "I'm sorry to hear that. He seems like a decent enough fella. But I guess I always have been kind of partial to a man with calluses on his hands. Lets you know he ain't afraid of a little hard work. And you know the way they make stuff these days, it don't never hurt to have a man who knows how to fix a thing or two."

I said, "Daddy, please. Would you stop already?"

He said, "What? I ain't trying to pick 'em for you. That's the kind of meddling I leave to your mama. Long as I get me a grandson out the deal, I don't really care one way or the other."

I laughed and told him, "I'll be sure to make a mental note of that."

Even though he was grinning, I knew he was halfway serious about the grandson thing. With five kids between them, it's not like my brothers haven't been trying, but thus far all the grands they've brought home to meet the old man have been girls.

After he left the kitchen, I couldn't help but wonder how my father might react to the secret I'd been keeping from him and the rest of the family for the past twelve years. Would his disapproval and disappointment eventually give way to acceptance and pride? And what were the chances of him ever coming to like Scoobie as much as he already seemed to like Carl?

I looked out the window that overlooked my folks' backyard and tried to imagine my son out there laughing, screaming, and acting a fool with the rest of his cousins. The only image I own of him is the one that burned itself into my subconscious on the day of his birth. All I have to do is close my eyes and within seconds I can see him—a big, pretty baby with an upturned nose and a headful of jet-black curls. According to Nora, who was right there with me, front row center through it all, he looked just like my daddy.

Of all the decisions I've been forced to make in my life, giving up my child has thus far been the most difficult and the one I've come to most regret. Not even the passage of time has helped ease the pain. Actually, in a lot of ways it's only made it all the more intense. Not a day goes by where I don't stop and think—if only I knew then what I know now, boy, would I have done it all differently.

HIM

On the way back home Nora insisted on taking the wheel and appointing herself the designated driver. And to tell you the truth, with all the ribs, spaghetti, potato salad, homemade ice cream, watermelon, and what have you stuffed in my gut, not to mention the homemade hooch swimming around in my head, I was only too happy to take the backseat and let the womenfolk commandeer the front. Once I got settled, I went so far as to pull a Faye and let myself cop a snooze. A couple times I even woke myself up snoring. I was caught up somewhere in that dreamlike space that exists between sleep and nod when I overheard a few snatches of the whispered conversation Nora was trying to have with Faye.

"Does he know about Oklahoma?"

"He who? Carl or Scoobie?"

"Either or? If you ask me, they've both damn well got a right to know."

"Well, ain't nobody asked you. Besides, this is neither the time nor the place to be getting into all of that. You know good and well every shut eye ain't sleep."

As far as what that particular exchange was really all about, man, your guess is about as good as mine. But what I heard lurking just beneath the surface of their words left me with the feeling that either something wasn't quite right or, worse yet, was on the verge of going horribly wrong.

But when we got back home, rather than press Faye for answers that I knew she'd only be reluctant, if not outright refuse, to give, I pulled her aside and told her that I'd only been kidding about all that stuff I'd said earlier about her coming over that night. I told her, "I know you're probably tired and I'm not out to sweat you. I want you to feel comfortable with your decision, not rushed into it. So when you make up your mind, just let me know."

"Sure," she said. "I'll do that."

"Of course," I said. "If you could tell a brother something by the end of the week, it would be nice."

She grinned and shook her head at me, like I was a lost cause, before she said, "I'll be in touch, Carl. End of the week at the latest. You've got my word, okay?"

HER

Wednesday night is usually when I put in my volunteer time up at Baptist East. But this past Wednesday evening I changed up and did something a little different. I went up to New Hope to assist in the weeklong career fair some of the elders had put together.

Since I'd already been informed that I was scheduled to be the first speaker for the night, I didn't even bother to look at the program that had been printed up and passed out for the event. When the deacon moderating the event introduced me, I just got up, went to the podium, and launched into the "So you want to be a pharmacist" spiel I'd prepared for the ten or so minutes I'd been allotted.

Anyway, I'm standing there with my VA lab jacket covering my conservative work garb and my reading glasses clinging to the end of my nose, doing my best to simultaneously engage and inspire the twenty-five to thirty youths who'd assembled themselves in New Hope's small basement auditorium, when in strolls who but my old friend Scoobie.

Rather than come in and pull up a chair, he found himself a nice spot against the wall in the back of the room, where he stood with his arms folded across his chest and with this *look* on his face. You know the *look* I'm talking about, girl, don't you? Umm-huh, that goofy-ass one our prez, George W., likes to aim at his girl, Madame Secretary Condi Rice, when he's got her standing up in front of folks, doing his dirty work? Yeah, well, that's the way Scoobie was staring at me and even though I'm sure he meant it as a compliment, there was something right yuck about it.

At the end of my presentation I went back to my seat only to nearly fall off of it when I heard the moderator announce that the next speaker would be none other than my boy, Chef Venard Nathaniel Payne. Honey, what you talking about? Before the brother could even climb up on the stage and open his mouth, I had all but made up my mind to find some kind of fault with both him and whatever it was he was fixing to say.

But the world has a funny way of turning on you sometimes, don't it, girl? Rather than maintain the level of evilness required to sit up in my church's basement and straight-up hate on the brother, I went ahead and lent him the fair chance and open ear I would have extended to just about anyone but him. And wouldn't you know it, before long I found myself slowly but surely being captivated and enthralled.

I kid you not, girl, Scoobie gave one of the most moving presentations I've ever heard, not only about his current position as Morris-Morgan's chief executive dining room chef, but the long, hard struggle he'd waged to get and stay there. I think it helped that in addition to touting the usual, such as the benefits of networking and the importance of seeking out mentors and internships, he openly addressed some of his own personal issues, including how he'd pretty much been forced into putting aside twenty-some years of bad habits (e.g., being lazy, trifling, and a womanizer) in order to achieve those things he wanted out of life. But I think the high point of his speech was when he went into the difficulties he'd encountered in trying to care for his ailing mother while pursuing his dream of becoming somebody's head chef.

At some point, during the course of Scoobie's talk, I caught a glimpse of the bright, charismatic, good-looking boy I'd fallen head over heels for way back when, and before he'd finished, I was all but fondly reminiscing about all those things I'd once adored so much about him. Lord knows I never could have imagined that the day would come that I'd be somewhere staring up at the likes of Scoobie and experiencing what can best be described as an immense feeling of pride. I can only hope that I hid it well and wasn't sitting up there with that dumb-ass look plastered across my face.

After the applause for Chef Payne's stirring presentation died down, a brief intermission was called. I was in the church's dining hall, sampling some of the refreshments that, come to find out, had been provided courtesy of the budding celebrity in our midst, when I felt him next to me and heard him say, "Chef Payne and Dr. Abrahams—it has quite a nice ring to it, don't you think?"

With a big slice of German chocolate cake in one hand and a fork, poised to do damage, in the other, I swiveled toward him and with a smile said, "You could have at least warned me you were going to be here."

He laughed and said, "What? And give you an opportunity to make plans to be elsewhere? Besides, I was hoping to surprise you."

"That you did," I admitted to him. "And in a good way, no less."

He soaked up the compliment and went fishing for more. "You're not actually giving me your stamp of approval, are you?"

Deciding it wouldn't hurt to let the brother have his moment, I told him, "You were incredibly impressive, to say the least."

With that bit of encouragement, I guess he decided the time had come to up the ante. He fingered my name tag and was like, "You're quite a hard act to follow, Dr. Abrahams. How could I help but pull out all the stops?"

Not about to let him rattle me, I took a step away from him and was all set to stuff my face full of cake, when he eased both the utensil and the plate out of my hands and said, "Ah, ah, ah—not until you tell me whether or not you're coming to my book party on Friday night."

"I don't know" is what I told him. "I can't say I've really given it that much thought."

"And why is that?" he said, jabbing into my dessert. And then, girl, on securing this itsy, bitsy piece of cake, devoid of so much as a lick of frosting on the end of the fork, he held it out for me to sample.

While I mouthed the stingy morsel, he kept talking. "You do want to see the inside of the house, don't you? And if I'm not mistaken, some small part of you very much wants to see if I am in fact the changed man I claim to be. Right?"

So I asked him, "Can I take that to mean you wouldn't be terribly upset if I brought someone with me?"

He gave me a right puzzled look and said, "You mean Nora?"

I laughed and told him "No, that's not exactly who I had in mind."

He was like, "Frankly, Faye, I was hoping you'd come as my special guest. There are a lot of things that still haven't been said between us."

"Huh, you got that right" is what I almost told him as I watched him dispose of my cake only to turn around and hand me a small saucer full of some ol' nasty dried fruit, bran, and granola mix.

HIM

All right, man, it's confession time. There's this chick I haven't told you about. Victoria's her name, but Ms. Vic is what I like to call her. She's in my marketing class and before Faye came along, I'd been entertaining thoughts of hooking up with her.

I've known her for well over a year now, but it's only been in these last two semesters that we've actually started hanging out. Initially, it was me, her, and a bunch of other students getting together after class to study every now and then. But in the past couple of weeks, it's just been me and her. And as of late, I've sorta gotten the impression that baby girl's highly interested in enlisting my services for some after-hours research of a more hands-on nature, if you know what I mean.

Now, back in the days BCAB—you know, "before Clarice and Benjamin"—I wouldn't have bothered to think twice about stepping to the honey and telling her to come on with it then. To be quite honest, I don't know too many brothers, married, single, or otherwise, with the wherewithal to "just say no" when it comes to some pretty young thing who's eager to put the naughty on 'em.

Yeah, man, baby girl is one of these young, hot fillies with legs and face for days, the type liable to put an old dog like me in permanent traction, trying to keep up with her ass. She kinda puts you in mind of a tall Lauryn Hill. Yeah, the chick that used to sing with the Fugees. You know, same ebony coloring, deep, expressive eyes, the same slim figure and petite frame, only much more statuesque.

So what's stopping me? Besides this thing I'm trying to cultivate with Faye, you mean? Come on, man, like I've told you on more than one occasion, I've just about had my fill of being out here trying to kick it with some of La-Dee, Da-Dee, and Everybody. At my age, I'm supposed to have enough sense to be cautious, if nothing else. And as pretty, book-smart, and mature-looking as Ms. Vic is, she's still a youngster. I'm talking at least twenty-some years my junior. And like I said, BCAB I wouldn't have had a problem with it. But having gone through my share of changes with Clarice, now I know, man, these young girls out here ain't nuthin' to play with.

Anyway, the other night after we finished up the project we'd been working on for class, I let her talk me into going with her and a group of her friends to this club that caters to the thirty and under hip-hop crowd. Yeah, in retrospect,

I guess I should have known better. But see, she lured me in by telling me that it was a real tame, afrocentric kinda clientele that frequented the joint and that on that particular night only poets and spoken-word artists were scheduled to perform. So I told myself, *Hey, why not? It's something different. And who knows, I just might like it.* Besides, quiet as it's kept, I tried my own hand at a little poetry back in the day.

Man, I wasn't up in that joint five minutes before I knew I had made a mistake. I'm saying, for all the noise, crazy-looking outfits, jacked-up hair-dos, and folks high on dope, I could just as well have spent a couple hours locked up in the high-risk ward of the nearest insane asylum. Maybe I am just getting old, but what I thought was gonna be a soulful showcasing of thought-provoking self-expression came off as little more than an opportunity for a bunch of depressed, disgruntled, dysfunctional types to holler, cuss, and act a clown in front of an audience of pseudo-intellectual wannabes. Hell, for less than half the price and none of the aggravation, I could have kicked back on my sofa with a bag of chips, a couple of cold brewskis, and my trusty remote and watched me some daggum *Comic View* on BET. Funny thing is, though, the entire time I was there I kept wondering what my girl Faye would have had to say about the whole scene.

Yeah, man, I'm not gonna lie. As long as Faye's in the picture, Ms. Vic don't hardly stand a chance. Earlier in that same day I'd been hit with this idea to do a li'l somethin' for ol' girl to let her know I'd been thinking about her. So after making sure my last paycheck had made it into my account and I had a few extra bucks to spare, I went out at lunchtime and pulled it all together.

Wasn't anything major, mind you, just a li'l somethin' with a hint of strawberry that I'm hoping will make her dimple-up in all the right places—if you know what I mean.

HER

I have to give it to him, girl, the basket was a nice touch. I found it parked in front of my door when I got home from church later that night. Almost immediately I recognized it as the same basket Carl had served me croissants from that Sunday morning he'd coaxed me into missing service. Only this time when I peeled back the cloth napkins covering the top of the basket, I found it chock-full of some of everything from candles to bubble bath, oils, potpourri, even a couple of those miniature jars of jelly and jam, and all of it strawberry related, whether by flavor, scent, or design. Wedged between the chocolate-covered strawberries and a bottle of strawberry-flavored juice spritzer, I found a note the brother had scribbled on a strawberry-shaped pad, no less. *Look here, girl, stop playing and call me. You know you want some more of this . . .* is what it said.

It was sweet, girl, no lie. And it wasn't like I wasn't incredibly tempted to walk on over and tell him so. But I knew if I did, chances were good he'd wind up talking me into staying awhile and ultimately engaging in a whole lot more than conversation. I'm sorry, that's just not how I wanted it all to go down, girl, especially after having just spent the last couple hours in Scoobie's company.

I didn't bother to tell Nora about the basket. I already knew how hard she was rooting for Carl, and I didn't feel like having to deal with the extra pressure or the guilt trip she was liable to try and lay on me.

As it was, I waited until the following morning to ask her if she'd be at all interested in going to Scoobie's book party with me on Friday night, only to have her shoot back at me with an emphatic "Hell, no!" before proceeding to describe in excruciating detail just how much she couldn't stand "Scoobie's monkey ass."

Had the refusal come from anyone other than Nora, I no doubt would have just dropped it and moved on. But what you have to understand is that I've long depended upon girlfriend to be sort of like my third eye. When it comes to certain situations, particularly those involving a group setting, she's always had a knack for picking up and pointing out those fine details and subtle nuances that ordinarily would escape my attention altogether. Besides all of that, the occasions in the past when I would have found myself lost, if not straight-up laid out somewhere, had Nora not been around to serve as my buffer and backup are way too numerous to even mention.

So in a desperate attempt to make the idea more palatable, I let it slip that in addition to some of the city's rich, famous, and influential, there would likely be a number of show-biz types attending the event. On noticing homegirl's eyes start to light up, I went all out and told her that there just might be someone there who could help her friend Ray-Ray get a leg up in the industry.

Girl, please. Ray-Ray is Nora's latest "boo." She met him after a bachelorette party at some strip club. No kidding, he's an exotic dancer whose big dream is to one day dance his groove thing onto the big screen. Lord help us all if it should ever happen.

When Nora turned around and asked if I really thought the chances were good that Scoobie knew someone who could help Ray-Ray get a solid foot in the door, you know it took everything in me not to break down and tell her the truth—besides a shake-'em-up joint, the only place brother Ray is ever likely to plant one of his big, crusty size 16s is in his even bigger mouth. But some things, girl, you just have to let die a natural death. Me trying to talk sense to Nora about a man is like trying to teach an old dog how to stop drinking out the toilet.

HIM

I was sitting at my desk at work, thinking about where I wanted to go for lunch, when she called and was like, "Hey, it's me. Is this a good time?"

I leaned back in my chair and told her, "Girl, you know when it comes to you, I'm willing to make any time a good time. Now go on and tell Papa just what it is you need."

She chuckled and said, "Well, I was just calling to thank you for the basketful of strawberry goodies. That was cute. I would have never guessed you to be such a hard-core romantic."

I said, "So how come you didn't bother to bring your butt over and tell me that last night?"

She said, "Oh, I think you know why, all right. Missing service this past Sunday was bad enough. I'm not about to let you start making me late for work, too."

I grinned and told her, "Yeah, girl, my whip appeal will straight-cold knock a sister out, won't it?"

She laughed again and said, "Anyway, like I said, I just wanted to let you know that I got it and I've been enjoying it and I thought it was a really sweet gesture."

I was like, "Uh-huh. So are you still thinking on what we talked about, or are you ready to give me an answer?"

She kind of hesitated before she said, "I thought you weren't going to pressure me."

I said, "What? Is that what you think I'm doing? No. Not me. Never." Then I got real and told her, "I'm just saying, baby, how difficult of a decision could it be? Either you want to do this thing with me or you don't. I mean, if the answer is no, Faye, that's cool, just tell me. I'm not gonna be mad. Maybe a little hurt. But I'm a big boy. I'll get over it."

She turned around and said, "Carl, if it were that simple—"

But before she could commence to ruffling any of my feathers, I cut her off. I said, "It is that simple, Faye, believe me. But hey, I'm not trying to argue with you about it. If the end of the week is what you want, then the end of the week is what I'm going to give you. Bottom line is, I just want you to be happy. All right?"

"All right," she said. "I'll be in touch."

Before she could hang up I told her, "You know, Faye, either way it goes, I'd still like to have that third time at bat."

And check this out, man, her noncommittal response to that was, "Okay, okay. I'll keep that in mind."

HER

Yeah, the house and the book party turned out to be something else, girl. Nora was right there with me, just like in the end I knew she would be, along with that fool boyfriend of hers, Ray-Ray, who for reasons known only to him had decided to come dressed like he was fixing to audition for that Will Smith/Kool Moe Dee *Wild, Wild West* video that came out umpteen-some years ago. For real, girl, I'm talking cowboy hat, leather chaps, boots, spurs, everything but the durn horse and saddle, though in Ray-Ray's case, a jackass would have been more his speed.

Anyway, as soon as we arrived, a proud and beaming Scoobie grabbed me by the arm and whisked me from one exquisitely decorated room to the next. Yeah, I was impressed. The place was laid. Marble and granite countertops, hardwood floors so shiny you could eat off them, original African and European artwork, and space! Girl, the brother has so many rooms he's pretty much designated one to his every fancy. I'm talking a full-scale library, a gym, a game room, a music room, a film room that's hooked up like a miniature movie theater. He's even got a cozy little setup with a fountain that he calls his "Prayer and Meditation" room.

To tell the truth, there wasn't a whole lot Scoobie got wrong at the party that night. He was incredibly attentive, to the point of treating me like I was the Queen of Sheba or somebody, and he seemed to get a particular kick out of introducing me to all of his friends and associates as "Dr. Abrahams." The talk he gave was short, eloquent, and chock-full of praise to all those who'd helped him along the way. The food, which showcased several of the recipes from his book, like braised short ribs and blackened catfish, was absolutely fabulous. The jazz quartet he'd hired to help set the proper mood jammed something fierce throughout the evening. And as far as I could tell, the guests, who'd turned out in droves, seemed both impressed and thoroughly entertained.

Besides Ray-Ray passing out business cards and telling folks he was available on an hourly basis for either clean or X-rated shake-'em-up shows, the only incident of any real significance occurred shortly after Scoobie had introduced me to the man he proudly claimed as his mentor, an older white gentleman by the name of Frank Dumas, and his lovely Black American Princess of a wife, Tina.

I'd met Ms. Thang briefly that night Scoobie had taken me by his workplace. She was a tall, slender, reasonably attractive sister, probably 'round 'bout my age. Even though the first time we'd met, I'd been able to tell in a glance that she was all about the bourgie, she'd seemed pleasant enough. But on this particular evening, girlfriend went all out of her way to show her durn drawers.

Now, you know as bad as I talk about Ray-Ray, even

I've got better sense and upbringing than to ever deliberately say anything to the man's face that might hurt his or Nora's feelings. But this cow, Tina, the first thing out of her mouth after Scoobie had introduced her to Nora and Ray was "Oh, so these must be some more of your hood friends."

I mean, come on, thinking something ugly is one thing, but saying it to folks' face is quite another. Then she had the nerve to make like she was going to clean it up. "Oh, dear me, did I misspeak? Ha, ha. I meant to say, friends from the hood."

Misspoke, my behind. Just minutes after that bit of clawing, girlfriend was up in my face talking about, "Darling, I hope you don't take this the wrong way, but in front of people like these, it might behoove you to drop the Scoobie bit and address our dear friend by his given name—Venard."

People like these?! Honey, please. I gave Lady T one of my "get thee away from me" looks and then, in the most countrified voice I could muster, I yelled across the room, "Scoobie! Oooh Scoo-oo-bay!" I sure did. Girlfriend was not finna worry me.

If anybody should have been concerned about appearances or impressions, by all rights, it should have been her silly behind. For starters, she's the one with nearly five inches of height, not to mention more than a couple feet worth of fake hair on her barely four-nine, sixty-some-year-old, Caucasian, combover-sporting husband. And that's not to take anything away from Mr. Dumas, who in spite of his obvious bad taste in women, seems like a really nice guy.

Somebody needs to tell girlfriend that before she starts endeavoring to get other folks straight, she needs to first make sure her own priorities are in order. And at the very top of her list ought to be her and Frank's four-year-old son, Evan, whom they'd somehow seen fit to drag along to the party and turn loose to do as he durn well pleased. You know how it is for most children that age, especially spoiled-rotten ones—the whole world is their playground. So quite naturally Evan was running around whooping and hollering it up like some warthog, skirting all between folks' legs and snatching food from people's plates, like he didn't have home training the first.

Now if there's one thing that hasn't changed about Scoobie, it's his heightened level of discomfort around kids, particularly those under the age of ten. In light of the situation, I was just about to compliment homeboy on the polite manner in which he seemed to be handling the antics of his rambunctious guest, when I heard the crash.

I didn't see what happened, but according to Nora's eyewitness account, it was no accident. According to her, little Mr. Dumas snatched the vase from its pedestal and slammed it to the floor like it was a football. I will say the child was definitely in the throes of what had all the makings of a victory dance when I turned around.

"Son-of-a-bitch, son-of-a-bitch" is what I heard Scoobie say under his breath as he rushed over to inspect the damage.

At least Frank had the decency to come over and apologize. He told Scoobie to send him the bill and he'd see that it was taken care of. But that grinning, fake-hair-slinging wife of his didn't budge so much as an inch from the spot where she'd been busy holding court on the other side of the room.

Poor Scoobie was still muttering what sounded like profanities under his breath when I bent down to help him clean up the mess. I could understand him being upset. Not only had he lost a beautiful, and no doubt expensive, vase, but he'd cut his finger on one of the shards and was dripping blood all over the place.

Still, I told him, "Try to keep in mind, he's just a baby. A mere four years is all he's been in the world."

Scoobie held his tongue until we'd finished gathering the broken pieces of the vase and were on our way into the kitchen. That's when he wondered aloud how much time he'd get for whacking the kid on the bottom one good time and strangling the mess out of his wench of a mama. My advice was to bypass the kid altogether and go straight for the mama.

I asked him, "What's with her, anyway? Her weave too tight or something?"

He chuckled and stepped inside this little bathroom off the kitchen. While rummaging through the medicine cabinet for something to put on his cut, he told me girlfriend used to have a thing for him when she first started at Morris-Morgan.

I was like, "You two worked together?" I told him it was kind of hard for me to imagine Lady T sweating up in somebody's kitchen.

He told me she'd come on board in some secretarial position. He made it sound like she'd seen in him a rising star and had tried to latch on for the ride. Spotting an opening, I just had to ask him, "And just how far up did you take her?"

Some of the devilish Scoobie of old spilled out as he smirked and said, "Isn't what you really want to know is how low did I let her go?" He sucked on his cut finger and said, "I'm not going to lie—I humped her first chance I got and every other time she was willing thereafter."

"My, how gentlemanly of you," I said, while cleaning and bandaging his cut as roughly as I could get away with.

He shrugged like it wasn't any big deal and said, "She had her agenda, and at the time, I had mine. After she got wise to the fact that I was strictly a solo act, she reset her sights and to her credit managed to snag my man Frank, a dude whose pockets run deeper than mine probably ever will."

I told him that for someone who was supposedly so sanctified he had to pray and meditate five times a day, he sounded awfully impressed with girlfriend's game.

He said, "Hey, if the girl can swing more bucks for the bang, who am I to judge her? At least she's getting something worthwhile out the deal—which, pardon me for saying it, is a lot more than whatever it is you call yourself doing with that chump-change friend of yours from next door."

I'd been wondering when he was going to get back around to talking bad about Carl. I batted my eyes at him and said, "The idea that I might actually like him just irks you to death, doesn't it?"

Rather than answer, Scoobie smiled, wagged his bandaged finger in my face, and said, "I bet a little kiss would really make this feel a whole lot better."

I laughed and told him, "If I didn't know any better, I'd say you were trying to come on to me."

HIM

Picture this now—I'm laid up on the couch, in my drawers, eyes half-closed, most of my brain cells spent from having blown close to an hour entertaining thoughts of me, Faye, and various fruity combinations, when one of those news stories touting some native son who's done good snares my attention. In a loud, animated voice, the news announcer goes into this big to-do about Chef So-and-so, and how he'd recently gotten a book of recipes published, and how he'd thrown this grand hoedown at his home to celebrate that fact, and how all the local la-de-da-dees and wanna-be-somebodies had turned out hoping to be seen . . .

You know, it was one of those upbeat "this here brother has got it going on" sort of pieces meant to inspire, if not make envious, those of us who ain't quite there yet. So, never one to deny some hardworking dog his props, when the newsfolk finally flashed the visuals, I glanced over, intending to give dude a quick thumbs-up, only to find myself sitting straight up and thinking to myself, "Say, I know this guy—"

Before I could even fully form the thought, the camera angle shifted ever so slightly and the sister at dude's side, who just so happened to be my good neighbor and occasional bed buddy, Margaret Faye Abrahams, burst into clear view.

Yeah, she was looking quite the picture of contentment, cuddled all up against dude, while the two of them conversed with some other fake-looking couple.

Both my head and my heart started pounding something fierce as the real of why Faye hadn't gotten back with me yet slowly sank in. Besides having access to a brother who owned more than his share of good looks and had obviously come into some serious bank, ol' girl was far too busy hobnobbing with the upper crust to want to be bothered with the likes of some ol' stale, tired, broke, regular-crust brother like me.

And who could blame her? It wasn't like I had anything particularly special to offer Faye outside of infrequent companionship, a whole lot of talk, and an occasional good time in bed.

Yeah, man, I know. I'm supposed to play it hard, like I really don't give a serious f—-. Like there's plenty more coochie out there where that came from. But on the real money, no brother who's got any kind of pride about himself ever wants to get caught coming in second—especially to some dude who underneath all the fancy wrapping ain't nothin' but a jerk.

Not wanting to add insult to injury by letting dude torment me in my own damn house, I clicked off the tube just as the a-hole was getting ready to deliver his well-rehearsed response to some supposedly off-the-cuff question. Afterward, man, I rolled over right there on the couch and fell asleep, only to wake up a few minutes later in the middle of a nightmare—a nightmare about that fool laying up in my bed with my girl Faye, straight working her body into a frenzy with some of my doggone strawberries. If that in and of itself wasn't bad enough, who do you think was standing up there next to the bed holding an empty fruit basket and looking right stupid?

HER

After the party, girl, is when things really got interesting. I'd planned to leave the same way I'd come, bumming a ride in the backseat of Ray-Ray's rim-spinning pimp mobile. But when Scoobie noticed me following Nora's lead as she got ready to go, he pulled me aside and was like, "What's your hurry? I was sort of looking forward to sitting down and talking with you after everyone had left."

So I asked him, "Does that mean you're planning on driving me home later or do you intend for me to stay the night?"

He assured me that all he wanted to do was talk and as far as anything else was concerned, according to him, we'd just play it by ear. Yeah, I know, girl, lame, huh?

And it wasn't like he had me totally convinced of anything at that point. I just let curiosity get the best of me. I couldn't help but want to see at what point he'd drop the good-guy masquerade and revert back to the hustling, hedonistic, "hurry up and give me some" Scoobie I knew and had grown to hate. The way I had it figured out, the sooner I gave homeboy an opportunity to really muck up, the sooner I could give him one last good cussing out for ol' times' sake and be on my merry little way.

When I peeped Nora to my plan to hang out with the

brother just a little while longer, she had the nerve to frown all up and say, "Why in the hell do you keep setting yourself up like this? You get a kick out of letting him play you or something?"

I told her to chill. I could handle it. I knew exactly what I was doing.

She was like, "Fine, but when your ass realizes otherwise, don't come running to me for help, hear?" Girl, I was too intent on trying to uncover flaws in this new and improved Scoobie to be studying Nora.

Shortly after he saw his last guest out, Scoobie strolled over to the bar and poured us both a drink before joining me on the couch. On sitting down, he pulled this remote out of a small case on the table in front of us and with a series of clicks, dimmed the lights, switched on the gas-log fireplace, and activated the stereo.

And get this, after adjusting the volume on the Dean Martin, Frank Sinatra, Sammy Davis Jr. set he had crooning in the background, dude clinked his glass against mine and said, "Well, I guess it's just you and me, babe."

Rather than tell the brother I was going to need something a whole lot stronger than the high-priced sparkling spring water he'd poured into my glass if he was going to have me sweating in front of some durn fireplace, listening to the likes of Sammy, Dean, and Frank all night long, I just smiled and said, "Yes, I guess it is."

He slid an arm around me, gave me a peck on the lips, then said, "You have a good time tonight?"

I told him the truth. "You did a nice job. Seriously, everything from the little talk you gave about your book, the food, the music, even the decor—deserved at least three stars."

"Only three?" he said, pretending to be insulted. "And what could I have possibly done to have earned a fourth star in your book?"

Ignoring the swelling of the brother's already big head—

and I do mean the one on his shoulders—I said, "Well, for one, you could have been just a tad more understanding about your young guest's mishap with the vase. And two, you know how you were going out of your way to introduce me to everyone tonight as Dr. Abrahams? Well, I kind of prefer to just leave my title at the hospital. Really, when I'm not on the j-o-b, plain ol' simple 'Faye from around the way' works best for me."

He touched my face and was like, "You earned that title, baby. I say you ought to wear it proudly and as often as you're able. Besides, 'Dr. Abrahams' has a certain ring of authority and power to it that to me is downright sexy." With that, he leaned over and kissed me. I mean really kissed me, girl, like he used to way back in the day, okay? And I'd be lying if I said it didn't stir just the teeniest bit of something within me.

But rather than let any of those old-time feelings get the best of me, I eased away from him, pulled myself together and said, "I thought you didn't indulge in that sort of thing anymore."

He said, "I don't. At least, not to the extent to which I think you're referring. I just didn't want you to think that I'd forgotten how." He caressed my lips with his bandaged finger and said, "I still know what you like, Faye, and I'm still very much capable of giving it to you."

Given his arrogance, I couldn't help but chuckle and say, "Well, now, is that a fact?"

"It is indeed," he said in a tone that let me know he didn't think there was anything funny about it either. Then he added, "But like I told you before, babe, all of that is going to have to wait."

When I ventured to ask, "Until when?" his response was, "Until after you've decided where you want to go with this."

I told him, "If the *this* you're talking about is *us,* Scoobie, I'd have to say in large part that depends on you."

That's when he got up, walked over to the fireplace, and rooted through one of the large baskets decorating the hearth. He brought the small wooden box he'd pulled out of the basket over to the couch and placed it in my lap.

On opening the box, the first thing I saw was what looked like handwritten letters—some folded, some stuffed in envelopes. Scoobie pulled one from the bunch, handed it to me, and said, "Go ahead."

I unfolded the stationery, took in the "Dear Scoobie" salutation, and immediately recognized the scrawl as my own. Yeah, girl, the box was full of, among other things, all the love notes, letters, cards, and things I'd given homeboy over the years.

He smiled and started reading from some mess I'd scribbled to him back when he had me believing our puppy love was the real thing, "My dearest, sweetest Venard. Words can't express the depths of my love for you. Every night I pray that our hearts will always beat in sync—"

Even though I couldn't help but laugh, I snatched the paper from him and said, "Stop! We were in the ninth grade. I'd dare say neither one of us knew any better."

"Oh, I always knew," Scoobie said, giving me that same look he'd given me right before he'd pressed his lips against mine and swept me back down memory lane.

"Knew what?" I said, shifting my gaze from his.

"That you were the one" is what he told me. "That you and I were destined to end up together. My mama knew too. In the years before she passed, she was always asking me, 'Whatever happened to Faye? She was such a sweet girl. When you get ready to settle down, promise me you'll look her up.' "

You know I started to roll my eyes and say something sarcastic, but in a glance I could tell, at least when it came to that part about his mama, the boy was being completely sincere.

He fished a bracelet out of the bottom of the box and asked me if I remembered it. Of course I did. It was the bracelet I'd given him on his sixteenth birthday. The one I'd saved up for and bought with my allowance and babysitting money. I'd even gone so far as to have the durn thing engraved with both our names—Margaret and Venard—as well as the words "forever" and "always."

Scoobie took my hand and guided my fingertips over the bracelet's lettering. "I was thinking that maybe one day soon we could give this to our son."

Since I didn't trust myself to respond to that without getting emotional, I didn't say anything. I just sat and listened as Scoobie made his plea. "I want another chance with you, Faye. I think we owe it to the child the Good Lord gave to us to at least try."

HIM

All it took was one look at her face to know that I was all but done for. "I'm not sure how to say this" is what she sputtered after coming in and having a seat next to me on the sofa.

"You don't have to say it" is what I told her, hoping to spare us both the pain and embarrassment of an "it's me, not you" speech. I said, "I already know. I saw you on TV with him the other night. Isn't he some big-shot chef who works for the rich and the famous and lives in some big-ass mansion on the hill?"

"It wasn't something I planned, Carl," she said, sounding genuinely remorseful.

"I thought it was over between you two" is what I told her. "I thought you weren't in love with him. So what happened? You spent the night with him and some of those old-time feelings that you didn't even know you had resurfaced, or something?"

She said, "It's not what you think. I haven't slept with him or anything. We've just been talking, really, about a lot of different things. And after thinking long and hard about some of those things, I've decided that it might be best if I tried to work it out with him."

Feeling like I'd just been kicked in the stomach, I said, "I see." But not wanting her to know just how bad she'd hurt me, I tried to be smooth with it. I said, "So I guess this means I don't get my third time at bat, huh?"

She stared down at a spot in the carpet, shook her head, and said, "Carl, did you hear anything I just said?"

I stood up and looked her in the eyes. "Sure, I heard you," I told her, "and that's fine. Go on. Be with him. I just don't see why that means I've got to be cheated out of my third strike, is all." Then I kissed her, and to my surprise instead of pulling away or going passive, she responded in kind.

But as soon as I made a move to draw her closer, she said, "Don't do this, Carl. It's only going to make it harder."

Rather than go for the obvious joke about it already being hard, I told her, "I don't see how. It's just a game, remember? And we're both adults." When she didn't say anything, I eased up off her, sat back down, and said, "Is this how you're gonna play it? You tell me one thing and then you up and change the rules and go and do another?"

She looked toward the door like she knew she really ought to be leaving, but when I tugged on the one hand of hers that I was still holding, she sat down with me. Before I could say anything she reached over, stroked my cheek, and said, "This isn't at all how I thought things would work out, Carl."

Man, now you know that was all the doggone incentive a brother needed. I buried my face against her neck and as I worked my hand beneath the back of her blouse, I told her, "Right now, right now, baby, all I want to hear from you is whether you're going to abide by the rules and play this thing with me all the way through the end or not?"

Rather than put forth any type of resistance, she went along with my advances—from my fingers on her breasts to my tongue's persistent forays between her lips. It wasn't until she heard me fumbling with my belt buckle that she muttered so much as a single word of protest. "Carl," she said, "if you think this is going to change anything, you're wrong."

I drew her hand against the bad boy in my pants, who at that point was all but begging to be let out, and I told her, "Baby, I just want my third strike. That's all I'm asking."

She ran her palm up and down my pride and joy a couple times before she searched my eyes and said, "And you promise you won't try to make any waves afterward?"

"Not a one," I said, knowing that she knew doggone well at that point I would have promised her near 'bout anything.

HER

Yeah, girl, I wanted it. Ain't no use in me trying to pretend otherwise. I did tell him I wanted to take a shower first, to which his laugh-riddled response was, "Dag, girl, I'll be dog if you ain't the cleanest woman I've ever met."

So anyway, I'm in the shower, right? And I guess I'm taking too long for him, because before I know anything he's jerked back the curtain and is stepping in to join me.

"What?" he said when I reached for the shower curtain and used part of it to cover myself. "We've been together twice already, remember? It's not like we haven't seen one another in the buff before."

"Carl, I was almost done. Do you mind?" is what I asked, even though what I really wanted to say was, *Excuse me, but if you think I'm the kind of girl who's going to play out some triple-X sex in the shower fantasy scene with you, you've got me pegged all wrong.*

But rather than take his tail out, Carl turned around and tilted his grinning mug toward the water cascading from the shower nozzle. Standing there, getting a right nice eyeful of his naked ass, I knew exactly what he wanted. He wanted me to touch him. And don't think I wasn't tempted. He's got these big, broad shoulders, a wide, muscular back, and one of those high, tight behinds—the kind you generally see on track athletes. Honey, please, just thinking about it gets me all . . . Anyway, fine specimen of Black manhood that he is, I knew if I touched him, it would be all over with. He'd either have me squirming on the hard, cold porcelain floor of the tub, or else in some awkward position all up against the wall. So rather than give in, I got out, wrapped myself up in his robe, and went and had myself a seat on the end of his bed.

The room pulsated with the sound of Carl's musical selection for the evening, Erykah Badu's "Orange Moon," on repeat, no less. The song is one of my favorites, but sitting there listening to it against the backdrop of my own rapidly beating heart made me somehow feel like I was hearing it for the first time.

Before long Carl came out and joined me, his body more wet than dry, but with a towel tied loosely around his waist. The latter I knew he'd done only out of a latent sense of courtesy toward me. On positioning himself next to me he took my hand, leaned over, and whispered into my ear, "You know your modesty is a turn-on, don't you?"

"What doesn't turn you on?" I asked him.

He chuckled and said, "When it comes to you, baby, there isn't a whole heck of a lot that doesn't. Even your bitchiness is, at times, extremely arousing."

He already had me way past hot and bothered. And knowing from previous experience how hard it was to get him to stop gabbing, once he got started, I said, "So are we going to talk or are we going to do this?"

"Oh," he said, "we are most definitely going to do this."

But instead of making a move toward my lips or taking me into his arms, he lowered himself to the floor and started rubbing my feet. At first I was like, I'll be durn if this man don't like himself some heels and toes. Rather than linger, though, he kissed a path up my ankles, past my shins, and over my calves. By the time he reached my locked knees, I had a pretty good idea where he was headed.

When he tried to peel his robe off my thighs, I grabbed his hands. He looked at me and said, "Why are you so tense? You act like we haven't done this before."

As far as I was concerned we hadn't. Well, not *that* anyway. *That* wasn't something I'd indulged in with anyone since . . . well, since Scoobie. Remember the whole Sunday morning, strawberry sex-capade I told you about? Even though Carl had tried to coax me into changing my mind, I'd drawn the line at letting him take his drip and lick act too far down into my lower divide.

Call me old-fashioned and out-of-touch with the current trends if you want to, but I still say casual sex ought to come with certain rules and limitations. And as far as I'm concerned that's just too intimate an act to be out here doing with some of any and everybody. Of course, this wasn't just anybody—it was Carl, a man truly unlike any I'd ever encountered.

And instead of giving up and turning his attention elsewhere, like he had the time before, this time the brother persisted. He rubbed his bristled chin against my tightly clasped knees and asked me if I trusted him.

I told him, "I suppose, or else I wouldn't be here."

He said, "So let me do this. Let me give you something to remember me by."

His cockiness cut through some of my anxiety. I smiled and said, "Come again?"

He guided my hand to the nape of his neck and said, "Go on, close your eyes, baby. If you get uncomfortable, all you have to do is take your hand away and I'll stop."

So with those durn "Orange Moon" flutes paving the way and my girl's sultry "How good it is," refrain egging me on, I unlocked my legs and let dude lower his head between them. He brushed his mustache and his closed mouth against the inner portion of my left thigh, before treating the right one to the wet press of his lips and just the tiniest bit of tongue. Moving slowly and steadily upward, he went back and forth like that, from one leg to the other.

The intensity was more than I thought I could possibly bear. He'd only made it to the halfway point when I eased my hand away from his head. And just like he said he would, he stopped. But with disappointment creasing his face, he looked up at me and said, "You sure? You're gonna always wonder . . ."

I knew he had a point. So without a word, I reached down with one hand and slid my fingers over his shoulders, up the back of his neck, and into his hair, which was still damp from the shower. After giving him the nod to go ahead and pick up where he'd left off, I closed my eyes again and waited for the music and the warm caress of Carl's tongue to take me wherever it was they wanted me to go.

He must have thought I just might catch another case of cold feet, because the brother's pace picked up considerably on the second go 'round, and before I knew anything, girl, he was there. If I had to describe it, I'd have to say it was kind of like the feeling you get on a diet when you deliberately deny yourself the one special treat you enjoy the most—Häagen-Dazs's black-cherry ice cream, for instance. And then after what's seemed like an eternity, you finally allow yourself a little. That first taste is so wonderfully exhilarating, it rolls through you like an electric shock might. Every cell in your body seems to suddenly come alive. In a matter of seconds, not only did I have both of my hands rocking against the back of the brother's head, but you'd best believe Ms. Badu wasn't the only sister up in that joint giving shout-outs about how durn good it was.

The brother has got skills, is all I can say, girl. I've never had anything close to what I had with Carl that night. It went beyond just good sex with an attentive lover who knows his way around a woman's body. No, this was some of that "get a sister all choked up and bring her ass to tears" kind of ecstasy that you generally only read about or see in the movies. Honey, I kid you not, somewhere 'round about that second orgasm the brother had me all worked up and crying so hard I think I kind of scared him.

He raised up and was like, "Damn, baby, what's wrong? Did I hurt you? I didn't mean to. Really, I didn't."

All I could do was shake my head and press my face into his chest. I couldn't even speak, girl. But what I wanted to tell him was, "Yeah, you put a hurting on me, all right, one I'm not likely to forget anytime soon."

I lay there for a little while wrapped up in Carl's arms, listening to the steady thump of his heart and dreading what I had to do next. It wasn't hard to tell he didn't want to let me go. Every time I so much as stretched a leg or wiggled a toe, he held me even tighter and said something along the lines of, "Not yet, baby. Just a couple more minutes."

When I finally did get up and go to the bathroom, I made sure to lock the door behind me. I had every intention of making my exit as quick and painless as possible, and the last thing I needed was Carl busting up in there, trying to throw more stumbling blocks in my path. I even forfeited the shower in exchange for a few hurried splashes here and there. After all, it wasn't like I didn't live right next door. Anyway, I got finished getting dressed and came out only to find him sitting up on the side of the bed, still naked as a jaybird and with my bag clutched in his lap.

He stood up as I approached him and even managed to summon forth a smile. But his eyes, which were bigger and sadder than any puppy dog I'd ever seen, said it all. On handing me the purse he said, "I guess this means I'm really *out,* huh?"

When I didn't answer him, he said, "It could have been good, you know?"

Wrong as I knew it was, I couldn't resist the urge to run my fingers over his chest one last time. I told him, "It was good, the best I've had thus far."

He caught me by the hand and said, "I wasn't talking about the sex, Faye."

After making myself look at the hurt written all over his face, I told him, "I know. Neither was I."

He looked like he was about to say something else, but I hushed him with a kiss. And then . . . and then I walked.

HIM

She walked out. She left me standing there butt-naked and begging. It was terrible, man. I felt so . . . so used.

Yeah, I know, it was my own damn fault for not heeding her warnings, right? Maybe if I hadn't drifted off so deep into my own little world I would have taken more serious note of the subtle resistance on her part. Maybe I wouldn't have been so ready and eager to carve out a permanent place for her in my life. But hey, all I'd wanted was to make her happy; to make her smile, to make her back arch in ecstasy as many times a week as she mighta wanted. Okay, so I admit, I was a brother who'd pretty much lost touch with reality.

I was still trying to reassemble the bent and busted pieces of my playa's mask the night I took my Uncle Westbrook up on his invitation to join him for a burger, a couple of beers, and a nice earful of some of them down-home blues. We'd just wrapped up our inspection of the quaint little spot I'll soon be calling home. I told you about the deal I worked out with him, right? Yeah, see, Unc owns a couple rental properties and he's agreed to let me move into one rent-free in exchange for helping him do a total rehab on the joint. Anyway, after walking through the place and checking out everything the old guy wanted done, I followed him to his favorite North Memphis getaway, Big Mama Mae's Cafe and Grill.

Big Mama's is this little dark hole-in-the-wall joint over there on Chelsea, the kind of place where you can order either red Kool-Aid, iced tea, or a cold brewski to wash down the great big helping of okra and peas that comes with your plate of fried chicken and hot-water cornbread; the kind of place where they've still got the likes of Muddy Waters, B. B. King, John Lee Hooker, and the three Bobbys—Rush, Blue Bland, and Womack—in heavy rotation on the jukebox.

Oh yeah, man, I'm a blues lover from way back. And if anybody's to fault for that, it's my music-loving former disc jockey of an uncle. Straight up, he's the cat who first turned me on to a lot of the old stuff I listen to now.

But getting back to Big Mama's, I'da probably been all right had I been able to get in and out of there without being forced to listen to that doggone song. I'm saying, man, me and Uncle Westbrook had finished grubbing and I was bobbing my head and tapping my foot to the closing lines of my all-time favorite Johnny Taylor jam, "Cheaper to Keep Her," when some fool went over to the jukebox and cued up, of all things, "Dimples." Yeah, man, it's this old John Lee Hooker cut about some chick with dimples in her jaws. And you know, having just been through all that I had with Faye, that particular song was the last one in the world a brother wanted to hear.

Still bobbing my head, I had closed my eyes and was sitting there determined to maintain my cool brotherman front when my uncle's voice bumped against the thin scab covering my blues. "So is what Squirrel said true? You and ol' gal done broke up?"

My cousin Squirrel, with his jive, meddling ass, had earlier in the evening taken it upon himself to publicly bust me on my apparent lack of luck with the ladies.

Instead of hollering, "Ouch," at the old guy, like I felt like doing, I opened my eyes and told him, "According to her way of looking at things, I don't think we were ever really together."

He passed me one of the beers the waitress brought to our table and took a long hit off of his before he asked, "You ever figure out what kind of volunteering she was doing up at the hospital?"

I took a hit off mine before I told him, "Nope."

On that note, Unc reared back in his chair and nodded at this big-legged chick who'd been eyeballing us on the sly from the bar. Knowing old dude like I do, I thought our conversation pretty much over, and I was on the verge of closing my eyes again when I heard him say, "You wanna know?"

I cocked my head sideways and looked at him like, "What you talking 'bout, Willis?"

With his sights still set on the chick, dude took another long swig before he said, "Listening to you and Squirrel talk about your lady friend's weekly trips up to the hospital got me kinda concerned, so I checked into. Just so happens I've got ties with a couple of fellas who work security out at Baptist East. I told 'em the deal—described ol' girl as best I could, said I thought her name was Faye—and come to find out they knew exactly who and what I was talking 'bout."

I leaned forward and was like, "Well, come on then, G, and tell me something already."

"For starters," he said, "it ain't nowhere near as bad as you and Squirrel was making it out to be. I went up there on my next free Wednesday and the fellas I know in security took me to the third floor and walked me over to that ward where they keep the newborns. And sure enough, that's where I saw her."

Now that threw me. "The infant ward? What was she doing up there?"

Unc said, "Not much that I could see besides sitting there rocking."

Dude wasn't making much sense and for a second I wondered if maybe his Barnaby Jones cover had somehow led him astray. "Rocking?" I said.

"Yeah, her and a couple of other women. They were all sitting there together in these here rocking chairs. And they were rocking . . . you know, rocking babies."

Babies? Even though the imagery was starting to click, it still wasn't exactly clear. I said, "Okay, so she sneaks up there every Wednesday evening to rock babies? What's that all about?"

My Uncle Westbrook shook his head and said, "Far as that's concerned, youngblood, your guess is 'bout as good as mine. But I will say this—any woman who makes time every week to go somewhere and rock other folks' chillren can't be all that bad."

HER

When I shared with Nora what Scoobie had said about his mother's affection for me and how she'd made him promise to seek me out when he finally decided to settle down, girlfriend was quick to dismiss it all with a snort and a curt wave of her hand. As if that wasn't rude enough, she went on to refresh my memory about the precarious state of Mrs. Payne's mental well-being.

"Scoobie's mama? Girl, now you know good and well Old Lady Payne spent more time in the crazy house than she did out. Hell, she's liable to have said some of anything. Remember that time she ran out in the middle of the street and was hollering and carrying on about some damn chipmunk mafia? And how all the neighborhood chipmunks had been meeting every night and were straight plotting to take her ass out?"

Yeah, girl, like Nora's really in a position to out-and-out call somebody else crazy. And if that didn't beat all, when I let her in on the news that I had broken things off with Carl, she went so far as to question my own sanity.

When she finally came to the end of her loud tirade, I told her like I'd told him: It was good while it lasted, but he'd had his three turns at bat and it was over. "Furthermore," I said, "if you really want to know the truth, the only reason Carl and I hooked up in the first place was for the sex. Basically, all it boiled down to was a relationship of convenience."

That only got her all fired up again. She said, "Oooh wee, Faye. You know you need to quit. Ain't no way you're fixing to sit up here and tell me Carl wasn't 'bout the best thing to come into your life since Just My Size panty hose. And what about Memorial Day? Huh? When was the last time you ever took anybody home to meet your mama?"

I said, "Heifer, that was your bright idea. Remember?"

And she was like, "Oh . . . yeah. But still, had he been any other brother you'da found some way to leave his butt behind. Say I'm lying."

What I chose to do was shut my mouth and not say any more about it. Nora just doesn't understand. I like Carl. Really, I do. And committing myself to a full-blown, honest-to-goodness relationship with him is something I fully intended to do. But this jones I've got for Scoobie runs deep.

After all these years I thought I'd shaken it, flushed it all out of my system, but obviously I was wrong and there's no sense in me lying to myself about it. Deep down, I still feel something for him. Could be, some small part of me always will.

Even if I did decide to turn away from Scoobie and step toward Carl, I'd be forever glancing over my shoulder and pondering all the *ifs*. What if Scoobie really has grown up? What if his heart finally is in the right place? What if he's sincere about the desire he's expressed to find our son and forge a new life for the three of us?

And how would any of that be fair to Carl? It wouldn't. No, girl, I've got to see this thing on through to the end or at least allow it an opportunity to run its natural course. If the point should arrive where I'm forced to yet again close the door on Scoobie and walk away from him, I want to be able to do it without feeling even the tiniest compulsion to look back.

HIM

Like I told Faye, it wasn't me who started that mess. I had every intention of handling our split in a civil if not outright cavalier fashion. For me that pretty much meant taking whatever steps were necessary to avoid running into her, dude, or, God forbid, the two of them together. And it wasn't like I was trying to hold a grudge. As much as I hated the idea of coming in second to dude, deep down I couldn't hold it against Faye that she wanted to try and work things out with him. After all, if getting back together with my ex had at any time been even a remote possibility, you'd better believe I'da crawled over a bed of hot coals on my belly at the chance.

But getting back to the unfortunate incident that I somehow ended up getting the blame for. Almost a week had passed since ol' girl and I had done the deed and agreed to go our separate ways. It was a Friday night and like I said, up until then the ol' duck-and-dodge routine had served me well. It was something after ten when I went out to my car to retrieve a couple of new CDs I'd left out there. But as luck would have it, just as I was headed out to my car, dude came sliding up in his. After parking and jumping out his pretty ride, he practically came running up the sidewalk that leads to Faye's place and mine. We met up midway and I'll be doggone if he wasn't wearing that same dumb-ass smirk he'd treated me to the last time I'd caught him lurking around there after dark.

Rather than return the nod, I was decent enough to extend him and keep on 'bout his damn business, dude stopped and said, "What you say, bro?" And while standing there with his hand all stuck out, as if he really expected me to reach out and shake it, he had the nerve to add, "No hard feelings, huh?"

I looked him in the eye to let him know he was treading on shaky ground before I told him, "Yeah, man. Whatever."

But instead of quitting while he was ahead, just as I was moving past his ignorant ass he says, "You know, Carl . . . It is Carl, isn't it?"

When I didn't say anything he went on with, "Well, anyway, I don't mean any harm, partner, but you might want to let this be a lesson to you."

I was trying hard to keep it in check, but I could feel the North Memphis thug in me getting ready to erupt. I stepped toward him and said, "Is that right? And how you figure that?"

"Simple addition, my brother," he said, backing away from me on tiptoe all the while. "One plus one equals me and Faye, minus you. So the next time you call yourself stepping to my lady, do yourself a favor and try bringing something to the table besides a big dick, all right?"

With that, I dropped down to his level and went all the way back-alley with him. "Listen here, man," I told him. "I don't know what kind of niggas you're used to dealing with, but if you think I'm about to stand out here and let you talk shit to me about Faye, the size of my johnson, or anything else, for that matter, you're sadly mistaken."

By that point he'd backed himself all the way up to the steps that lead to Faye and Nora's front door. He opened his mouth, but before he could pop off again, I snatched him up by the collar and told him, "What? You think I'm joking? Fool, I will jack your shit so tough you won't know whether you're coming or going."

'Round about then is when Faye and Nora came flying out the door, both of them doing about seventy miles per hour. While Nora stood back, Faye came over and put her hand on my shoulder. I guess she called herself trying to calm me down, but it was a move that only made me think about the way her fingers had caressed my shoulders and the back of my neck the last time I'd made love to her. My response was to grip dude even harder and raise him even higher off the ground. When he started gurgling, Faye sank her nails into my arm and said, "Carl, don't. You promised me you weren't going to do this."

I let go of dude's collar and watched as his punk ass bounced off the steps and hit the ground. I turned to Faye and told her, "I kept my end of the damn deal. It's your smart-mouthed boyfriend here who somehow saw fit to bring that shit to me. If you're looking to lecture somebody, you need to start with him, all right?"

While dude sat on the ground, coughing and massaging his windpipe, Nora finally summoned enough courage to come over and jump into the mix. "Okay, Carl," she said, "it's over, baby. Why not squash this now before it gets way out of hand?"

"Yeah, you're right," I said, staring at Faye, who was standing there shaking her head. "Consider it squashed. But over? Uh-uh, not hardly."

HER

I wasn't sure if I was supposed to take Carl's "it ain't over" declaration as some kind of threat, just another testosterone-inspired act of bravado, or what. I do know that he wasn't totally to blame for the round of fireworks that nearly blew up outside the condo that night.

Nora and I both heard Scoobie out there thumping his chest and talking trash, as if he really had the balls to follow up all his silly posturing with some kick-butt sho' 'nuff. And I most certainly want to go on record as saying that I've never discussed the intimate details of Carl's anatomy or what went on between the two of us in the bedroom with Scoobie. So where he was coming from with all of that mess is anybody's guess.

When I asked the brother to explain himself and his behavior, at first he tried to blow it off as just a whole bunch of sour grapes on Carl's part. And when that didn't get a rise out of me he went in for the kill. "What would ever possess you to get involved with a roughneck like him anyway? Hell, I'm willing to bet all it would take is one missed car note and his ass would be back on the corner with all the rest of the bums."

Not wanting to add any more fuel to the petty little fire Scoobie called himself trying to build, I just left it alone. I see little to gain from allowing myself to get all worked up on behalf of a man who, one, I'm no longer seeing, and two, has shown himself quite capable of defending his own honor without my or anyone else's help. I've gotta tell you, girl, given the way Scoobie was out there acting, had Carl hauled off and straight-up smacked the brother one good time, I really wouldn't have felt all that bad about it.

HIM

When Nora stopped by early the next morning to check on me, I told her, "I guess I looked like a pretty big fool out there last night."

I was shocked when she grinned and said, "Based on what I overheard, I'd say dude damn well had it coming."

After all the laughing and joking died down, I asked her, "So . . . is she in love with this guy or what?"

Nora got serious and said, "The only thing I can tell you, Carl, is what girlfriend keeps telling me—she just feels like this is something she's got to do."

I had a sense that there was actually a whole lot more than Nora could have told me had she allowed herself. But rather than force the issue, I just listened and kept my mouth shut until she up and said, "Well, what's your plan? Maybe I can help."

I was like, "Plan for what?"

She said, "Duh! For getting your woman back, what else? I know you're not about to just step aside and let this fool take her—especially after what you said last night about it not being over."

I told her, "You know I wasn't doing nothin' but talking junk. Besides, Faye's already made her choice pretty clear. I've got far too much pride to keep going back to her groveling and sniveling in hopes that she'll give me another chance. Nope, I'm afraid that there is some tail I'm through chasing."

Nora wouldn't let it go, though. She kept insisting that

it was too early in the game to give up yet. When I finally got right tired of hearing it I said, "Well, what about you? You wouldn't happen to need the services of a good man, would you?"

It was only a joke. You know, an attempt on my part to lighten the mood. But without so much as a moment's thought homegirl broke out with a loud, "Psst, Negro, please! I ain't trying to chump on you or nothin', 'cause you ain't half-bad in the looks department, but be for real! You got way too many chillren and not hardly enough cash to be trying to roll with my flow. Besides, all that sitting 'round watching videos and conversating you like to do woulda been done drove me crazy. No, sweetheart, I'm afraid when it comes to men, me and Faye's tastes are worlds apart."

I know, man. How's that old saying go? Be careful what you ask for 'cause you just might get smacked dead upside the head with it?

HER

I had just arrived back from my Saturday morning stint at the grocery store when I spied them—Carl's two little girls, Renita and Renee.

For a moment they were too engrossed in what looked and sounded like some newfangled version of Miss Mary Mack to notice me. But soon as I slammed shut my car door they stopped their clapping and chanting and came running over.

They said, "Hey, Ms. Faye," before almost knocking me over with a joint hug.

Renee, the one who sounds and acts most like Carl, asked if they could help with the groceries.

I told them sure. I mean, they're ten-year-olds. All I figured they were looking for was something to do and possibly a little spare change.

While we were carrying the bags into the house, Carl came out and poked his head over the fence. Still obviously upset about Scoobie, the fight, the breakup, and everything else that had gone down between us in the last week or so, he looked at me with eyes so cold, girl, I nearly lost my grip on the sack I had pressed against my chest. A couple of ice-filled seconds ticked by before he eased up on the freeze and said, "They bothering you?"

I told him, "No, they're fine."

He'd started back to his condo when all of a sudden he spun around, threw the twins a look, and said, "Ladies, don't forget what we talked about."

"Yes, Dad," they said in unison. "We won't."

It didn't take a Ph.D. to conclude that whatever they'd talked about had something to do with *moi*. But since what was done, was done, I wasn't trying to sweat it.

After the girls finished helping me bring in the last of the groceries, I pulled out my wallet and was about to give them a couple dollars apiece when Renita, the twin who I'm guessing takes after her mother's side of the family, piped up and said, "That's okay, Ms. Faye. I don't think our daddy would like it very much if he found out we'd taken money from you."

So I offered a couple of Twinkies and a glass of milk as a possible substitute, which, after a bit of whispering between the two of them, they decided to accept.

I joined them on the opposite side of the breakfast bar with a snack and a glass of milk of my own. Everything was cool and we'd giggled our way through a good three minutes' worth of girl talk when, with her mouth partially full, Renee just up and out of nowhere said, "Ms. Faye, are you mad at my daddy about something?"

"Now, what would make you ask something like that?"

I said, trying my best not to get rattled, even as the other child started coughing and shaking her head, like something might have gone down the wrong way.

Renee said, "I don't know. I was just wondering why you guys didn't seem particularly happy to see one another. I hope he didn't cheat on you like he did my mama."

That did it for Renita. She jumped off her stool and snatched her sister by the arm. "Renee! Don't mind her, Ms. Faye. She runs off at the mouth like she don't have a lick of sense sometimes. Come on, girl. It's time for us to go."

I was like, uh-uh, hold up. "Is that what your daddy told you? I mean, that he and I were boyfriend, girlfriend?"

Renita's eyes got all big, bless her heart, and she took it upon herself to try and answer for the both of them. "No, ma'am. Our daddy's never said anything like that."

Renee, who'd already proved herself perfectly capable of speaking for herself, said, "But my mama did say you guys were probably more than just friends."

I told them, "Okay, look, I'm not mad at your father. But sometimes people don't always agree on things. And that's what happened between me and your dad. We had a disagreement of sorts. You understand?"

They both nodded and yes ma'med me, but Renee still wasn't ready to let the issue die. She said, "I understand, but I guess what I really want to know is if it's the kind of disagreement that's going to keep you from coming to see us in the wedding?"

Renita slapped her forehead. "I don't believe you. Renee, you're gonna get us in trouble."

I asked them, "Is that what this is all about? Me coming to the wedding? Did your father put you up to this?"

Renee said, "Yes, ma'am. I mean, no, ma'am. I mean, he didn't put us up to anything. Tell her, Renita."

Poor Renita looked like she was about to hyperventilate.

I stopped and thought about it for a moment before I told them, "I guess I did kind of promise to do you all's nails."

"You also said you'd come to the wedding," Renee reminded me. "Will you? Please, Ms. Faye. Please, please, pretty please?"

I told them I'd have to talk it over with their father.

Renee seemed satisfied enough with my answer, but as I escorted them to the door I overheard Renita tell her twin, "You know Dad's gonna flip when he finds out about this. He specifically told us not to say anything to Ms. Faye about our nails."

"And we didn't," Renee said. "All I did was ask her about the wedding. Ms. Faye brought up the nail thing herself. Isn't that right, Ms Faye?"

Girl, I was much too busy trying to piece together what I was going to say to Carl to come up with any kind of child-appropriate response.

HIM

I should have known something wasn't right when my daughter Renee came in and tossed me a package of Twinkies she claimed had been sent to me by Ms. Faye. The first question in my head was why after all that had transpired between me and chick would she still be interested in sending me goodies? Besides, I knew enough about the chick's ways to appreciate that a trick of some sort generally lurked behind her generously tendered treats—and any indulgence on my part would most certainly come with a price.

On the other hand, I also knew that not unlike myself, my daughter Renee has a slick side to her. Consequences be damned, she'll run a con in a minute, especially if she thinks there's something worthwhile in it for both her and her sister.

I zeroed in on her and said, "You were over there doing exactly what I told you not to do, weren't you?" After confirming the obvious, I'd barely launched into the opening lines of my "I'm terribly disappointed in you" speech when they both fell all to pieces and amid an intense shower of snot and tears, began blubbering their apologies.

"It was all my fault," Renee admitted. "But all I really wanted was for Ms. Faye to come see us in the wedding and for you guys to be friends again."

Then my other daughter, Renita, who's always striving hard to be the good girl, had to up and ask, "Daddy, you aren't going to say anything mean to Ms. Faye, are you?"

It's hard to stay mad at folks whose motives are that pure—especially when they're two cute, precocious ten-year-olds with eyes deep enough to swim in. I was standing there trying to decide how to handle the situation when I got the call from Faye, asking if I'd mind joining her outside for a second.

So I went out only to I find ol' girl in her usual patio pose, butt backed up into a lawn chair, romance novel and cigarette in hand. I'd braced myself for the worst, but right away I detected something different in her demeanor. Not only was her cigarette unlit, but absent too was any sign of the bad attitude she generally keeps on simmer, just beneath the surface. Still, not wanting to take any chances and hoping to beat her to the punch, I stepped to her with, "Look, if this is about the girls and the whole nails and wedding bit, I gave them specific instructions *not* to be up in your face with any of that."

She nodded for me to take the seat next to her. After I did she said, "First, let me just say that I know you're not solely responsible for what jumped off the other night. I heard Scoobie out here doing his best to egg you on. I hate that it went down like that. But as far as your girls are concerned, well, I did make them a promise. And if it's okay with you, I'd really appreciate the opportunity to make good on it."

To be honest, after the blowup between me and her boy, Faye's willingness to take the civil route wasn't at all what I'd expected. I took it as a sign that maybe—just maybe—ol' girl was having second thoughts about the decision she'd made to be with dude. Never one to bypass what has all the appearances of being a legitimate opening, after we agreed that I would drop the kids by her place after their rehearsal dinner on Friday night, I went ahead and told Faye that the invitation to the wedding was still open if she cared to join us.

Before she could piece together some feeble excuse to tell me No, I assured her that my sister-in-law had already given me and the girls the okay to bring a guest if we wanted, the ex was fine with it, and she didn't even have to go with me, if she thought it would cause problems between her and dude. I'd be only too happy to give her the address and directions. As a final bit of enticement I said, "You know, it would really mean a lot to the girls if you came."

HER

Yeah, I know what you're thinking, but the only reason I went was for the girls, okay? Even though I never let Carl in on my plans, one way or the other, when I got to the church, he was the first somebody I spotted when I walked through the door.

And I must admit, he looked exceptionally dapper and

dignified standing up there in his charcoal-colored, Sunday going-to-meeting suit, even though he almost ruined the effect with the stupid reflector, aviator-like glasses he had perched on his nose.

"Glad you could make it," he said, grinning at me as he peered over the rims of the shades.

"Just remember," I told him, "I'm only here for the girls."

His sunny disposition disappeared and he was like, "I know the deal, Faye. I'm good with rules, remember?"

After escorting me inside and leading me to a seat, he said, "It is okay if I sit next to you, isn't it?"

No, I didn't snap back at him. Things having gone down between us like they had, I guess I sorta felt like he was entitled to cop some kind of an attitude. Actually, I had expected as much, if not worse.

We must have sat there side by side, neither of us saying a word, for a good four or five minutes as we waited for the wedding to get under way. I'm so used to Carl running off at the mouth, I just knew at any second, he'd be the one to break. But as fate would have it, I was the one who made the first attempt at breaking the ice between us, mainly because I've been raised to believe that God don't like ugly. And being ugly is about all Carl and I were really accomplishing, sitting up in the Lord's house with our lips stuck out, not speaking and acting like we hated each other's guts.

On braving a peek in his direction, rather than tell him how silly he looked, sitting up there with those durn blind-man glasses on, I told him he had what looked like a couple of grease smudges on his lenses and offered to clean them for him.

When he pulled off the shades and raised his gaze to meet mine, the softness I saw there stirred the reservoir of ice I generally kept around my heart.

"What?" he said, in response to the smile I couldn't for

the life of me keep from creeping across my face. "I got a booger hanging out my nose or something?"

"No," I told him. "I was just noticing how well our color choices complement one another. You in your gray and white pinstripes, me in my peach and cream. We probably couldn't have done any better coordinating wardrobes if we'd tried."

He smiled and I felt him relax a little. But after stretching one arm across the pew behind me, he reached down with the other and took the glasses in order to slide them right back onto his face.

It wasn't until all the bridesmaids and groomsmen had marched in and the ceremony had started in earnest that I finally grasped the reasoning behind Carl's protective eyewear. This guy with this great voice had taken the stage and he'd barely finished belting out the first few bars of Kenny Lattimore's "For You" when I heard all this sniffling.

Girl, I glanced over at Carl and there he was with all these big ol' crocodile tears just pouring down his face. I'm like, I know this man is not sitting up here next to me boohooing like some big ol' baby. Please, that's exactly what he was doing. And when I realized he was either too ashamed to dig out his handkerchief or else had neglected to bring one, I whipped out a couple of tissues and passed them to him.

While he dabbed at his eyes and cleared his nasal passages, I looked away in order to keep him from feeling any more embarrassed than he already did, and that's when I locked eyes with one of the bridesmaids.

Even though I called myself checking out each of the five ladies in the bridal party when they'd first strutted in, it wasn't until that moment that I realized one of them was Betty—you know, Renee and Renita's mom, and even more to the point, Carl's stunningly gorgeous ex-wife. Yeah, you heard me right, Ms. Betty has got it going on. And I'm not talking about your average pretty-girl good looks. No, I'm talking that Halle Berry, Vanessa Williams, "make a sister wanna hate your ass" kind of looks. As if that alone wasn't enough, girlfriend also appeared generously blessed with all the curves the brothers like.

I could tell she recognized me too, but before I could start getting paranoid about the possibility of her trying to trip, the little grin I saw twitch across her face assured me that she was more amused than perturbed about seeing me there.

That's when I started pondering the likelihood of Carl still being in love with the woman who'd been his wife for eight years. A wedding is always good for stirring up painful memories of what woulda, coulda, and might have been—even for someone like myself, who's never even been engaged. Excusing the fact that the brother is sort of a sentimental sap anyway, that was the only other reasonable explanation I could come up with for the way he was carrying on.

HIM

Yeah, I cry at weddings. I'm an emotional kind of guy, all right?! Besides, I don't think it makes me any less of a man than the burly macho sports figure who breaks down after his team loses the game. And to some degree that's how I felt that day—like a player who'd flubbed up several times during the course of a big game and who in the end cost the team the win.

I couldn't help but think back on me and Betty's wedding day, our marriage, the promises we'd made and in turn, all the promises I'd broken, like they were little more than dry spaghetti noodles destined to be tossed into a pot and boiled until they were no longer fit for consumption. Hey, if that makes me a wuss, I'm sorry, but I'm just the kind of guy who deep down truly does respect the institution of marriage and all that it's supposed to represent.

Then there was Faye sitting next to me looking like some fine, ripe Georgia peach, waiting for the first right somebody to come along and take a big bite out of her. Man, as hypocritical as it may sound in light of all my past and previous behavior to the contrary, I actually do want a stable, loving, committed relationship with one woman. Now why I can't for the life of me seem to make that happen is, I suppose, just another one of the many grand mysteries of my all too pitiful existence.

As touching as the ceremony was, I couldn't wait for the doggone thing to end. Even for an openly emotional guy like myself, there's a limit to just how long you're willing to sit up somewhere with your eyes watering and your nose dripping.

I have Faye to thank for coming through with a steady supply of tissues, even though every few minutes I'd catch her cutting her eyes at me, as if to ask, "What's up with this fool?"

I'd just finished blowing my nose and was in the process of pulling myself together when who but my girls should come prancing down the aisle, looking cute as they wanted to be in all their ribbons, bows, and frills while swinging their little baskets and tossing flower petals every which-away. Man, you know I started blubbering all over again.

Finally, after all the "I do's" had been said and the blushing bride had been thoroughly tongued, I wiped my face one last time before turning to Faye and venturing to ask if she planned to go on home or if she'd like to stay for the reception.

To my surprise she opted for the latter, and on agreeing to partake of each other's company just a little while longer, we were on our way to the reception area when I heard an all too familiar voice behind me. "Carl? Aren't you going to introduce us?"

Now, had I a real say in the matter, when I turned around and saw my ex, Betty, standing there, my answer would have been "No! Oh, hell, no!"

Bet, who's always been quick to read my mind, stepped forward and initiated the honors herself. "Hi, you must be Faye. I'm Betty. I've heard so many wonderful things about you from Carl and the girls . . ."

I stood back with my arms folded and watched as the two exchanged a good forty-five seconds' worth of pleasantries before Bet got called away to rejoin the bridal party for pictures. "Sorry, got to run," she said in her little cutesie-pie voice. "But it was so nice meeting you, Faye. Are you staying for the reception? Great! Hopefully, we'll get a chance to talk again."

Before running off to strike her pose with the others, Bet paused to extend me a smile and what was supposed to pass for a parting pat on the cheek but went over more like a quick smack to the jaw.

We went downstairs to the reception area, where I had the pleasure of introducing Faye to several members of my former wife's family. Man, you know I got some sho' 'nuff crazy looks, don't you? But the attitude I copped was one of "Yeah, that's right. I'm here with somebody. So what! Later for all y'all player-haters."

Everything seemed to be going along fine. We'd gotten our grub, found our table, and were sitting there eating, making light conversation and having a fairly decent time. The twins stopped by briefly to swirl and twirl and get our praise-filled feedback on their joint performance, before racing off to cut up with all their other little badass cousins and friends.

I'd been sitting next to Faye thinking how nice it might be to slow-dance with her one more 'gain and wondering if she'd go for the idea, when the time came for the bride and groom to have their first dance together as newlyweds. The song they'd chosen turned out to be Luther

Vandross and Cheryl Lynn's rendition of "If This World Were Mine." Even though I personally think the version by Marvin Gaye and Tammi Terrell is the better jam, I was still digging it. I reached under the table and on finding Faye's hand I gave it a squeeze and said, "One last dance. You and me. What do you say?"

She smiled. But right as she parted her lips to give me a reply, the twins redescended upon our table, screaming and climbing all over me like a couple of overdressed and much too excited chimpanzees.

"Electric slide, Daddy! It's electric slide time!"

You know it, man, the newlyweds' dance had ended, and the electric slide line had begun to form. At my darling daughters' insistence, I took off my shades and shifted into boogie mode. But before storming the dance floor, I asked Faye if she cared to join us.

She told me, "No, you all go on. I'm going to sit this one out. Check back with me on the next one."

Maybe I shouldn't have, but I took the last part of ol' girl's statement as a clear indication that her answer to my previous question was a resounding "Yes. Yes, I'd be honored to dance with you, Carl dear, just as soon as the next slow jam comes on."

HER

No, see, I had every intention of dancing with Carl. What happened was, while I was sitting there, trying not to get too tickled by the sight of him and his girls grooving together on the dance floor, this big muscle-bound stud of a brother parked himself in Carl's empty seat and commenced to getting up-close and personal.

"Hey there, Miss Lady. The name's Lenny," he said,

while licking his lips and eyeballing me all up and down like I was a pork chop dinner with generous portions of rice, redeye gravy, and buttermilk biscuits on the side, and it just so happened he was a hungry man with a country boy's appetite. "And who," he asked, "might you be?"

After shaking his hand and telling him my name, I quickly shared with him the fact that I was there with Carl.

The fool grinned and bobbed his head like he'd just heard a good joke or something before he up and asked, "So, ah, you here as Carl's guest or his girl?"

I could have lied and saved myself a whole lot of grief, but being that we were still in the church house, I went ahead and confirmed the fact that Carl and I were just friends.

He said, "So, ah, if I give you my number there's a pretty good chance you just might call?"

For the sake of preserving the peace and in the hopes of getting rid of him, I told him I might, even though I knew I wouldn't. The good Lord will just have to forgive me on that one because as cute and broad-shouldered as the brother was, he had a right crazy look in his eyes. The last thing I wanted to do was to get the fool riled up enough to start tripping.

His next thing was, "So, ah, how's about a dance?"

I told him basically the same thing I'd told Carl. "Sure, check back with me later."

Of course, Lenny insisted on knowing how much later. "Not that I wouldn't love to spend the rest of my afternoon getting to know you better," he said. "But I'm due to split this joint sometime in the next ten minutes. You know how it is. I'm a busy man with lots of places to go and peeps to see. A brother handling his business is what it's all about—you know what I'm saying?"

I started to ask him the nature of his "business" but decided I didn't really need to know. Instead, I told him I wasn't really much of an electric slider—which is true, I'm not.

He said, "Well, what about the next dance, which by the sounds of things is coming up shortly? Unless you'd rather wait until Carl comes back to the table so we could ask his permission."

Yeah, brother was trying to crack wise. But right about then is when I had a brilliant and an all too in living color flashback of Carl choking the stew out of Scoobie in front of the condo that night. The last thing I wanted was Carl coming back to the table, nutting out, and catching a public butt wiping on account of something that wasn't even happening between me and this goon.

"Let's go," I said, practically dragging big man to the dance floor.

Another up-tempo number is what I was counting on. Something quick and dirty so me and this boy could get out there, hit it, quit, and be done with it. But no, girl! The DJ, in his infinite wisdom, decided to switch back over to some Luther. Yeah, as soon as I heard that slow thumping bass and the first few taps of the drumbeat I knew I was in for a world of trouble. "Anyone Who Had a Heart" is a song you can't do anything but slow-dance to.

But before I could breathe a word about the ground rules, this boy snatched me against him and started in with the hands all up and down my behind. And I was like, "Hold up, Tarzan, this ain't Jane you dealing with here, okay? You'd best back up before you get beat down."

For real, girl. And he was like, "My bad, my bad. You just felt so good, baby, I couldn't help myself."

Once I had brother Len in proper check, I started searching the room for Carl 'cause getting bum-rushed from behind was not how I intended to go out. Knowing the brother like I do, I figured he'd be somewhere pacing and working himself into a slow and steady burn. Instead, I found him standing off to the side with his hands jabbed down in his pockets, staring at me like I'd just wrenched his heart out of his chest, slammed it to the floor, and stomped on it.

It never fails. No matter what I do I always end up stabbing Carl in the back. Had I been a better woman, I might have just told Lenny, "Look, I'm sorry, I think Carl wants to cut in here," and then waved him on over so he could get it all out of his system. But being the low-down skank he thinks I am anyway, I didn't do anything other than look away.

At the song's end, I thanked Lenny for the dance, took the phone number he insisted on giving me, then trekked back to the table to wait for Carl. Quite naturally, he pulled a disappearing act on me and after about fifteen minutes of sitting there twiddling my thumbs I said, "Psst, later for this."

My first thought was to head for home, but something made me decide to wait it out a while longer. After a quick trip to the ladies' room, I stepped outside for some air, where, once again, I came face-to-face with Sister Betty.

She turned on the glamour-girl smile when she saw me and said, "I was hoping to catch you alone. There's something I'd like to discuss with you, if you have a moment."

You know me—I'm thinking the worst—either it's some garbage about Carl she's getting ready to dump on me or else it's some bone she wants to pick about something I said or did to her daughters. Nonetheless, I agreed to take a walk with her across the church grounds, banking on her being too much of a lady to start some mess that might ultimately lead to the ruin of her sister's wedding.

She started off with, "I don't know if you know this, but Carl's got a birthday coming up, near the end of next month. And the girls, well, they've been sort of hounding me about throwing him this big birthday bash. A surprise party sort of thing. So I thought, you know, maybe you'd like to be in on the planning of it."

After I got over being stunned, the response that stuttered out of my mouth went something like, "Well, the thing is, Carl and I aren't really together—if you know what I mean. We're just friends. And to be perfectly frank, after today, I'm not so sure we'll even be that."

She looked confused but said, "Oh, I see. Tell you what, then, why don't we just exchange telephone information. That way, if you happen to have a change of mind—or heart, as the case may be—you can just give me a call. And if not, well, just look for me to call and invite you as a friend to both Carl and the girls."

I wasn't so sure about all that, but I pulled out one of my business cards and jotted down my home phone number for her on the back, which is a whole lot more than I did for Lenny.

Before leaving me to myself she said, "The girls really do speak highly of you, as does Carl. Hopefully, the two of you will be able to work things out."

I'm saying, girl, she said that mess like she actually might have meant it. I was so shocked, I broke down and pulled out a smoke in order to clear my head. I'd found a nice, clean concrete bench under a shade tree and was sitting there with my lips folded around a cigarette when Carl's pouting butt wandered up.

In a loud voice and obvious reference to the unlit end of my cigarette, he said, "What's wrong? You forget to bring a light? Maybe you oughta go back in and ask that thug I saw you all hugged up with out on the dance floor."

I told him, "Don't even start with me. He asked me to dance, I danced with him and that's all there is to it. And as far as this is concerned," I said, waving the cigarette at him before shoving it back into its pack, "I'm trying to quit. Okay?"

Carl straddled the bench opposite the one I was seated on, and wearing his best pissed-off expression, he took off on a verbal mission to set me straight. "He's got a record, you know. Bad checks, burglary, dope-slanging, gang-banging, you name it, he's done it. Fifty to one the police are probably looking for him now. You happen to notice anything bulging around his ankle? Or were you too busy concentrating on that bulge between his—"

That's when I jumped in and said, "Carl, I'm warning you. Don't go there with me."

He said, "And what if I do? I don't get you, Faye. Why is it you've got time and a half to waste on roughnecks like Lenny and that fake-ass Chef Boyardee character but none to spare for an honest, hardworking brother like myself?"

Girl, even mad as he was, I couldn't keep myself from laughing. I said, "Chef Boyardee? How many times do I have to tell you his name is Scoobie?"

HIM

Yeah, seeing her out on the dance floor with Lenny got me hot, man. And I'da probably said something to her that I would have later regretted had the twins not come running from out of nowhere, armed with a couple of disposable cameras and insisting that we pose for them.

Proceeding with extreme caution, I got up and went over to where Faye was seated. After positioning my legs on either side of her bench, I sat down and took the liberty of snuggling up behind ol' girl. Being that she seemed fairly okay with that, I went ahead and slid my arms around her.

To my surprise, she didn't seem to mind playing along. Not only did she mug and grin through several clicks of the camera, but at my suggestion she even turned her head so the kids could get a shot of me kissing her on the jaw.

And what with the warmth, the closeness, and her scent circling all underneath my nose, you know I was digging it, so much so I didn't make any effort to move once the girls had exited the scene. Nor, to my surprise, did Faye ask me to. Without so much as a grumbled word of protest she sat there and let me massage her shoulder, caress her arm, and run my hands over her hips and down the length of her thighs.

Yeah, man, what you talking 'bout? Working my mack for all it was worth, I pressed my chest into her back, rubbed my chin across the top of her shoulder, moved my mouth to her ear, and whispered, "It's not too late to change your mind, Faye. I'll take you back—right here and right now, no hard feelings, no questions asked—you know I will."

She grabbed hold of my hands and squeezed them, I think to keep them still as much as to calm herself before she whispered back at me, "I know that, Carl. And if by some chance it turns out that this thing between me and Scoobie isn't going to work, and assuming that it's not too late for you and I to pick up where we left off, I'll give you a call."

Before I could ask her to promise me as much, ol' girl wiggled loose from my grasp and stood up, and I knew without her having to utter another word that it was all over with and our day together was done.

I walked her back to her car, but before we could complete our final farewell, Faye informed me that she had a couple of items she wanted me to pass along to the kids. She went into her trunk and pulled out this nice-sized gift bag, which she promptly shoved into my arms.

"What's this?" I asked, even though I already had a pretty good idea.

"Just a couple of going-away presents. Something for the girls and a little something for your son" is what she told me. It wasn't until later that I found out that in addition to purchasing some fancy nail-care kit for my daughters, Faye had gone back and gotten those boots for my son—you know, the same expensive pair I told you we'd both admired that day at the mall but that I'd ultimately vetoed due to a lack of funds.

After peeking into the bag, I just kinda smiled before asking her, "So . . . what'd you get for me?"

Instead of grinning back, the expression on her face fell completely somber as she looked at me and said, "I already gave you everything I had to give. Maybe one day you'll come to understand and accept that."

Then she turned and left me standing there without bothering to extend me so much as a kiss, a hug, a handshake, or even a proper goodbye. But before she could duck behind the tinted window of her open car door, I called her. "Faye," I said. And when she looked toward me, I told her, "Thanks . . . you know, for everything."

She smiled and said, "You're welcome."

I guess it goes without saying that it wasn't exactly one of my better days. If sitting up at my former sister-in-law's wedding, slinging snot every which-a-way wasn't bad enough, I don't know what was worse, having to stand by while ol' girl slow-danced with dude or watching her drive out of my life. On top of all that, my doggone glasses, which I'd last seen at me and Faye's table, turned up missing, though, it wouldn't surprise me at all if they'd somehow ended up in Lenny's thieving, ashy, butt-groping hands.

But anyway, man, that was that. Or so it seems. A part of me is still not totally convinced it's really time to turn loose. Maybe Nora was right. Maybe what I need to do is sit down and come up with some kind of plan, because on the real, man, I'm not ready to just walk away and start over with somebody new. I can't close the door on my feelings that easily. And in spite of what she says, I don't think Faye can either.

Part Three

HER

Aside from Scoobie's silly and woefully misguided attempt to jump bad by picking a fight with Carl, he has yet to do anything major that would justify me giving him the boot. No, in most respects, he's been the dream man I always thought I wanted. In much the manner of the well-bred, adequately home-trained Black Southern gent (that I know him durn well not to be), he opens doors, pulls out chairs, arrives on time for dates, calls when he says he will, and even attends church with me on a regular basis. Financially speaking, he's been generous to a fault—buying me gifts, treating me to expensive outings, and when he found out I was sending one of my nieces money for books and tuition every semester, he even went so far as to offer to help me out with those costs. I'm saying, being with Scoobie definitely has its perks—moonlit jazz excursions on the river, dancing under the stars on the rooftop of the Peabody Hotel, bumping elbows with a slew of Memphis-connected celebs at a variety of red-carpet events.

On the surface, it seems all good, but when you get right down to it, girl, something's missing. Some essential ingredient, aside from sex, mind you, just isn't there. It's an absence that's most noticeable to me when we laugh, when we touch, when we gaze into each other's eyes for one or two seconds too long. And it's gotten so bad with me here lately that when we've been out together, rather than enjoy the good time the man has gone out of his way to show me, I find myself focusing on all that I'm not feeling. I know the torch I've long held for Scoobie is still there, somewhere deep inside of me, waiting to be stroked and rekindled into full flame. On occasion, it'll flare up and burn brightly, but the simple truth is, the intensity isn't at all what it used to be.

Of course, having to contend with all the usual little annoyances that undermine even the best of relationships doesn't help. At the top of the extensive and detailed list I have on homeboy is all that durn late '50s and early '60s white-bread music he likes to unwind to. Girl, please, what self-respecting, twenty-first-century, thirty-some-year-old Black man willingly sits up and listens to that mess? I swear if I have to hear "I Did It My Way" or "The Candy Man" one more durn time, I'm either gonna croak or lose my mind.

And while I'm on the subject of both croaking and losing one's mind, let me tell you about the all too bizarre habit homeboy has of talking to his dead mama. And I do mean fully animated, gesture-filled conversations, girl. Soon as Nora learned about it, she was like, "Uh-huh, and the first time you hear Mama Payne say something back to his monkey ass, you need to grab your shit and be up outta there."

But anyway, Scoobie had his mother cremated and he keeps the urn containing her ashes in his study. I was over to his place not too long ago when I heard all of this fussing and cussing going on. I thought maybe he was on the phone chewing somebody out. But when I peeped in the study, all I saw was him, minus a phone or even a headset, just standing there straight raising Cain with that durn urn. When I asked him about it, he initially tried to blow it off, before finally confessing that every now and then he still feels the need to consult with his mother on certain matters.

See, unlike Nora, it's hard for me to laugh at the brother when it comes to that sort of thing. I don't know, but maybe it has something to do with him being an only child who at an early age lost both of his parents, his father to drugs and his mother to mental illness, which eventually led to her having to be permanently committed. But I've always felt more than just a little bit sorry for Scoobie and the bad hand life seems to have dealt him from the start. According to Nora, it's a weakness on my part and one that as far back as junior high she was predicting would one day lead to my undoing.

But getting back to the present, if I had to narrow it down to the one thing about Scoobie that really gets my goat, I'd have to say it's what appears to be his growing obsession with my weight. These extra pounds I'm packing evidently irk homeboy to no end. If he's not badgering me about going to the gym, he's trying to coax or coerce me into sticking to the starvation plan he took it upon himself to have his staff nutritionist design for me.

And it's not like I haven't been trying to both cooperate and be a good sport about his efforts to help me be a "better" me. But I'll be durn if a sister don't just need a freaking break sometimes. Take last week, for instance. After being talked into skipping breakfast and accompanying him to the track for a grueling three-mile romp, I was already sore, tired, winded, and this close to being pissed off as it was when right there in the middle of our cooldown lap he said, "I hope you don't have anything special planned for the Fourth of July weekend, because I'm going to need you to make this trip to Atlanta with me."

I told him I thought he was going to be busy playing in some kind of golf tournament, not to mention doing promotional work for his book.

He said, "I am. Still, I want you to go with me. You're my good-luck charm. Plus, there's going to be someone there I want you to meet."

"Yeah?" I asked him. "Like who?"

He smiled and said, "Like, I can't tell you, babe. It's supposed to be a surprise."

Being that I wasn't in the mood for any surprises, much less entertaining the thought of having to spend my holiday weekend watching homeboy play golf and sign autographs, I told him, "Well, Nora and I had talked about driving over to Nashville to spend the Fourth with her brother LeRoi and his family. You remember LeRoi, don't you? He and his wife just had another baby—"

Girl, he had the nerve to jump up and cut me off. "Oh, so you mean to tell me you'd rather do Nashville with Nora than go to Atlanta with your man? Don't you spend enough time with Nora as it is? Frankly, I've never understood what it is you see in her anyway."

"Funny," I told him, "that's the same thing she says about you."

"Fine," he said, knowing all too well that was a battle he was bound to lose. "Since you're not going to let me surprise you, I suppose I'll just have to tell you now. The detective that I hired has come up with what he thinks is a good solid lead and he wants us to meet him in Atlanta—"

I slowed to a stop on the track and was like, "What detective? What are you talking about?"

He said, "Our son, Faye. I'm talking about sitting down with this detective and letting him fill us in on what he's found out about our son."

As would be expected, that particular tidbit of information changed everything. On notifying Nora of my sudden change of plans and the why behind it, she got all excited, then said, "If dude keeps this up, I guess I'll have to go ahead and cut him some slack. Sounds like he's really trying hard to make up for all those years he dogged you."

About all I could say to that was, "Sure sounds that way, doesn't it?"

But knowing me as well as she does, Nora was quick to fire back, "So what's wrong? You having second thoughts about your boy? Or is it finally starting to dawn on you what you could have had with Carl?"

Not ready yet to own up to either, I told her, "Actually, I'd been kind of looking forward to going to Nashville—if only to hang out with you and get away from it all."

Nora said, "Stop lying. If you were looking forward to anything, it was hunkering down over a plate of LeRoi's barbecued ribs without all the grief and guilt that doing so in front of Drill Sergeant Scoobie is liable to bring on you."

Rather than yuck it up with her, I said, "Seriously, Nora. Besides meeting with this detective, which will no doubt be the highlight of my holiday weekend, the majority of my time will be spent standing off on the sidelines somewhere with my stomach growling while I watch Scoobie wield a pen or a golf club."

That's when Nora stepped up and made me an offer I could hardly refuse. "You know, I am scheduled to be in the Atlanta area earlier in that same week. The Bulk Mail Center has me going down there to oversee some employee training sessions. But I'm only supposed to be there until Thursday, which means I could hang around and keep you company if you want."

HIM

Sure, I still think about Faye. Even more, as much as it pains me to admit it, I miss her. I miss the insights we shared, the private thoughts, the laughs, the kisses, the way her legs wrapped around my back when we were . . . No, but all kidding aside, I do miss very much playing man to her woman—if you can relate to that.

Just last week when I found myself standing, of all places, outside Baptist East's infant ward, who do you think was uppermost on my mind? And before you even go there, man, no, stalking the girl was neither my intent nor my primary reason for going out there.

If you wanna know the truth, I try to stay as far away from baby wards as I can, the one at Baptist East, in particular. Being there stirs up too many memories and mixed emotions. And it's not like there aren't some fine people working up there. It's a great facility, one of the best in the area, I'd dare say. Me and Bet went up there for all our kids—the twins, as well as the other two. Yeah, man, in the years prior to giving birth to our two girls, we suffered a late-term miscarriage on one occasion and on another, had a baby who was with us all of a week before he passed. Those were some rough times.

And that's why I don't hardly blame Bet for tossing my butt out when she found out about Benjamin. I'm sure every time she's forced to look at him or hear about him, she can't help but think about the two little boys we had to bury.

Anyway, man, the last thing I intended to do that night I went out there with my Uncle Westbrook was to wind up in the baby ward, reliving any of that. No, see, me and Unc went out there to visit a friend of the family who's recuperating from having his prostate operated on. After we'd finished joking and chatting with our friend, Unc asked if I'd mind him taking a few minutes to rap to some ol' girl he'd met in the infant ward on his last visit. While the old dog trotted off to work his silver-tongued magic, I strolled through the unit until I spied the window with the babies and the women in the rocking chairs behind it.

From the looks of things, it's one of those preemie programs where volunteers come in and provide the extra time and attention that for whatever reasons the nurses or parents can't. But the glow of utter contentment I saw radiating from some of those women's faces as they cuddled and cooed over the infants in their arms let me know that, for at least a few of them, the experience went a whole lot deeper than simply the desire to comfort a needy or sick child. It made me wonder if tending to those babies fulfills some deeply buried need within Faye's soul or psyche that she doesn't want too many people to know about. Why else would she be so intent on keeping something so admirable such a well-kept secret?

HER

We flew out of Memphis International late that Thursday evening and we hadn't been in Atlanta two solid hours when Scoobie started backtracking about the meeting with the private investigator. Lounging in the plush rear seating of one of Morris-Morgan's chauffer-driven Lincoln Town Cars, we were on our way from the airport to the hotel when Nora called, looking to coordinate our schedules. So I asked him, "When did you say we're supposed to meet with the detective? Was it Saturday afternoon or after your book signing on Sunday?"

The brother reached for my free hand and started patting it. I guess it was his way of trying to soothe me before he delivered the bad news. "Actually, sweetheart, we just might have to catch up with Detective Clarke some other time altogether. He called right before we boarded the plane and told me that something urgent had come up on another case he's working on in L.A."

Nora, who'd obviously heard it all on her end, said, "Uh-huh, what did I tell you? But did your ass listen? Nooo!"

Sensing my displeasure, Scoobie leaned over and whispered into my ear, "Don't worry, babe, detective or no detective, I'm going to make all of this worth your while, starting with dinner tonight. Just wait, you'll see."

Yeah, right! is what I started to tell him. *The only thing I've seen thus far is the extreme length to which you're willing to go to tell a bald-faced lie.*

But no, I didn't go off, girl. I actually kept my mouth shut for once. After checking into the hotel and freshening up a bit in my room, I went downstairs and joined him for dinner like nothing at all was wrong.

He greeted me in the lobby with a kiss and said, "I hope you don't mind, but I invited one of my golfing buddies to join us."

Turns out, this golf pal of Scoobie's, one Jacob Goldstein, just so happened to be a doctor who specializes in cosmetic surgery. At first I didn't think anything of it. The doc seemed like a nice enough guy, even if the brunt of his conversation never veered too far from his work and the inpatient clinic he runs in Florida. But while I was sitting there striving to be cordial and polite as I sipped ice water and nibbled on the rabbit food Scoobie had taken upon himself to order for the two of us, it started dawning on me that this was no incidental meeting or innocent introduction. All this talk about minor body-shaping procedures, the cost involved, and the average length of stay at Dr. Goldstein's state-of-the-art facility, all of that was aimed directly at me.

Yeah, girl, evidently the twelve or so pounds I've lost thus far aren't doing it for homeboy. Apparently, he's got his mind set on some much speedier results, because when I up and asked him, hypothetically speaking, mind you, just how much work he proposed I get, girl, he started talking lypo, a tummy tuck, a boob job, and the whole freaking nine! Had his surgeon buddy not been there, honey, I'da probably leaped over the durn table and, like Carl, straight started choking the hell out of him.

Later, after we'd parted ways with Dr. Goldstein and Scoobie was seeing me back to my room, I turned to him and said, "Of all the stunts you had to go and pull, why this one? You used my son to lure me down here just so you could sit me down in front of some stranger and tell me what an undesirable cow I am?"

He tried to act all hurt and innocent, as if I was the one who'd just publicly humiliated him. "How could you ever think such, much less say it? All I've done since we got back together is try and help you. That's been my only intent."

I told him, "Has it ever occurred to you that I don't need or want your damn help?"

He was like, "You know, you can really be one hard-headed, evil Black woman when you want to be."

I said, "Maybe if you fed a sister something besides sticks and twigs every once in a while you'd get a more chipper response."

Suffice to say, rather than go out like we'd originally planned, we bid each other some right chilly good nights before marching off to our separate suites.

A half an hour or so had passed and I was sitting on the side of the bed getting ready to dial up room service and order me the burger and fries I'd been craving, when I heard a knock at the door. Yeah, it was him, girl. And he came in talking about, "I don't want us going to bed angry with one another."

"Why?" I said. "You thinking it might throw off your golf game tomorrow?"

He strolled over, stretched out next to me on the bed, and said, "Come on, babe. Aren't you at least willing to let me try and make it up to you?"

"Depends on what you have in mind," I said, thinking

to myself that a little nookie in lieu of a burger and a side order of seasoned fries might not be such a bad trade.

Unfortunately, breaking his vow of celibacy isn't exactly what brother Scoob had in mind. He said, "For starters, as far as dinner tomorrow is concerned—how's a filet mignon, a twice-baked potato, a nice-sized Caesar salad, and a slice of chocolate cherry cheesecake for dessert, all lovingly prepared by your very own personal chef, Venard 'Scoobie' Payne, sound to you?"

I couldn't help but smile and ask him if the potato came fully loaded and, even more important, if a pitcher of sweetened iced tea accompanied the whole shebang.

He chuckled and said, "I'll do you one even better. Why not call Nora and have her come and join us? Matter of fact, I'll go so far as to set her up in a room here and have all of her expenses added to my tab. I'm serious, babe, I'll make sure everyone here is informed that you're both my guests and that you're to be treated accordingly."

And, girl, if that in and of itself wasn't rich enough, no pun intended, mind you, the brother reached into his jacket and pulled out a thick envelope. "And this," he said, "this is just a little something extra—you know, in case you're out somewhere and you or Nora see something you really, really like."

With that, he leaned over and planted a wet one on my cheek. But before he got up to go he told me, "If you need me, I'll be downstairs in the kitchen. After all, I do have a cheesecake to tend to."

After he left, I got on the phone with Nora and on hearing the deal, the first thing she had me do was count the money. Turns out it was an even grand, all in brand-new, crisp fifty-dollar bills. Nora said, "You know the slick bastard is up to something, don't you?"

"Look, girl," I told her, "we're here, so we might as well make the most of it and try to enjoy ourselves. Besides, with Scoobie footing all the expenses, it's not like it's gonna cost us anything."

Nora was like, "Don't fool yourself, Faye. Everything comes with a price, especially when and where Scoobie is involved."

HIM

I keep trying to tell Ms. Vic I got way too many real kids to clothe and feed to be out here fronting like I got enough extra to spare for the role of sugar daddy. She acts like she ain't trying to hear me, though. Not only has she repeatedly told me that money wasn't no thang, she's even gone as far as to inform me that her last two boyfriends were older than me. I think she said the one dude was on the other side of fifty and the other was in his early sixties.

I was like, "Dag, girl, is you got a geriatrics jones, or what?"

Older guys just treat her better is what she told me. She said, "Take yourself, for instance. As long as you and I have known each other and as many times as we've been alone together, you have yet to try and work your way into my drawers."

And that's true enough. I haven't tried. But between you and me, man, there's been many a night, especially since Faye's been gone, that I've laid up in bed thinking about doing just that and then some. Ain't no need of me lying, it's tempting, not to mention extremely flattering to have a young hottie like her jocking me.

But I don't know, man. It's more than just the age thing. I'm saying, in between all the petty bickering, me and Faye actually did have quite a few insightful and stimulating conversations about books, music, sports, sex, Black folks, and the stuff of life in general. Even given the nine to ten years' worth of age difference between us, I wasn't always having to stop and bring ol' girl up to speed when it came to certain cultural references and icons. But with my friend Ms. Vic, it's a whole 'nother kind of party, and the longer I hang out with her, the more I realize that.

Take the other night, for instance. She called and asked what I was up to. It was a Friday and I told her I'd just buttered my popcorn and I was getting ready to sit down and watch one of the movie classics I'd rented.

She was like, "You're an old-movie fan? See, I told you we had a lot more in common than meets the eye. I'm something of an old-movie buff myself. Elvis's *Blue Hawaii,* Jimmy Stewart's *It's a Wonderful Life,* and Doris Day and Rock Hudson's *Pillow Talk* are some of my all-time favorites."

Now you know I was through at the mention of Elvis and *Blue Hawaii* but rather than bad-mouth the girl, I just told her, "No, I'm talking the quote-unquote Black classics—like *Carmen, Cotton Comes to Harlem, In the Heat of the Night.*"

She said, "Ooh, *In the Heat of the Night,* sounds pretty steamy. What's that all about?"

I said, "You know, *In the Heat of the Night*, featuring the one and only *They Call Me Mr. Tibbs*, Sidney Poitier?"

When all I got back from her was silence, I said, "You do know who Sidney Poitier is, don't you?"

"Yeah," she said, real sheepish-like, before confessing to the unthinkable. "I sorta know his face, but I don't think I've ever seen him in anything."

I was like, "Uh-uh, wait a minute. You've never seen a Poitier flick? Never? Come on! No *Guess Who's Coming to Dinner*?! No *Raisin in the Sun*?! Dag, girl, I mean, what about the stuff he did with the Cos—*Uptown Saturday Night*? *Let's Do It Again*?"

Shocked doesn't even come close to describing what I initially felt, man. Try appalled. Pardon me if I come off sounding pompous, but in my book that's like somebody saying they're a jazz lover, but they've never listened to a single note of Miles or Coltrane.

She seemed so embarrassed about the whole thing that I couldn't help but start feeling sorry for her—so much so that when she turned around and asked if she could come over and watch the movie with me, I almost fell for the bait.

But just in the nick of time, a fuzzy image of me and baby girl naked, sweating and getting straight buck in the middle of my living room, flashed before my eyes and I came to my senses. I lied and told her, "Ah, you know my ex is supposed to be dropping the kids off by here tonight, so maybe we'd best save that for another time."

HER

Even with both of our BS barometers sitting right up there on high alert, don't think that Nora and I didn't take full advantage of homeboy's guilt-laced hospitality. Late Friday afternoon, after having spent several hours running around town, spending dude's money like it wasn't no thang, we'd come back to the hotel and stepped into its full-service salon and spa, looking for a massage and a chance to sit in the sauna, when we should bump into who but Tina, that worrisome wench I told you I'd clashed with at Scoobie's party. And just like the last occasion, she had that wild child Evan with her.

Actually, Evan is who we bumped into first, and I do mean that in the literal sense. Apparently, after having wreaked a wide path of destruction throughout the spacious lounge at the spa's entrance, the pint-sized tornado was trying to avoid capture when he came tearing around the receptionist's desk and collided with us, screaming like a banshee all the while.

Nora recognized him first, probably because she's the one who ended up on the floor with him after having caught a head-butt in the abdomen. She said, "Hey, isn't that the same little badass who terrorized everybody over at Scoobie's that night?"

I was in the middle of scolding homegirl for mouthing off like that in front of a minor when his mama suddenly appeared. "Oh, my dear," she said, trying to sound like somebody who was sincerely horrified and genuinely remorseful. "I am so sorry. Are you all right?"

As soon as she saw it was us, she dumped the front and went back to her witch ways again. "My, my. Don't you two get around?" she said, trying to pass off mean-spiritedness as a playful jab between old friends.

Rather than pop open a can of whup-ass, I smiled back at her and said, "Nice to see you again too, Ms. Tina. It just so happens we're here on Scoobie's invite. And you?"

The heifer had the nerve to bat her eyes and say, "Oh, you know when you have your own money, dear, you're free to come and go when and where you please."

Nora, who by this time had picked herself up off the floor, grunted like she does when she's about to dive tongue-first into her 'round-the-way-girl routine. The only thing that kept her from going there was the "slow your roll, sister" warning glance I shot her.

In true diva fashion, and totally oblivious to how close she was to getting some of that yak hair snatched out of her head, Ms. Tina brushed what looked like a freshly manicured hand over her Diana Ross–like do and said, "In any case, I have some urgent business that needs tending to, so I must be on. But truly, it was lovely seeing you again."

At that point, believe it or not, the wench actually leaned forward and extended me one of those puckered-lip, cheek-brushing air kisses. She probably would have treated Nora to some of the same if homegirl hadn't been standing there wearing an expression that clearly said, "Honey, try that mess with me and I will deck your hainty behind from here, clean into tomorrow . . ."

Before gathering up her son and gliding past us, Tina said, "Oh, and do have Venard give me a buzz while you're here. Time permitting, perhaps we could all get together and, you know, have lunch, drinks, or something."

Nora waited until the two had skipped their happy little butts on out the door before reading me the riot act. "Girl, you must be slipping. I can hardly believe you let Ms. It get away with that 'when you have your own money' bit."

I was like, "You're right. Maybe next time I oughta just backhand the 'ho and be done with it."

Nora grumbled, then reiterated the sentiments she'd expressed after our first formal meeting with the Dumas clan. "I still say there's something funny 'bout those folks, especially that kid."

"Funny like what?" I asked her. "You think the boy might have a set of triple sixes in his head or something?"

She looked at me with her eyes all bucked as if to say, "Hey, now that's a thought." But after a few more seconds of consideration she was like, "Well, I haven't exactly figured it all out yet. But when I do, I'll be sure to let you know."

Naturally, I had my own suspicions, particularly about the coincidental timing of slim's visit to Atlanta. But instead of rushing off to jump up in Scoobie's face about it, my plan was to wait until homeboy and I were alone to broach the topic.

I didn't have to wait all that long. Later that evening, after treating me and Nora to the dinner he'd promised and that, I must say, was both filling and absolutely scrumptious, Scoobie invited me up to his room for a nightcap. Caught off guard by the request, I was about to tell him that Nora and I had already made plans to scope out the late-night happenings around the hotel's outdoor pool.

But the kick girlfriend was quick to issue me beneath the table brought me back to my senses. Here was my opportunity to try and further peep the game I suspected Scoobie of playing. So, yeah, I accompanied the man to his suite, sat out on the balcony with him, had a glass of wine, and, for nearly the umpteenth time, listened to his larger-than-life image of himself and his even grander plans for blowing up in the future.

You know after spewing so much bull, your mouth has a tendency to get dry, so when he finally stopped to wet his palate, I slid on out there with the ol', "Guess who I bumped into today?"

I'd expected him to ask, "Who?" then take another sip from his glass, at which point I was going to tell him, "Tina," and watch as he either sprayed wine everywhere or else started choking and gagging.

Instead he sat his glass down, looked at me with the sweetest smile, and said, "Well, my first guess would be Mrs. Dumas."

He seemed so pleased with himself on having guessed correctly, I couldn't help but try to put a damper on his spirits by jumping straight to the point. "So, you two still screwing around or something?"

Again, he looked me straight in the eye and said, "Absolutely, positively *not.*"

I said, "So you want me to believe her showing up here was just one of those weird coincidences that sometimes happen in life?"

Still staring at me, like he was some kind of expert shrink and I his newest basket case, he leaned back in his chair, clasped his hands, and said, "As if I couldn't very well ask the same of you about your friend, Nora. Oddly enough, you seem to be forgetting this is both a free country and Morris-Morgan's corporate headquarters. Tina could be here for any number of reasons, whether to accompany her husband, Frank, on some legitimate business or for some purely social purpose. Whatever the case, it neither involves nor concerns me."

None too thrilled with the haughtiness of homeboy's tone, I got up in a huff and walked over to the balcony railing. After a quick, calming sip of wine, I said, "Oh, you've just got it all worked out, now, don't you?"

He laughed behind that and said, "I know I'm not detecting a little jealousy on your part, am I? I told you, love, what happened between Tina and me is history. After all, why would I want to settle for second best when I could have top of the line?"

I narrowed my eyes, swirled the wine in my glass, and said, "Man, please. Why don't you just admit it? All that stuff you said about the detective and searching for our son was a farce, wasn't it? Why not stop with all the bullcrap, Scoobie, and tell me exactly what it is you have in mind besides shipping me off to some fat farm and having your surgeon friend carve me up like a plate of prime rib?"

"What exactly do I have in mind?" he said, letting his smile fade before he came over to where I stood and handed me an open box. "I suppose marriage is as good a place as any to start."

I lowered my gaze only to have it greeted by the sparkle of a ring—a ring with the biggest freaking diamond I've ever seen up-close and personal in all my life. Good thing I was standing near the balcony's railing, because what I'd wished on Scoobie earlier boomeranged back on me. I'm saying wine shot out of my nose every which-a-way. And when I finally stopped coughing and dripping, all I could get out was a, "You're joking, right?"

HIM

What? Ain't no crime in a brother updating his look, is there? Okay, fine, I let Ms. Vic sweet-talk/sucker me into it to some degree. Believe me, it could have been a whole hell of a lot worse. Had I really let baby girl have her way with me, I'd no doubt be sitting up here looking like a broke cousin of Dennis Rodman. I'm talking tattoos, nose rings, multicolored hair, and all.

See, what happened was, I was sitting at home one night, minding my own, when she called and asked if I was interested in riding over to the university's student center with her and shooting some pool. Being that I wasn't doing nothing, I told her sure, I'd go hang for a minute. So she came by and picked me up, right? But instead of heading straight for the U, she told me she needed to swing by the mall for a sec.

I didn't say anything, but all the while I was thinking to myself, now if this is some kinda slick ploy to get me to buy her something, baby girl has another thang coming. But no, turned out it was on the up-and-up. She stopped by this little shop and, without so much as a sideways glance in my direction, she picked up and paid for a pair and a half of earrings.

And you know my slow tail. Just before her transaction was complete, I picked up the tiny, single silver loop and asked, "So how come you're not buying the match for this one?"

She was like, "Oh, that's for my belly button."

Yeah, man, I've been trying to tell you, quiet as it's kept, baby girl's got a right healthy dose of freak in her. To look at her, you'd never know she's got a navel piercing as well as a doggone butterfly etched high up on the upper portion of her left butt cheek.

Anyway, she'd paid for the jewelry and we were about to leave when the gum-cracking chick behind the counter flashed me a grin and said, "What about you, good-looking? You ever thought about getting an earring?"

I could have lied and told her no. It would have spared me some time, if nothing else. But like I told you, man, I wasn't operating at the top of my game that evening. So, like a fool, I went ahead and told her, "Actually, I have thought about it, but—"

Mind you, I did say "but" followed by a multitude of reasons why I'd thus far opted *not* to go the earring route. Of course, neither she nor Ms. Vic was trying to hear any of that. They kept stroking my ego and telling me how much more like Michael Jordan an earring would make me look. And, man, before I knew anything, I was standing up there with not one but two throbbing earlobes, and the doggone refrain to one of Prince's old songs —"You need another lover like you need another hole in your head, baby, baby . . ." riding my brain waves in a forty-second rotation.

Pretty much the same sort of deal went down with the hair bit. I'm saying, it wasn't something I set out to do, but once it was done, there was no turning back. All I call myself doing was stopping by Ms. Vic's house to drop off a class assignment she'd missed. It just so happened that her brother Darnell was there getting his hair done.

Now I gotta tell you, that whole pimped-out Nick Ashford, Al Sharpton, dippity-do look ain't never been my thang. No, sir, unlike a countless number of other nappy-headed brothers who broke beneath the pressure, I was one of the proud few who refused to buckle when the Jheri-Curl craze descended amongst our folk with a drip and splash in the early eighties. But the waves Ms. Vic had put in Darnell's head weren't all that bad-looking. None of that hard, caked-up, greasy-looking mess or those big bouncy-ass curls you see some brothers out here rolling with. No, dude's waves looked really natural. But instead of keeping my thoughts to myself, I made the mistake of complimenting Ms. Vic on her handiwork.

She thanked me, then stared at the buckshot on the back of my head for a couple of long seconds before telling me, "You know, Carl, I could do yours if you'd like. It's a no-lye product, so it doesn't burn. And given the length of your hair, it shouldn't take all that long . . ."

That's when my boy Darnell chimed in with his forty-nine and a half cents' worth, "Yeah, dog, go on and let sis hook you up. I got a couple partners who won't let nobody but her come near their heads."

You right, I should have known better. What's good for a young wolf like Darnell and the wild pack he runs with ain't necessarily the best bet for some old table scrap–fed mutt like myself. But, yeah, I sat on down and let baby girl slap that mess all up in my head. And when she finally announced she'd done all she could do and reluctantly passed me the mirror, it took everything in me not to break down crying. Man, my head looked like something my doggone cat Sapphire had spent an afternoon licking and lapping on. Instead of waving up or even laying down flat, clumps and bunches of little hairs were sticking up some of everywhere.

All Ms. Vic could say was, "I'm sorry, Carl. I guess the texture of your hair calls for something a bit stronger. But you know, after the chemical grows out you might want to think about going dread."

Come on now, man. What in the world am I gonna look like walking around with some nappy-ass locks hanging off my big ol' half-bald head? A zip-dang fool, that's what! Had she not been a woman, I'd straight cussed her tail out for coming at me with some junk like that.

I went right out the next day and had my barber take all that mess off. And to help balance things out, I told him to go ahead and clean up some of the hair on my face.

So, to make a long story short, that's how I ended up with the earrings, the bald head, the trimmed mustache, and the new goatee. Even though it wasn't something I'd planned, overall I'd say the look is something of an improvement. Wouldn't you?

HER

Scoobie came over with a handkerchief and ran down his rap while wiping and dabbing at the wine I'd dribbled on myself. "Faye, for the last year or so I've been praying for God to send me the right woman—that one special lady who would make the picture complete for me. And when I saw you at the mall that night, I knew not only had my prayers been answered, but my mama had been right all along. You're the only one for me, babe. We're supposed to spend the rest of our lives together."

Girl, right then and there is when I should have broke for the door and made a run for it. But with Scoobie's hypnotic eyes hitting me from one angle and the twinkling sparkle of that durn ring coming at me from another, my feet got all confused. Had I moved, I'da probably tripped. Nonetheless, I tried to tell him, "Wooh! Listen, I don't know what kind of dream world you're living in, but it's way too soon for us to be talking about marriage. And frankly, at the rate we're going, I'm not sure if we'll ever—"

"Yeah, baby, you're right," he said, cutting me off. "I am living in a dream world, and one that would be absolutely complete if only I had you—the one woman in my life who I could always count on to be there for me, come what may."

Having said all of that, the brother leaned forward and pressed a light but lingering and suitably wet kiss on my lips, after which he said, "Take some time and think about it. I'm open to giving you as much as you want and whatever it is you need. You know that, baby."

To keep from getting distracted, I snapped shut the lid on the ring box before I told him, "Okay! Right now, Scoobie, what I need more than anything are some straight answers. You want me to start? Fine! The truth of the matter is, the only reason I agreed to come here with you at all is because you led me to believe we were going to find out something about our son."

"Babe," he said, reaching out to touch my face. "Haven't I more than proven myself since in the last four to five weeks? Do we not serve a God of second chances?"

I peeled his fingers off my face and told him, "You know, Scoobie, it's one thing to play with my feelings, but it's quite another to play with the Lord."

"Okay," he said, throwing up his arms and looking angrier than I'd seen him in a long time. "I'm a liar and all of this has been one extremely expensive charade!" He turned and walked back into the suite, leaving me out on the balcony by myself. After a few minutes of standing there, letting it all soak in, I went inside as well. I walked over and set the box, with the ring still inside it, on top of one of the white, fluffy pillows sitting atop his bed.

Scoobie was standing in front of the suite's fireplace, thumbing through some papers in a large brown envelope. On noting that his face was still flushed red with emotion, I told him, "I'm gonna go on back to my room now. I think we've both said enough for one night."

But before I could make my move, Scoobie whipped a sheet of paper from the envelope and said, "Before you go, you might want to take a look at this."

I remember sighing and opening my mouth to tell him that I was too tired to play any more games with him, but before I could get anything out he said, "What? You don't want to see your son? He looks just like your daddy. Tell me I'm lying about that, why don't you?"

HIM

I stopped by to check on the girls the other day, and the first thing outta my ex's mouth when she caught a glimpse of my two new gold loop earrings and my big, shiny, bald head was, "So how old is she?"

I was like, "How old is who?"

She turned away from the sink where she'd been washing dishes and said, "Who? The silly chile you done let talk you into that god-awful foolishness, that's who. What's it going to be next, huh? A tongue stud, four or five platinum teeth, and some beaded hair extensions?"

My girl Bet don't pull no punches. Good thing she didn't see me right after Ms. Vic fixed me up with that whacked-out perm.

"Come on, now," I said. "Haven't you and the girls been getting on me for the longest about updating my appearance and freshening up my wardrobe?"

Dishrag in hand, she came over to where I was seated and commenced to scrubbing like mad at a spot on the kitchen table right in front of me. "Umpf," she said. "Had I known that was going to translate into you going out and having two extra holes drilled into your head, I'da sure kept my mouth shut. You need to start acting your age, Carl, and stop running around out here like you're twenty-something and part of Lil Jon and Nem's crew.

"Anyway," I said, raising my voice in an attempt to drown out hers, "I think I look good."

"Yeah," she said with a laugh. "I imagine you do." She

cocked a hand to her hip and said, "And what's Faye had to say about all of this?"

"Ain't nobody trying to hear what Faye's got to say" is what I told her, hoping she wouldn't look too deeply into my eyes and spot any of the scars and bruises I was still sporting from having been kicked to the curb. "She's not even in the picture anymore, anyway."

Bet shook her head and said, "Uh-huh, just like I figured. You done gone and let some little tramp come between you, huh?" She pulled out a chair and sat down like she was tired before she added, "When are you ever going to learn, Carl?"

"Learn what?" I said. "That nothing I do is ever gonna be good enough?"

Shaking her head again, Bet shot me the same pissed expression she issues the kids when she's had enough of their mess. "So what happened?"

Knowing all too well that any attempt to skirt around the issue would only make it harder on myself, I just went ahead and told her, "She dumped me, that's what. Sound familiar?"

Bet took my sarcasm and tossed it right back at me. "I know it didn't happen clear out of the blue. You must have done something."

"Obviously," I said, like a man who didn't know when to leave well enough alone. "Once a dog, always a dog in your book, right?"

"You want to talk about her?" Bet asked, her face drawing up into a tight frown. "Or would you rather talk about us?"

Sensing a full-fledged fight coming on, I backed down and told her, "I really don't care to discuss either one. You're the one who's so intent on dredging it all up."

"Well, excuse me for trying to care" is what she said. "I thought your allowing Faye to interact with the girls and come to my sister's wedding meant she was someone special, someone you were planning on keeping around for a while."

I wanted to say something, but I knew I couldn't without peeping Bet to some of the emotional junk I was trying to keep tucked beneath my mask. But I'll be damned if she didn't hone in on it anyway.

"You still have feelings for her, don't you?" she said with a smile after staring at me all of ten seconds. "Does she know?"

Unwilling to go that deep into it with her, I got up from the table and said, "I told you already, Bet. The girl dumped me. She's got another man. All right?"

Before I could leave the room and go off to fetch my girls, Bet came over to me, and with a tenderness that I haven't been privy to in quite some time, she squeezed my arm and said, "For the record, Carl, I've never thought of you as a dog. Not even when you were out there whoring around like somebody who didn't know he had a wife and kids waiting at home for him. No, if anything, I'd say you were something more along the lines of an alley cat—the reckless, foolish type who at some level truly believes he's been blessed with more than one life to spare."

I hate that about Bet, man. Even after all the crap I've put her through, she still has the gall to want the best for me. I told her, "I hear you. And even though it might not look like it, I want you to know that I have been making more of a conscious effort to do better by you, the kids, and myself."

She smiled and said, "I'm glad to hear it."

I kissed her on the cheek and was about to turn and walk away when I heard her go and add, " 'Cause if you don't stop messing around with these here young girls, you're going to find yourself laying up broke, dead, or in a hospital somewhere."

I thought to myself, *Yeah, but I'll be laying up there with a big ol' smile on my face.*

HER

In a glance, all of the guilt and hurt I'd been keeping dammed up inside for so long came spilling out in one sobbing wave after another. There was no refuting the honest-to-God truth of what Scoobie had said. The little boy who smiled back at me from the eight-by-ten head shot was and is my very own daddy's spitting image. According to Scoobie, it was a copy of our son's first-grade photo we were looking at. The investigator he'd hired had managed to get it from our son's adoptive grandparents, an elderly couple who made their home somewhere in the Atlanta metropolitan area.

But that was pretty much where the good news ended. The grandparents had no clue as to the current whereabouts of the little boy they called Tariq. Not long after they'd received his school picture, their daughter—our son's adoptive mother—had been killed in a car accident. For whatever reason, in the years after her death, the adoptive grandparents had fallen out of touch with their daughter's husband and subsequently lost track of Tariq. Basically, the only thing they could do was confirm a few of the bits and pieces the detective had already uncovered—like the fact that their former son-in-law, now Tariq's sole legal guardian, was a military man who moved every few years. Rumor also had it that he'd remarried and could quite possibly be living somewhere overseas.

I'm telling you, girl, that was one mind-blowing night. And me seeing my son's picture wasn't even the half of it. I wept so hard and so long there came a point when it was all I could do but crawl up into Scoobie's king-size bed and rest my head on the same pillow where I'd left the ring. And don't think anyone was more shocked than me, when after having spent a good fifteen minutes listening to the brother pray and petition the good Lord for both of our forgiveness, I felt him crawl into the bed and lay down next to me. I stayed with him through the rest of the night and well into the following morning. Not that anything of a sexual nature happened, mind you. Scoobie held me and periodically whispered promises and reassurances into my ear while I cried myself into a fitful sleep.

The next day I wasn't sure what to think or feel about anything. I was so out of it, I seriously wondered if the brother might have slipped something into my drink. And Nora wasn't the least bit of help. When I finally caught up with her again, told her how I'd spent the night, and showed her the ring Scoobie had talked me into holding onto until I'd made up my mind, she nearly pitched a hissy.

"Ain't this some bull . . . Girl, have you lost your ever-loving mind?!" she shouted, before grabbing me by the shoulders and shaking me. "Margaret Faye Abrahams, tell me you are not seriously thinking about marrying this fool!"

Rather than give her a straightforward answer, I told her about Tariq and showed her the picture I hadn't been able to stop looking at or leave anywhere since Scoobie had given it to me. In a matter of seconds, the expression on Nora's face skipped from one of bitter outrage to one of complete shock and horror before coming to rest on something that appeared to be a mixture of pity and sadness. On handing me back the photo, she said, "Okay, girl. Just promise me you're not going to rush off and elope or anything—at least not before I've had a chance to do some investigating of my own."

"Of course not," I told her, even though I wasn't thinking a bit more about her than I was Scoobie or even Carl at that moment. No, the only somebody on my mind was the little boy whose happy face looked so much like my daddy's it was downright spooky.

A couple days after we came back from Atlanta, I was

sitting in the kitchen gazing at the picture again, wondering where Tariq was and how life had been treating him, when Nora came in and slapped a small white envelope down on the table in front of me.

"What's this?" I asked her.

"Oh, just some pictures I took by the poolside at the hotel in Atlanta while you and Scoobie were off doing whatever in the hell it is y'all do when you're alone together," she said. "Go on. Look at 'em and tell me who you see."

I thumbed through the photos for a second before I told her, "What? All I see is Tina's hellion of a kid, Evan."

"Yeah," Nora said. "But who, outside of his badass mama, does he remind you of? Uh-huh, that's right. I told you I was going to do a little snooping around of my own."

I wasn't exactly following homegirl, but before I could respond she threw another picture down in front of me. It was a school portrait, similar to one I have of Tariq, only wallet-sized, and the snaggletoothed boy in it was none other than our old childhood chum, Venard Nathaniel Payne, aka Scoobie.

Nora slid one of the snapshots she'd taken of Evan next to the first-grade photo of Scoobie and said, "See, I told you there was something funny 'bout that kid. Tell me you don't see the resemblance!"

Girl, it was a body-double moment, if I've ever experienced one. But still, I didn't want to believe it. I looked at Nora and said, "You really think this might be Scoobie's kid?"

Nora rolled her eyes and said, "Might, my behind. The real question is, does old man Dumas know? I think it might behoove you and me to sit down and see if we can't write us an anonymous 'Dear Mr. Dumas, you know damn well that baby ain't none of yours' type of letter."

Now, see, I didn't want any part of that. Far as I was concerned, whatever was going on between Scoobie and the Dumas crew was best off left between the four of them. I was about to tell Nora something along those lines when the telephone rang. Thinking it might be Scoobie, and not wanting to get into it with him about Evan in front of Nora, I told her, "Wait, don't answer that. Let's see who it is first."

When the answering machine clicked on, me and Nora both scrunched up our faces as we listened and tried to place the voice of the woman who'd obviously been getting her drink on. "Hey, this is a message for Faye. Look, I don't mind sharing him, okay? But it would be terribly unwise for you to think for even one split second that I'm going to just step aside and let you have him. You feel me? All right, then. So don't act like you ain't been told."

I sat back in my chair and was like, "Who in the world . . . ?"

But Nora said, "Uh-uh, don't even play. You know exactly who that was. I told you we should have gone ahead and beat that hainty heifer down when we had the chance. Who does she think she is, calling here and threatening somebody?"

Girl, at that point, I was too outdone to say anything. All I could do was stare at the pictures of the three little boys—Scoobie, Evan, and Tariq—and shake my head.

HIM

Nora called the other day and asked if she could come over and check out my new pad. "Yeah, come on" is what I told her, secretly hoping that she'd find a way to convince Ms. "You Know Who" to tag along.

Even though I called myself trying to hide my disappointment when Nora caught me peeking behind her, she took it upon herself to scold, "If you'da wanted her to come, you should have asked her."

With my grin fading fast, I told her, "If she'da wanted to come, her ass woulda been here."

Nora let it go for all of ten minutes. Just long enough to tease and compliment me on the noticeable changes in my appearance before taking off for a quick look-see of my new place. We were on the last leg on the tour and had just opened the door to my bedroom, when she stopped in midstep and started squealing. "Dag, Carl! You went all out in here, didn't you?"

After checking everything out and letting me know how impressed she was with my impeccable style and taste (thank you very much), she took her busy butt on over and bounced it up and down on my mattress a couple of times. "Faye said you had a real nice bed" was the comment she let slide on stretching out and shifting into maximum relax.

I laughed and told her, "Yeah, and I'm willing to bet that's not all Faye had to say about the time she spent in my bedroom."

A big ol' grin busted out across her face and she was like, "I told you, you oughta call her sometime."

I took a seat in the rocker next to my bed and told her, "Nothing doing, sister. I'll have you know I fully intend to keep the few shreds of dignity I do have left."

Nora got quiet and I saw the playful expression on her face give way to one much more serious. "Something wrong?" I asked her.

She sat up and shook her head. "I'm just kind of worried about her is all." Remembering what a chump dude had been that night outside the condo, I stopped rocking and said, "She's not letting ol' boy smack her around or anything, is she?"

"No, nothing like that," Nora said. "Actually, he's just

asked her to marry him." She went on to give me all the gut-wrenching details about their recent trip to Atlanta and the big-ass ring Chef Boy had given her. It hurt like hell to hear that shit, man, but rather than let on, I said, "Wow! She must be happy, then."

Nora made a face and said, "Happy, my ass. Stuck, is what she is. Stuck on stupid and ain't even trying to find a clue. What are we gonna do, Carl? Have you given any more thought to coming up with a plan?"

I told her I had a plan, all right. A plan to mind my own damn business, same as she needed to do.

She said, "Chances are you'd be humming a different tune if you knew Faye like I know Faye. See, you weren't there when she went through her little nervous breakdown episode behind some of Scoobie's ignorant-ass mess and I thought I was gonna have to call somebody to come and put my girl in a freaking straitjacket."

I was like, "Hold up! Faye had a nervous breakdown?"

Realizing she'd revealed way more than she'd intended, Nora fell back against the pile of pillows on my bed and tried to blow it off. "It was one incident that happened years ago. Matter of fact, forget I even brought it up. The last thing I want is for you to start thinking the girl is straight-up Looney Tunes."

Too curious to just leave it alone, I said, "If you don't mind me asking, did this 'little episode,' as you described it, by any chance take place in Oklahoma?"

Nora's eyebrows shot straight up on her forehead like my little girls' do when they know they're in trouble. She jumped up off the bed with, "You know what, Carl? I shouldn't even be talking about this. Faye would kill me if she found out."

"So who says she has to find out?" I said, stepping in front of her as she headed for the door. "And what difference would it make now anyway?"

She squeezed her eyes shut and for a second I thought she was gonna go ahead and give it up. But when she opened them again she said, "As much as I'd like to tell you, Carl, I can't. I made a promise to Faye a long time ago—a promise that I'd never tell anyone. So if you really want to know, I'd suggest you call her up and ask her—the sooner, the better."

HER

Yeah, girl, I've been getting a lot of weird calls lately. Remember Betty, Carl's ex-wife? Well, she called me the other night. She and the twins are throwing this big surprise birthday bash for Carl and they want me and Nora to come.

I'da probably told her thanks but no thanks and kept the invite to myself had Nora not been sitting there looking dead in my mouth when I took the call.

Soon as I hung up the phone, she was like, "A party for Carl? And we're both invited? Oh yeah, girl, we going! So don't even try and trip, 'cause we are most definitely going."

For real, girl, the heifer is about this close to getting on my last freaking nerve. And if she says one more thing to me about what she perceives as my hesitancy to go ahead and confront Scoobie about Evan, I swear, I'm gonna straight take her out.

Hell, it's not like I'm afraid to nail homeboy's behind to the wall. Nor do I doubt for a second that girlfriend hasn't straight cold cracked the case and that the little devil-in-training's real daddy is our very own Chef Scoobie Payne. I've just decided to bide my time and take a wait-and-see approach about it all. Eventually the truth is bound to show itself, not only about the nature of Scoobie's relationship with Tina and Evan but the earnestness of his intentions toward me and our son as well.

You'da thought that us acquiring our son's picture would have had Scoobie all stoked about the possibility of us seeing the child in the flesh one day soon. But outside of his initial display of concern for me and my feelings, the brother has pretty much donned the role of Mr. Nonchalant. The only thing he's said to me at all about Tariq since our return from Atlanta is, "As soon as Detective Clarke turns up something else, you, my dear, will be the first to know."

I told you, girl, the only thing Scoobie seems to have any real interest in discussing with me, other than himself, of course, is my body and what he obviously views as its current state of total disrepair. "So how much weight have we lost this week? Are you still sticking to that food program the nutritionist recommended? You did go to the gym last night, didn't you? Have you used any of that stretch-mark cream I bought you? Let me know when you've made up your mind about Florida."

"Right," I told him. "You really think I can just walk up into my job and talk those folks into granting me an extended leave of absence for some surgery that ain't hardly necessary for my continued health and well-being?"

He was like, "So quit. I told you, baby, I want you to be my wife. I want to take care of you and all your needs."

Girl, please. I am not fixing to let Scoobie worry me. True enough, the changes I've made thus far—like losing weight, kicking my smoking habit, moving more, and eating healthier—are ones I've needed to make for a long time. And certainly I'm grateful to Scoobie for helping me get back on track, even if he is the one who knocked me on my butt in the first place. But if he thinks I'm about to hand him my life on a platter to shape and mold as he sees fit, he's got another thing coming.

HIM

Man, me hooking up with Ms. Vic on my birthday is something that just sorta happened. Really, it did. If anything, my plan was to be as far away from her ass as possible because I knew good and well if we went out that evening and had so much as a halfway decent time, later on that night we were destined to be laid up somewhere buck-naked, humping like a couple of mad dogs in heat.

I promise you, man, I called up some of everybody—including the good Lord—in my desperate attempt to keep baby girl at bay, only to come up with absolute zip. My cousin Squirrel wasn't picking up his phone or responding to any of the messages I left him. My Uncle Westbrook claimed he had himself some hot date he didn't dare break. And everybody else either already had other plans or for some reason I wasn't able to touch bases with them.

I was all set to spend my birthday nursing a beer by my lonesome, either at the bar or else holed up in one of the dark booths at Big Mama Mae's. But baby girl chucked a nice-size wrench in those plans.

She'd been bugging me for days about my birthday plans and I'd pretty much been giving her the brush-off. So when she called me at work that afternoon, I decided to take the easy route and just not call her back. But lo and behold, as I'm clocking out for the day, who do you think I spot in the parking lot standing next to my car? I'm saying I guess she called herself straight gonna stalk a brother.

She was like, "So what's it gonna be, birthday boy? You gonna let me treat you to dinner tonight or are you gonna keep running?"

I said, "Victoria, look, I don't want you to think that I don't appreciate the offer, 'cause I do. But like I've told you before—"

"Yeah, I know, I know," she said. "You're still hung up on the age thing, but that's okay. I guess that means I'll just have to give you your birthday gift now, as opposed to later."

That's when she stepped to me, man. And before I could get a proper hold of the situation, her lips had locked against mine and the sister was straight working on trying to suck the tongue out the back of a brother's head.

"Happy birthday" is what she had the nerve to tell me when she finally turned me loose.

Tell me 'bout it, man! Baby girl ain't a day over twenty-two, but her skills and abilities are on par with those of any forty-some-year-old who has been around the block more than a time or two.

I made the mistake of watching her walk away. And, man, what I do that for? She had on these hip-hugging, low-riding jeans, and I'll be damned if that doggone butterfly riding her ass wasn't winking at a brother.

I don't know what to say, man. I just lost it—all my cool, all my resolve, everything. "Wait up," I said, chasing behind her like some mindless, punked-out zombie. "You, ah, you think you could be ready by say 6, 6:15 or so?" is what I asked her. "My daughters want me to drop by around 6:30 and pick up the present they got for me. I mean, I could come and get you later, if you like."

"No," she said, sealing my fate with a grin and a seductive lick of the lips. "No, 6:15 is fine. I'll see you then."

HER

I wasn't gonna go. It had been nearly a month and a half since Carl and I went our separate ways. But the more I thought about it, the more I realized I really did want to see him again.

To keep Nora from hounding my behind, I finally just told her, "Look, I'll go to the durn party, all right? But I'm only gonna stay a minute. You know Wednesday night is the night I do my volunteer work. So it would probably be best if we went in separate cars." She rolled her eyes and said, "You need to quit. How you gonna plot a getaway before you even get there?"

See, that's why homegirl is always sitting up somewhere crying the blues. She don't know the game like I know the game. If she did, she'd be hip to the fact that one of the basic rules of play is leaving a convenient out for oneself—just in case something right funky goes down.

As for what Scoobie might say, I really wasn't worried one way or the other. The fact of the matter is, he's been in Europe for the past couple of weeks. Yeah, Morris-Morgan sent him over there to take part in some international culinary program. It's a three-week deal. And don't think I haven't been thoroughly enjoying the break homeboy being umpteen thousand miles away has given me.

But anyway, getting back to Carl and his birthday, after batting a couple of ideas around, Nora and I decided to split the cost of getting him an iPod. After we brought the gadget home, I took the liberty of hooking dude up with some of those old tunes he's so partial to. You know, a little Luther, a little Barry White, some Kenny Lattimore, a song or two by Jarreau. For good measure, I even threw in those two slow jams he asked me to dance to back when we were first feeling each other out—"You Got Me Going in Circles" by the Friends of Distinction and "Baby I'm for Real" by the Originals.

Yeah, girl, I'm not gonna lie, listening to all those songs brought back more than just a few memories about Carl and some of the things he and I did together. But then I got to thinking about our breakup and the fight between him and Scoobie and that last nasty exchange of words.

I stepped up in the place not really knowing what to expect but praying all the while that if nothing else Carl and I could at least be polite to each other. Betty was gracious, as always, and the twins nearly trampled Nora and me in their excitement to see us—all reactions I'd pretty much anticipated.

Now, what I never expected was to have such an intense physical reaction when dude finally made his appearance. A surge of warmth started at the top of my head and slowly spread throughout the rest of my body. If that wasn't bad enough, I felt a certain part of my female anatomy straight up start to clench and swell, girl, as if it had a mind and more than just a few memories of its own.

And I have to give it to the brother, he wasn't looking half-bad. Not only did it look like he'd been hitting the weights and gotten more muscular, he'd cut his hair and had trimmed his beard into a nice little goatee. He was also sporting these itty-bitty gold hoops, girl, I'm saying, one in each ear. Altogether it was a look that made him appear considerably hipper and fresher, if not several years younger. And given the youthful appearance of the fast-tailed slim who came skipping in two steps behind him, *not* looking his age was the whole point.

I'm not sure why, but not once did it ever occur to me that Carl just might show up with a date. If it had, you'd best believe I would have kept my big butt at home. I don't know, girl, seeing him there with slim just made me feel weird. Not jealous, not angry or upset, just weird.

Nora looked at me and said, "You all right?"

I lied and told her, "Of course I am. Why wouldn't I be?"

She said, "Well, it ain't everyday that some half-dressed hoochie shows up at a party with your man."

"First of all," I told her, "he's not my man. And secondly, we were never more than—"

Nora threw a hand up in my face and said, "Uh-uh! Spare me the sad little speech, girlfriend, 'cause ain't nobody 'round here trying to believe that mess but you. Okay?"

That got me hot, and I told Ms. Smart Mouth, "Look, all I'm saying is that what happened between me and Carl has been over and done with. He's free to see whomever he pleases without any unnecessary interference or drama from me."

She fired back at me with, "Yeah, and all I'm saying is you ain't got to worry 'bout getting your hands dirty. If you want me to do the honor of going over there and busting that up for you, just say the word, 'cause you know I will."

I grabbed her and said, "Nora, I swear if you embarrass me in front of all these people, I'll never speak to your ignorant butt again."

She settled down and said, "Well, aren't you at least gonna go over and speak to the man? I ain't never known a freaking 'hello' to hurt nobody."

I snuck a glance over at Carl and slim before I turned back to Nora and shook my head. "Not now. Maybe later."

She frowned and shook her head back at me. "Girl, please," she said. "Later for later. I'm going over there now and I'd advise you to stop being such a big chicken and bring your silly butt on with me."

She headed off like a woman on a sho' 'nuff mission to make matters worse, and the only thing that slowed her down and bought me enough time to get myself together was the sudden appearance of Carl's cousin Squirrel and Uncle Westbrook square in homegirl's path.

HIM

A birthday party? Yeah, I was surprised, all right. And so too were quite a few other folks, apparently. I'm saying, surprised that this ol' boy hadn't exactly arrived on the scene by his lonesome.

Even so, my showing up with Ms. Vic probably wouldn't have caused such a big stir if baby girl hadn't shown up all hooched-out. She'd traded in the hip-hugging jeans she'd had on earlier for a pair of slacks that were twice as tight and provided even more of a behind-the-scenes peek—I'm saying, man, butterfly, ass crack, and all. If that wasn't bad enough, her shirt only came to her midriff and was mostly cutaway in the back. I'd never seen baby girl with that much skin exposed, which leads me to believe she'd only done it as some sort of birthday treat for me. And let me tell you, it was most definitely a show and one I probably would have enjoyed had it not taken place in the presence of my ex, my two little girls, and the dozen or more friends and relatives who'd shown up to help me celebrate my forty-second.

The ex didn't waste any time in sharing with me her opinion with regards to my choice of company and her provocative attire. Smiling politely and chattering pleasantries all the while, she hurriedly parked my crazy cousin Constance on the sofa next to Ms. Vic before dragging me aside and promptly getting all in my face. "What in the hell would ever possess you to grace my doorstep with some two-bit video 'ho?!" I told you, man, preacher's daughter or not, get her mad and my girl Bet will straight cuss you worse than any drunk, one-eyed sailor.

I was like, "A video 'ho? You actually think I'd show up here in front of my children with a doggone 'ho of any kind?"

"Well, it damn sure looks that way," Betty said, with those jaws of hers so swoll you'da thought she had a bunch of sour grapes shoved up into each cheek.

That's when my cousin Squirrel jumped in and, with an arm around my shoulder, said, "You tell 'im, Bet. Carl know he ain't right."

I looked at him and said, "Did somebody ask for your opinion?"

He said, "Hey, you know it don't make me no never mind what kind of 'ho she is. I mean, just so long as before you leave here tonight, you pass me the name and the number of the pimp you know that can hook a brother up like that!" He bust out laughing, then dapped me up and hollered, "Dag, Carl! Baby got it going on. Hook me up with some of that, playa! You know what I'm saying?"

Still looking like a mad chipmunk, the ex waved a finger in my face and said, "Uh-huh, I should have known. That explains why you've been walking 'round here lately looking like a Black Mr. Clean or somebody."

"You tell 'im, Bet," Squirrel piped up again. But before he could contribute any more of his special brand of stupidity to the conversation, Betty ordered him to hush up before proceeding to drag him off to the kitchen to help her with the punch.

I was standing there feeling a little lost and just a tad embarrassed when who but Nora should come up and tap me on the shoulder. Rather than give her the standard "it's good to see ya" embrace, I picked her up and spun her around.

She said, "Better save some of that, lover boy. Your girl Faye's here."

I was like, "Faye?! Where?"

An honest-to-goodness double take is what I did when I turned and saw ol' girl. She was standing over in a corner talking to my Uncle Westbrook and looking as fine as all get-out. I'm saying, man, she's lost so much weight, I hardly recognized her.

"And you'd best be nice to her," Nora said. "It took a whole lot for her to come here tonight."

Knowing Faye, I didn't doubt it. And not wanting to waste any time, I was on my way over to holla at her when Ms. Vic suddenly slid back up in the picture. On handing me a glass of punch, she smiled and latched her arm around mine. Baby girl ain't no dummy. Chances are she'd gotten a good whiff of the scent I was onto and had decided it probably wasn't in her best interest to let me wander off too far without her.

What was I supposed to do, man? Leave her standing there while I ran over and wagged my tail all up in some other woman's face? I'm sorry, it's just not in me to outright dis a chick like that, especially a chick I brought to the dadgum party in the first place. See, and therein lay the problem in a nutshell. I mean, had I known there was gonna be a gathering in my honor and my girl Faye was gonna be there, I'da straight left Ms. Vic sitting at home alone.

Ain't no sense in me denying it, man. I've still got feelings for the girl. I can hardly be in the same room with her without wanting to touch her, talk to her—I'm saying, just be close to her. Every time I looked her way, I got this big fat knot in my chest. And of course it didn't help any that on one of my many glances in her direction, she stopped playing coy and went ahead and acknowledged me with a quick flash of dimples and a nod.

I was hurting somethin' awful, man, and feeling on the verge of being straight-up sick when Nora, with her slick self, came to my rescue.

HER

Nora is the only somebody I know who carries her own condiments everywhere she goes. I'm talking little packets of ketchup, mustard, soy sauce, Tabasco . . . you name it and she's probably got some stashed away in the bottom of her bag.

So I really didn't think twice about it when I saw her squeezing a packet of hot sauce into the bowl of cheese and salsa dip she was walking around with. But I should have known better than to think that homegirl was going to be deterred from her stated goal of arranging a face-to-face meeting between me and dude before the party was over.

She'd worked her way across the room and had even managed to peep Carl to my presence, only to come up short when sistergirl popped her half-naked booty back into the mix and made it clear that she wasn't 'bout to let dude go anywhere without her.

Nora looked over at the pair and, with a scowl on her face, said, "I wonder just how spicy she likes her dip?"

Figuring she was just out to poke fun, I chuckled but didn't comment.

Then Nora looked at me real serious-like and said, "You think Betty's got any jalapeno?"

I said, "Jalapeno? Girl, if you make that stuff any hotter you're gonna be sick as a dog up in here."

That's when Nora winked at me and took off. Next thing I knew, she had Betty by the arm and they were making their way to the kitchen, grinning and bobbing heads all the while.

It wasn't hard to tell that the fit was about to hit the sham. Not wanting to wind up with any mess on me, I decided to be an adult about the situation and just go on over and speak to dude and Ms. Thang.

As it was, Carl kept glancing over at me with this weird, almost pained expression on his face. I couldn't tell if he was growing increasingly uncomfortable with my presence or, like me, was simply trying to figure out a way to navigate the distance between us.

But before I could make my move, Nora was out of the kitchen and making room for herself on the sofa next to Carl's date. There was a brief exchange of words before Nora raised up the bowl of chips and doctored dip and offered sistergirl a taste.

As mean a stunt as it was, girl, I couldn't help but laugh. I'm saying, a bug-eyed catfish fresh out of the water and headed for the nearest frying pan is what the poor chile reminded me of.

Nora, with her crazy self, waited until the girl's huffing and puffing turned into some straight-up coughing and gagging before she summoned Betty over to escort their unassuming mark to the bathroom.

Even though Carl appeared genuinely concerned about sistergirl's well-being, as soon as she was safely out of sight, he was off the couch and headed in my direction.

HIM

When she spread her arms and offered me a hug, I pulled her toward me and squeezed her tight, savoring as much as she'd let me of her warmth, her scent, and the leaner-than-I-remembered contours of her sweet, brown frame.

Upon pulling back and checking her out up-close and personal, the most I could get out of my mouth without slinging slobber every which-a-way was, "Damn, girl, you look good!"

I'm saying, man, in spite of the damage she'd done to my ego, I couldn't help but be happy to see her. She did a little spin for me and said that in addition to counting calories, she'd been working out at the gym four to five times a week.

I said, "I guess that means you and ol' boy are still tight then, huh?"

She said, "Now, why you want to start up with that? Besides, it hardly seems like you're hurting for company. Didn't you come here with somebody?"

Wasn't nothin' I could say but "Yeah, I guess I did."

Faye said, "She's cute—your girlfriend, I mean."

I was like, "Who? Victoria? No, see, we aren't, like, together, together. I mean, she's just somebody I hooked up with from school."

She looked at me with a grin and said, "Oh, she's college-age, is she?"

"See, now you wrong for that, Faye" is what I told her. "Dead wrong."

Those dimples of hers got even deeper as she batted her eyes and she said, "Am I?"

Yeah, shucking and jiving with Faye took me back and almost made me forget that anything foul had ever happened between us. The whole time I was standing there, all I could think was that maybe her being there was a sign—you know, a sign that possibly she'd changed her mind about ol' boy and was ready to pick up where she and I had left off. After all, I didn't see any sign of that big-ass ring Nora had told me about. With the vibe between us growing thicker by the second, I finally just broke down and cast my line, "Look, baby, why don't you come hang out with me and the girls next weekend? Alvin Ailey's American Dance Theatre is gonna be in town and—"

She put her fingers to my lips to keep me from finishing

and motioned with her eyes for me to turn and look. When I did, I saw that Ms. Vic had come back into the room. But Nora and my ex were doing their damnedest to keep her hemmed up in a corner.

When I turned back around, Faye was like, "You should probably go and rescue her."

To show ol' girl I wasn't about to run scared, I stood my ground and reached for her hand before stepping to her again. Without a shred of amusement in my voice, I asked her point-blank, "Why you so worried about her, when it's obvious that I'm the one who's drowning here?"

HER

Girl, when he took my hand and put it on his face, all I could think was, *Lord, please don't let this man try to kiss me.*

First of all, I knew if his lips came anywhere near mine, I'd hardly be able to resist the urge to kiss him back. And secondly, I wasn't at all looking to get into some nasty catfight with the slim he'd arrived there with.

I tried to ease away from him, but that only made him move closer and hold me tighter. He pressed his mouth to the heel of my palm and said, "Do you at least plan on saving a dance for me?"

I stroked his jawline and fingered one of his earrings before I caught myself. I cleared my throat and told him, "I don't know. That might not go over so well with, you know, your new girl."

He locked his gaze with mine and said, "I told you already, she's not my girl."

'Round about that time is when slim finally managed to slip free from the tight clutch Nora and Betty had her in.

And in the blink of an eye, she was right back at Carl's side, hanging onto his arm for dear life. Thinking she had something to prove, girlfriend went so far as to plant a noisy kiss on the brother's cheek and say, "Hey, ya miss me?"

Instead of coming right out and telling her the truth, which would have been, "Not one durn bit," Carl introduced us. "Victoria, I want you to meet Faye. Me and Faye used to be . . . neighbors."

Before reaching out for slim's hand, I smiled at Carl, who was standing between us looking like his drawers had suddenly become violently twisted. Girlfriend, for her part, grinned and greeted me cordially enough, even though it was clear that she'd done peeped the deal between me and dude.

Carl opened his mouth to say something, only to be cut off by Renita and Renee, who busted in on the scene and temporarily stole the show. "Daddy! Daddy! It's Bow Wow! Remember, you said you'd dance with us when his song came on?" With a look of resigned relief on his face, Carl shrugged before letting the twins drag him off.

Not knowing what to say to each other, me and slim stood there for a moment and watched as Carl and the girls danced. In an attempt to try to break the ice, I said, "I guess we know who has his heart, huh?"

Girlfriend looked at me real funny-like and said, "So, exactly how long were you and Carl . . . neighbors?"

I don't know if she was simply digging for information, trying to start something, or what, but just as I was about to give her the goods on me and dude, Carl's Uncle Westbrook came over and launched into an interrogation of his own.

"You ladies doing all right?" is what he started with, before turning on slim and saying, "Excuse me, but don't I know you from somewhere? Didn't you used to go with a tall, gray-haired cat, owned a red Caddy? Went by the name of, ah, Sonny Boy?"

She grinned and said, "Yes, sir, I most certainly did. I haven't seen him in ages, though. How's he doing these days?"

Mr. Westbrook was like, "Who? Sonny Boy? Oh, he's dead."

Looking right shocked, girlfriend hollered, "What?!"

"Yup." Westbrook nodded. "Passed away 'bout four, five months ago. A massive heart attack is what I heard."

While they danced back and forth around the details, I snuck my butt on away from there and slid up next to Nora, who was busying herself at the buffet table.

She smiled and said, "What's up, girl? Don't tell me you need me and Betty to buy you some more time."

"Thanks, but no thanks" is what I was quick to tell her.

She glanced over at slim and said, "So, what she talkin' 'bout?"

Nothin' besides the number of old-ass men she done put out to pasture is what I almost volunteered. But not wanting to get Nora all riled again, I just said, "Honey, please, you don't even wanna know."

HIM

Women are funny, man. If ol' girl showing her face up in the place wasn't shocking enough, not in a billion years would I have ever banked on Nora and my ex teaming up to run a doggone screen on my behalf. And Ms. Vic . . . man, had anybody told me baby girl had it in her to cut up sideways like she did that night, I'da called them and their mama both a liar. But I was an eyewitness, if not a reluctant participant, in some of her tricked-out madness.

Take the li'l stunt she up and pulled when somebody made the mistake of treating me to some of Al Green's

"Love and Happiness." I'd just finished proving to the twins that their ol' pops was still capable of busting a move or two when I heard those smooth, rhythmic strings segueing into the last few notes of Bow Wow's spastic hip-hop beat. Yeah, man, you know how it goes. Bump-bump-bump, bump-bump-bump-bump, bum . . . bum . . . bum.

I'm saying, dog, it's just something about those licks that make the hair rise up on a brother's back. And it wasn't like I needed a partner. It's one of those songs I'm just as content to groove to all by my lonesome. But as my quote-unquote date for the evening, Ms. Vic obviously somehow felt obliged to join me—which I probably wouldn't have minded all that much had the circumstances been different. Say, for instance, had the audience watching us do our thing not included my two highly impressionable little girls, my already pissed-off ex, my fickle former lover, and her scheming-demon of a best friend. Or, let's say, if Ms. Vic hadn't been out there grinding her butterfly all up in my groin, dropping it like it was hot, and whatnot. I'm telling you, man, the girl was popping that little butt of hers every which way but loose. And anybody who's ever heard "Love and Happiness" knows it ain't even that kind of jam.

I thought for sure at any second my girl Bet was gonna fly into a stomp-footed rage and snatch both our asses off the floor. And it wasn't like I didn't have a good mind to pull baby girl aside and tell her to slow her doggone roll. But hey, all my boys were there—my cousin Squirrel, my Uncle Westbrook, and all the rest of 'em. Short of letting myself be seen getting straight punked, wasn't nothin' I could do but go with the flow.

And even after all was said and done, I might have still been okay with it if at a certain point I hadn't looked up and seen what looked for all the world like hurt in Faye's eyes. *Come on, baby. This ain't even about you!* is what I wanted to yell across the room at her, even though on Ms. Vic's part, I'd dare say it most certainly was.

To my surprise, we managed to get through the song and finish the dance without any subsequent loss of life or limb. But it was right about then that I realized if I kept hanging out with the likes of Ms. Vic, the chances of me making it to yet another birthday unscathed and with all my wits about me were somewhere between slim and none.

After bowing to the round of cheers and applause I got from most of the fellas, I joined Ms. Vic in downing another glass of punch. Of course the whole time I was drinking, I was looking around for Faye, in hopes that she'd be open to hearing me out about what had just gone down.

With ol' girl nowhere in sight, I made up my mind to go off in search of her. But in order to facilitate a clean getaway without Ms. Vic feeling the need to trail me, I had to drum up a lie about having to go take a leak.

On my way across the room, I ran into Squirrel, who said, "You know something, man? Since Big Red lost all that weight, she kinda puts you in mind of a nice voluptuous cross between Faith Evans and Toni Braxton, don't you think?"

"Sure, man, whatever" is what I told him. "You seen her anywhere?"

He was like, "Who, Red? Yeah, she just left. What, you didn't know?"

Man, that's when I saw Nora. She swung a hand up on her hip and shook her head in my direction as if to say, "Umm-hmm, you know ya blew that, don't cha?"

HER

Ordinarily, that kind of mess doesn't even phase me. Wasn't like I didn't know exactly what girlfriend was trying to pull with her pointedly nasty imitation of Lil Kim, Foxy Brown, and Beyoncé all rolled into one. But I'm here to tell you, "bootylicious" it wasn't. More like a whole lot of booty-stank.

Even so, I might have halfway understood it had I said something nasty to the chile or done something to indicate that I was out to claim her man. I almost stuck around just so I could tell her that she needn't waste her time worrying about me, because for all practical purposes I'd already been there, done that, and moved on to other things.

I guess more than anything, what really irked me was just how much Carl seemed to be enjoying the whole trite Player's Club set, especially given the fact that just seconds before he'd been all up in my face talking that yang.

Now, how was I supposed to believe anything he'd just said to me after seeing him let little Ms. Hot Draws back that thang up on him? Like I'm really gonna want to stick around, much less dance with his silly behind after having stood by and watched him get his jollies with this girl. Honey, please. Had I been in the mood for a freak show, I'da stayed at home and watched the durn Spice channel.

So, yeah, I left. What else was I supposed to do? I told you, girl, I'm not even trying to waste my time like that. But if it makes you feel any better, then fine, I'll admit it. Yeah, I was a little hurt, but only because I'd momentarily let myself buy into the con that Carl really cared.

HIM

Soon as she realized Faye had split the scene, Ms. Vic went ahead and loosened the choke hold she had on my leash. I was standing 'round with a group of the fellas, soaking up the praises they were showering on me for having bagged such a hot, young cutie, when the ex walked up and dragged my airborne ego back to the ground. "Yeah, go 'head, 'Mr. Big Stuff.' Out there in front of your children showing your natural black ass, like you ain't got good sense the first. I swear, when the barber shaved off all your hair, he must have taken a damn good chunk of your brain right along with it."

After she stormed off, my cousin Squirrel stepped to me in all seriousness and said, "You know, as much as I enjoyed it, dog, that was a pretty foul thing to do, not only because of the kids, but I mean, dang, especially with your girl Red being here and all. That's not like you, dog. Did ol' girl say something to make you mad or what?"

Instead of answering him, I turned to my Uncle Westbrook, who was standing there with a slightly amused expression on his face. "All right," I told him. "Go 'head and let me have it."

Unc slid an arm across my shoulder and said, "Look here, son. I'm just gonna tell you what a smart man would do. A smart man would take that li'l ol' hot-tailed gal back home, give her a quick smooch goodbye, and then go on and see about his woman. That's what a smart man would do."

Squirrel said, "Hold up, now, Unc. I'm all for being smart and what have you. But I think the brother's entitled to a little something more than just a quick smooch before he ups and makes that final exit. I'm saying, ain't no harm in making that butterfly bounce a time or two before you go and make things right 'twence you and Big Red. You feel me?"

Man, the only thing I was feeling right about then was bad—because deep down I knew my Uncle Westbrook was right. I needed to leave Victoria's hard-bouncing butt alone and go see about my woman. Only thing was, I wasn't sure where to even start with that task. So, quite naturally, I did what I usually do when in doubt—I winged it.

On the ride back to Victoria's place, "Say Yes" by Floetry came on the radio and she told me, "Oooh, Carl, turn that up! That's my jam."

While she was sitting there snapping her fingers, bobbing her head, and mouthing the lyrics to "Say Yes," I was over there in the driver's seat twitching and squirming and trying to figure out a nice way to just tell her ass no.

When the moment of truth finally arrived and we were standing up at her door, instead of being cool with it, I held up my watch and went straight goober on the girl. "Man, time sure does fly when you're having fun, don't it?"

She smiled at me and said, "Is that a polite way of saying you're not coming in?"

I told her, "I'd better not."

"Why?" she asked, prior to reaching over and dancing her fingers across my chest. "You scared?"

"Something like that" is what I said, after reminding myself to breathe.

"I had a little sumthin'-sumthin' of my own planned for you," she said, while alternately thumbing my nipples, neither of which wasted any time in jumping up to greet her touch.

I was like, "Ahh, I can well imagine."

She narrowed her eyes and went on. "A little Sidney Poitier, a little champagne, a little coconut-flavored massage oil, a brand-new black teddy . . ."

I'd started sweating and I was trying to back up offa baby girl when she pressed her body against me, laid her head on my chest, and said, "Carl?"

"Yeah, baby," I said. And I'ma tell you, man, by this time the girl had my nose so wide open, I was straight up smelling Girl Scout cookies. I'm talking Trefoils and Thin Mints. Seriously.

"You're going to see that woman, aren't you?" is what she asked me. "The one who left the party early?"

I told you, man, chick ain't no dummy. And inasmuch, I kicked it to her like this. I said, "To tell you the truth, Victoria, I'm not really sure what I'm gonna do after I leave here tonight."

Easing off me a bit, she smiled and looked down at the heat-seeking missile, which despite my best efforts was now boldly asserting its presence between us. She said, "So is that for me or for her?"

"That's certainly because of you" is what I told her. "But if you want me to be honest, baby, I gotta say no. I'm fairly certain it's not for you."

"Well, as always, I appreciate your honesty, Carl. And when you see your lady friend, make sure you tell her I ain't mad at her. Tell her I didn't mean any real harm. I just thought that maybe I had a chance."

I kissed her on the forehead and told her, "Hey, don't worry about it. It's all good. And thanks for being there for me. It meant a lot. Really."

She said, "Sure, anytime. And just so you know, if things don't work out between you and your friend, you're always welcome to stop back by here, be it tonight or any other night."

Man, I nodded my head and took off out of there like a jet before I lost what little resolve I had to keep away from all the sinful goodies I suspected were lying in wait for a brother at the bottom of baby girl's cookie jar.

HER

After I left the party, I went home and changed clothes before driving over to the hospital and doing my volunteer bit. Come the end of my shift, I'd started back to the condo when I remembered that I was only three days into my weeklong stay at Scoobie's place.

Initially the plan had been for me to stay at the godawful plantation brother Scoobie calls a home until his return from Europe, which would have had me holed up out there in misery a full three weeks. But thankfully, he'd been having some renovations done in his kitchen and two of his bathrooms and the completion of the work had taken a couple weeks longer than expected. That, at least, cut my sentence down to a somewhat tolerable seven days.

"It's a great house, babe" is what he told me before he left. "And I'm sure after you've spent some time out here, you'll come to love it as much as I do."

Girl, please. Just because living up in the durn "big house" with Prissy, Mammy, Uncle Ben, and 'Nem is Scoobie's idea of the good life doesn't make it mine.

Anyway, that's where I was when the phone rang around eleven that night. I wasn't asleep. Matter of fact, the phone was on the bed next to me 'cause I'd just hung up from talking to my girl Terri. The only reason I let the answering machine take the call was that I figured it would probably be Scoobie again, calling to twist my arm some more about going to Florida, marrying him, or some other such nonsense.

Suffice to say, I was more than just a little shocked when after the beep, I heard Carl's voice talking 'bout, "Faye, it's me, the birthday boy. I was calling to thank you for my gift."

I picked up and told him, "Hey . . . you're welcome. I

suppose I have Nora to thank for telling you how and where to find me."

"Of course," he said. "But in her defense, your girl didn't exactly volunteer the information. So if you're gonna be mad at anybody, make it me. In case you haven't noticed, persistence is my middle name."

I told him, "Ain't that the truth."

Rather than waste any more time, he jumped right to his real reason for calling. "So tell me, why'd you leave so early?"

"Tonight's the night I do my volunteer work at the hospital, remember?" I said, deciding to play along.

"Yeah, but you could have at least told me goodbye. You owe me a dance, I want you to know."

I said, "Uh-huh. So how come you're not out somewhere celebrating with your girlfriend?"

He was like, "I told you, she's not my girlfriend. Is that why you left?"

Yeah, like I was really supposed to cop to that. I said, "Please."

He paused before slipping down into his Barry White voice. "You know, when I was dancing with her tonight, I looked over at you and for a split second there I saw something in your eyes that made me wonder if you weren't just a wee bit jealous."

I said, "Umpf, you've been drinking, haven't you?"

He laughed and said, "You left before I got a chance to cut the cake. I saved you a piece and I was wondering if I could bring it over."

My heart started racing a bit because having to see him again so soon wasn't something I'd exactly prepared myself for. I said, "You mean now?"

He said, "Yeah, why not? You expecting your boy Chef Cootie home sometime tonight?"

Without bothering to stop and correct his deliberate mispronunciation of Scoobie's name, I said, "Carl, it's late and, well, I'm supposed to be house-sitting. I don't know if you coming out here is such a good idea" is what I told him, hoping that the agitation in my voice would be enough to make him change his mind.

"I won't stay long, I promise," he said, trading in his Barry act for some Keith Sweat. "Come on, Faye. It's my birthday. All I'm asking for is a little company."

Yeah, girl. He tried to play me like Sally Simple. But you know a sister wasn't having it—at least not on those terms anyway. I told him, "Oh, like I'm really supposed to believe that once you get over here, you're not gonna try and make some kinda pass."

That's when he broke down and said, "Look, woman, I'm on the phone at the Exxon not too far from you and not only is it starting to rain, but there's a young thug out here who looks like he might try to bust a cap in my behind any second now. Just let me drop the cake off. If you'd rather I not come in, then fine, I won't."

Hoping the frustration I heard in his tone was a sign that he was ready to hang it up and call it a night, I told him, "Fine. Come on then."

HIM

Dude lives way out in the county in this big antebellum monstrosity. And, yeah, I know going out there was a risky, if not outright reckless, move on my part. But hey, the way I see it, Nora's just as much to blame as me for how the whole trip out there came to be in the first place. After all, she's the one who kept pestering me about coming up with some kind of plan. To Nora's credit, though, prior to giving me the full 411 on her friend's whereabouts, she did grill me rather extensively about my intentions.

"Look, Carl, you can't be going out there and acting no fool" is what she told me. "I'm saying, don't make me regret this, okay? 'Cause on the real, my brother, if I find out that you was up in there cutting up and carrying on, I will hunt your ass down and . . ."

I gave her my best mad Black-man scowl and said, "I done already told you, this ain't Mike Tyson or Kobe Bryant you're dealing with. All I want to do is see the girl. Besides, when have you ever known Faye to let somebody take advantage of her without a fight? And believe me, if I've got to whup her for it, she can damn well keep it."

Faye's instructions over the phone had been for me to take the circular drive around to the rear of the property. She met me at the back door, like she said she would. And I'm not gonna lie, just the sight of her standing there waiting on me in her robe, and bare feet, and with a hint of a smile on her face, got me good and tingly in all the right places. And if I'm gonna come all the way clean 'bout my motives, I've got to admit that the canine in me was pumped by the very idea of kicking it with ol' girl up in dude's house while he was way on the other side of the world somewhere.

But instead of ushering me in out of the rain, Faye reached for the sack I was holding. In handing it over, I told her there was enough inside for the both of us if she felt at all like sharing. Then I stood there for a moment, staring and looking stupid, I'm sure. Finally, I said, "I guess you're not up to having a slice with me right now, huh?"

When all I got from her was a shrug, I nodded and turned to leave. A flash of lightning lit up the path that led back to my car and I was about to pick up the pace when I thought I heard her call my name.

I glanced over my shoulder, and sure enough, her mouth

seemed to be moving, but I couldn't quite make out what she was saying for all the thunder and the sudden downpour of rain. When I trotted back up to the porch, she pushed open the door and shouted down at me, "It's starting to look pretty bad out here. Maybe you ought to come in—at least until things die down a bit."

Dude's kitchen is where I found myself once I stepped inside. And let me tell you, man, I've never seen anything like it outside of an episode of *How I'm Living*. I'm talking granite countertops galore, wood floors polyurethaned so tough you could practically see your reflection in them, cherrywood cabinets, top-of-the-line appliances, recessed lighting, and more. All I could say was, "Dag, this boy really does have it going on, huh?"

In total awe of all the space, wealth, and luxury, I was just standing there trying to take it all in—with my mouth open, no doubt, when some of the water dripping off my head made its way into my eyes. "Here, let me," Faye said, coming to my rescue with a big, fluffy dish towel that smelled like it had never been used.

While she dabbed my face, my neck, my head, around my ears, and across my brow, I shut my eyes and quietly reveled in the warm caress of her breath on my skin. My mind became little more than a jumble of Faye-centered thoughts. I started thinking about that evening she'd made me let her in so she could help me with my son, Benjamin; the day we'd spent at the amusement park; and the night we'd made out on my sofa after the Jarreau concert. I started thinking about the naked press of her body against mine; the pinch of her nails on my back; the run of my tongue along her thigh; and that doggone dance that had started it all.

I'm not sure what she was thinking or feeling while I stood there fighting against the urge to pull her into my arms and tell her just how bad I'd been missing her, but when she finally lowered the towel and spoke to me, her tone was considerably softer than it had been before. "There's coffee if you want some, or I could make tea if you like."

"No, coffee's good," I told her.

While she busied herself with the cake and the brew, I made a beeline for the fancy sound system I spotted near the kitchen table and popped in the *Love and Happiness* CD I'd brought in with me. I'm saying, man, she owed me a dance and I had every intention of getting it. After lowering the volume on the music until it was just a hum, I sat down at the table and tried not to let my nerves get the best of me.

I was sitting there, playing with the oversize number 42 candle that had been on my cake when I noticed Faye staring at me from the other side of the room. She said, "I suppose this whole new-look thing was your girlfriend's, excuse me, I mean Victoria's, idea?"

I said, "No, not all of it. Really, just the earrings. The rest I came up with on my own. Why? You think it makes me look stupid or something?"

She bit her lip and spent a few seconds mulling either the question or her answer before she said, "No, actually I think it's kind of cute. A bald head does you justice."

Always a sucker for a compliment, I said, "Yeah? What about the goatee?"

She laughed and said, "Anything beats that scraggly-ass beard you were wearing."

I was like, "Hey, if you didn't like my beard, you should have said something."

She said, "Sure, and just like that you would have gotten rid of it?"

Spotting my opening, I told her, "To make you happy, yeah, I would have. I thought you knew."

Her dimples deepened. I know they did. Yet and still, rather than go for the bait, Faye being Faye chose to skirt around it. After clearing her throat, she said, "So the girls have you taking them to see an Alvin Ailey production, do they?"

On informing her that the dance outing was an idea I'd come up with and had been looking forward to attending, I asked her if she'd ever seen *Cry.* I told her it was an Ailey classic. "Matter of fact," I said, "I've got a copy of it on tape with Judith Jamison performing it, no less. Couple of nights ago, I pulled it out and watched it. And I'll be dog if it didn't remind me of a certain somebody."

HER

Sure, the brother having the wherewithal to show up on Scoobie's doorstep in the middle of the night in a durn thunderstorm looking for me was flattering, to say the least. So, yeah, I invited him in, but even so, I hadn't meant to let him stay any longer than it would take for him to partake of some cake and maybe a cup of coffee. Yeah, that was the plan, all right, until he up and started talking about *Cry.*

In case you didn't know, girl, *Cry* is a modern dance number that the late, great choreographer Alvin Ailey put together in tribute to his mother. Not only does it capture the very essence of the Black woman's experience in America, it's one of the most moving combinations of music, dance, and emotions that I've personally ever witnessed. So when Carl brought it up, I couldn't help but wonder if it was a subtle ploy on his part to get me to open up about my son, Tariq.

"Carl, why don't you save us both some time and just tell me why you really came all the way out here?" is what I asked him before bringing the coffee and the cake over to the table and having myself a seat.

"Same reason you showed up at my party tonight" is what he told me. "Same reason you're willing to sit here with me now. Face it, baby, we never got to finish what we started. And as long as ol' boy is standing between us, I don't guess we ever will. You really thinking about marrying this joker? Is that what you want?"

Rather than answer, I watched as he lit the candle and jabbed it into his piece of cake. He looked up at me and said, "It seems to me that any woman in her right mind would know better than to settle for frosting when she could have cake." Then he reached over, poked a finger into the thick chocolate icing covering my slice of cake, and after licking the cream from his finger told me, "Another layer, baby, and we'da been there. You hear what I'm saying?"

Stifling the urge to laugh, I asked him, "Carl, what makes you think what we had would have even lasted? Tell the truth, cake or no cake, I'm not even your type. You like young, skinny girls. Young, skinny, and from the looks of this latest little honey, just a tad on the airhead side."

He had the nerve to get hot behind that and say, "Now, how you gonna tell me what my type is? And based on what—Clarice? A woman I hooked up with at a party one night when I was drunk? Or Victoria? A woman whose affections I respectfully declined to partake of tonight because I wanted to be with you. Seems to me it's rather obvious you've got something I like or else I wouldn't be over here trying to beg up on some more of it."

HIM

I pulled out my billfold, flipped it open to the picture section, and set it down in front of her. When she looked down, the first thing out of her mouth was, "Wait! Dag, Carl, that's you?! Get out!"

What I'd taken the liberty of showing her was one of my old prom pictures. Yeah, man, you know how we kicked it back in the '70s with the big fro, the baby-blue polyester, the stack heels, and all? Well, add a big ol' lopsided grin to that bit of imagery and you've got me at age seventeen, tipping the scales at 250-plus pounds and, according to my cousin Squirrel, looking like a black disco version of Baby Huey.

Faye tripped so hard at my doofus-looking butt, she almost didn't take full notice of the heavyset girl in the picture beside me. But soon as she did, an "Oh, my goodness!" slipped out of her. She picked up the photo and held it closer to her face before she frowned and said, "You mean to tell me . . . I mean, that's . . ."

I laughed and told her, "Yup, that's my girl Bet, all right—sixteen years old and probably somewhere around a hundred pounds heavier than she is today. Now, what was that you were saying again about the kind of women I like?"

Still staring at the photo, Faye nodded and said, "Point well taken. I suppose there is a lot about you I don't know. And by the same token, there's quite a bit you don't know about me."

"So how about we change that, starting now?" is what I said. "Go ahead, ask me and I'll tell you anything you want to know."

I didn't really think she'd take me up on the offer. So when she asked if I was still in love with my wife, I was thrown a bit off guard. "Yeah, I am," I managed to stutter. "But it's not like you think. There's absolutely no chance of us ever getting back together."

On her next pitch, ol' girl switched up on me and went from a fastball to a curve. "So why were you out in the streets humping around in the first place?"

Even though sharing the raw, intimate details of my marriage was the last thing I wanted to do, rather than throw up my hands and say, "Okay, game over. I quit," I sucked in a deep breath and slowly released it before I laid it out for her. "I suppose I was searching for a way to feel better about myself."

Apparently she thought I was out to make light of my misbehavior, because she said, "Oh, that's one I've never heard before—extramarital sex as a cure for self-esteem."

I told her, "I'm being as straightforward with you as I can, Faye. Several years into what I thought was a near-perfect relationship, I found out I wasn't making my wife happy in bed. She suffers from this condition, I don't know the clinical term for it, but it pretty much renders her unable to reach the big 'O.' Come to find out, all those times I'd thought I had her climbing the walls, she'd actually been faking it."

That's when Faye truly surprised me, man. Rather than go for the cheap shot, she slipped into what I assumed to be her friendly neighborhood pharmacist voice and said, "In case you didn't know, there are a lot of really good medications on the market specifically designed to treat what Betty suffers from."

I told her, "Believe me, we tried several. And right before Bet and I split up is when her doctor finally lucked up on one that worked for her."

"So why the divorce?" Faye wanted to know.

"In a word," I told her, "Benjamin." See, man, my sleeping around, as bad as it was, Bet was still willing to forgive and even forget to some extent. But the fact that I went out and had a child outside of our marriage, that was just too much for her.

After I finished breaking it down for ol' girl, I told her it was my turn and, upon flipping the script, I said, "Assuming that you're still maintaining that you're not in love with this guy, I really would like to know just what it is you're getting out of this. There's gotta be a payoff of some sort, Faye, or else you wouldn't be here. This joker throwing down something so tough beneath the sheets that it's got you content to sit here alone and wait for him rather than laying up butt-naked somewhere next to me?"

I could tell she thought that was funny, but when she saw how dead serious I was, she told me, "For all it's worth, Carl, technically speaking I haven't been with anyone since I was with you. Scoobie's been celibate for the past year or so and his preference is that we abstain from any sort of premarital sexual activity."

Now, man, you know I'm sitting there with this blank expression on my face and thinking to myself, *Celibate, my ass! I'll be damned if I ain't messed around and lost my woman to some trash-talking, closet sissy! And if my cousin Squirrel should ever get wind of this shit, I'm liable to never live it down.*

But you'll be happy to know I took the high road and opted not to go there. Instead, I turned around and asked her if it was about the money and the bling. I told her, "I gotta be real with you, baby—barring me hitting it big on the slots in Tunica, financially I'm probably never gonna be able to afford to have you living in this type of luxury. But what I can and would very much like to do is give you all of me . . . and in time, possibly a kid or two, if that's what you want."

She lifted her gaze from the picture she'd been staring at and appeared to search my face for a few seconds before she said, "You know . . . don't you?"

I was like, "Know what? That like a lot of women over thirty, you hear your biological clock ticking? Isn't that why you go up to Baptist East and rock infants every Wednesday night? That's not a problem for me, Faye. I'm not opposed to having more kids, even if it means I've got to take on a third job. Matter of fact, something tells me if you and I ever did get together and did this thing right, we'd make one hell of a pretty baby."

She rubbed her eyes and sighed before she told me, "Carl, the truth is, I already had a baby."

HER

There it was, and instead of me trying to maneuver around it or shuck it off, I decided that after all I'd taken the man through, I owed him at least some small portion of the truth. So after swallowing a couple times to keep back the bile I felt rising, I finally just told him. "Twelve years ago I got pregnant with Scoobie's child. Instead of trying to help me figure out what to do, Scoobie left me to deal with it on my own. After contemplating my choices, I decided to go through with the pregnancy. Being that I didn't want my folks to find out, I packed up and moved to Oklahoma. Nora's got relatives out there. She came along and helped me get set up. She was also there when I gave birth to him. I had a boy, eight pounds, nine ounces."

"Okay," he said. "So you had a child under what could best be described as less than desirable circumstances, not unlike what transpired in my situation. What I still don't understand is why you would feel the need to keep something like that from me."

"Because," I said, "the deal was we weren't supposed to get emotionally involved, remember? There was only so much of myself I ever intended to give you."

He asked me, "So what happened? With the baby, I mean?"

My mouth opened, but nothing came out. After a good thirty seconds' worth of trying, I just dropped my head.

But there were no tears, at least not on my part. No, that's a hurt I've long felt honor-bound to keep bottled up inside.

Carl, on the other hand, was so choked up, it wouldn't have surprised me if he'd broken down and started blubbering enough for the both of us. "Damn. I'm so sorry, Faye. I'm so awfully sorry" is what he kept repeating.

After extending him a sincere apology for all the times I'd been less than nice to him, I told him, "If I didn't give you as much as I should have, Carl, it's only because I don't feel as if I have all that much to give—to you or anyone else."

He insisted I'd given him plenty. A rediscovered love of poetry. A newfound appreciation of jazz, an ear for his troubles, a soft place to lay his head. He told me, "If you think I came here tonight looking for something other than just to be with you, baby, you're wrong."

In an attempt to clarify his muddled understanding of the facts concerning me, Scoobie, and our son, I said, "Carl, you don't understand—"

And he was like, "Oh, you think not? Well, let me just say this. Not every man is as sorry as your friend Scoobie. My guess is, as soon as you stop beating yourself up about your past, you'll be able to see that."

"My past?" I said, allowing myself to get pulled all off track with him. "Carl, the grief you feel when you lose a child doesn't have a statute of limitations. Hell, it's been twelve years, and my arms still feel empty. I sincerely hope that's not something you'll ever have to experience first-hand."

I could tell in a glance that not only had he felt the sting of the jab, but it had cut him pretty deep. Instead of backing away from the pain, like a lot of other men might have, he stayed put and told me, "Actually, I do know some of what you're feeling. I've been there . . . twice. Me and Bet had the misfortune of burying two babies before the twins came along. The first one, Bet miscarried in her last trimester. The second was born but only lived about a week. In part that's why when I found out about Clarice being pregnant, I went and talked her out of having an abortion. Even though I wasn't a hundred percent sure it was mine, I simply couldn't bear the thought of losing yet another child I'd helped bring into existence."

HIM

After I finished saying my piece, neither one of us uttered another word for what seemed like an eternity. Finally, I went over and turned up the volume on the CD player and let brother Green break through the wall of silence between us with a few bars of "Love and Happiness."

I stretched out my hand to her, but rather than oblige me she folded her arms across her chest and said, "Please don't take this the wrong way, Carl, but I'm really not up for any of that right now."

I flipped over the CD case and pointed to the list of songs on the back. I told her that No. 4, "What a Wonderful Thing Love Is," was a song that reminded me of the first two years of my marriage to Bet. In hopes of defusing some of the melancholy in the room, I put the song on and told Faye I'd like to experience that feeling again with the right someone.

Determined to hold true to form, Faye drew her arms tighter around herself and said, "And I wish you the best in that. Really, I do."

Rather than tuck tail and run, I held my ground and told her that one of the songs on the CD reminded me of her. I handed her the case and asked her to guess which one. It was a gamble and, as unpredictable a woman as Faye is, it wouldn't have surprised me at all had she opted to chuck the case right back and ordered me to get the hell out.

Instead, after heaving a heavy sigh, she went ahead and lowered her gaze to the list. And in light of titles like "I'm Still in Love with You" and "Look What You've Done for Me" I thought it interesting that she would choose "For the Good Times."

It wasn't a bad guess, but I told her the right answer was song No. 5, "Simply Beautiful." At first she didn't appear terribly impressed and I thought for sure I was done for. But as soon as I put the song on, the hard, jagged lines in her face began to soften. Just to be sure, I waited several bars into the tune before sitting back down and reaching out for her hand again.

Even though she didn't say a word, slowly but surely she slid her palms across the table. I met her halfway and for another minute or so we just sat there with our hands raised and clasped together, mine on either side of hers, almost as if in prayer. And then, unable to resist the urging we both heard in brother Green's voice, we stood up and let the music work its magic.

HER

I know, girl, my first mistake was letting Carl up in the house at all. And yes, my second was not immediately correcting the conclusion he'd jumped to about the fate of my son. In my defense, all I can say is that by the time the brother got around to playing "Simply Beautiful" I'd gotten so caught up in all those things I'd been trying so hard not to feel that there wasn't much I could do but get up and dance with him.

But come the end of the song, I told him it was getting

late and he'd best be getting on home. To let him know I was serious about calling it a night, I went over and pressed the Stop button on the CD player.

He gave me a right pitiful look and said, "But it's my birthday. Can't I at least have a good night kiss?"

I broke down and told him, "Fine, but first close your eyes."

He pulled me toward him and said, "What? And have you blast the hell outta me with some of that doggone mace Nora tells me you never keep too far away? Uh-uh, I don't hardly think so."

I laughed and asked him, "What makes you think I'd ever deliberately hurt you?" before ordering him again to close his eyes.

When he finally dropped his lashes and puckered up, I kissed my fingertips and pressed them first to both of his eyebrows. I kissed the same two fingers before moving down to his nose and then his chin.

When I was through, he opened his eyes and smiled before turning around and treating me to some of the same, only his fingertip kisses didn't end at my chin. He stroked one of my earlobes and wet a space alongside my neck before moving down to the exposed skin of my shoulder. Had I let him I'm pretty sure he would have ventured well beyond the open neck of my robe. But as soon as I felt his just-kissed fingertips traveling toward the harnessed plunge created by my twin sisterfriends, I cleared my throat and gave him a look that said, *Don't even think about it*.

He laughed before leaning over and whispering in my ear, "You mind if I ask you one last question?"

I said, "Like what?"

He said, "Like, you ever, you know, fake it with a guy?"

I told him, "I never faked it with you, which is what I think you really want to know. Now, having said that, shall I stroke your ego even further and tell you just how good it really was?"

He was like, "I'd much rather you stroke something else and let me do all the talking."

I told him, "You do all the talking anyway. And like I've already told you more than once tonight, that other thing ain't hardly gonna happen."

"Umm," he said. "Maybe not tonight, but in case you need any reminding, I haven't blown out my candle yet."

"Which means what?" I said.

He said, "Which means I've still got a wish left to make."

Oh yeah, girl, the brother was talking some serious junk. And before I knew anything, talking wasn't all he was doing. In spite of my best efforts, an involuntary moan squeezed itself out of my tightened throat when I felt the sweep of his mustache across my collarbone.

"Carl," I said, trying to summon the strength from somewhere to pull away from him as he worked his way up my neck.

He said, "I hear you calling my name, baby, but until you say something that sounds like 'no, stop' or 'don't' I'm gonna keep going for what I know."

"And what is it that you think you know?" I asked when his mouth finally reached mine.

He stared into my eyes and said, "That deep down inside, you want me as bad as I want you."

Even though I didn't laugh outright, I did get kind of tickled and said, "Sounds like a line you stole from Marvin. I thought you were rapping to brother Green tonight."

That's when he lowered his lips to within a hairbreadth of mine and sang the verse like I'd never heard it sung before, "Oh, I want you . . . and you want me. So why don't we . . . get together after the dance?"

When I opened my mouth to give him an answer, he was quick to claim the space with the full thrust of his tongue.

He wasn't holding me tight. I could have easily pushed him off me. So let there be no mistaking—I was an eager and willing participant in what turned into a full two minutes' worth of unbridled passion. He didn't waste any time in untying my robe. All I had on underneath it was a thin cotton nightgown. But rather than go for the easy grope, the brother bypassed all of my hotspots to press his hands into the small of my back and draw me even closer. He seemed intent on me feeling every swollen inch of what he was feeling, if you know what I mean. And, girl, if you only knew how close I came to hiking up my gown and giving it up right there in the middle of the kitchen floor . . .

It was only when Carl stopped kissing me long enough to mutter my name that I somehow found the wherewithal to exhibit some kinda restraint.

"Faye," he said.

I knew where he was headed. And rather than let him get there I placed two of my fingers over his lips before they jumped back on mine and I told him, "Baby, I can't. Not here, not now."

He placed his mouth against my ear and in a hoarse whisper he said, "Then tell me when, tell me where."

I'm saying, girl, that's one begging brother. But before I could respond, the phone rang. And when the answering machine picked it up, I'll be durn if the voice on the other end of the line didn't turn out to be Scoobie's.

"Faye . . . it's me. I know you're there. So why aren't you picking up? Anyway, I've got some more good news for you. Detective Clarke's found us some more pictures of Tariq. Yeah, according to Clarke, our boy Tariq looks like he might be around eight or nine years old in these. I told him to go ahead and FedEx them to you. So look for them to arrive sometime tomorrow. All right? Cool. Oh, and call me back when you get a moment. Love you, babe. Later . . ."

After Scoobie hung up, Carl was just standing there, waiting for me to say something, and when I didn't he said, "I suppose Tariq's the son you were telling me about."

I nodded, then winced at the mixture of disgust and disappointment I saw descend over his face as he stepped away from me and said, "I thought you said you lost him."

"I did," I said. "Lost him as in gave him up for adoption." I reached out for his arm and said, "Why don't you sit down and let me try to explain."

He snatched his arm away from me and in a voice that showcased his hurt like an open wound, he said, "What's the point, Faye? You're no more ready to break loose from this joker than you are to stop playing games with my feelings. Until you're prepared to do both, I think it might be best if we just kept our distance from one another."

I don't know if it was pride, fear, or some other unknown factor that kept me from reaching out, grabbing him, and telling him, "No, baby, that's not at all what I want." A part of me desperately longed to, but in the end, girl, I just couldn't. So instead I went over and got his CD out of the player and, on putting it back in its case, I handed it back to him.

Rather than take it, Carl shook his head and said, "No, you keep it. Maybe one day, if you're lucky, one of these songs will remind you of me." Then he went over and blew out his candle before turning away from me and calmly retracing the steps that led him out the door.

HIM

Rather than head straight for home, after I left Faye, I drove back to Ms. Vic's. I mean, after all, she had extended a brother an open invitation. I parked in front of her apartment with every intention of going in and getting some. But before I could climb out of the car, I spotted the iPod Nora and Faye had given me for my birthday.

"It was Faye's idea" is what Nora had told me. "She put some music in there for you too."

I slid on the headset, sat back in the driver's seat, and had myself a listen. It was all there, man, all the songs we'd danced to, fought to, made love to, and then some. And beneath the music, I heard the pain, the passion, and the truth of all those things Faye still, for whatever reason, wasn't able to tell me.

I'm saying, man, all ol' girl had to do was hip me from the git that there was a child involved. She and this fool had a kid, made the mistake of giving him up, and now they're trying to find him and work things out as a family. What's there left for me to say but hey, I wish you all the very best. For real, man, having already busted up my own family, I'm not ashamed to admit that homewrecking ain't exactly the kind of business I'm looking to make a career of. Had Faye just told me the truth, I wouldn't have made such a big f-ing deal about stepping back and letting her and homeboy do their thing. Instead she led me on and had me believing in the possibility of us finally getting it together enough to kick it right.

Man, I sat out there in front of Ms. Vic's place, listening to the music for I don't know how long. I was sad, frustrated, and horny as all get-out, but I knew if I broke down and went up there and tapped on Ms. Vic's door, the most I'd be getting would be a weak substitute for what I really wanted. So to make a long story short, I declined yet another opportunity to get up-close and personal with Ms. Vic and her butterfly, and chose instead to go home alone and crawl into bed by myself.

But at some point in the wee hours of the morning, I got this phone call. And it wasn't like it woke me up or anything, 'cause all I'd been doing was tossing and turning and thinking about everything that had happened earlier that night. My "hello" was met by silence, but a feeling way down deep in my gut wouldn't let me put down the receiver. "Faye?" I said. "Say something, baby. I know it's you."

Even with all the drama and BS she'd just put me through, had ol' girl stepped up and been a woman about the situation, you know doggone well I'da been ready to forgive it all. I'm saying, man, all I wanted her to do was make an honest effort for once.

As it was, she hung up without saying anything. I started to call her ass back, but then I told myself, "You know I can't keep putting myself out there only to have this girl reciprocate with the same ol', same ol'. If she wants to keep shortchanging herself, then hey, so be it. But this is one brother who's through begging to partake of her precious time and attention." Well, at least for now . . .

HER

Yeah, I called him. But as soon as I heard his voice, I knew I still wasn't ready to say everything he wanted and needed to hear, so I hung up. And there was still the unresolved matter of me, Scoobie, and Tariq.

I was lying in bed praying for either a sign of some sort or else an easy way out, when the phone rang. Thinking it might be Carl, being that only fifteen minutes or so had passed since my call to him, I grabbed up the phone and had his name halfway out of my mouth when I caught myself. "Ca—Ahmm, hello?"

"Hey, and just where have you been all night?" Scoobie asked.

"Why?" I shot back at him. "You suddenly feeling a need to keep a watchful eye over me?"

He said, "That's a good question. Do I need to?"

Not up to doing battle with him just yet, I told him, "I spent part of the night up at the hospital and part of it hanging out with Nora and some friends." It wasn't the whole truth, but it wasn't exactly an out-and-out lie either.

After inquiring as to whether I'd gotten his message about Tariq, he said, "Something tells me we're real close to finding him, babe. Real close."

"You think?" I said, desperately wanting to believe on the one hand and not willing to risk letting my hopes get too high on the other.

"Yeah," Scoobie said. "Make sure you let me know if you get those pictures tomorrow. And also, even though I know it's late there and you're probably tired, I wonder if you might do me a favor? There are some important papers I need you to look for in my study."

In hindsight, girl, I wonder if it might have been a setup. I wonder if the brother had known all along that once I'd gained entry into his study, I wouldn't be able to resist poking around and that I'd end up finding out some, if not all, of what I did.

See, what happened was before he'd left for Europe, Scoobie had basically given me free rein of his house. "I'm going to need you to help me keep an eye on things around here while I'm away" is what he'd told me. "Besides, I'm willing to bet the more time you spend out here, the sooner you'll start to feel at home."

To be honest, I couldn't have cared less about lounging around up in Scoobie's big house, keeping company with the ghost of his dead mama and listening to Frank Sinatra, Sammy Davis Jr., Dean Martin, and the crew. But as soon as Nora heard that homes was going to be out of the country and was leaving me with the keys, she couldn't stop grinning. She was like, "Oh yeah, girl, now we're free to see what the real deal is with dude."

When I asked her what she was talking about, she smirked and said, "I'm talking about getting our snoop on—

that's what. Drawers, closets, medicine cabinets, under the bed, inside the toilet tank—all that."

On playing dumb and inquiring as to just what we might be looking for, she answered me with a "Duh! Whatever in the hell it is he's been trying to hide from you. Mark my words, as big a rat bastard as Scoobie is—there's bound to be something. I mean, besides the fact that he's our girl Tina's baby's daddy."

So we searched for a couple of hours on end one night, only to come up with absolutely zilch. I'm talking no illegal drug paraphernalia or semiautomatic weapons; no filled or unfilled prescriptions for Viagra, Levitra, Cialis, or Prozac; no women's lingerie, girlie magazines, homoerotic literature, or even so much as one lewd snapshot of ol' Ms. Nasty Butt Tina.

The only thing of any real interest that we stumbled upon in our snoop-filled trek through Scoobie's place was that I had free access to every room except for one—homeboy's study. Not only did we find the double doors to the study sealed shut, but on closer inspection we discovered that the lock was equipped with an electronic keypad.

Nora said, "Uh-huh, how much you wanna bet the smoking gun we've been looking for is stashed somewhere on the other side of these doors?"

At the time I'd shrugged it off and told her it wasn't like I was a complete stranger to the room. I knew it was where Scoobie went to write up his menu and recipe ideas, finish paperwork, pay bills, and the like. I told her besides a safe, a couple of locked file cabinets, some books, and a bunch of office-related equipment and supplies, about the only thing of any real interest we were liable to uncover in there was the urn housing Scoobie's dead mama's ashes.

I remember Nora shaking her head, laughing, and talking about, "Girl, you trying to tell me homeboy still feels the need to keep his poor mama locked up somewhere and her nutty butt's been dead how many years now?"

But as I stood there punching in the numerical sequence that released the study's electronic lock, I started wondering if Nora might have been on to something. I wasn't sure what to expect when I first walked in, but the anticipation had my poor heart skipping to a double Dutch beat.

A quick visual survey of the room turned up little that I hadn't already seen. There was a huge desk, built out of what looked like real mahogany wood and equipped with a phone, a lamp, and a laptop. On one wall there were some nice built-in bookshelves and, on the other, a large series of built-in cabinets and drawers, both apparently constructed out of the same dark, rich wood as the desk. I was walking past the cabinetry on my way to the desk when I heard a distinctive hum. I stopped and eased open the door of the cabinet where the noise seemed to be coming from.

What I found inside the cabinet surprised me, but by all rights really shouldn't have. It was a monitor, you know, the kind that's generally attached to a camera of some sort and used for security and surveillance purposes.

Before he'd left, Scoobie had shown me the camera he had trained on the front entrance of the home as well as its corresponding monitor, which he kept in an area off the kitchen. He'd even shown me how to work them and had told me that he was still in the process of setting up additional surveillance elsewhere on the property. That was the main reason I'd had Carl drive his car around to the rear of the house. I'd even tinkered with the angle of the camera that Scoobie had set up to capture the comings and goings of the cars and people who visited his house and had double-checked the monitor's view, just as an added precaution.

What I hadn't counted on was the existence of yet another electronic eye, mainly because I'd taken Scoobie at his word that the one was all he'd had time to set up thus far. But there it was—what looked to me like a fully functioning monitor and on it a tight shot of what else but the back side of Scoobie's property.

I pushed a couple of buttons on the monitor's control panel until I got the machine to stop and the tape to rewind. And sure enough, on pressing Play my worst fears were confirmed. Carl's arrival at the house, my inviting him inside, and even our brief exchange of words on the back porch had all been recorded.

I was standing there biting my lip and trying to decide if I wanted to attempt to erase the incriminating evidence or remove the tape from the machine altogether, when the phone on Scoobie's desk started ringing. Of course it was him, wanting to know if I'd managed to get into the study all right and if I'd been able to locate the work-related information he'd previously called about.

It didn't take me but a few seconds' worth of shuffling through the basket on his desk to find the particular set of papers he needed. I'd hoped after I'd finished reading him the info, he'd thank me and let me get off the phone so I could hurry up and figure myself a way out of the mess I'd gone and made. Instead, Scoobie up and started telling me about his durn plans for the day.

But after a few minutes of rambling with little if any response from me, he stopped and said, "Hey, babe, you feeling all right?"

I was quick to tell him, "Yeah, I'm fine."

He said, "You sure? 'Cause if you need me to come home sooner rather than later, it can easily be arranged."

Girl, my conscience was all but begging me to go ahead and confess. Instead of scheming, just tell it all and be done with it. Besides, it wasn't like Carl and I had really done anything besides kiss. And even if we had, so what? Scoobie and I were neither married nor even officially engaged.

But ultimately the coward in me won out and I told

him, "It is well after 2 in the morning here. Once I get some shut-eye, I'm sure I'll be fine."

After Scoobie finally let me go, I got up from behind the desk and had every intention of heading straight to bed when a name on an envelope caught my eye. Dr. Jacob Goldstein.

I picked up the envelope that was sitting atop a small stack of mail on Scoobie's desk. On turning it over and finding it already open, I didn't waste any time in removing the letter and sitting back down to read it. Basically, what the good doctor had sent was the list of dates he'd be available to perform the extreme makeover Scoobie had been trying to convince me to have.

But that wasn't even the stunner, girl. No, what got me durn near hot enough to reach for the phone and cuss Scoobie's conniving ass was when I came across the portion of the letter that dealt with the coordination of all my nip, lift, and tuck procedures with homeboy's own pending vasectomy.

I was sitting there mad as all get-out, ranting and raving aloud to myself, when I swear if I didn't hear what sounded like somebody clearing their throat. Girl, I kid you not, I eased myself up and kind of tipped over to the bookcase, where I thought I'd heard the noise. You know, there wasn't anything over there besides that durn urn containing Scoobie's mama's charred remains and an antique-looking Bible.

Since I wasn't about to get caught asking Scoobie's dead mama if she'd said something, I reached for the Bible with the desperate hope of finding a verse upon which I could draw some much-needed strength and solace. But when I opened the Good Book, what I discovered wedged in the middle of Revelations was anything but the peace of mind I'd sought.

HIM

The first thing I did when I saw my ex again was apologize and promise that nothing of the sort would happen ever again, at least not in her and the girls' presence. Let's face it, man, wasn't no sense in me coming at her with a whole bunch of lies and excuses when Bet and I both know that had the script been flipped and it been her out there in front of our kids, doing the freak nasty with some joker, I'da straight been ready to jack somebody.

And it's not like I'm crazy enough to think that me and the ex will ever hook up again. She trashed any notion I might have had about that the day she found out about Benjamin. But even after all the mess I've put her through, man, not once has Bet ever dogged me out in front of the twins, made it particularly difficult for me to see them, or asked me for so much as a penny over and beyond what the court ordered me to give her and the girls.

Besides that, man, me and Bet got a history dating all the way back to elementary school. I was her first love and she was mine. Old as I am and as much as we've been through together, I'd be a fool not to appreciate the girl. So I'm saying, wasn't nothing I could do but come correct and give her nothing short of her due.

She accepted the apology, but not without sharing just a few more of her thoughts on the matter. "You know, Carl, that's all fine and dandy, as far as me and the girls are concerned," she said. "But what about Faye? Her feelings were probably hurt more than anyone's. And I sure as hell would have never invited her had I known you were going to be waltzing up in here with Ms. Butterfly."

The swipe at Victoria didn't bother me in the least, but the mere mention of ol' girl's name got me riled and I said, "I don't mean no harm, but I wouldn't waste my time worrying about Faye or her feelings. Believe me, if she's not already over it, she will be."

Rather than drop the ball, Bet snatched it up and ran with it. "Does that mean you've talked to her since the night of the party?"

The last thing I wanted to do was share with the ex the full extent to which I'd just been hurt and duped, but knowing better than to attempt an outright dodge, I said, "Look, if you must know I went by Faye's place after I dropped Victoria off that evening. But as far as the two of us ever hooking up on a regular basis to do some kind of cutesy couples thing, forget it, 'cause I really don't see that happening."

Man, had you seen the snarl Bet aimed in my direction, you'da thought my name was Rover and I'd just gotten caught trying to ride all up on her rear. She said, "I guess not, if the best you can do is sneak by the girl's place late at night and hit her up for some after-the-party boot-knocking."

That's when I jerked off the kid gloves and hit her with, "For your information, sweetheart, if getting sexed up and slobbed down is all I'd wanted, I'da capped off my evening snuggled beneath the sheets with the woman I came to the party with in the first damn place, rather than drive way out in the boonies somewhere only to get rained on and chumped by a woman who's repeatedly made it clear that she ain't hardly trying to hook up for more than a couple of nights with the likes of somebody like me."

I fully expected Bet to come flying back at me with some wild combination of flurries. But her counter, when it finally came, struck me as more of a rub than a blow. "So help me out here," she said. "Should I take that little outburst to mean that you really do care about Faye, or would that just be another bad assumption on my part?"

I gave it to her straight, man. I said, "Let me put it to you like this—had I known about the party and that you had invited Faye, I wouldn't have needed a Ms. Vic, a cake, or even any doggone presents, 'cause just Faye's presence alone would have been gift enough. Hell, yeah, I've got feelings for the girl—most nights, I'm up to my neck in 'em."

Yeah, man, so I'm a wuss, all right? 'Bout the only thing I didn't do was come right out and commence to weeping on the woman's shoulder. But I ain't gon' lie, it was straight-up touch-and-go there for a few seconds.

Extending me more sympathy than I would have ever previously thought possible, my ex said, "She probably just needs some time, Carl. I mean, what sensible woman wouldn't be somewhat apprehensive about letting herself fall in too deep with a self-confessed knucklehead who's saddled with three kids, an ex-wife, a baby's mama, and a long history of infidelity? You want me to talk to her?"

"No, no, and hell no!" is what I told her. "I think you and Nora both have done enough instigating as it is, don't you?"

And speaking of Nora, man, I'll be dog if her ass ain't about to make me lose my mind. Ever since the party, she's been hounding me something awful. I'm saying, if she's not blowing up my pager, she's leaving multiple messages on my answering machine at home for me to stop tripping and call her.

What she needs to do is take that mess on somewhere else, 'cause I'm through. That's right, I'm through letting her and ol' girl play me like some kinda sucker who's too hard up to know any better. Like that old blues song says, "I can do bad, all by my damn self."

HER

Oh yeah, girl, wait until I tell you what I found locked up in Scoobie's study, tucked in the pages of his Bible and being guarded by his dead mama's ashes. It looked like something a child in one of those classes for slow kids had put together. So imagine this if you will: a notebook-size piece of paper with four photocopied head shots of yours truly, plastered onto four different emaciated women's bodies—and two of them white!

I'm saying, bad as it was, girl, I might not have been quite as outraged had the body types Scoobie chosen for me been more realistically within my reach. You know, had he gone the big-hip, thick-thighed, Serena Williams or Beyoncé route? But no, apparently this brother was out to mold and shape my big butt into some anorexic, right-sickly looking type of heifer.

Dying to see just who the bodies belonged to, I peeped under the first head shot only to find the songstress Whitney Houston's hollow-cheeked mug grinning back at me. And don't get me wrong, 'cause I don't have a thing against my girl Whitney. I think she's both talented and beautiful. I just ain't trying to look like her skinny ass, is all. And that goes double for the actress Calista Flockhart, who's pasty, pinched face was the next one to peer up at me when I snatched off the photocopied cover. Hell yeah, girl, horrible barely even comes close to describing what I was feeling and it only got worse from there. I don't know if it was Mary Kate or Ashley, but one of those durn Olsen twins popped out from under the third version of me. And the fourth one! Girl, don't you know I was too through when I peeled back that last piece of paper and discovered that Scoobie had taken it upon himself to paste my face on top of that wench Tina's yak-headed, flat-chested, no-butt body!

I was so worked up, rather than do any more snooping, I gathered together the bits and pieces of Scoobie's paper-doll project, stormed out of the study, and took my frazzled nerves to bed. But the very first thing I did upon rising that next morning was to call Nora, who, like me, wasn't scheduled to be at work until later that afternoon.

After listening to all I had to say about my venture into Scoobie's study and having herself a good, long laugh behind it, homegirl didn't waste any time in coming out to join me. Though she claimed all she wanted to do was take a peek at all the incriminating evidence, I think what she really wanted was to help me edit some of the less than flattering surveillance footage.

As it turns out, it didn't matter much what her plans were, because when I punched in the code that Scoobie had previously given me for the door's lock, the durn thing wouldn't budge. After double-checking the numbers and reentering them a couple more times, Nora said, "You know what? I bet that sneaky bastard's got this mug rigged up some kind of way so that you need a different code every time you try to open it."

I told her it wasn't a big deal because when Scoobie got back home I fully intended to tell him that our journey together had come to an end. Even with the possibility of finding our son seemingly so close, there wasn't any way that a long-term relationship between the two of us could ever really work—not with all the lies and unspoken truths steadily growing between us, and I meant his as well as my own.

Of course, within seconds of me making the grand announcement, the FedEx package with the new pics of Tariq arrived at the door. Good thing I had Nora there to remind me of all I stood to lose by not letting go of Scoobie—like my dignity, my self-respect, and the opportunity to fix all that I'd messed up with Carl.

"Don't you go getting weak on me" is what she'd said on noticing the tremble in my hands as I fumbled through the new glossies of the little boy my arms still longed to hold. "If Scoobie's sincere about wanting to find this child, he's gonna do that whether the two of you are together or not. Hell, for all we know, the lying SOB may have known about Tariq and his whereabouts from the git. No, I'm saying, girl, think about it. There might not even be a detective Clarke. It's not like you've ever actually seen or talked to the man. And these pictures—pssst, how do we know they haven't been in Scoobie's possession for years now?"

As far-fetched as it initially sounded, over the next couple of days, I found myself wondering if Nora wasn't on to something. It was entirely possible that Scoobie had been using my desire to reconnect with our son as a way of getting whatever the hell it was he wanted from me.

Yeah, I spoke to his jive tail quite a few times after my visit inside his room of horrors. But since I knew a long-distance war of words wouldn't give me the type of closure I needed, I let him go ahead and think that everything was hunky-dory. I'm telling you, girl, I went so far as to write myself a script and was planning to have Nora rehearse it with me. But as fate would have it, Scoobie's flight put him back in town much earlier than I anticipated and he was already at the house waiting on me when I stopped by there after work.

"Are we celebrating something?" I asked on accepting the warm kiss on the lips and the cold glass of champagne he'd met me with at the door.

"Indeed we are," he said, grinning at me like he'd already had one glass too many and had bumped his head, to boot. "We're celebrating us. Me, you, our son, Tariq, and the wonderful life that lies ahead of us."

"Umpf," I said, before downing a couple sips of the bubbly. Just because I understood and fully accepted the necessity of confronting Scoobie on the sorriness of his actions and letting him know it was time he took a flying leap, didn't make the task of doing so any easier. A part of me had actually wanted things to pan out the way he'd been insisting they eventually would: I'd let go of the past; we'd fall in love; we'd find our son, safe and sound and willing to forgive us for abandoning him; Scoobie and I would go on to get married; and we'd all live happily ever after. But as I sat there on the sofa, swirling the champagne in my glass and trying not to grit my teeth as Scoobie talked about finalizing our plans for Florida, I realized there was no way in hell I was going to spend so much as another hour with this man.

"So when do you want to do this?" he asked, passing me a calendar with all the dates I'd seen in the doctor's letter marked off.

I set the calendar on the coffee table in front of us and looked at Scoobie before I told him point-blank, "I don't."

He was like, "Oh, come on, Faye, there's nothing to be afraid of. Dr. Goldstein is one of the best surgeons in the country. We've talked about this a dozen times already."

"No, just because you've found a way to interject the subject into durn near every conversation we've had in the past month or so doesn't mean we've actually talked about it" is what I told him. "So hear me loud and clear," I said, raising my voice over the durn Sinatra homeboy had crooning in the background. "I'm not the least bit interested in letting any of your surgeon friends meddle with the size of my breasts or suck any of the fat outta my ass, okay?"

He shot me a look of disgust and said, "Now, why do you have to say it like that? Look, babe, it's not like I won't be right there with you every step of the way. Matter of fact, I'm thinking about having some procedures done myself."

"Yeah?" I said, surprised to hear him confess even that much. "Like what?"

He stood up and said, "I don't know. I could use some tweaking here and there. Maybe a little Botox around the eyes, some collagen for my lips."

I said, "Tweaking, huh? Is that what you call a vasectomy—just a little tweaking here and there?"

He frowned and rubbed his forehead. "Is that what this

is all about? So what's the deal—you're going behind my back and reading my mail now?"

I pressed my shoulders against the couch and stared at him. "You weren't going to tell me, were you? You were just going to have this thing done without letting me have a say about it."

He stared back at me and was like, "Faye, you've always known how I feel about kids. I've never wanted any. Never. So don't act like this suddenly comes as some big surprise to you."

"Well, damn it, Scoobie," I said. "What about what I might want?! Did it ever occur to you that I just might like to have a family one day? And since you're so adamant about not wanting any kids, where in the hell does that leave poor Tariq?"

He'd started pacing, but he stopped long enough to say, "I'm not trying to be cruel, Faye, but you made the choice to have Tariq. Had it been left to me, I would have done things differently. But since he's here now, I plan to see that he's well taken care of."

"Should I assume that the same goes for Evan? Or is that something you'd rather I take up with Tina?"

"Forgive me," he said, stepping over to the bar to refill his glass, "but I fail to see what Tina or Evan have to do with you and me and our plans for the future."

"Man, damn the future" is what I told him. "What I want to talk about is the here and the now. Are you or are you not Evan's father?"

Scoobie grimaced and finished off the champagne in his glass before he looked over at me and said, "I take it you already know the answer to that."

I said, "So when were you going to tell me? Before or after you told me about the vasectomy? Face it, Scoobie, you haven't been completely honest or forthcoming with me about a lot of things, whether it be Evan, the vasectomy you were going to have behind my back, or the sick and twisted plan of yours to mold me into some kind of skinny-ass Stepford wife!" Girl, I reached down in my bag, whipped out the paper bearing his bizarre-looking cut-and-paste project, and threw it at him.

Oh yeah, now that really set him off. Through partially clenched teeth he said, "*You* accusing *me* of being deceitful? Now, that's funny, especially when it's obvious that you're still getting some on the side from that crowbar-toting chump with the ten-year-old Corolla. What's he do for a living anyway, pump gas?"

On managing to suppress the sudden urge to get up, go over, and in true drama-queen fashion toss what was left of my champagne into his all-too-smug mug, I offered him an icy stare instead and told him, "Your ass needs to quit."

He laughed and said, "What? I know you're not going to sit here and deny that he was here, are you?"

Even though I knew good and well what was coming next, when the brother snatched up his all-purpose remote and started clicking buttons, I couldn't help but wince and brace myself. "Correct me if I'm wrong," he said, pointing to the image of Carl that flashed up on the television screen, "but isn't that your boy getting out of his raggedy-ass ride, or are my eyes playing tricks on me?"

"Yeah, he was here," I said. "He stopped by and dropped off some of his birthday cake. But it wasn't like we did anything."

"No?" Scoobie said, looking like at any second he was going to start frothing at the mouth. "Then what do you call this?" He clicked from the image of Carl's back door entry to a close-up shot of me and the brother in the kitchen with our lips and bodies fused together.

With his mouth all twisted up like he had a good mind to spit, Scoobie folded his arms across his chest and said, "I haven't been able to view any of the other tapes as of yet, but believe me, looking at this for any length of time is enough to turn my damn stomach. So why not be a good sport and save me both the time and the trouble by just telling me which room you *did* him in?"

Starting to feel for all the world like a scolded child, I dropped my gaze to the floor as I tried to explain. "I told you already, Scoobie, we didn't—" Then it dawned on me, and I looked up and said, "Hold up, are you saying you've got some kind of hidden monitoring system set up in all of these rooms?"

An ugly, downright evil grin spread across his pretty face as he laid it out for me. "Rooms, hallways, closets, you name it" is what he said. "Trust me, if your boy so much as sat his rusty behind on one of the commodes up in here, I have it somewhere on tape. Got to, babe. I'm a busy man. How else am I supposed to keep up with all my valuables while I'm away?"

Not wanting to believe what I thought I was hearing, I stood up and said, "Spying on folks while they're sitting up on the toilet? I hope and pray that is not how you're getting your jollies these days."

Trying to look all contrite, he came over, put his arms around me, and was like, "Oh, come on, babe, you know that whole bathroom thing was just a joke. What's this really all about, huh? Sex? And the fact that I haven't been giving you any? Because if that's all it is, babe, I can fix that right now. And I will. Just give me a moment to pray about it . . ."

Girl, I pushed that fool off me, grabbed up my purse, and told him, "You're one sick puppy, you know that? Next time you talk to your surgeon friend you might want to see if he can't refer you to a reputable shrink, 'cause I swear if you ain't 'bout as crazy as—" I would have finished, but the rage I saw come to life in homeboy's eyes made me momentarily lose my train of thought.

"Crazy as who?" he asked, coming toward me with his

fists all balled up and his face turning a deep red. "My mama? Is that what you were going to say?"

See, if I had really wanted to be mean, I would have been like, "Hey, man, if the durn shoe fits, kick yourself in the ass with it." But knowing how sensitive Scoobie's always been about his mother and her mental illness, I couldn't go there, nor had I planned to in the first place. And that's what I told him. "Scoobie, in all of our years together and with all the verbal knockdown, drag-outs we've had, you've never known me to stoop that low. What makes you think I'm going to start now?"

On reaching into my purse and pulling out the engagement ring he'd given me, I told him, "Bottom line is, I'm just not willing to give up any more years of my life trying to love you, Scoobie. I thought I could, if only for the sake of our son, but I can't."

And having said my piece and returned his ring, girl, I walked out of that cold, unwelcoming, camera-rigged relic of the old South that Scoobie calls a home and didn't look back.

HIM

Ms Vic? Sure, I still see her around campus sometimes. But all that studying in the library and hanging out after class we used to do—that's over. I told you, son, I'm too through letting these young girls out here make a monkey outta me.

And it's just as well, 'cause last I heard baby girl had reset her sights on none other than my poor ol' Uncle Westbrook. On the real money, ol' dude called me and was like, "What the hell you give that li'l ol' hot-tailed gal my number for? You got a life insurance policy out on me or somethin'?"

I assured him that it wasn't me who gave Ms. Vic his number. I've got better sense than that. No, see, that's the type of stunt that's got Squirrel written all over it. If anybody's liable to cold straight set a brother up, he's the one. I still owe dude some payback for the number he pulled on me a couple nights ago.

There I was, laid up on the sofa, listening to some music and trying not to nod off after having done my eight hours and then some when the phone rang. On seeing my cousin Squirrel's number flash up on the caller ID, I picked up and was like, "Yo, partner. What's shaking?"

He said, "You got it, cuz. What you doing tonight and who wit?"

I told him, "Same ol' same ol', man. Nothing and nobody. Why? What you into?"

He sorta laughed and was like, "Since I'll be in your neck of the woods in another five minutes, why don't I just stop by and let you see for yourself?"

I had a hunch he wasn't exactly riding solo that night. So when he turned up on my doorstep a few minutes later, the fact that he had a woman with him didn't surprise me. But when I realized that the woman in question was none other than ol' worrisome-ass Nora, I didn't even bother trying to suppress the "Damn!" that jumped up outta my throat in one loud, mad bark.

Nora grinned, pinched me on the cheek, and said, "Nice seeing you again too, sweetie."

I pointed a finger at Squirrel and told him, "Now, how you gonna do me like this, man? Haven't I always had your back?"

He shrugged and was like, "Hey, man, when it comes to making the ladies happy, a brother's gotta do what a brother's gotta do. And if I'm not mistaken, it was you who first hip me to that sweet fact of life."

Nora said, "Don't go blaming Nigel. If you'da answered your phone or tried to call somebody back sometime, it wouldn't have had to go down like this."

In my head I'm thinking, *Nigel?* It'd been so long since I'd heard anybody call dude by his given name that I'd almost forgotten it. The realization that these two coconuts had gone and gotten quite chummy since the night of my party kind of threw me for a minute. But on regrouping, I let Nora know that if she'd come to plead on her girl's behalf, she was wasting her time, *Nigel's,* and mine. Not only had I lost interest, I'd already moved on to bigger and better things.

That's when Nigel—I mean Squirrel—jumped all in the mix with, "Man, you know you oughta stop telling that tale. Ever since you and Red fell out with one another, you ain't been doing nothing 'sides laying around here whining, pining, and wearing the grooves out on all of them old dusty Al Green albums you got."

I stopped pacing the floor long enough to look at that fool and say, "Keep on, hear. I'd hate to have to up and whup your ass in front of company."

Nora said, "Carl, I know you're upset, but if you'd just calm down for a sec, I think I could explain to you how that whole situation with the kid transpired."

I threw up my arms and was like, "Hello! News flash! Being that I do have three of my own, I think I pretty much know everything I need to about how that whole thing with the kid transpired."

Nora invited herself to a seat next to me and said, "Don't play, Carl. You know damn well that's not what I meant." Then, looking all serious and teary-eyed, she took both of my hands into her own and squeezed them before she said, "She wanted to tell you, Carl. Really, and I'm sure she would have had things not gotten so muddled early on between the two of you. But what you need to try and understand is that very few people in Faye's inner circle know that this child even exists. The shame and secrecy of it all is something I've watched her struggle with for years. Hell, it's been over a decade and to this day she still hasn't found a way to tell her folks."

Squirrel butted in with a "Yeah, go on and cut the girl some slack, dog. Ain't like none of that mess you did behind Bet's back while y'all was married was any less foul." Before I could fix my mouth to cuss him out, he picked up my phone and tossed it to me and said, "Call her up, why don't you? From what I understand, she and ol' boy done already went their separate ways. Ain't that right, Nora?"

She nodded and said, "Umm-hmm. I don't know what you waiting on. You know she's had you sprung since that first night y'all hooked up to watch videos."

Determined to stand my ground, I shook my head and told them both, "Nope. Not gonna happen. Not this time around. If Faye wants to make things right, she knows where and how to find me. Until then, I'd kindly appreciate the two of you leaving me the hell alone to enjoy all of my musty, dusty Al Green albums in peace and by my damn self!"

On her way out the door, Nora pulled up short, cocked her head to one side, and said, "Al Green, huh? You know, Faye listens to him a lot these days. Marvin too. And for some reason here lately, that *After the Dance* track is one she can't hardly seem to get enough of."

HER

I was milling around in the bakery section of the grocery store the other night, trying to decide if I was in the mood for the chocolate doughnuts or the French twists, when I heard this voice behind me: "Goodness, girl, you've lost even more weight since the last time I saw you, haven't you?"

When I turned around, the smiling face that greeted me belonged to none other than Miss Betty, Carl's ex. Always the friendly one, after embracing me with a warm hug, she looked at the pastry boxes I was clutching in each hand and said, "That's right, girl. Go on and get it out your system. A binge every now and then ain't never hurt nobody—just so long as you don't let it turn into an every-other-night affair."

I laughed and assured her that I only planned to buy one box and I'd have to find a way to sneak that past Nora's greedy tail.

We stood there like old friends, shooting the breeze about this, that, and the other for several minutes. She told me she'd just dropped the girls off at a friend's house for a sleepover, while she herself had made plans to spend the evening with her friend Charles—the tall, strapping, chocolate chunk of eye candy I'd met briefly at her sister's wedding. And evidently the prescription her physician's got her on is doing the trick, because every time girlfriend said her boy Charles's name, she looked durn near on the verge of wetting on herself. Too polite to come right out and ask me if I had anything on my Friday-night itinerary besides the box of pastries I was hanging on to for dear life, Miss Betty instead asked me why I hadn't been by her place to pick up the pictures.

Yeah, girl, about a week prior to our run-in at the grocery store, Betty had called and left a message with Nora about some pictures from the wedding that the twins wanted me to have. Now you know durn well I'd just about had my fill of pictures of any kind, so I hadn't been in what you might call too big of a hurry to get back with her.

After I fibbed and told her I'd been busy but that I fully intended to drop by her place one day soon, she went and did me one better. She said, "Well, guess what? You're in luck. It just so happens that I've got them with me."

Hell! Wasn't anything I could do but follow her over to one of the little cafe-style tables they have in the store's bakery section and watch while she dug around in her purse. On finding the package, she first passed me all of the cute snapshots of the twins and said, "They insisted that I made sure you got these."

I smiled and was about to tell Betty that I'd have to call the girls later and thank them, when she added, "And oh, don't let me forget these."

A tremor raced up my back as I stared down at the photos the girls had taken of me and Carl cuddled up on the bench beneath the trees. Totally speechless, I just sat there for a moment gazing at the pictures and trying not to let on that they made me feel one way or another.

Betty took it upon herself to fill in the pause with a surprisingly tender "You really do make a nice couple."

I looked up and without the slightest hint of humor in my voice said, "You think? I bet people said the same thing about the two of you when you were together."

Being the lady that she is, she ignored my saltiness and asked if I'd talked to Carl lately.

I shouldered up my pocketbook, like I was ready to go, looked hard at Betty, and said, "I'm sure you already know that I haven't."

She stared back just as hard and said, "Yes, but what I don't get, for the life of me, Faye, is why? I know you're not going to stand here and deny your feelings for him. Anybody who was paying the least bit of attention to the two of you that night at the party could tell otherwise. Don't think I missed the way he was looking at you or the way you were trying not to look back at him."

"Listen," I said. "I don't have any problems with saying that Carl's one of the sweetest guys I've ever met, bar none. What woman wouldn't be attracted to him?"

"So what's the *but?*" she said. "Because if it has anything to do with that little hoochie who was shaking her little stank behind—"

"It doesn't," I told her. "I'd already messed things up between me and Carl long before she showed up in the picture."

To my surprise, rather than try and coax all the sordid details out of me, Betty looked on in silence as I studied the pictures of me and Carl. After a few seconds or so, she placed a hand on my arm, dropped her head closer to mine, and said, "Hey, now here's a thought. Why don't you call Carl up and offer to bring a box of these baked goodies by his place tonight? Given that it's a Friday evening, you and I both know it's highly unlikely that he's doing anything other than sitting up somewhere with his hands in his pants, watching some ol' Pam Grier video."

Even though we'd both enjoyed a good laugh behind the comment, don't think I didn't give it several minutes' worth of serious thought after I left the grocery store that night. I even went so far as to pull out my cell phone a couple of times with the intent of calling him. In the end, though, I chickened out and decided it best to sleep on it, rather than do anything rash. Good thing I did too because as fate would have it, the following day is when I accidentally caught sight of the brother out frolicking in the park with his kids and some woman.

Yeah, girl, I was driving past Audubon Park late that Saturday afternoon when out of the corner of my eye I spotted them—Carl, the twins, Benjamin, and this woman. No, not his friend from the party. It was some other slim. And you know I circled back around just to be sure. In any case, given the grand ol' time they were all having, chasing one another and rolling around in the grass, Ms. Thang was obviously someone Carl and the kids knew very well.

Seeing them out there like that pretty much messed me up for the rest of the day. From the looks of things, the worst had happened—I'd waited too late and homeboy had decided to move on without me. Even though on a certain intellectual level I could accept that, what I couldn't do was just let it go. I was still in dire need of some sort of resolution to all that had happened between us. So come nightfall, I squared my shoulders, mustered up my courage, and made myself go to a place that emotionally I'd rarely if ever permitted myself to go before.

HIM

She called. It was a little past eleven on a Saturday night and I was laid up in bed, fully engaged in my favorite fantasy-dream sequence starring Angela Bassett, Vivica Fox, Lela Rochon, and yours truly. Irritated by the interruption, I snatched up the receiver and said, "Yeah?"

She said, "Hello, Carl?"

The voice sounded familiar, but I was still somewhat on the groggy and confused side, so I guessed, "Nora?"

"No," she said. "It's me . . . Faye."

"Faye?!" For some reason, man, I shot straight up in bed and bunched the sheets between my legs, as if I suddenly felt the family jewels in danger of being kicked, smacked, or in some manner assaulted.

"I'm sorry if I woke you," she said.

"I wasn't really asleep," I said. "I was just laying up here, well—" I glanced down at my hand and gripped the sheet a little tighter before I said, "Anyway, what's up on your side of town?"

"You were busy, weren't you?" she asked, voice cracking around the edges. "You've got company?"

"Yes and no," I said. "Angela, Vivica, and Lela were just leaving . . ."

She said, "Oh . . . I see. Maybe I ought to call back tomorrow then."

I said, "Faye, I'm just joking. Are you okay? Is something wrong?"

"No, no, nothing's wrong," she said. "I was just thinking . . . about you . . ."

"About me?" I said. All of a sudden my grogginess was gone and my interest extremely piqued.

"Yes, you and the fact that I still have something that belongs to you," she went on to say.

"Yeah, you do—my heart," I whispered, half-joking, half-serious, and fully aroused at that point.

True to form, she ignored the comment and said, "Well, actually I was referring to your videotape—*Wanda Does Watts*. And if I'm not mistaken, I think you still have my book—*Jungle Passions*. So I was wondering if we could possibly get together and exchange them?"

I said, "Great. How soon can you get here?"

She had the nerve to be offended. "Carl, this isn't a booty call. I'm not looking to get laid tonight."

"That's too bad," I said, before I could catch myself.

After I agreed to meet her at Tom Lee Park, the following Saturday, she said, "Fine. Thank you very much. Goodbye," and proceeded to hang up, but not before I managed to slip in "Hey, Faye . . . I'm glad you called, but you don't need an excuse to see me, you know. My Friday nights are still free. Most Saturdays too."

Naw, man, player, player, my behind. I was just trying to give ol' girl an opportunity to stop playing and come correct with it for once. See, the problem with Faye is she always wants to make things more complicated than necessary. Granted, the fact that the sister even picked up the phone and dialed my number indicated a definite crack and thaw in the ice, but instead of hatching up some silly scheme to see me, all she had to say was, "Carl, honey, I was wrong. I've been lonely and miserable without you, and I'm ready to kiss and make up."

As it was, more than a couple of months had passed since we'd last seen or spoken to each other and I'd all but given up on any chance of us getting back together. Mentally and emotionally I'd graduated to a whole 'nother sphere—or so I thought. Her calling didn't do anything but upset the delicate balance of things in my world and make me mad. And the more I dwelled on it in the days to come, the madder I got. She obviously had me pegged as some kinda Howdy Doody type whose strings she could twist and pull whenever it suited her fancy. Why else would she want to meet me on some mosquito-infested downtown riverbank rather than in some quaint little cozy restaurant, or better yet, her place or mine?

Well, I'd had enough of her self-indulgent, childish games. When Saturday finally rolled around, I went prepared for the worst, intent on doing my own share of damage, and slightly on edge from having spent the night before tossing, turning, and having bad dreams. I was hoping and praying my nightmare wasn't some kind of awful premonition, 'cause in the dream, man, the real reason Faye had asked to see me was so she could let me know she was with child—mine, I assume.

Yeah, I know it sounds crazy. It had been months since our last intimate encounter. And she sure as hell didn't look pregnant that night we hooked up after my birthday party, but hey, with my luck, anything's possible. I had been slow to rubber up that last time. And on one of those slips in—who knows—something just mighta slipped out. Now, while the two of us sitting down and mutually agreeing to have a child within the confines of a long-term, committed relationship is one thing, having a kid unexpectedly sprung on me is yet another.

Check it out, though—in the dream, man, I didn't waste

any time waiting to see what the sister had to say. As soon as I caught sight of her and that big baby-filled belly, I took off running. Bad thing about it, though, is she took off after me. Yeah, man, chased my ass all up and down the muddy banks of the Mississippi. And if that wasn't bad enough, somewhere along the way she was joined in the chase by my son, Benjamin, his mama, Clarice, my ex, the twins, even my study partner from school, Victoria.

I'm telling you, man, the whole damn crew of 'em was running and screaming and grabbing at me, like a pack of evil, demented, swift-footed Cheshire cats. Yeah, you laughing, but I woke up on the floor next to the bed, drenched in sweat and babbling like an idiot.

I breathed a sigh of relief when she finally arrived at our agreed-upon meeting place, looking fit and trim and even finer than before. The only thing was she had on these dark glasses. It wasn't until she reached me that I realized they were in fact the very same shades I figured I'd either misplaced or lost at Bet's sister's wedding. It was drizzling and the sky was way too overcast for her to need sunglasses, so I didn't know if she was trying to make fun of me or just being her usual coy and manipulative self.

I frowned, snapped up my raincoat's collar, and was fixing my mouth to say something nasty when she smiled, said hello, and thanked me for coming. I'm saying, the dimples alone almost did me in, man. And she sounded so soft, sweet, and delectable—not only did I have to lick my lips to keep from drooling—but it took every drop of determination in me not to just grab hold of her and start laying on both the lines and the moves.

But the warrior in me wasn't fixing to have it. Sounding for all the world like Mr. T, the voice in my head barked, "Have some balls about you, boy! After all ol' girl put you through, I know you're not 'bout to let her off that easy."

That's right, it was at Mr. T's insistence that I returned Faye's warm, friendly greeting with a somber face and a stiff nod before I said, "Here's your book. You got my tape?"

After we'd finished with the fake formality of the false exchange, I said, "Cool. I guess maybe I'll see you around sometime," then turned and started back to my car.

"Carl," she called after me. "I thought if you had a moment, maybe we could talk. You got someplace you need to be?"

I stopped, turned around, looked at her, and said, "Nope. I just figured we were done here. You got something you wanna say?"

She shuffled her feet, thrust her hands in the pockets of her jacket, and said, "Well, I was just wondering—you know—how you've been?"

Far as I was concerned, she may as well have shoved a thorn bush up my behind and given it a good twist. With my arms folded across my chest I stared at her long and hard before I asked, "How the hell do you think? Listen, Faye, if you've got something to say, come on and spit it out already."

I thought for sure she'd react defensively to the undisguised venom in my voice. Instead she just stared back at me from behind the shades for a moment before saying, "My mama asked about you."

"Yeah?" I said, as I walked back toward her. "You tell her I'd already used up my three humps and been sent on my merry little way?"

Rather than curse or even curl her upper lip at me, Faye turned her face toward the river and in that same quiet voice said, "She wanted to know if you were coming down on Monday for the Labor Day barbecue. I told her I hadn't asked you yet."

I reached out, slid my hand beneath her chin, and tilted her face back in my direction. "So what's up?" I said. "You asking or just making polite conversation?"

She brushed my hand off and shuffled her feet again.

"Come on, Carl. Don't you see me trying? Why you got to be so hard? I mean, didn't you once tell me if I ever had a change of heart to let you know?"

"That's funny," I said, " 'Cause last time I checked, you didn't have a heart."

Bull's-eye! I could tell by the way her jaws tightened and her lips twitched I'd finally hit her where it hurt.

She said, "Fine. If that's how you feel, Carl, fine. Just forget about it."

"Besides, it's too late," I said, aiming my words at her back as she walked away from me. "As of last night I'm officially seeing someone. But just out of curiosity, what kind of game were you and I supposed to play next? Isn't baseball season just about over?"

She picked up her pace and toughed her tone. "Like I said, Carl, that's fine. Are you through? Is there anything else?"

"Yeah, one more thing," I said, still hot on her trail as she hoofed it back to her car. "Give me back my damn glasses."

We nearly bumped noses when in midstep she swung around and said, "What?!"

I backed up a bit and said, "You heard me. The glasses. Give 'em to me. They're mine and I don't want you having any more excuses to call me up and waste my time."

Her hand flew up, and thinking I was about to get the taste smacked outta my mouth, I'm not ashamed to say I flinched. But instead of lashing out, she slid the shades from her face and held them out to me. Stunned, I watched as her eyes blinked, her lashes fluttered, and a couple of big, fat tears rolled down her reddened cheeks. "Here," she said, tossing the glasses at me. "You happy now?"

Call me stupid, but the last thing I'd intended to do was make her cry. As she stood there with tears streaming and her nose starting to snot, all the anger I'd ever felt toward her melted. "Faye, wait," I said, reaching for her as she turned away. "Listen, baby, I'm sorry. I didn't mean to—"

"No," she said, slapping my hand away and resuming her done-had-enough strut. "You've more than made your point, Carl. I really don't care to hear anything else you have to say."

I could feel myself falling like a water-filled balloon tossed from the top of some tall building, and in a last-ditch effort to keep from going splat, I said, "Well, what about your mama then?" Of course, ol' girl didn't take it quite the way I meant it.

This time when she swirled around there was some sho' 'nuff hellfire in her eyes. "My mama?! What about my mama?!" She took to emphasizing her words by poking me in the chest with the book she was holding. "Man, I know you're not about to stand up here and play the durn dozens with me 'cause if that's what you think . . ."

"Faye, Faye, Faye," I kept saying until she finally stopped her yapping and hollered, "What?!"

I said, "When you talk to your mama tonight, tell her that I'm looking forward to seeing her on Monday, if not before then. Tell her I'd take her daughter anywhere on God's green earth that she might want to go. I mean, assuming we could get there and back on a tank of gas or two."

Her face softened for a moment, then soured again. "Right. And what about your girlfriend? What's she gonna be doing? Riding in the backseat giving directions and pointing out landmarks?"

"What girlfriend?" I asked. "I made that up. I'm not seeing anyone. I'm not."

She rolled her eyes and said, "Carl, I saw you with her. Last Saturday? Audubon Park? You, her, and the kids?"

I started laughing and said, "You're right. That was me you saw in the park—me, my kids, and my sister Sheila.

She was visiting from out of town. It's true. Okay, where's your phone? I'll call her and let her tell you herself. You believe me?"

She flipped the pages of the book—*Jungle Passions*—over her thumb a couple of times and looked toward the river again before turning to me and saying, "I want to."

"So do," I said.

She nodded and pursed her lips.

I started to kiss her, but then I got a better idea. After tossing my shades, the video, and her book into the grass, I started unzipping her jacket.

"Carl, what are you doing?" she said. "It's raining out here."

"Don't worry, baby," I said, unfastening my own coat and pulling her against me. "If I don't do anything else, I'm gonna keep you safe from the storm."

When I wrapped my arms around her, pressed my cheek to hers, and started rocking from side to side, she responded with an "Uhumpf. I should have known. And what, pray tell, are we supposed to be dancing to?"

I said, "Oh, I don't know. What do you say we try a little 'Carl and Faye, sitting in a tree, k-i-s-s-i-n-g . . ."

She looked at me and cracked up.

I circled a finger around one of her dimples and told her, "You know, baby, all I want, all I've ever wanted since that very first night we danced together was to make you happy and give you a reason to smile like that."

Her face turned serious and she said, "I know and I'm sorry, Carl, about everything, especially not telling you about my son. I wanted to—a lot of times. But when I realized how much you loved and were willing to sacrifice for your own children, it only made me that much more ashamed . . ."

"Stop," I said. "You only did what at the time you thought was best for you and the kid. Now, as far as you going outta your way to hide the situation from me—

yeah—you should have damn well known better than to think that I'd ever try to stand in judgment of you. Me? 'Mr. Sho' 'Nuff Less-than-Perfect himself? Come on, baby, I thought you knew me better than that. The fact that you didn't think that I could be a man about the whole situation is what really hurt me more than anything, Faye."

She told me, "I was scared, Carl. Too scared to trust you. Too afraid to even let myself want you. To tell you the truth, I'm even more afraid now than I was before."

"But you're here anyway," I said, holding her a little tighter. "And I want you to know that means a lot to me."

"Thank you," she said.

"For what?" I asked.

She was like, "You know . . . for wanting me, in spite of . . ."

I looked at her and said, "Baby, I want you because."

She said, "Because?"

I told her, "Yeah, because you're beautiful, because you're smart and sexy, and because right here and right now, you're all the woman I'll ever need."

That's when she went all the way out and broke one of her unspoken rules. She reached up, cupped my face in her hands, and kissed me. I'm saying, in the past, I'd always been the first to initiate any of the tongue-twisting that kicked off between us. And if that in and of itself wasn't shocking enough, after easing her lips from mine she ran her hand over my chest and said, "I missed you, Carl. And first chance I get, I'm gonna show you just how much."

I was like, "Well, damn, girl, what are we wasting time 'round here for? Let's go do this."

And so without further ado, we did.

And thus far, man, it's been good, real good. 'Course I know this ain't no fairy tale we're talking about here. Like me, Faye's still very much a work in progress. There're bound to be a few challenges on the long road ahead of us—if only because we're both two extremely prideful, passionate, headstrong individuals who've yet to properly deal with our own private pains. But I'm not finna let any of that have me punked and running scared like I did with Bet, man. You know?

I'm saying, on the real, son, I want this. I want to be the man in this woman's life—the one she picks up the phone to call in the middle of the day; the one she reaches across the bed for in the middle of the night; the one she lets love away some of the emptiness in her arms. I want to be all those things to her and more.

And if that makes me whupped, man, then hey, so be it. I'm whupped and loving every doggone second of it, 'cause when all is said and done, player, it beats a brother laying up somewhere butt-naked and by himself. It beats that by a long shot.

HER

After the dance? Well, after the dance we kissed, we agreed to leave my book and his tape on the riverbank where we'd dropped them, and before the day was done we ended up at his place making . . . well, let's just say, making up for lost time.

I'm sorry, girl, as much as I really do adore Carl, it's going to take some time for me to get accustomed to using the "L" word in reference to him. I suppose in that regard I could take some notes from Nora. Yeah, girlfriend doesn't seem to have any reservations when it comes to expressing to some of any and everybody the fact that she's head over heels about her boy Squirrel. Excuse me, I mean Nigel.

But as far as Carl is concerned, one of the things I've come to treasure most about him is his willingness to accept me as I am—big hips, bad attitude, and all. Seriously, being with him has taught me that I don't always have to come so hard with it. I can be soft and sweet and tender sometimes if only because he makes me feel safe and secure enough to do so. He's the first man I've dealt with who's ever cared enough to confront me about my issues, much less flat-out call me on my selfishness. He's the first to ever make me wanna stop, look at myself, and as a result turn around and do something altogether different.

Scoobie? I still run into him at church every now and then, even though I switched from one service time to another in an effort to keep our paths from crossing as much. It's not like I don't hate that there's bad blood between us. One day, not too long after I gave him back his ring, I tried mending the rift by calling him and letting him know that I hadn't meant to take all of Tariq's pictures and that I'd be happy to have copies made for him. He told me not to worry about it. "You go ahead and keep them" is what he said. "I'm sure they mean more to you then they probably ever will to me."

And if that wasn't bad enough, when I asked if he was still in touch with the detective, all he said was, "When and if there are any new developments, I'll let you know," before coldly rushing me off the phone by informing me that he was right in the middle of something important.

Carl, on the other hand, has been incredibly supportive. Lately he's been encouraging me to do what I've been absolutely dreading for the longest—to sit down with my parents and tell them about Tariq. He's even offered to come along with me just to rub my back and hold my hand.

Lord knows I never thought I'd be saying this, girl, but yeah, I think this one's a keeper—if not forever, then at least for a little while. And I'm okay with that, really, 'cause right now all I want to do is maintain the courage to keep stepping out there on faith, instead of running as fast as I can in the opposite direction. I, at least, want to be open to the possibility that Carl has it in his heart to do right by me and that he actually means what he says when he tells me I'm beautiful or that he thinks we could make pretty babies together. I've been missing that kind of sweetness in my life, you know?

So yeah, girl, I guess the plain and simple truth of the matter is, I do love him. And I think I've finally made up my mind to go ahead and do this thing and enjoy it. I'm talking the strawberries, the frosting, the cake, and all that, for however long it lasts. I'd be crazy not to, don't you think?

A READING GROUP GUIDE

AFTER THE DANCE

Lori Johnson

The following questions are intended to enhance your group's discussion of this book.

DISCUSSION QUESTIONS

1. What, if anything, made this story different from some of the other love stories or romance novels you've read? Discuss some of the features and/or elements this story has in common with them.

2. Have you ever had a friend like Nora, one nuttier than a fruitcake but whom you couldn't help but love nonetheless? Discuss how this person impacted (and/or continues to impact) your life, whether good or bad.

3. Could you see yourself being attracted to a man like Carl? A woman like Faye? Why? Or why not?

4. Faye wasn't an easy person to like. What did you find most annoying about her? At what point, if any, did you start to like and/or understand her?

5. Why is it that some women, like Nora, can offer good advice but don't seem to have the same good judgment or presence of mind when it comes to the choices they make in their own lives?

6. At what point do you think Carl's feelings for Faye changed? What do you think Carl found most attractive about Faye?

7. What do you think attracted Faye to Carl? At what point did her feelings for him deepen?

8. How did Benjamin influence Carl and Faye's relationship? What type of influence did the twins have on Carl and Faye's relationship? How might the story

have been different had Faye and Carl's kids not gotten along?

9. Were you surprised, amused, or annoyed by the discovery of Faye and Scoobie's secret love child?

10. Do you think Scoobie was lying or telling the truth about his desire to reunite with their son?

11. What do you think was behind Scoobie's desire to reunite with Faye?

12. Why do you think so many women, like Faye, are willing to grant men like Scoobie second chances? Why do you think Faye so desperately wanted to believe Scoobie had changed?

13. Do you think Scoobie was lying or telling the truth about his relationship with Tina? Do you believe it was over between them or do you suspect they were still involved?

14. Do you think a relationship between Scoobie and Faye might have worked had she not been overweight?

15. Do you think Faye had a real problem with her weight, size, or body image? Which scenes illustrate your opinion?

16. Why do you think Betty was rooting for Faye?

17. Do you think Scoobie was at all sincere about his newfound sense of spirituality?

18. What did you think or feel about the book's depiction of the church?

19. How did the depiction of the "family" differ from some of the other books you've read?

20. Which scenes made you laugh out loud? Which scenes touched you? Which scenes struck you as unbelievable?

21. Which two secondary characters did you like the best and why? Nora, Uncle Westbrook, Squirrel (aka Nigel), Betty, the twins (Renee and Renita), Ms. Vic (aka Victoria), Tina Dumas, Benjamin, or Clarice?

22. Which character(s) would you have enjoyed seeing more of?

23. In the end, did you think Scoobie was mean, trifling, mentally ill, a fool, or some odd combination of the aforementioned?

24. What kind of challenges do you think Carl and Faye will face as a couple in the future? Where do you envision them in five years?

25. Can you see Betty, at some point, changing her mind about taking Carl back? If so, how might that affect Carl's relationship with Faye?

26. How long do you think Squirrel and Nora's relationship will last? Five years or longer? Five months or less? Five weeks, at best?